The Cindra Corrina Chronicles
BOOK 3

THE WAY OF THE HART

MARK RUDE

ISBN 978-0-9848275-3-4

Printed in the United States of America.

For my new friends and readers who share my love for a nice, long story.
And also for Rowena Z, my biggest fan.

Acknowledgements

I want to thank everyone who has spread the word and helped me to find new readers. Even in this Information Age, I still find that word-of-mouth is the best endorsement.

Also, a big "thank you" goes out to Gini Koch and Marsheila Rockwell for their friendship and for making me part of *The Inner Circle*.

Contents

Chapter One

Cordoshome

Sir Jaron had been defeated. He felt it in his heart and in his weary limbs; there was no more fight left in him and he hung his head in surrender, resigned to his fate. The battle had lasted for weeks, covering many miles of ground, and he was now looking forward to whatever fleeting peace he could achieve.

"Fine," he said, as he glared at his smaller opponent's big hazel eyes. He threw up his hands as she beamed with victory, "But Sir Cord has the final say. It is his school after all."

Cindra had been confident in her ability to wear down the knight and bring him to her side, but the admission was satisfying nonetheless. "You mean it? You'll support the idea when he arrives? Oh, Jaron!" The girl flung her arms about his neck and kissed him on the lips, making him blush. She had avoided using their newfound love as a lever to move him, but it would do as a reward.

During the last few weeks she had become more adept at the fencing style of male reason, forming counter-arguments to points he had not yet made. It had been a particularly difficult battle, since the idea she had been promoting was by all measures absurd.

It had been nearly two years since Lady Cindra Corrina was placed on an ill-fated ship bound for an arranged marriage, and her father's knight, Sir Jaron Dunlorden, was banished for a scandal following their very public kiss. Her ship had been attacked by Minozhian bull-men who were hired to kill her, but she had escaped thanks to a magical bracelet that had since gone missing.

Cindra had spent the last nineteen months living among a family of Galindri nomads who disguised her as one of their own, and it had been the most trying yet wonderful time of her life. Then fate had brought Jaron and her back together. Now they were heading home to beautiful Portshia, the only hitch being that there was a dark conspiracy to murder her and prevent what alliance her marriage could bring. Cindra's solution to this little problem was the source of the argument she had just won.

Cindra crossed the spacious room and opened a window that overlooked the coastal town of Cordoshome. The afternoon sun cast ridged shadows upon the familiar clay roof tiles, and plastered brick walls glowed with warm colors as the buildings marched down the cliffs toward the Emerald Sea. The smell of fishing boats and salty ocean air filled her nose and made her yearn for home.

"You know," Cindra began, shifting from verbal warrior to diplomat, "If this is to work, there must be some changes in how you and I... that is, we both must learn different ways."

Jaron wanted a tankard of ale and a nap, not another discussion. "I suppose we must," he conceded, hoping to end it at that.

"For example," Cindra said as she paced about the

room, unaware of Jaron's head drooping to his chest, "If we are to avoid suspicion, we must change our sleeping arrangements. If I am to truly be your squire, I can hardly be seen in the bed while you are on the cot."

"Lady Cindra, dearest, if this is to work we are going to need a miracle. I don't even know where to start, but you will have to be retrained to do *everything*." He rubbed his eyes, not caring if he got the bed, or the cot, or even the floor tonight; he wondered if she would permit him to sneak away and hide.

"What do you mean?" she asked indignantly, with hands on hips, "I hid among the Galindri for well over a year. You didn't know me yourself when you first saw me."

"You were disguised as a Galindri *girl*." Jaron explained, as he had tried to do for the past few weeks. He had been avoiding bringing up the practical difficulties, not wishing to challenge her pride. One did not tell Lady Cindra she could not do a thing unless one wanted her to try. "You must learn to act as a young knight-in-training. The other lads will study you for weakness, judging your place in the pack, like dogs. If you seem too feminine or refined, they will taunt you and make life miserable. If you seem too timid or shy, such as a girl might among men, they will sense it." He took a deep breath and sighed. "I think I will regret agreeing to this."

Cindra lifted her chin defiantly, "Yet you have agreed nonetheless. We have all winter to sort me out, so I suggest you prepare your lessons." She smiled and ruffled his hair while he looked miserable. "Shall we begin with spitting and belching practice?"

"I think I will need to sleep on it," he said, taking her shoulders and kissing her forehead. "Why don't you walk about in the town and watch other boys for a start." He turned and headed for the cot, then checked himself and went for the bed, lest she bring it up again.

"I think I shall," Cindra said happily. She grabbed her jacket and floppy hat, tucked her long auburn hair under it, and headed for the door.

Once, she would have bristled at being shooed away by a mere knight, but her noble upbringing had been suppressed for some time and now she thought it funny, like a kind of game. When she had played games with the peasant children in the castle she had always been in charge; she'd been a general shouting orders to her Army of Mischief. Now she was going to be taking orders and would have to do so willingly. She briefly wondered how long this game would remain funny. Soon it would be all about her survival and she would be tested sorely. Resolved to face any challenge, she went down stairs and left the manor house to walk in town.

Cordoshome was a pleasant little community with buildings and streets descending the sloping cliffs like steps, switching this way and that in a lazy path to the modest sea cove below. The houses were painted in earthy tones, from the cool greens of spring to the warm shades of autumn. Some of the red clay roof tiles looked ready to slide off onto the street, yet held fast; somehow defying the wind, weather, and abuse of seabirds. The cobbled streets had deep gutters, giving the tall narrow avenues the distinctive smell of human habitation. Part of the waterway that fed the town was diverted to keeping the gutters flowing so the stench did not linger, and the sea breeze took care of the rest.

Cindra walked with her hands in her pockets as she had seen some men do. It not only kept her hands warm but hid them as well; she had a girl's dainty hands and hopefully always would, but they did little for her disguise. Her breasts were hidden by the loose shirt and vest, and the baggy trousers served to conceal her slight waist, wider hips, and lack of other manly... traits.

*I wonder how Jaron and I shall solve **that** little detail, and need it be a **little** detail after all?* Her lips curved in a wicked smile as she imagined the look on his face, and the furious blush that would color it. She did love making him blush.

Turning another corner to the next street down, she found a row of what looked like taverns and inns, as well as the office of the watch. Trouble was managed efficiently, with the strangers and drunks collecting within sight of the sentries and their jail cells. A group of rowdies laughed boisterously near a tavern door, so Cindra crossed to the opposite side of the street, where some women were gathered. A fiddle played on the balcony, and the smell of incense and perfume lingered about the open front door.

As she approached the women they smiled and gestured, calling out, "Here's a pretty boy!"

"Make a man of you, love?"

"Ask yer daddy fer a couple o' silvers."

The women laughed and made wooing noises at Cindra, and now it was her turn to blush furiously.

*They really **do** that? How disgraceful!* she thought. Cindra had no idea that women, even whores, would act so... so *improper*. She'd always assumed that men did all the brazen banter when seeking impolite company. She hunched her shoulders and hid her face under her hat, wondering what other indignities awaited her. *Pretty boy... hmmph.*

Further on, a group of lads ran by and she was reminded of Nixy DuQuayne, the young boy who had pinched her purse on the night she slipped out of her father's castle. *He would be about twelve years old now,* she thought, *the same age as my then-husband-to-be, Duke Haynyyd.* She made a face at the memory of her engagement; she had not been informed until the celebratory dinner that the duke she was to marry had died mysteriously, and his little brother was now her betrothed. She wondered if she would ever forgive her father for that.

Twelve. Unbelievable.

The lads, ranging in age from perhaps eight to fourteen, were playing with some kind of leather ball, following rules that Cindra could not fathom. They shouted and bumped into each other, heedless of injury as they dashed and dodged about. Cindra stood in a doorway and watched, cringing as one boy fell face-first on the cobblestones. The game paused while he tended a bloody lip and skinned hands.

One older boy noticed her watching and shouted, "Hey! You with the hat! Want to join?" He motioned for her to come over as the injured boy tried to look able and unharmed.

Cindra shook her head, realizing too late that her curiosity had been confused with interest. The boys came over and stood around her, making her nervous.

"Come on, it's easy." The lad offered the ball and the others looked on with appraising eyes, trying to gauge her worth. Or *his* worth for all they knew.

Cindra shook her head beneath her large hat and said timidly, "No thanks, just watching." She self-consciously crossed her arms, just in case the jacket didn't quite hide the curve of her breasts. She was as tall as the tallest boy, but she didn't feel tall at the moment.

The boys looked at her with disappointment and perhaps a touch of scorn, and then returned to their game; the injured boy looked happy he had not been replaced. Cindra watched for a bit longer before moving on, wondering if she had failed some kind of test. It felt that way.

———

The month grew colder day by day and much of Cindra's time was spent caring for Vortigras, Jaron's chestnut stallion, and her own Galindri bay pony T'ózha. Since stable duties were expected of a squire, it was deemed good practice for the boy-in-training, plus it had the added benefit of keeping Cindra busy while Jaron wondered what to do with her. He was not eager to start teaching her 'the ways of men,' for he was not entirely conscious of them himself. He simply was what he was.

He counted the days until Sir Cord returned from

Portshia to his family estates. Jaron had always been able to turn to Cord Freekirk when his head or heart were troubled; the older man had a way of cleaving through all the nonsense that the younger knight found so daunting. Even when Jaron and Lady Cindra had caused a scandal with a passionate kiss in public, it was Sir Cord who had uncovered a plot involving roses enchanted with a love spell, pointing to another's guilt. That had spared Sir Jaron an executioner's blade and reduced his sentence to banishment for two years, a period that would end with the approach of spring.

During one of his glum, introspective strolls along the terrace, he encountered Lady Mytha, Baroness of Cordo and Sir Cord Freekirk's mother. She was a large woman in height and girth, though not unpleasantly so, and she had given the baron six large sons. She counted Jaron as her seventh, though not of her blood.

"Good afternoon, Lady Mytha," he called, as he had since boyhood. She bred familiarity in a way that appalled some nobles.

"Good afternoon, dear Jaron," she replied, the heavy woolen dress and cloak of blue barely moving with the chill breeze. Her round features and blue eyes reminded Jaron of the moon, and her sandy hair was plainly braided, covered with neither hat nor veil. Her northern blood was strong and she didn't mind the easy winters of the southern coast. "You seem to be in a lesser mood of late. Do you find having a squire in your care is more of a burden than you imagined?" She stood next to him on the terrace overlooking the covered garden.

Jaron smiled wearily and nodded, "Indeed it is. When Cord took me as a squire, I thought he had the best of it, letting me tag along and telling me what to do. I didn't realize he was trying to guide a young fool into manhood."

The baroness laughed and nodded in agreement. "Much like raising children, I suppose." She placed a hand on his arm saying, "I have tried to guide six young fools into manhood, though not always successfully."

Jaron grinned, "I'll try not to mention it to Cord when he arrives." The baroness chuckled, and then was silent for a moment.

"Your squire, what is his name again?" Lady Mytha asked.

Jaron's heart skipped a beat. They had not decided on a name for Cindra to use publicly, and he had taken to calling her 'lad' when others were around. He cleared his throat and answered, "Dillan." It was the name of one of the wizardry students he had stayed with the year before.

"Dillan," she repeated as she looked over the garden, "from Casselvane province?"

"Eh, no." His mind raced to whip up a false biography. *Why was she being so interested all of a sudden?* "From the north. Alva province... near the town of Aldrig."

"Aldrig," she mused, "The Mystic College is based there, is it not? Is he from a wizard family, or nobles perhaps?" She raised her eyebrows questioningly.

Jaron was getting flustered. "His family is wealthy but not noble. I expect they considered the Mystic College, but the lad begged to become a squire; wore me down for weeks, actually." *The first bit of truth I've uttered.*

"Ah, so much less of a money burden on the parents, I suppose. Still, soldiery is a most dangerous profession, especially in these times." She moved to his other side, making Jaron feel like an opponent was flanking him. "It was good of them to give him a pony; such a fine animal.

He nodded and saw no need to elaborate. Lady Mytha knew that Jaron could not afford such a beast; naturally she had assumed it was a gift to 'Dillan' from 'his' wealthy family.

"When were you near Aldrig, by the way? It has been so long since I traveled north, I have forgotten how it was." She looked over the garden and breathed in the scent of the evergreens.

Jaron responded honestly, "It was last winter; I

stayed in town until the school closed, then escorted some students home through the snow. It was quite lovely, though bitter cold."

"And there you met young Dillan... what did you say his family name was?"

"Uh," Jaron stammered, "It's er..."

She turned towards him and asked, "Do you know what happens when you raise six boys, Jaron dear?" The sudden change of direction unseated him and he shook his head stupidly. "Nothing surprises you... or fools you. I have listened to six different versions of the same story hundreds of times before. Most of my sons managed a better lie than you can, sad to say."

The knight reddened and sputtered, wondering where he had gone wrong. He opened his mouth to protest but the baroness silenced him with a raised finger. "What is the girl's name?" she asked.

"How... how did you know she was a girl?" he whispered, awestruck. *Had we been spied upon or careless?* Then panic struck him, "Who else knows?"

She smiled triumphantly, "No one else. I was not sure until now, but I had my suspicions." Jaron's face was so perplexed that she almost laughed. "You said 'he' is from the north, but the accent places him here in the south. You said you stayed in Aldrig over the winter, but that Gali foal would have been born in spring if it could be helped, and that pony in the stable is not yet a yearling."

Jaron frowned, keeping his voice low as his eyes darted about, "But how did you know 'he' was a 'she?'"

"I am a mother, and a lady besides. I have tried to raise my boys with proper table manners, but they all ended up eating like their father, forking their meat like they had to kill it first, shoveling food into their mouths, elbows leaning on the table, holding knife or fork or spoon all the same way." She shook her head in resignation.

"But this 'Dillan' eats like I do, with a mind to proper manners," she continued, "Not the sort of thing one would expect from a boy, noble or base. Dillan held fork and spoon like a lady would, and arranged cup and cutlery properly about the plate by habit, even as I had the servants set them incorrectly."

Jaron was astounded that she had not only suspected, but had tested her presumptions right under his nose at the dinner table.

She smiled slyly at him and said, "I have seen my boys invent many a means to be alone with a girl, though I must say making her wear men's clothing is extreme, illegal even. I assume you wished to gain your father's approval for marriage upon returning home, but how to sleep in the same quarters with your betrothed without scandalizing your hosts?" She clucked her tongue disapprovingly. "Most inventive, but you have always been a terrible liar." She tugged his beard in the manner she scolded her grown sons. "You have not answered my question, sir knight. What is the name of the young lady staying with you in my house?"

Jaron looked at his boots in shame, but a thought stirred him. He could trust Cord, and Lady Mytha was like the mother he never knew, since his own had passed when he was very young. The woman obviously had a certain insight about boys, so who better to instruct a girl? A feeling of relief washed over him, as it seemed he might not have to tutor her alone.

"Lady Mytha, can you keep a secret? I tell you this is not what it seems, and the matter must not go beyond these walls, even with the gossip of servants." He looked pleadingly at her and the lady's interest piqued. She nodded, for all women loved to hear secrets, whether they could keep them or not, though certainly the lady meant to.

Jaron's voice dropped low and conspiring as he leaned closer, "The girl's life is in danger; she has already survived an attempt at murder, though most think it succeeded, and we must keep it so." He looked into the baroness's round face and waited for the import to sink in. When her eyes told him she understood, he continued. "The girl in your house is Lady Cindra Corrina, daughter of Count Casselvane."

The baroness gasped and her eyes darted about the terrace and garden, making sure they were not overheard. "Lady Cindra? But surely she died at sea?"

Jaron shook his head, "Saved by the intervention of Ildric Finnael, by means of a magical bracelet. It bore her safely to shore after she fell overboard."

The lady took him by the arms, "But the count and countess! They must be told!" She was a mother after all and knew what House Corrina must be going through.

Jaron said, "They will be, after we arrive in Portshia, but it must be handled carefully. There might be spies and assassins inside House Corrina, like Cindra believes there were in House Cordobal."

"House Cordobal!" she hissed, her face going paler, "the royal family!"

"Yes, the late king. His lengthy illness was poisoning; Cindra learned this herself." The lady's eyes went wide at the news. "There are forces plotting against us, possibly the Dissenter Houses that want to break from the realm. Until we can uncover the traitors, it is not safe for Cindra to be revealed. The duke in Rokvynnar was murdered to prevent the alliance by marriage, but the count arranged for Cindra to marry the younger duke, so the Minozhian pirates were hired to attack her ship and kill her."

The baroness gripped the railing of the terrace to steady herself as the weight of the knight's story bore upon her. Sir Jaron was always a rascal but a terrible liar, and his eyes held no falsehood. Either all of it was true or he believed it so fervently that it made no difference. She looked concerned and asked, "Are you sure this girl is Lady Cindra Corrina? There might be some mistake..."

Jaron smiled humorlessly saying, "Milady Mytha, you must have heard the details of my banishment." The baroness nodded as she conceded the point. "I know her quite well," and he quickly added, "though *not* in the way that has been rumored. I care for her deeply but I am still her father's honorable knight." He wondered if that was entirely accurate. He hoped it was.

She took his arm, leading him from the railing, "Let us go someplace more private and discuss this. Is 'Dillan' in your quarters?"

"Sh-he should be," Jaron corrected himself. "Probably finished in the stables by now."

The baroness huffed in dismay as she considered how the count's daughter had been spending her time grooming horses and sleeping on a cot while under the Freekirk's roof. At least she hoped *one* of them had been sleeping on the cot.

Boys...

Cindra sat in a chair by the fireplace across from the baroness, while Jaron stood by the hearth, his arm resting on the mantle. The fire crackled slowly, having not yet taken possession of the fresh logs. The smell of burning sap and a hint of horse manure mingled in a not-unpleasant manner, and the last light of day shone through the slats on the windows, illuminating the motes of dust that floated like faerie bugs.

Cindra had not been properly introduced to her hostess before now, but considering their ruse, that was necessary. She was relieved that the sharp-eyed woman was no longer being lied to, but now she must be trusted if not to assist, then at least not to hinder their plans.

The baroness, for her part, was at a loss for words. The girl sitting across from her was unkempt and smelled of horses, dirt smudged her elegant face and nose; her auburn hair was dirty, with wavy tangles from having been tightly braided; the loose trousers and linen shirt were poorer than her house servants wore; yet the girl was the scion of a major house. She would be a duchess by now if she had made it to her wedding. Lady Mytha tried to picture the girl in a fine dress and styled hair, looking like the noble lady that she knew her to be.

Jaron just stood by, keeping his mouth shut. He was outclassed here, so he briefly explained the circumstances of the sudden meeting to Cindra, hinting that the lady of the house might be of help. He would let them sort out the rest.

"Forgive my appearance baroness," Cindra said, "I'm afraid I have not had the chance to bathe." She sat straight in her chair facing the elder woman, while the lady of the house turned to the left slightly in deference. Though Cindra held no real title, and therefore no real authority, her pedigree counted for something. She decided that winning the lady's help would require taking up the mantle of the high peerage once again. *I will need all the help I can get*, she thought.

The baroness sat with her hands folded in her lap and waived a dismissal in the air, "Think nothing of it milady, I understand your life has been out of sorts for a time." She smiled and offered, "I can arrange for a bath to be drawn, if you wish."

"That would be kind of you, baroness. But I must ask that no special care be given; we cannot let it be known that anything unusual has happened." Cindra rested her hands on the arms of the high-backed chair, making it look like a throne despite her grubby appearance. "Now I am afraid I have a great favor to ask of you, a service that may help me to survive my time in Portshia until our enemies can be discovered."

"Anything, milady, I would be happy to assist in any way!" the baroness began.

"Please Lady Mytha, hold your enthusiasm until you hear my proposal." Cindra smiled, waiting to see the look on the kindly woman's face when she told her. It was important to give her time to think it over; she owed her that much for her trouble. Lady Mytha sat patiently as Cindra gathered her words. "What I must ask of you baroness, if you are so willing, is that you use your extensive mothering experience to teach me to act as a young man."

The baroness frowned at the strange request. "I-I believe this can be done... but why would you wish to pass as a young man?" Looking to Jaron and upon seeing him pinch the bridge of his nose as if to suppress a headache, her confusion turned to apprehension.

Cindra cleared her throat, which was suddenly dry. "I have asked Sir Jaron to go through a great deal of danger and trouble to assist me, and I must ask your son Sir Cord to do the same. I intend to stay at the Freekirk Fighting School in Portshia." The baroness gaped at this, but Cindra wasn't finished. "What's more, I intend to train there with the other students while disguised as Sir Jaron's squire."

There, I have said it.

She waited for the woman to absorb the news.

Lady Mytha's blue eyes widened and the color left her cheeks. A series of emotions played across her round face as she wondered what madness she had stumbled into. *Train a highborn lady to act as a boy, so she might train in a fighting school?* **Our** *fighting school?* It was the most bizarre idea she had ever heard, and she had thought nothing more could surprise her. *Perhaps I was lucky I bore only sons?*

"You need not answer right away; I know this will be a burden upon your house, for all must be kept as secretive as possible." Cindra sat back in the chair and waited for a moment, then sniffed a bit and said, "I think I will have my bath while you consider my request, baroness."

Chapter Two

Special Luck

The winter was colder than any he could remember, but Nixy DuQuayne was warm despite the chill. His life had taken a fair turn among the brotherhood of thieves that he called his family. The Circle of Gold was often harsh and unforgiving but Nixy had shown his true worth. He sat in an old abandoned wine cellar under what used to be a famous tavern in the Silver District. Once the mines petered out, the business moved on and the cellar was forgotten. The tavern became an orphanage and the cellar became the parlor, headquarters of the Circle's operations near the Market Square. The parlor was part of a maze of tunnels and catacombs known as the Warren to its inhabitants; dozens of young men and boys trained and lived there, emerging to comb the streets for fat purses, untended merchandise and unwary marks.

Nixy reclined in an antique upholstered chair that may have belonged in a manor house at one time, but was now part of the parlor's eclectic furnishings. The chair was near an iron fireplace that gave the room its orange glow and merry heat. The room itself had a high arched ceiling and cracked plastered walls. Decorative rugs covered the cold stone floor, muffling the echoes. The musty smell of dust and damp permeated the chamber, masked by hanging herbs and burning coals. Dripping candles lit the gloom, painting the curved walls with dancing shadows; pale wax lay spattered and frozen about the feet of the wrought iron stands like ghostly gore.

The boy's clothing was simple but of good quality and fit. He wore blue trousers, a white linen shirt with gray vest, a coat of dark blue wool, and a pair of leather boots wrapped with extra material for warmth. It was by far the finest outfit he had ever owned, and he found himself brushing dust and lint off it from time to time.

His hair was a mop of light blond shag that hung in his eyes and stood in a cowlick on top. It had grown out from the bowl cut he had received during his time in Casselvane Keep and he had not bothered to trim it again. The lad's youthful face was ruddy in the cheeks from too much wine; a treat he was given for a job well done, which described most of his jobs. He was small for a boy of twelve years, but his limbs were strong and nimble from a life of dodging in and out of trouble. Blue eyes stared sleepily into the fire, but his ears were sharp and attentive. He had to be wary, because he was not alone.

The chamber still contained the old wine casks from the tavern's glory days. The only person allowed to draw from the casks was the boss of the Silver District, the man who made the parlor his personal study. For the time being, Dexer was that man. The tall, gaunt figure was walking the length of the room now, enjoying the trappings of his position. He ran a velvet-gloved hand along the face of one of the large wine casks, tracing the faded markings of the original vintner's seal.

Dexer dressed head to toe in dark burgundy or black,

his skin was concealed but for his face, which emerged as a grotesque oval mask from a close-fitting hood. The man had unfeeling gray eyes under a thin ridge of brow, hairless and weathered like a stone relief. His straight, sharp nose and thin lips gave him a predatory look that well suited him.

Dexer was a killer, pure and simple; a man with lethal talents that had been placed in charge of a flock of wayward children, and ordered to bring them up in a manner that best suited the interests of the Circle. He didn't love his job, but it had its benefits.

He poured himself another goblet of wine from his favorite cask, swirling the dark liquid as he breathed in the aroma. Such treasures weren't meant for the boy, the cheap stuff was good enough for those purposes. He walked towards the lad in the chair and smiled his ghastly version of a friendly expression.

"You done well, Nixy my boy. This past year... I can't say how proud I am." Dexer sat in a nearby chair, balancing his goblet on his knee. "I always knew you were quality material."

Nixy smiled tightly, not wanting to seem too overjoyed. The man was almost like a father to him, despite the occasional death threats and scary speeches. His real father had been more of a misery to live with, so he had left home at an early age to find his fortune in the city. Now fortunes seemed to be finding him.

"Thanksss Dexer," Nixy said, his words slurring a bit from the wine. Drinking the strong burning grape juice made him feel grown up, but his head hurt if he had too much. The little cup he had been poured was almost empty.

Dexer said, with a twinkle in his eye, "The Boss tells me I should make you a housebreaker, seeing as how you've got the knack. Everyone was impressed by your break into Clavemont Manor, stealing right from the lord's study, no less! An over-achiever, that's what you are. You done what no one's done before or since, and lived to tell."

Nixy lowered his eyes and picked at his fingernails nervously. "What'd ya tell him?" He asked the gaunt man, "The Boss, I mean?"

Dexer's eyes narrowed as he read the boy's face and fidgeting hands. "I told him I'd wait till you're older; it's too much to lay on a kid so young."

Nixy relaxed noticeably; he hated housebreaking and never wanted to do it again. In truth he was very lucky to be alive at all; Lord Clavemont turned out to be the third monster Nixy had met in the last two years. The first had been Black Will, a man possessed by a demnox that gave him frightful powers; the next called itself a Guadim, and it looked like a corpse with horns, sharp teeth, and big bat-wings. It wanted Nixy's blood for some reason, and used Black Will to get it.

The third monster, Lord Clavemont, was one that no one suspected. He was popular and rich, throwing parties in his manor by the River Walk. He was an albino with white skin, light blue eyes and pale blond hair. He was well-liked, charming and generous with his fortune, and apart from his odd appearance, was as ordinary as a noble socialite could be. He had also *died* hundreds of years ago and was inhabited by a vemlok, a thirsting spirit from the Abyss. Instead of becoming a ravening ghoul, he had tamed the intruding spirit. The man had saved Nixy's life, killing Black Will on the roof of the cathedral and chasing the Guadim from the city. If Dexer was like Nixy's scary second father, Lord Clavemont was like a creepy rich uncle that watched him from afar and made secret plans for his life. Not an ideal family.

"The last thing I wanna do is push you in the wrong direction." Dexer said as he leaned forward, sipping his wine. "You've the talent to be whatever you want, kid. You're already the best pinch I got, day or night. I want you to build on that. Be like a ghost. That's you, Nixy Shadowskipper, best in the trade." Dexer got even more spooky when he was being encouraging; his eyes were all intense and staring.

The man's gaze always made Nixy squirm, though he was pleased to hear his new brotherhood name used. Once he became a made brother, Nixy had given up his old surname and took one that would carry his reputation. 'Shadowskipper' sounded skillful and harmless, like Nixy wanted to be. He could never go with a name like 'Nix the Nasty' or 'Nixy the Knife' like his mates suggested; that just wasn't *him*.

"One thing I gotta ask," said Dexer, admiring him like a prize pig, "How did you do it? How did you pull off the greatest break in the Circle's history? Clavemont Manor!" The gaunt man shivered dramatically. "No one *ever* came outta there who went in uninvited. But *you...* you go in with less than a month of training and nab a pretty thing from the lord's own desk!"

Nixy well recalled the jeweled dagger with the lord's symbol, propped upright on the nice desk. It was called a 'letter opener' but Nixy couldn't imagine a letter that needed to be stabbed open. He had tried to tell the story several times before, but there was a big part he had to leave out; his entry was strange enough, but his escape was completely unnatural.

"Um... it's kinda blurry. I was scared an' all." He tried to think of another way to avoid talking about it, but the wine made him want to talk. Wine was funny that way; his old rule of 'keep yer eyes open and yer mouth shut' was strangely reversed when he had some wine in him. "Like I said, I went in through the sewer drain and had to wash up in the cellar so no one could smell me. Then the door was spelled..." Dexer leaned forward to listen, making Nixy pause, "I *think* it was spelled anyway, and I just wished real hard that nothing bad would happen... and nothing did." He didn't know what to think of that himself, strange as it was. He had always been told that doors and windows protected by magic could hurt you or kill you without the right counter-spell to unlock it. He remembered touching the door and feeling the pulse and tingle, like something draining through him; like all the magic was being sapped away by his touch. Even Lord Clavemont had no answer for that.

Five months after the break-in, the vemlok nobleman had called him somehow, drawing him to a room where they had a little chat. The lord had asked many questions about Nixy's parents, his past, and about magic. Clavemont revealed that Nixy had blood more noble and powerful than any he had ever felt. Nixy supposed he had meant 'tasted.' But is it 'tasting' if you drink it through your fingers?

Dexer stirred impatiently. "You *wished* real hard and the ward spell let you pass?" His eyes searched Nixy for any clue that the boy was lying. He was definitely hiding something. "If it's a trade secret, I can respect that." He sipped his wine, "You don't have to tell the lads; I wouldn't expect you to. But there are no secrets between us, hmm?" He drew an imaginary tether between them with his finger, smiling like a cat in a birdcage. "We gotta have trust, and I have to know there isn't something *funny* going on." His pale face was stark against the dark hood and shadows, floating like a disembodied skull.

Nixy fought the stupor and shook his head, suddenly alarmed at the threat in the man's voice. "No Dexer! There's nothing funny going on, honest! I dunno how it worked out like it did... I figured I'd guessed the trick is all." He waited nervously for the menace to leave the gaunt man's eyes.

Dexer nodded slowly, accepting that answer... for now. "And how did you get away again?" he asked, "You always get 'blurry' on that part too."

Black Will pulled me out a window and took me to the roof of the cathedral to kill me, but Clavemont flew up there and knocked his head off. That was the truth, but it was the last thing he would say. The vemlok had made it very clear that if Nixy let his secret slip, there would be death and more death. He hadn't said as much, but he didn't have to. Clavemont had a way of getting in someone's head.

"I made it out a window and tied off a rope, that's how I got down," he squeaked, "I dunno which window it was, I just ran and found one that was in the clear." It sounded good to Nixy; he hoped Dexer would think so too. Dexer sat back in his chair and sipped more wine, so Nixy relaxed a bit.

"No spells on the windows? No noise, no pain when you opened it?" Dexer asked, "Or did you pull your little trick again?"

"There was one opened already," Nixy answered quickly. Wine made the lies tumble out, but were they good enough?

"It was raining like horse piss that night, but they had a window open?" Dexer's jaw muscles clenched like he was chewing leather.

Not a good lie, Nixy decided. *Of course it was pouring! Why didn't I think of that before I opened my big, stupid mouth?* A vein at Dexer's temple was standing out, so Nixy needed to think of something fast. He fought to keep calm and not stammer.

"It... it kinda smelled, like maybe somebody dumped out a chamber pot. I didn't stay to find out." *That sounded good, didn't it?* He looked expectantly at Dexer to see if the man had bought it.

It seemed he had. "You're a good kid Nixy," Dexer said, turning his gaze to the fire. "And you done well. There's a special luck about you, that's for sure. Maybe Tavenji's got his eye on you." He touched the side of his nose and pointed at Nixy; it was the Circle's hand sign for keeping a secret. "Maybe you got something you don't even know about."

That was true enough. As Nixy thought about the last few years of his young life, there were more and more things that popped up in his memory, black wolves watching him from afar, even appearing in the castle bailey. While on the cathedral roof, the troll monster said they couldn't save him this time. *Save him?* Nixy was *terrified* of wolves; black ones especially. Then there was his talent for hiding. Lord Clavemont had looked right at him and later told Nixy he hadn't seen him; he thought he was looking at a shade, a ghost. *Maybe what's special about me is the reason I keep running into monsters*, Nixy thought, as he made the connection at last. He had always assumed he had rotten luck, but now it seemed he had 'special luck' that came with a special price.

He preferred ordinary, rotten luck.

Chapter Three

Dillan DePort

Lady Mytha had taken until morning to decide and came to the conclusion that the girl's life depended on her help, whether her son agreed to take her as a student or not. It would be a great tragedy if the count's daughter was discovered and killed because the baroness had not made the effort to teach her a few boyish mannerisms.

Cindra's training began with getting dressed in the morning, learning to hide her feminine features. Jaron, who could return as an assistant instructor, would be assigned private quarters that he would share with Cindra. This would allow her to take certain precautions before dressing, such as wrapping her breasts with a length of fabric, flattening them as much as possible. She had always been self-conscious of her slow development, but now she was happy that there was not more to hide. If she were as well-endowed as the girls she had envied, her life would be taking a cruel turn about now.

The real trick was teaching Jaron to help her get dressed without becoming overly distracted. The baroness was present during the first few attempts, and this caused some anxiety for them both. However once he and Cindra were alone, they fumbled and giggled their way through it more comfortably, if not more efficiently.

The main trouble with her disguise turned out to be the hosiery, for while she had too much to hide above the waist, she had too little below. Jaron was reluctant to offer opinion, so Lady Mytha was consulted.

"What if we used a codpiece?" said the baroness as she and Cindra examined the fit of the hose in a large polished mirror.

Jaron glanced over at the girl. The green fabric was tight and left little to the imagination, not that Jaron needed to imagine; he had seen her bathing once, thinking she was a dark-skinned Galindri girl until she rose from the water and her dark skin ended at the waist and mid-thigh. The memory made him blush and he turned away.

"You don't think that's a bit much? What if we just stuffed it with something?" Cindra said, turning her hips to and fro while lifting the hem of her shirt to see.

"Perhaps a roll of linen?" said the baroness, as she looked about for something suitable. Finding a clean hand towel, she rolled it up and handed it to Cindra while making sure Jaron was looking away. The knight was looking at the ceiling, shaking his head.

"What do you think?" said Cindra after she had finished. She presented the new packaging for their approval and the baroness broke out in laughter, while Jaron's mouth dropped. It was far more... *conspicuous* than necessary and not something he wished to see on the woman he loved. Lady Mytha's laughter made Cindra giggle and soon they were adjusting it back and forth, trying to get Jaron to stand by for comparison.

"I will not!" Jaron cried, and sat in a chair, crossing

his legs. This only made them laugh harder.

"This won't do," Cindra said breathlessly, her face red with mirth. "What about a plum?"

The baroness laughed anew, "A pear!" she exclaimed.

"A sausage!" Cindra barely finished the word as she doubled over, holding the arm of the baroness for support while they laughed hysterically in a manner quite unsuitable for mixed company. Jaron endured as long as he could and finally left, unexcused.

The women looked up at the sound of the closing door, looked at each other, and laughed all over again.

Later in the hour, a servant delivered a summons to Jaron, who was sulking on the terrace. Reluctantly he returned to his quarters, wondering what the ladies had in store for him. He was in no mood for jokes, so he was relieved when he found Cindra posing by the mirror in a pair of bombast-breeches that cinched at the waist and mid-thigh. It not only hid her feminine hips and behind, but freed her from having to wear a mockery of a male member. For this, Jaron was exceedingly grateful.

"Much better," he said as Cindra turned for him, and the baroness smiled in approval. "That is a northern fashion, actually. How did you come by them?"

"I bought them on a whim at last year's trade fair," Lady Mytha explained. "I have a small horde of old and new clothing; in hope of grandsons, you see. But so far, my sons have been blessed with girls."

"I think it looks a bit silly; it makes everything rather shapeless." Cindra pouted as she looked in the mirror.

"That is the point, my dear." The baroness gave the pants an adjusting tug.

"On me yes," said Cindra as she pulled at the hose under the pants. "But I rather prefer a more revealing look on a gentleman, from behind, I mean. It helps to verify good tone and breeding; rather like a horse." She and the baroness shared a sly smile as they watched Jaron in the mirror. Seeing his stupefied expression, Cindra sputtered in laughter and snorted, making the baroness burst forth as well. Jaron shook his head. It was going to be a long winter.

————

Sir Cord returned home from Portshia in early Kraamoth, the last month of the year. Cordoshome usually received only a dusting of snow, but this year the snowfall was much heavier and it was all the knight spoke of as the family and servants greeted him by the fireplace in the main hall. His wide shoulders cast a huge shadow upon the wall, and his barrel chest gave him a voice that reverberated about the high ceiling. He hung his cloak on a hook in the foyer and stamped his booted feet to remove the snow. It resounded like the footfalls of a giant.

"Father, good to see you! I feared I would not make it up the road with all this ice." Cord brushed the snow from his shoulders and embraced Lord Saul, who met his son with a bit of formal stiffness, or it might have been the cold affecting his joints. The baron had become doddering and eccentric in his old age, and seldom made public appearances anymore. His white hair looked hastily combed and sat oddly about his head, and his eyes showed confusion for a moment, but he smiled readily as they parted their embrace.

"Mother!" He smiled as the Lady Mytha came forward to hug him. "Quite a winter, eh?" The big knight's beard had gone a bit long and his mother tugged at it.

"Not so cold that you need the extra hair, my dear," she chided, looking him over to see if he was adequately fed. "All is well at the school, I trust?"

"Well enough, I suppose. We graduated most of the lads this class, and have a new batch of students to look forward to come spring, though fewer than I'd like." He removed his beret and scratched his sandy hair near the binding of the *tipok* knot at the back of his head. The braided locks needed to be rebound and drooped wearily.

"I might have one more for you," called Jaron from the stairs. A young boy followed close behind, his auburn hair trimmed short with longer forelocks. Cord looked up in surprise and tossed his arms in the air with joy.

"Jaron! You lucky fool! I was hoping I'd see you here before your time was up. How was your exile?" The big knight hugged the smaller man in a bear-like grip as he reached the foot of the stairs.

Jaron groaned, "Two years without being crushed or smacked about, I'd say it was a holiday!" He slapped the man on the shoulders as he grinned from ear to ear.

"And who is this?" Cord looked behind Jaron to the boy on the stairs. "Did you rescue a puppy in your travels?" The big knight's smile was charming and friendly.

"This," said Jaron, presenting the lad, "is Dillan DePort, my squire, who will be training at your school if you'll have him." The boy stepped down the stairs and bowed low.

"Dillan! Did this scoundrel tell you he was a knight?" Cord bellowed, "He's just too lazy to groom his own horse!"

Jaron thumped the big man in the stomach. "Don't demoralize my squire any further. It's bad enough that I told him *you* were the master of the Freekirk School."

The lad smiled meekly, as if unsure whether to laugh or not. "How do you do, Sir Cord?" Dillan asked. The lad's voice was light and high, and had not yet dropped to a manly tone.

"I do as I can, young Dillan. Welcome to House Freekirk. We will talk more over dinner." He looked to his mother, "I do hope I'm in time?" he asked.

"As if you were ever late for a meal?" Jaron muttered.

The baroness inclined her round face and said, "There is still time for you to draw a bath and change, my dear. I have sent most of the staff home for the winter, so the cook needs a bit more time."

"Ah," said the big knight, "That is my mother's way of

telling me that I smell. Very well, off with me. Good to meet you young Dillan." He stomped upstairs to his room and disappeared.

Cindra looked around at everyone's faces and smiled, elated. Months of acting lessons from Jaron and the baroness had just been tested on Sir Cord, who had only met her once two years ago. If she could continue to fool him successfully, her confidence would gather much needed strength.

Lord Saul frowned and looked to his wife, muttering in her ear. "What's this about the girl attending the school? You never said she would be at the school."

Lady Mytha whispered to him, "It is how she will get into the city undetected. She might stay there awhile until other arrangements are made. Sir Jaron says it is all a secret mission you know, very mysterious."

Lord Saul brightened as he recalled what his wife had told him hours before, "Ah yes, the girl is a spy looking for the count's enemies! I recall, yes..." He blustered, "You don't think the villains are in the school?"

The baroness led him to the chair by the fire saying, "Possibly, it's all very hush-hush. Let's not spoil the surprise now, hmm? If she can fool Cord, then we'll know her training has not been in vain." She sat him in a warm chair and poured him a glass of mulled wine.

"Cord?" he asked, "Ah yes, a fine boy, as I recall."

Dinner was served an hour later. A long table was placed in the main hall and the family gathered around for the evening meal; the lord and lady sat at one end with Cord and Jaron on either side. Dillan sat beside Jaron, where she was meant to pour his drink and serve his food, as a squire's duties required. The rest of the table was conspicuously empty. The other five Freekirk sons had estates of their own or lived modestly elsewhere; only Cord preferred to winter with his parents rather than spend the colder months in the city.

After the baroness led them in prayers to Obesh for the bounty of the sea and Jayda for the bounty of the land, the feast began in earnest. Venison and fish were served on copper trays, steamed crabs awaited the crack of breaking stones; three kinds of bread came fresh and steaming from the oven, served with whipped butter and olive oil; a selection of vegetables from the garden were set about the table in decorative ceramic bowls; cups of wine and flagons of winter ale were set upon fire-heated flat stones to keep them warm. The meal was not overly fancy but there was plenty of food. What could not be finished was shared among the cooking staff, so they probably made larger portions on purpose.

After serving Jaron, who was still not used to the idea, Dillan grabbed fork and knife and attacked the food like a growing lad ought to. She held her elbows in the air as she sawed the meat into smaller bites. It was one of the hardest things for Cindra to break herself of, so ingrained had been her table manners.

Cord talked around a portion of fish as he addressed Jaron and the lad. "So how did the two of you meet up? Have squires dropped their standards?" He looked at Dillan and grinned, happy with his little pun.

"Cord, do behave. Show some respect to Jaron in front of the lad." Lady Mytha scolded.

"It was an honest question mother." He turned to Jaron and asked, "I assume you told the boy's family about the details of your errantry? They deserved to know, surely." He was being serious now, for it was an important matter.

Jaron nodded, "They know that I was banished, yes. They also know I am to return to the count's service after my exile."

Dillan noticed that Jaron looked uneasy; he was a terrible liar, but he wasn't really lying, just omitting certain pertinent facts.

Cord looked to Dillan and asked, "I am not familiar with House DePort; are they an old family?"

Cindra gave her prepared biography, "My parents are not nobles, Sir Cord; my father manages orchards in Waynwell." The city was to the northwest, beyond the

Shadowood Forest; it was where Cindra had said goodbye to her adopted Galindri family before she and Jaron made for Cordoshome. "There were no knights in the city that wanted a commoner for a squire, except for Sir Jaron." She made sure she didn't finish chewing before speaking; she was surprised at how boyish it sounded.

"Ah, I see." Cord nodded. "Some knights seek to train boys from impressive families, hoping to improve their own fortunes. I've always been more concerned with quality myself." He drank several gulps of ale, trickling a bit down his beard.

Jaron added, "Dillan's parents know my father was made a knight by brave deeds in battle, but before that he was a farmer." It was simply easier for Jaron to speak the truth, or partial truths, but he noted that Cindra was far more at ease with her false biography, having made up most of it herself. It seemed she was playing at pretend, still unmindful of how serious her deception would be.

Dillan said between bites, "Dad and mum were happy to see me off. Being a knight is all I ever talked about." She had to be careful not to get too chatty.

"Was that your horse in the stables then?" Cord asked.

Dillan nodded, "Yep. T'ózha is his name." She flinched a bit, not sure if she should have made up an alias for her horse.

"Tozha?" remarked Cord, mispronouncing the strange word. "What manner of name is that?"

Jaron looked sidelong at Dillan who responded, "Galindri sir. My parents bought the foal from a caravan for a good price and trade." Cindra had seen it done before in her travels, for Galindri horses were a fine breed and highly sought after. "T'ózha means 'he is fast' in their tongue." She spoke the language rather fluently herself and liked to instruct.

"Well, I hope they dealt honestly with you. The animal looks fine enough, but I'd not trust them." Cord remarked. His prejudice was not uncommon but it made Cindra bristle. She had not only lived with the Galindri but was made to look as one, so she knew firsthand how 'Outlanders' treated them. She was about to refute the remark when Jaron nudged her under the table.

"It's good that you have your own horse though," Cord amended. "We train in mounted combat but few students have their own mounts. Most have to purchase one from a breeder after a lord has retained them; for some it's a choice between mount and armor." He knew Jaron and his father Sir Fedrick had been in the same predicament but there was no gibe in his remark; it was simply a fact of life if one was not very wealthy.

The rest of the meal was spent talking of news from Portshia, which Cindra found to be particularly gripping. She had been so long without word from home that she had to restrain herself from blurting out questions, which would have been improper for a boy at table, especially if he had never been there. She had to count on Jaron to ask the pertinent questions and she prodded him under the table with her foot when he lagged behind.

Cord was saying, "So there was a year of mourning; all the city was hung with black banners, and prayers for the departed were made each Highday. They were only taken down during spring of this year but there is still a pall over the city." His eyes were downcast. "House Corrina is a sad place, though life goes on, as it must."

Jaron had admitted to hearing of Lady Cindra's death over a year ago, but still hung his head in feigned sorrow; he'd given in to despair and nearly been ruined.

Cindra was quite familiar with the city's official mourning rites, having lost her baby brother years before; she was far more concerned for her mother and father. She nudged Jaron's foot saying, "Her poor parents..."

Jaron looked into her expectant eyes and asked, "Yes, what news of House Corrina? How fares the family?"

Cord was a knight of House Corrina but spent little time at the keep, unless it was to visit Jaron's father Sir Fedrick, who lived in modest quarters in the castle. He took a deep breath and said; "I have not seen them much, for they only leave the Highcourt to go to the cathedral once a week. It is said that the count is working on the alliance with Rokvynnar still, hoping to gain their support for the king... the *new* king, that is." Murmured prayers for the departed Galen II went around the table. "I hear the pirate hunting is not going well for the navy," Cord continued. "They're scouring the coast for Minozhian longships but they could be up a river in the woods for all we know."

"Bad business, bad business," the baron muttered into his beard.

Cindra's eyes flashed at the mention of Minozhians; the bull-headed beast men had killed poor Mineth, her handmaiden and life-long friend. Her face reddened and she looked to her food, trying to eat despite her loss of appetite.

"You know, I almost forgot the strangest news of all." Cord exclaimed, "Later that spring, there was a bizarre story about the cathedral. It seems a body was found on the *roof*, up on one of the buttresses."

The baroness was appalled. "Oh, how horrible! Was it a worker that fell? Poor man."

"No one knows for sure who he was, but they say he was no worker; no work was scheduled. And the oddest part," Cord leaned forward and lowered his voice, "was that they never found the head. Not on the roof, not on the ground."

Cindra shivered at the memory of Black Will, the demnox-possessed man who could scale walls like a lizard. "Was... was it a boy's body?" she asked meekly. If anything had happened to her young friend Nixy, she would be devastated. She had left him safe and sound at the castle, where he could start a new life.

"I heard it was a man, and a filthy one at that." Cord smiled reassuringly, "But don't worry lad, you'll be safe enough at the school."

Dillan asked, "Sir Jaron, may I be excused?"

Jaron was still not used to having the count's daughter ask leave of him. "Er, yes, Dillan. I think we shall talk with Sir Cord after dinner." Dillan bowed to the baron and baroness, then to the men before heading upstairs.

"Well, I seem to have put the young man off his dessert." Cord said as he grinned at his mother, who returned his look with raised eyebrows.

"Dessert?" said the baroness, "There is no dessert, my dear."

"No dessert?" Cord bellowed, "Why, surely House Freekirk is crumbling! Sad times have befallen us! No dessert..." He crossed his arms and hung his head in mock despair. "Why did you send so many servants home this winter?"

The baron, also distressed by the lack of desert and the apparent decline of his house, looked to his wife for answers.

"I think Sir Jaron can explain that, but it is not a subject for the dinner table." She raised her cup of wine and smiled.

"Oooh, hehehe," Lord Saul chuckled and winked slyly at his son. *Now* he remembered. Deception and intrigue was most entertaining, especially if one was in on it.

Sir Cord grumbled as he followed Jaron to his quarters, questioning the back of the smaller knight's head. "What in the dark Abyss is going on here, Dunlorden? What are you up to and why are my mother and father acting like cats with cream?"

The windows were shut against the cold and a fire was burning in the hearth. Dillan, who was sitting in an upholstered chair, did not rise when they entered; the lad looked rather pleased with himself for some reason. There was a cot on one side of the room and a bed on the other, with several piles of new clothes neatly stacked on the dressing table. Sweet grass was added to the fire and gave off a calming scent, though Cord was not soothed by it; things were too strange in his ancestral home to be lulled by incense.

Jaron closed the door and checked the windows as if someone might be listening below, even though they were high above the ground. The big knight stood there with his hands on his hips, wondering if Jaron had come back from his exile with delusions, or a new sense of mischief. He looked at Dillan just sitting there, watching him as if in amusement. It was unnerving.

"Do you know what this is all about, Dillan?" Sir Cord asked, guessing that the lad was a part of the puzzle.

"Dillan *is* what this is all about," Jaron said as he stood by the chair. "Sir Cord Freekirk, may I present to you... Lady Cindra Corrina." He gestured to the boy in the chair.

Cord stood in shock, his look of astonishment turning to a slow angry burn. "I'd laugh if that was remotely funny Dunlorden."

"Why Sir Cord," said Cindra, "I thought you made it a point to know your betters," she used her proper voice and accent, choosing words he had spoken to her two years before.

The big man's jaw dropped as he stared hard at the boy, seeing for the first time the shape of his face, the set of his eyes, the auburn hair as it might be if it were longer and styled differently. He, no *she*, was the spitting image of the noble girl he had met in better times; her face and nose like her mother's, her eyes like those of her father, Count Casselvane. He sat heavily on the bed, not taking his eyes from the girl lest she vanish in a puff of smoke.

"But you died at sea..." He covered his mouth.

She shook her head gently and smiled, her hazel-green eyes shining in the firelight.

"It's a long story," said Jaron as he walked to the door. "I shall get us something to drink."

Chapter Four

Nixy the Spy

Dexer took a carriage on a roundabout route through the streets of Portshia to DuShonmaer, the impressive estate of Kobus DuChat, the wealthiest man in the entire province. DuChat was a product of a growing trend towards a third class of people between noble and common, rich and poor. He was filthy rich but had no title or lordship, making him unequal in the eyes of the peerage, even as they scrambled for a slice of his wealth. It was funny if one thought about it, and Dexer smirked as the carriage rolled through the gates of DuShonmaer, bearing the coat of arms that DuChat had purchased the honor of displaying.

Kobus DuChat was many things to many people, but only a select few in the city knew him as the Boss. As the Boss, DuChat had secretly created an alliance between competing gangs, forging the Circle of Gold; a brotherhood of thieves that was organized, successful and feared. None but the district bosses knew his true identity and fewer reported directly to him. Dexer was boss of the Silver District, which included the Market Square, making it the juiciest fruit of the bunch; it was a reward for faithful and ruthless service.

Now the Boss wanted to talk to Dexer about a matter of some importance and had summoned him through the city's courier network. The courier's guild had a number of operatives in each district that were in the Circle's employ, sometimes unknown even to themselves. Messages bearing certain addresses or marks were rerouted or given special significance, speeding them to the bosses and muddling their origin. Dexer had received his parcel less than an hour ago; it came as a package for Sister Bethley at the Silver Sunrise Orphanage, via three other stops. The contents were unimportant, but the parcel to the non-existent priestess was a summons not to be ignored.

As he stepped out of the carriage and paid the driver, Dexer saw a man and woman exiting the front door, chatting happily. He had noticed them around the area lately, the man was Julen Gordon, a shipping merchant or some such thing; the woman was his wife Lemorea, an insufferably cheerful wench. They supposedly lived in the Silver District and the word was handed down that they were under the Circle's protection; there would be no predation on their property or interests. Dexer stared at them as they passed him by, the couple smiling at him stupidly as though he were a member of decent society. Little did they know that if DuChat gave the word, Dexer would terminate their business agreement with a late night visit and a pair of knives. They climbed aboard the waiting carriage and departed, gabbing together like a pair of old women.

The gaunt man entered the foyer and nodded to the butler, who bid him wait while he announced his presence. The smell of incense could be detected in the hall; a rich cloying scent that lulled the unwary into relaxation, making them more pliable to the will of the renowned merchant. It also helped to cover any other smells that might hint at a darker side of his business dealings. The butler approached and beckoned to Dexer silently, leading him down the hall to DuChat's office.

The door opened and revealed the opulent study of the underworld boss, decorated with rare, strange items from years of travel. There was a bookshelf full of ledgers and manifests, and a portrait of the late elder DuChat hung above a polished dark wood desk, behind which sat the master of the house. Kobus DuChat motioned for Dexer to enter as he leaned back in his chair, taking a pinch from a silver snuffbox. The man was dressed in a silk doublet with voluminous sleeves ending in frills at the wrist. His hair was black and curly, trimmed shorter on the sides, and his beard was a neatly brushed border around his lips and jaw. The man's most noticeable features were his eyes; large gray orbs under heavy eyelids and a dark brow that many women found so alluring. Dexer always wondered at the scar on DuChat's left eyelid that made it sit a little more heavily than the other.

"Welcome, Lintroth." DuChat used the killer's family name to nettle the man, reminding him that he knew where he came from. Not that Dexer cared much for family he had left behind long ago. "How have things been in the Warren? Not too stressful I trust?"

Dexer sat in the offered chair and went right to business; otherwise the man would dally about with pleasantries just to test his patience. "Things are good. I got your summons. You have something for me?" DuChat snorted a laugh, or it might have been because of the snuff.

"Have you heard news of the count's attempts to save the alliance with Rokvynnar, despite the loss of his poor daughter?" Kobus turned the snuffbox around, admiring it and ignoring Dexer's blank stare.

"No Boss, I haven't." Dexer didn't keep track of such things, and the Boss knew it; if they had nothing to do with business in the Silver District, it was none of Dexer's business.

DuChat put the snuffbox down and spoke in his lecturing tone, "Two years ago, Count Casselvane had secured an alliance through marriage with a ducal family in Rokvynnar, promising trade and mutual assistance in the event of a civil war. The Rok have a fine navy, making them important allies to the king. As we all know, the bride's ship was attacked and the wedding never happened; yet the alliance is so important that the count is still trying to make it work." DuChat stood and paced behind his desk, fingering dust from the frame of his father's portrait. "They are very tight-lipped about it, keeping all the details secret. I need to keep track of the lord's progress so I can plan accordingly."

Dexer said, "I thought you had two people inside the keep already?"

DuChat smiled, "My main source of information is one of the count's men; an honest fellow, if a bit arrogant. I generously loaned him money in a time of need, and now he has me over each week for lunch."

"He was bought that easily?" Dexer marveled.

"The man does not know he has been bought. He still keeps the count's secrets, but he likes to gossip like an old woman. One just needs to sieve his words." DuChat shrugged, "The other fellow is not so close to the lord and lady, but he has his uses."

He looked at Dexer, as though an idea had just struck him. "You had a boy in the castle for a time, the one who was saved by the count's daughter on the night of her engagement. Is he still alive?"

Dexer shifted in his chair. "Nixy, yeah, my best boy. He's the one I told you about, the one who broke Clavemont Manor last year." DuChat had a long and precise memory and Dexer knew it well. He realized that Nixy was the reason he'd been summoned, but the Boss liked to playact.

"Ah, the prized apprentice housebreaker! Yes, I recall now. You said he was not ready for advanced training, that he was better off on the street, pinching purses.

Well, I have decided that he would make a better spy inside House Corrina. His closeness to the departed girl may allow him access to his lordship, and that may lead to insight that I would find vital."

Dexer recognized an order when he heard one, but he had some issues. "I'm not sure the boy would make a good spy. He's a good kid, but he's still young. He might have some attachments to the family... some doubts..."

"He needn't know he's a spy. You can spin him any story you wish, so long as he knows to keep his eyes and ears open. There is no betrayal involved, just good business planning." DuChat waved his hand, "Make him think we are doing the family a favor, helping them secretly. I don't care. But I need to know if the mood of their lordships changes for the better. Such a diplomatic success will surely improve their temperaments."

Dexer nodded glumly; there was no telling if the lad would return to the Circle this time. *That's all I need, to lose a prize pupil like him*, Dexer thought as he stared blankly at the desk. "What if they don't take him back? He left on his own, ducked out on them. They might not be so... charitable this time."

"Never underestimate the power of sentiment, my friend." DuChat waved a finger like a master to a foolish student. "A familiar face on a particular day will change the Gold Cat to a kitten. As for the lad's conscience, I leave it to you to set him at ease." The Boss grinned with his last remark, for Dexer could set no one at ease.

The gaunt man was at a loss to argue any further, besides it was unwise. His prized pupil would be taken out of his hands yet again, not by fate this time, but by a direct order. He wasn't sure what the Boss thought the boy could accomplish, but the man had a way with people, even ones he'd never met. Dexer sucked up his misgivings, nodded his head, and donned his wide-brimmed hat. "It'll be done," he said and stood to leave.

As he did, DuChat reached for a quill and a scrap of

parchment. "Before you go, let me give you the date and time of his dramatic reintroduction." He scribbled on the scrap and handed it to his underling.

Dexer read it as he walked out. It said simply '*Evening, 28th of Kraamoth.*'

Nixy wasn't sure what to expect. His life had taken another odd turn when Dexer told him he would no longer be working in the market like he wanted, but would be going back to House Corrina to live if they would have him. It made no sense. When he had gone missing from the Circle of Gold last time, Dexer had threatened him, telling him he had better remember who his *real* family was. Now he wanted him to go back and spy. It *was* spying, he was sure of it, though Dexer had made it sound so harmless. Nixy was to go back and look for signs of happiness in the count and countess, like a secret joy they couldn't quite contain. He had explained that the Circle was interested in lots of different things and had to know which way the tide turned. If they were happy, it would be good for everyone and the Circle could make plans. If they weren't happy, then there was nothing to bother with. It sounded harmless enough, but the Circle was always up to something. The last thing he wanted to do was bring pain on Cindra's parents; they had more than their share.

He was stopped at the Highcourt gate, the road that went up past many noble villas and ended at Casselvane Keep. The night sentries looked him up and down, taking in his common clothes and young innocent face, their trained mistrust judging him as having no business within. He presented the parcel he was given to deliver, marked with a seal of the Trade Guild. He also carried the seal of a city courier, which he held up for their inspection. They let him pass, just as Dexer said they would.

The trek through the Highcourt was uphill and slippery, for the cobblestones were slick with ice and light snowfall. The moon shone overhead, giving the night a pale glow as Nixy's cold nose took in the scent of firewood crackling in well-kept hearths. Torches at the castle gate burned in the distance, flickering like candles above the short, iron braziers that gave off warming heat to the night watch. It was the deepest part of winter, just past the equinox when the days began to grow longer again. It was also Lady Cindra's birthday if he remembered right.

His mind swam with memories of two years ago. It was a night warmer than this, but he had shivered more. He had been nervous because it was the night of his big test and he had to prove himself to become a made brother. He had picked a girl walking alone near the Market Square, looking at the lights and not the shadows. He made the grab, but she ran after him and caught him.

What happened next was forever burned in his mind.
Black Will...
Being unable to scream...
The girl saving him with his own knife...
The ghastly black bones of smoke and fire...
He later found out that *Cutter*, the knife his mother left him, was a magic knife and wouldn't have driven off the monster otherwise. It was his most prized possession and he kept it with him now at all times. Black Will was dead but there were worse things out there, wanting to snatch him away.

He reached the castle gate and showed his credentials, getting a similar treatment from the gatekeepers. The castle bailey was just like he remembered. He looked at the stable quarters where he once lived, and to the kennels where he spent happier times with the count's hounds. The dogs howled as if welcoming him home and he felt warmer inside. The gloom that had driven him away from this place had lifted and he felt only good things now. He wondered if he might get his old cot back in the stable house or if someone else was sleeping there now. He also wondered if Stable Master Gorin would smack him around for leaving on his own. He almost missed the squat potato man and his bellowing voice. Almost.

The main hall was dimly-lit and gloomy, but there was a small, solemn feast taking place nonetheless. The grand table, once an impressive ring seating dozens, had been reduced to a small arc. To Nixy, it was a sorrowful sight. The great hall meant feasting and parties and music; it was the heart of the castle and all who dwelt within. Now that heart seemed dark and broken; stripped of joy, laughter, and all good things. He felt a lump in his throat as he saw the count and countess dining quietly with a handful of guests.

The count wore a robe of blue and gold, embroidered with the gold cat of House Corrina. His graying, chestnut-colored hair was looking thinner and grayer, and his beard was longer than Nixy remembered. The lord's face was drawn and cheerless, creased and wrinkled from years of worry.

The countess was younger than her husband by nearly twenty years, and rather beautiful. Her high cheekbones, and long, elegant nose were traits she had passed on to her daughter. Her hair was golden blond and braided in a simple manner, hanging down her back without veil or ornament. The lady's most striking feature were her emerald green eyes, which now were downcast and sad.

The guard escorting Nixy announced him as a courier bearing a parcel from the Trade Guild, but the lord and lady barely raised their eyes from their plates. Nixy walked to the table and placed the parcel before the count, bowing clumsily. The count, finally looking up at the face of the courier, stood in amazement.

"Nixyalderthor!" he cried, his eyes alight. "Zara, see here, it's young Nixy!"

The countess was agape and her eyes welled with tears as she beheld the boy. She reached for the count's hand and squeezed, her eyes never leaving the child. "Is it true? Nixyalderthor DuQuayne?" Her voice, accented from her old home in Aurilon, shook with emotion. The other dinner guests looked on in confounded silence, perhaps grateful for anything that would shatter the melancholy of the feast.

Nixy was shocked that they remembered his name, for it was almost two years to the day they had met him. He stood before the lord and lady, quivering inside, worried that he would either fail Dexer or further ruin the lives of the Corrina family. He too mourned the death of Cindra and had nothing but gratitude for the lord and lady for taking him in so long ago. He ventured to speak, though it might be out of place in this company.

"Yes, yer lordship, it's me." He squeaked the last word as his stomach turned. He gave an unpracticed bow and stood rooted under the gaze of the rulers of the province, not sure what to do next.

Lady Zara looked as though a ghost from the past had returned; she spoke with an uneven voice, "We heard you had vanished and feared the worst. Our dear Cindra had risked so much to save you from that monster." Her voice cracked as she spoke her daughter's name, and Nixy cast his eyes to the floor.

"I... I left because..." he had practiced what to say, but he was not one for words, "because it hurt too much to stay, the sadness I mean. I had to get away..." He was surprised to see both the count and countess nod in understanding, the grief plain on their faces. "I'm sorry," he said hurriedly, "I didn't mean to make anyone mad."

The countess shook her head, "No, we did not wish to keep you longer than you could endure, child. But we feared the worst when you vanished."

"Well, now you have returned," said the count, his face creasing in a rare smile. "This is the young boy that our dear Cindra saved and brought home two years ago." The guests looked at each other in wonder. Was this strange return of a lost child a sign from the gods?

"I was hoping..." Nixy cleared his throat, which felt suddenly tight. "Things in the city were getting dangerous and... I was hoping I might stay here again, if you'd have me." Nixy mumbled the request. He didn't *want* them to accept him back, not if it meant he had to spy on them. He also didn't want to upset Dexer or fail the Circle of Gold. *I'm not a spy,* he reminded himself, *I'm not spying on 'em, not really.*

"Of course, child," said the countess. She arose, walked around the table, and placed her hands upon his shoulders. "You are always welcome in our house," she said. Some of the light had returned to her eyes, and they seemed to smile once more. Nixy grinned uneasily, his happiness mixed with guilt.

"Thank you, milady. Should I report to the stables then?" Nixy asked. The countess's eyes widened slightly, and then softened as she turned to her husband.

"I think not, my boy," said the count. "We shall find a place for you here. You shall be given a wardship." Quiet murmurings of amusement and approval went around the table.

Nixy was confused, "Wardship? Is that like a-a sailboat?" The guests chuckled and the lord and lady smiled.

"No child," said the countess, "It means that you shall be in the care of House Corrina and raised here in the castle."

Nixy just stood and blinked, his knees wobbled and threatened to buckle as he teetered on his suddenly weak ankles. *I'm going to be raised in the castle instead of mucking out the stables? I'm going to eat food from the kitchen instead of getting scraps! I'll be sleeping in a nice bed by a fire, not an old dusty crypt in the Warren, or a smelly cot above the stables! Ha! What would Dexer say to that?*

What *would* Dexer say? He suddenly felt a chill down his spine as he recalled the reason for his return. He was supposed to tell Dexer when the lord and lady were secretly happy about something so the Circle could make plans. He was supposed to spy on his new family for his old family. Nixy Shadowskipper, Circle of Gold spy in House Corrina. He didn't like the sound of that; it made him kind of sick.

The gathered guests began to applaud, and Nixy looked into the kind faces of the count and countess. He recalled the first time they had granted him a place to stay; Nixy had told them of Cindra's bravery, and had begged that she be treated like a hero, not punished. Maybe it was his praise of her that led to their present kindness, or maybe they wanted to have a child in the castle again. Nixy knew that he didn't want to do anything to betray them, but crossing Dexer was a really bad idea.

Things had been going so well in the Circle lately, and he liked the respect the other lads gave him. Even Daymi and Cricket, the former favorite pupils, had learned to back off. They had been the ones who picked Clavemont Manor for his breaker test, hoping he would get himself killed. Now his special luck had placed him in Dexer's favor. That same special luck was also working for him now and he wondered what the price would be later on. Would he have to choose between the Circle of Gold and the Gold Cat?

"Thank you, milord." He bowed low, feeling cold and slimy, like a worm in an apple.

Chapter Five

Lady Woodkin

Wenyssaya gazed down the road at the dwivayiin city in the distance, a massive collection of wood and stone that spanned from the base of the mountains to the carved channel that diverted river water past its walls. The city extended farther still, spreading out like seepage from its enclosed center; cottages and huts clustered together for protection on the verge of the untamed lands beyond. A canopy of haze from countless hearth fires hung over the expanse, irritating the eyes and nose. It was much like the other settlements she had ridden past on her journey, though she had seldom seen one so large.

The dwivayiin had never learned to moderate their creations or their lives, short and fleeting though they were. Her teachers had explained that the dwivayiin had always been determined to ask questions and find answers; it was why they changed constantly, rising and falling, only to rise again, lessons forgotten and relearned.

She stroked the neck of the white mare that had borne her so many leagues, apologizing for the burden with her soothing fingers. She whispered in the horse's ear, promising rest, oats and fresh water daily when the journey ended. The horse snorted with satisfaction, replying that the burden was neither great nor the road difficult.

Wenyssaya smiled and sat back, adjusting her riding dress across her legs to diminish the winter draft. It was early in the year by the calendar of these lands and the weather was unusually cold, even this far south. It was a time of change when great events would transpire; all of the elders agreed that the signs were clear. The gods who dwelt in the outer realms had fallen silent since the Great Thinning, but the gods of nature were a part of this world, and could still speak to the learned through sky, water and earth. A tempest had been seen on the horizon and Wenyssaya's training had been advanced in preparation. The summons from the west had been troubling, but anticipated.

The call of a raven echoed overhead in the crisp blue sky, its shadow crossing the road before her as it glided past the noonday sun. Navithwi was his name; he had delivered her summons, and they had since become fast friends and traveling companions. He spoke of a clear road ahead and smells that meant food aplenty, but Navithwi could dine on a decomposing rat and be overjoyed; so the maiden had learned to be skeptical of his opinions. Cities meant the best and worst of the dwivayiin; they were a tight collection of the kind and cruel. If she was lucky she would encounter more of the former.

As she passed farmhouses and little clusters of cottages near the road, she drew looks of curiosity from the townsfolk. It happened everywhere she went; there was no denying that she was different and a raised hood could not hide it all. Wenyssaya's clothing was beautiful and elegant, though she thought it rather simple. The dress was made of gossamer silk dyed green like spring leaves and embroidered with vine patterns that twisted and intertwined playfully. Her vest was fine linen, the color of deep earth tones, bound at the sides and tied up the front with laces of braided leather. Her boots were made of tanned doeskin, stitched with twisting leafy branches. They were also immaculately clean, as though her feet never touched the ground on her journey.

Her hair, when it could be seen beneath the dark gray hooded cloak, shone like gold in the sun, and hung in curls that bounced with the horse's gait. The back of her hands and fingers were painted with dark markings of reddish brown, and they rested on the mare's back, smoothing her snowy coat. Perhaps more than the quality of her garments, people stopped and stared because she wore so little for the winter chill; her dress would not have been out of place on a fine spring day.

As the maiden rode further towards the wall, the traffic on the road grew more crowded, and the dwellings were raised so close that they were leaning upon each other in places. The smells of dense humanity assaulted her and she wrinkled her nose, trying to adapt to the odors. Fires were cooking the midday meals, and the smoke stung the eyes when the breeze turned; pits used for tanning and waste disposal were located far from the road, but not so far they went undetected; livestock pens concentrated the stench of animals as they jostled for position at the feed troughs. Under it all was the sour sweat of working people as they went about their daily lives, so used to the constant reek that they hardly seemed to notice.

She rode past the buildings of the Outwalls, through the space between the outer city and the defensive moat. Children played in this vacant strip of land that would be a killing ground in times of war; dogs ran after them, joining in the fun as they made up games on the frosty ground, trying to stay warm by dashing back and forth. Steam arose from the droppings of horses and livestock, which were swept away by men with wheelbarrows when the road traffic ebbed. Guardsmen manned the gate entering the city, asking the business of those they deemed suspicious or undesirable. Weapons were checked and carts were searched for contraband. Through it all the traffic flowed efficiently, like the lifeblood of the city that it was. Few if any were turned away, for the gate guardians did not wish to make their lives more difficult either.

Wenyssaya rode to the gate, stopping her mare when a guard raised his hand, his face going slack as he peered under her hood. He cleared his throat before he spoke, though he had been shouting directions all day. "G-good afternoon miss. What's yer business in Portshia?" The other guard turned to look at her as well, his eyes wide with awe.

"I am an emissary from the eastern wood, in the shadow of the Gartethan Mountains. I am looking for a friend." She smiled at the man, making him flush.

The guard took a moment to recover and ask, "Eastern wood, ya say? What province do *you* hail from?" He was as polite as he could manage whilst keeping an air of authority.

"No province of human kind; I hail from Du-Velthathwe, The Hidden Grove of the Ilvayiin." She removed her hood momentarily and the guards gasped, the traffic around her stumbling to a halt.

Her shining golden curls were partially braided and bound with an ornate polished wooden comb, she had delicate ears that swept up into faerie points; her skin shone like cream mixed with golden honey, flawless and smooth; her generous lips held a natural pout that gave her the look of both child and woman; her thin nose was perfectly straight, as if formed by a master sculptor's hand. Most alluring were her eyes, large and striking with the richest violet hues dancing about deep pupils of fathomless black. Her brows arched like graceful wings over those remarkable eyes, crowning her face with arcs of dark gold.

She replaced her hood and the spell was broken. The

crowd began to disperse uncertainly, some fighting the urge to turn and follow her back into the city. The guardsmen mutely waved her on, unable to find a reason to hinder her, and unwilling to risk her turning a frown upon them to break their hearts. Wenyssaya spoke to the white mare and the horse moved on into the city beyond the massive gatehouse.

"An elf!" exclaimed the guard as he watched her ride away. "Never thought I'd live to see one." He rubbed his eyes and blinked.

His companion agreed as the elf disappeared into the crowd, "That was a Woodkin, sure enough; right out of the old stories! Gods above and below, but she was a sight!"

It was a few more moments before they remembered their duties and returned to checking the comings and goings at the gate. There would be a tale to tell in the guardhouse tonight; that was for certain.

Wenyssaya led her horse through the streets, which were bustling with people wrapped in warm cloaks and slipping on the frosted paving stones as they went about their daily affairs. Her destination could not yet be seen beyond the high roofs of the quad buildings and the towering spires of the cathedral; she had witnessed the white tower from afar, but it was concealed now as a tree in the forest. She approached a curved avenue that encircled the cathedral and a row of lesser temples devoted to the gods of the city, turning left towards the southeast. She was rewarded shortly as she spied the white tower in the distance looming over a wide-open marketplace, full of vendors and customers buying and selling goods from distant lands; a cacophony of languages reached her ears and the scent of exotic spices, rich foods, perfumes and peculiar smoke tantalized her nose. The cold air made the small crowds move slowly, but the enthusiasm was there to greet the first of the trade caravans. Winter was ebbing and there were things to do out-o-doors beside purchase more firewood. Young boys darted through the throng here and there, bumping clumsily into people as they played in the market. Wenyssaya pressed on towards the white edifice; a satisfied smile came to her face as the end of her journey seemed close at hand.

The Tower of Sight loomed over the buildings of the Market Square, its white walls gleaming like a pillar of ivory. A long patch of snow remained in the city shadows, out of reach of the late winter sun. The tower wore a skirt of ivy around its base, crawling twenty feet or more up the white stones. A door could be seen recessed in an arch amid the ivy drapery, partially concealed by the crisscrossing vines. The maiden peered at the massive structure, sensing the weave of power that twisted up from the ground and infused the very stones with its energy. Navithwi, having followed her from the air, circled the tower and glided in a gentle spiral down to meet her.

The raven suddenly gave a squawk of dismay as it was set upon by a larger creature that launched itself from the tower, roaring like a young lion. Wenyssaya raised her arm to defend her companion, power flowing from the raw source of the spirit well into her outstretched hand. But the creature's dive was only a warning and the raven escaped to land upon her arm, ruffling his feathers and cawing an insult at the attacker. The maiden checked her spell as she recognized the creature from the tower; it was dragon-kin with a body as large as a house-cat, a long neck, and longer tail. Bat-like leathery wings caught the air, and its scales reflected the afternoon sun, casting purple and crimson sparkles against the cerulean sky. Wenyssaya was shocked and delighted, never thinking to see such a creature living in a human city.

"Dwimathii!" she called to the creature in her native tongue, which the Beloved Goddess had bestowed with a nearly universal capacity; whether spoken or written, it had great power and effect, "Dwimathii, nin yudome-diis."

The little dragon-kin arrested its flight, beating its wings furiously to stop and stare at the newcomer. It cocked its little head, blinked in wonder, then flapped down to the ground to land upon four clawed feet, sitting up on its haunches and stretching its neck to gaze up at the woman on the horse. The raven chattered insults from the woman's arm as the horse sidestepped uncertainly.

"Those words you spoke," said the little dragon in a high masculine voice, "what did they mean?" He folded his wings, wrapping his tail about his feet.

Wenyssaya smiled down at him and spoke in Calilesh, the human language of the region, "Why, I asked you to come and be friends."

The little dragon nodded to himself. "I thought so," he said as he clasped his fore claws together, "but you said something else when you called to me."

"Dwimathii," she told him, "It means 'new dragon.' What is your name, little one?"

The creature looked uncertain and then cleared his throat in a very human manner, dropping his high speaking voice to a low draconic rumble. "*Drahnizhlomazhith*," he hissed and growled. It made the white mare shy away and toss her head, so he quickly added in his normal voice, "But most people call me Dwahn, er, Drahn."

"Hello Drahn, I am Wenyssaya of Du-Velthathwe. This is Thasimé," she stroked the horse's mane to calm her, "and I believe you have met Navithwi." The raven croaked something unkind at Drahn, making the maiden click her tongue in disapproval at him. "Be nice Navithwi, we are all friends now."

Drahn was excited, "You are Ilvayiin, what humans call Ilves or Elves!" He clapped his fore claws. "I have never met an elf. It is said they all returned to Alhanna after the last Great War." Drahn's scholarly instincts were fully engaged now as the woman dismounted her horse, slipping gracefully to the ground. He knew she was likely much older than she looked by the standards of humankind, and the stories she might tell thrilled his imagination.

"Not so," she said, "Many remain in the eastern woods by the mountains, and some reside in far-off lands." She whispered to the horse and placed the raven upon the mare's bare back. "But I have come a long way to find someone, and I was told he lives here." She looked up at the tower. "He is a human who has learned to weave what they call magic."

"Master Ildwic, er, Ildric Finnael!" He was determined to improve his pronunciation in front of the maiden. "Yes, this is his home. I shall announce you if you like."

"That would be wonderful, Drahn." She straightened her traveling dress with a flick of her wrist, throwing back her hood and unfastening her cloak.

Drahn walked to the vine-covered door, raising his claw and muttering a Celvestrian phrase to move the foliage aside and keep it from ensnaring them. With the door exposed, he stretched up on his toes to reach the latch, speaking the command word while focusing on a mental picture that completed the unlocking charm. The door swung open and he stepped aside to show the lady in. "After you," he said. Wenyssaya glided into the tower as Thasimé the horse prepared to loiter outside, Navithwi the raven perched on her back.

Inside the door was a wide circular sitting room furnished with simple but comfortable chairs and benches; three evenly spaced fireplaces lined the walls, and in the center of the tower was an impressive spiral staircase that twisted all the way to the pinnacle, far beyond the high arched ceiling. "Please wait here and I will inform Master Ildric." Drahn bounded cat-like up the stairs, wings tucked in close, tail swinging to help him balance.

Wenyssaya let out a deep sigh of relief, sinking into a padded chair by the cold fireplace. Upon raising her fingers and whispering "S'heth," a warm cozy fire sprung forth from the bare stone, smokeless and soothing. She basked in the glow of the flame as she awaited the wizard, letting the power of the spirit well upon which the tower was built wash over and renew her.

Spirit wells were precious fonts of magic that rose to the heavens like pillars of soft light. They had been formed when Lu-Duella of the Radiant Face danced upon the land in the early days; her footfalls created a thinning of the boundaries between Alsuvath and Alhanna, the world of elements and the world of spirit. It was a shame that so many had been discovered by humans, who always built their stone circles, temples, and towers upon them.

The dwivayiin, the 'new people' who called themselves humans, had little sense of the power that flowed around them; they had learned to use tools and techniques to do what Wenyssaya could do naturally. But then, Wenyssaya herself was uncommon among her own people.

At an early age the girl had shown gifts that other children never developed. Like her ancient fore-bearers, she could manipulate the elements and speak with plants and animals. Even her ethereal beauty was reminiscent of the old Ilvayiin legends. Her mother named her Spring Song, for within her was the promise of all that blossomed and grew to great splendor.

Then there were the dreams. As a child she had been troubled by visions both in sleep and waking, dreams that both fascinated and terrified her, dreams that bordered on memory and madness. She told her parents about her dreams and they had wisely consulted the elders. It was then that Wenyssaya began a special training that was to prepare her for greater things. When the message came from the western wood, she knew her time had come; it was as if she had been waiting all her life to complete something left undone.

Footsteps descended the spiral stair and Drahn came

slinking down, preceding a man in a violet robe trimmed with golden glyphs of human magic. His hair and face spoke of advanced age among his kind, and a silvery, metallic mechanism had replaced his right hand. Embedded within the palm of metal hand, Wenyssaya perceived an artifact of great power.

"Mistress Wenyssaya, may I introduce Arch Mage Ildric Finnael." Drahn presented the wizard as the lady arose and curtsied. "Master Ildric, I pwesent Wenyssaya of Du-Velthathwe."

The wizard, though taken aback by the sight of her, smiled and said, "Welcome to Portshia, milady. I am honored to receive an emissary of the Ilvayiin. To what do we owe the pleasure of your company?" He gestured for her to be seated as he took an opposite chair, noticing with mild surprise that the fire was burning without fuel.

"I have come at the behest of the lord of the western wood, for there is a matter of great urgency that requires his attention, but alas, he cannot abandon his duties."

The wizard's eyes narrowed and he asked, "The lord of the western wood? Do you mean the Shadowood Forest?"

Drahn, who had not been dismissed, climbed onto a footstool to listen.

Wenyssaya nodded, "Yes that is the name your people have given his domain. The lord has been watching from afar, sending his agents to do his bidding, but they are hindered by the human city. It was his wish that an ally be found within to assist in my mission, and you were the one he recommended."

The wizard stroked his chin with the peculiar silver talon as Drahn looked back and forth between the maiden and the old man. Finally, unable to restrain himself, the dweedragon asked, "Who is the lord of the western wood, and how does he know Master Ildwic?"

Ildric glanced at his impatient pupil and said, "He is known as the Shadow Lord in the old stories of the forest. He is the source of the power that keeps the forest for its creatures and drives away any who would delve too deeply." He looked at the maiden who only smiled. "If I am not mistaken, he is an Ilvayiin of great age, undiminished by the passing of generations."

"You know much of our kind, Master Ildric," said the maiden. "It is true, he is very old; he arrived in this land long, long ago and made his home in the great dark woods. His power is great, but he is not without weakness."

"But how does he know you?" Drahn asked the wizard. "And how do you know so much about him? And why haven't you told me this before?" The little dragon almost whined his last question.

"There are secrets one must keep until the proper time," said the wizard, casting a disapproving look at his pupil. "But I told you much of the story already. Do you recall when I traveled north to Syngmore nearly two years ago, seeking information about the boy Nixy?" Drahn nodded. Wenyssaya stirred at the mention of the lad, but neither the wizard nor the dweedragon took notice.

"I told you that I was there thirty years prior, before I lost my hand," he wiggled the silver replacement. "I was searching for a little girl that had wandered into the Shadowood. After being sorely tested by the power there, I found her sitting safely within a spirit well."

Drahn perked up, "She had the magic knife that the boy Nixy has, the one with the raven head carved on the handle." The dweedragon glanced at their guest and said in a whisper, "She was accompanied by a waven, master. It's outside." Drahn hoped the raven was not befouling his master's tower in revenge for their earlier misunderstanding.

The maiden spoke, "Navithwi, the raven, came to the eastern woods bearing a message from the Shadow Lord, as you call him."

"Then the power that challenged you as you searched for the girl..." Drahn said, looking from Ildric to the maiden, "That was this Shadow Lord, the ancient elf lord of the forest?"

"The same," answered Ildric. "Though I did not meet him in his proper form, whatever that may be. He has a gift for the theatrical and chose to appear as a pair of disembodied eyes floating in the deep shadows of the forest. He assured me the girl was unharmed but I told him I would not leave without her. He relented and a path appeared, leading me to her."

Wenyssaya said, "He knew then that you were a human of good character. It was later that you drew his attention again; it was with some difficulty that he kept your vision in the dark." She glanced at the stone eye in the palm of Ildric's silver hand.

"The boy," Ildric said, nodding slowly. Something had always clouded his divinations when seeking the boy, Nixyalderthor. It was as if he were cloaked in shadow, being kept from sight.

Drahn was perplexed, "But why was the Shadow Lord hiding Nixy from your divining? After all, we sat and spoke to the child face-to-face."

Wenyssaya leaned forward in her chair. "You have spoken to the boy? Do you know where he is?" Her lovely face became anxious.

Ildric said sadly, "For a time he was living in the castle, but he left there a while back. I have not been able to find him, but I think he is safe for now."

Drahn interrupted again, for something was confusing. "So on your last visit to Syngmore village, you learned that the little girl grew up and had a son named Nixyalderthor, but she died in childbirth. Now the elf lord wants to hide the boy like he once hid the mother. But why?" The dweedragon sat in earnest with his hand on his chin, determined to help his master figure out the puzzle.

"Don't be dense, Drahn," Ildric said with frustration. "Nixyalderthor DuQuayne is obviously the son of the Shadow Lord." The dweedragon's jaw dropped and his wings fanned in surprise. "It all fits," the wizard explained. "From an early age the girl Kirana did not fear the power of the wood. He gave her the magic knife as a gift. Later as she grew, he came to love her, for she was reputed to be a great beauty. She had an overlong pregnancy and died of the strain, for there were none who knew the cause. Then there is the boy Nixy and his encounter with the demnox Black Will..."

"A demnox!" the maiden cried as she nearly jumped from her chair. "You said he was safe!"

"The boy was saved by the count's daughter, using the magic knife he inherited from his mother; it was how he came to be in the castle. But fear not, for I believe that the demnox has been thwarted for the time being, yet we must be vigilant."

Drahn nodded in understanding, "That was what Black Will meant by Blood Magic, needing Nixy's father's blood. Just like in the days of the Sorcerer Kings, powerful blood can be used against the family. That was why the empires of old died out; the Sorcerer Kings killed their blood relatives and descendants so their enemies could not capture them and use Blood Magic to harm the rulers." He paused and his eyes grew wide, his vertical pupils dilating, "But that means that Nixy..."

"Yes," said Ildric gravely. "Nixy is the heir to that power. He is half-elven, son of an ancient Ilvayiin, just like the Sorcerer Kings of old."

"And if our enemies find him," Wenyssaya said urgently, "they can use him to strike at the Shadow Lord and do untold damage."

Drahn was greatly alarmed and he gaped at the maiden, "You don't mean to kill the boy to protect the elf lord, do you?"

Wenyssaya raised her lovely eyebrows in surprise. "Kill him? No little one, we are not fearful half-human emperors. The lord of the western wood sent me to protect his son from harm."

Drahn sighed in relief. "Forgive me lady, I did not mean to offend. I've never known any elves before today, and I only know what I've read in the human stories."

Wenyssaya reached out to stroke Drahn's head saying, "No offense taken little one. But is it true that you know so little of us? I would think that you knew of the bond we share, your people and mine." Drahn only blinked at her.

"The Dwimathii and Ilvayiin have long been friends since the elder days." She looked curiously at the little dragon as he fidgeted, the tip of his tail clasped in his fore claws. "Was it not among the stories of your *dimcuthe*?" Drahn lowered his head, looking uncertain. "Your Age of the Shell?" she explained.

Ildric intervened, "Drahn was separated from his mother before he was hatched," the wizard said quietly. "He never learned all that he should." Wenyssaya looked at the little dweedragon with sadness, her heart welling up with great pity for the creature. She now understood why he had chanted the human words to pass the vines and unlock the door to the tower. He knew no other way, the poor thing.

Drahn felt as though he was a disappointment to the new visitor, especially since she had exceeded his expectations of what an elf might be like. He drooped his head and sniffed, not wanting to look her in the eye anymore. She probably knew more about his kind than he did.

The maiden wished to comfort the dweedragon, but more pressing matters drove her; she was on a mission after all. "Master Ildric, I must find this boy, Nixyalderthor. His safety is paramount and time is fleeting."

Ildric nodded and sat forward in the chair, his curiosity getting the better of him, "I agree, he must be found and safeguarded, but I am led to wonder what would be gained by those who seek him?" He held the maiden in a searching stare, looking for signs of evasion. If he were to be trusted as an ally to the elves, he would know more about what was at stake.

Wenyssaya gave him a perplexed look, "I told you, the enemy could use the boy to work great harm upon the Shadow Lord."

"The enemy, whomever *that* might be, wants to harm or kill the Shadow Lord, but why? What is so important about this one elf lord in particular? He keeps the forest safe from the encroachment of humans, but that is surely not worth all the trouble. Why is he such a target?"

Drahn perked up, for it seemed that his master had struck upon an important question, one that had not occurred to him. The maiden looked uneasy about this line of inquiry, but after a few moments of gathering her thoughts she said, "It relates to the return of the Ilvayiin to the world of Jayde. You have heard that most of the elder generations left for Alhanna, the spirit world where our kind were first created?" The wizard and dweedragon nodded, both well versed in the scant histories that survived the Time of Chaos. She continued, "Your stories do not tell of how they left, only that they left. The truth is," she paused for a brief moment, "that the path lies within the depths of the Shadowood Forest, and the way is guarded by the Shadow Lord."

Drahn raised his neck, his wings unfolding with excitement. "There is a... a portal to Alhanna in the woods? A way to the world of spiwit?" He looked excitedly at Ildric, "Master!" The dweedragon wanted to see it immediately and maybe poke his nose through to have a sniff. The wizard rested his chin on his hand of flesh as the silver talon tapped the arm of the chair thoughtfully.

"So you see," the maiden coontinued, "if our enemies take the boy, they can take the portal in the woods and the Ilvayiin can never return to aid us."

"Grim news indeed," said Ildric, trying to ignore his apprentice, who was jittery with academic excitement. "If there is such a war coming, we will need their aid. The gods cannot help us now; there will not be another demigod ruler like Kraal to lead us. Humanity is left to its own devices."

"If such a war is coming, it will affect more than humanity," the maiden replied, folding her hands in her lap. "All the creatures of Jayde are at stake if the old prophesies are true, which I doubt not. The First Ones spoke of many evil times to come before they departed Jayde forever, leaving their children to rule in their stead. The blood of the Countless God has been the undoing of many an empire, and may yet be the undoing of all things."

Drahn shivered, "The blood of the Countless God? W-what might that be?" He hoped it was not common knowledge among his kind, for he did not want to seem more lacking in the eyes of the elf maid than he already was.

"You may have heard of it by another name," said the maiden, "In human history it is called the Dark Heart; it is the blood of Llomaak the Countless God, for he is one and many, and it was spilled upon the earth at the end of the First War. Just a drop fell, but it soon became as a precious stone, a corrupt jewel of dark crimson. It was recovered by his faithful human priests and made its way into the hands of the greatest of the Sorcerer Kings."

Drahn nodded, eager to show off his knowledge of the story, "It turned him fwom a pawagon of Order into an agent of Chaos, and his empire fell into terrible ruin. When next it surfaced, the Anointed King Orthicus took it as a spoil of victory after cwushing the Llomaakitte Temple in the land of Maanok, east of the mountains. It cowwupted him as well, making the chosen of Arathus into the vile mockewy who brought about the Time of Chaos."

Wenyssaya nodded approvingly, "That time is known as the Great Thinning among my people."

Ildric added, "And after giving a child to a mortal woman, the King God Arathus closed the portals between Jayde and the Outer Realms, sealing us off from the influence of the gods. His divine son became Kraal the Great, who destroyed the Dark Heart once and for all."

"Did he?" Wenyssaya asked sullenly. "Our people do not tell of the fate of the Dark Heart, only that it was cut from the chest of Orthicus and taken far away. Kraal may have destroyed it, or we can hope as much, but the prophecies of the First Ones say otherwise." She looked into the fire as she recalled the stories of her teachers. "There are few Ilvayiin who dared to look into the future, to see the path the world would take. The first to try did so out of folly; he became known as Iluvdim, the Blood Star. It is by the shining of his red face that we can read the signs of the times, for he was fated to see only the blood spilled upon the world he so loved, and by the brilliance of Iluvdim can violent times be known. He shines very brightly now.

"Others sought the future with wisdom, but only with the help of the Dwimathii could the riddles be unraveled." Drahn stood upon his hind legs, his neck stretched; his head now even with the maiden's. "Yes, little one. The dweedragons helped us to write the prophecies of old. Eldest of races, your kind was wise and learned; the most powerful artifacts of sight were created by the Dwimathii, even the relic held within the palm of your master's silver hand."

Ildric turned the palm of his talon-like metal hand upward and he and Drahn looked anew at the Eye of Omithys embedded there, sealed with glyphs of binding. The polished stone eye was draconic, green and yellow with a vertical pupil that dilated when Ildric used its power. It was obviously a dragon-like eye, but neither master nor pupil imagined it was crafted by dragon-kind.

"Omithys was a dweedragon?" Drahn asked, secretly wondering if the eye might be his by some convoluted right. He shook the thought from his head immediately; it was an honest treasure-hoarding instinct but had no bearing on reality.

"No," answered Ildric, "Omithys was an ancient human diviner who lived in the time of the Sorcerer Kings, but I always assumed he was the eye's creator."

Wenyssaya smiled, "He may have helped in a way, or perhaps it came into his possession by other means. Regardless, humans have no talent for the craft; it takes elder blood to create artifacts of such power."

Ildric's pride was stung, both as a wizard and a human, but he did not show it... much. "I'd beg to differ, milady. There have been many things created by wizards that have magic power, meager though they might be." He thought of the bracelet that saved Lady Cindra's life; not his creation, but that of an 'untalented human wizard' to be sure.

"But nothing that lasts, Master Ildric. Trinkets crafted by humans only borrow from the spirit realm; their spark fades over time like a dying ember. True spirit craft endures, even grows stronger with age. You hold your artisans in high esteem and rightfully so, but know too that there are still Ilvayiin living in the world, and their blood flows in many peoples. Though the power of their fore-bearers may diminish with each generation, there are still what you call 'half-elves' living among you."

That gave him pause, for it was known that there were others who practiced magic besides wizards. Some, like witches, learned the art from unsanctioned sources, while others had a more primal power that came from within. Few of these were trusted in the community of wizards, so it was not unthinkable that such a one, fearing persecution, might pass as an ordinary human and use his special talents only when it would not appear unseemly.

Drahn broke the uncomfortable silence, "What are these prophecies that the dweedragons helped the elves to write?" He wanted to hear more about his people and had little care for professional rivalry.

Wenyssaya turned her attention to the eager little dragon and said, "I do not remember them word for word, but I recall enough; it was said that the Dark Heart would thrice plague the age of mortals, each time leading to disaster. The final time would hail the ending of the worlds, when all that was created would be undone. Even the gods would fall, all but the first three, Jayda, Arathus and Llomaak. The Mother would begin a world anew and the Brothers would continue their unending battle of Order against Chaos." She lowered her eyes, "The reign of Orthicus marked the second emergence of the Dark Heart, over a thousand years ago. I was raised on stories of that war, on prophecies of the fall of creation, but I hoped those days would never come. The spirit realm of Alhanna will not be spared; all of my fore-bearers that reside there, even our beloved goddess Eyorona will perish for all time."

Ildric was silent and Drahn was cowed. He hung his head low and his wings drooped. "H-how will it happen?" he asked with barely a whisper.

"None are certain, but there are prophecies on that matter as well." The maiden's eyes were pained as she looked at Drahn, a great sympathy welling within her. "One such prophecy was acted upon in recent years, but I fear it was a tragic misinterpretation. The Ilvayiin were able to put an end to it, but..." she sniffed back a tear and Drahn felt a tingle down his spine. "The damage had been done. It was an ancient dragon prophecy that foretold of the last dragon born. Upon the birth of the last dragon, the world would burn in endless fire, along with the heavens and all creation."

Drahn said carefully, "All dragons are hatched, not born, so that prophecy must be about *Kraowjomazh*," he growled and hissed the name, "the dragon god of fire. Jayda the World Mother never gave birth to him, keeping him locked within her womb for all time. He tries to escape, sending fire and ash hurtling into the sky, but she restrains him."

"Yes," the maiden said, the grief plain in her voice. "That is the correct understanding of the prophecy. When the dragon god of fire is born, all shall be laid waste. But there were those who misunderstood and sought to bring about the end by another means. They thought they could end the world by ending the race of dragon-kind. The Dwimathii were hunted..." Her voice broke, choked with pity.

Drahn felt his body melt like soft wax. His wings hung like wet blankets at his sides, his tail drooped from the footstool, and his scales turned first pale then dark.

Hunted. His kind had been *hunted.*

Someone thought the last dragon born meant the last dragon alive. Some maniac sought to end all creation by murdering Drahn's race, all because they misread an old fable... He felt sick, his throat closed up as the tears came, remembering once again the youthful impressions within his egg, the voices, the screams of draconic rage and pain, the tumbling and spinning. He never before understood what had happened but now it all made sense. His family was the victims of fanatics, mad men who wanted to end the world. His mother and clutch mates might all be dead; it was a fear he carried always, but now that he knew the circumstances, his last remaining hope was extinguished.

Men came upon the nest and sought to crush the eggs. His mother tried to stop them but was murdered and only luck sent his egg tumbling away to safety. After he hatched, he could not make sense of his ordeal, and it was all so confusing. The wizards who raised him treated him well enough, but they had no answers. When he met Ildric, he thought the diviner might teach him to see beyond, to learn of his past and the fate of his family. Now he knew. Now he knew it all.

"Excuse me," Drahn muttered. He slunk from the footstool and climbed the stairs to his little room, leaving a trail of tears upon the winding steps.

Chapter Six

Homecoming

The last time Cindra had passed the Copper Gate into Portshia, she and Jaron were returning from a riding lesson and a rather curious nap under a tree. Mineth was with them, poor sweet Mineth, and the traitorous bodyguard Sir Earnold Greenfellow. His hatred and jealousy had led him to betray his vows, bringing shame to House Corrina for no other reason but to kill his rival, Sir Jaron.

Now they were riding along the Red Coast Road once again, this time as knight and squire. Jaron's spirits seemed to be lifted as they drew closer to the city he had not seen in two years. It would be a bittersweet homecoming for him, for he was returning as a stained knight who would have to regain his lost honor in the eyes of many. Jaron sighed aloud once again. Sir Cord was riding next to him on Champ, his blond sorrel charger, and shook his head at the young man's theatrics.

"You sound like a lovesick maid when you do that, lad." Cord remarked.

"Don't get your hopes up, I'm spoken for." Jaron replied, and he turned to wink at Cindra.

"Ha!" the big knight barked a laugh, "Seems exile has improved your humor at least."

Jaron said, "You'd be surprised how many practiced conversations you can have on a lonely road."

Cindra was seated behind Jaron on Vortigras, with T'ózha in tow. Her heart was racing in anticipation, and her mind was full of worries; she was finally returning home, but the evil priests who had arranged for her death might still have a presence in the city, and she feared for her parents' safety. A castle had been no protection for the king, and there might already be spies and assassins within Casselvane Keep. From her vantage on the road, she could clearly see the low parapets of her family's fortress on the sea cliff, dominating the harbor. Her heart ached for her parents, knowing they grieved a second time for a lost child. She desperately wanted to gallop to the castle and fly into their arms, but the need for secrecy was paramount. *In time,* she thought, *in time...*

"Home at last, eh?" said Cord as they approached the Copper Gate. "Your father will be happy to see you again, then you can return that sword to him." Cord eyed the hilt of the weapon strapped to Jaron's side. Valdiroth the Firebrand was one of three honor swords crafted for House Corrina by commission of the crown, and Jaron had managed to lose and recover it in the course of his travels. It was not one of his favorite stories to relate.

Jaron put his hand on the hilt and said, "Not to worry old hound, he will hear the tale and I'll present the sword back to him. I'm not a child anymore; I need not hide my deeds or misdeeds."

"Oho, look here young Dillan! Sir Jaron is finally a man! All it took was to kick him out of the house for a few years. Congratulations, lad."

Jaron muttered curses under his breath. Cord laughed heartily, and Cindra smiled at their backs.

As the trio started across the bridge to the gatehouse, Cindra's eyes searched the edge of the canal looking for the tree she had destroyed with cannon shot. It could not be seen among the foliage growing on the banks, for it had been cut to a stump and the reeds had grown up around it. *It is in disguise,* she thought. *It now serves as a warning to other trees to lay low.*

The guards recognized Sir Cord, though they were surprised to see Sir Jaron. They let them pass with a salute and wave of the hand, not bothering to question them. Cindra mused, *What disguises could the assassins have taken, I wonder? Perhaps they can pass gate guards without a second glance as well?*

Within moments of riding through the thick gatehouse, Cindra was once again within the walls of her home city. She felt excitement growing within that threatened to overwhelm her, and thought she heard music in the distance, though it might have been her heart singing.

I have returned, alive and well. I am home. Yet, it didn't quite feel like home. *Home is supposed to feel safe.*

Red roof tiles and high plastered walls painted in warm earth-tones greeted her eyes. The worn paving stones made their mounts' horseshoes clack merrily as the striders made way before them. The massive Tower of the Silver Moon dominated her view, rising high above the rooftops of the buildings that lined the avenue. The polished copper orb that topped the patina structure caught the sunlight and cast it about for miles, while at night it mimicked the phases of the moon.

They were in the Lowcourt, or Copper District as it was often called. Long ago, wagons loaded with copper ore from the west came down the coast road through that gate; much of it was used to plate the tower which had long since turned to a green patina. Now it was a poorer district, where copper kenmarks were seen more often than silver calimarks. Still, the people seemed busy and lively. Winter was fading quickly.

"It's been a rough winter," Cord said, indicating the snow lingering in the alleyways. "We're used to a dusting, but this was nearly to the boot tops."

Jaron laughed, "Save your sobbing, old hound. Dillan and I spent our last few winters in the northwest, where the snow stacks as high as your head!"

Cindra shivered at the memory. As a southern girl, she had been unprepared for the reality of living in a wooden caravan in the northern winter. There had been some nights she thought they would all die, but the Galindri were survivors.

Shops near the gate exuded the welcomed aromas of cooked food, tempting newcomers arriving with full purses and empty bellies. Cindra was not very hungry, but found she could not help salivating like a dog at a feast. Street vendors carried racks of twisted bread and pastries, and tavern barkers called to one and all, announcing the fresh catch of the day. As they rode on, she took in the odors of sea air and dense humanity, familiar if not overly pleasant. There was a bakery nearby, teasing the nose with the scent of Portshia's famous sour salt bread. That scent brought tears to her eyes; so strongly was it tied to her childhood. She remembered breakfasts in the castle, peeling the upper crust from a hot, round loaf.

Sir Cord guided Champ to the left at the first major cross street and the party headed north up the Arrow's Flight, the longest and straightest thoroughfare in the city. While crossing the canal bridge to the next district, Cindra watched a loaded barge make the hazardous turn from the main canal into the city waterway; the barge driver called out to his team of water oxen, pulling the reigns as the powerful horned beasts fought the currents. Their humped backs rose and fell, throwing up white spray as the steersman strained on the rudder, guiding the turn. Those barges were sturdy and their drivers well-trained, that was for certain.

Soon Cindra and the knights were over the bridge and in the Temple District, most of which was taken up by the cathedral, the surrounding temples and their support buildings, as well as blocks of wealthy private estates that ran to the western wall. They passed DuShonmaer, the home of Kobus DuChat, a rich merchant who had attended her birthday-betrothal dinner two years ago. Under different circumstances, she would have liked to stop by and thank him personally for the five lovely dresses he had given her; they were probably drifting with the currents around the Emerald Bay thanks to Minozhian pirates, but still...

"Been to any good plays of late?" Jaron asked, gazing ahead at the copper dome of the theater.

"As if I'd know," Cord smirked. "I'm not for sitting and watching mummers play at love and war."

Jaron grinned, "I've seen you play at love and war; the mummers do it better."

"Aye, but most of their 'girls' are boys," Cord remarked, looking back at Dillan.

Cindra laughed merrily, drawing the gaze of passing striders.

Further on they entered the Gates District, named for its two main gates and the moated prison located within one of the horseshoe-shaped sections of the northern curtain wall. Its boundaries were marked by the road that ran from the Wood Gate, past the Grand Portshia Theater, around the northern Temple Walk, and ending at the Golden Path.

Memories of the night Jaron escorted her to dinner and the theater swam in Cindra's mind; she thought of how handsome he had looked, how giddy she had felt, and how dear Mineth had chaperoned the affair, clucking her tongue when one of them misbehaved. Those were happier, simpler days, or so it seemed now. Cindra remembered thinking the worst of her predicament at the time; being sent off to marry a stranger was the ultimate nightmare in her sheltered life.

They passed behind the theater, turning right onto an east road called Procession Way; it was one of the more crooked roads in town, kinking at nearly every other intersection. The road led directly to the cemetery, and most funeral processions turned onto the street at some point. Many superstitious townsfolk who weren't in a hurry to get somewhere would avoid the road for this reason, so it was often lightly trafficked.

As the road turned southeast, they saw over the rooftops a large roaring dragon made of polished brass, perched atop a tower and clutching a staff topped with a silvery orb.

"Is that the wizard school?" Cindra asked.

"It is," Cord replied sourly. "Local chapter of the Mystic College. Spell spouters and swellheads."

Jaron said, "I hear they bought the land for an enormous sum from one of the city's first temples, back before the gods went silent. They wanted access to the little well of magic it was built on."

Cord just looked at him.

Jaron added, "The castle and city were built here to secure the magic areas. 'Spirit wells' they call them. It's a rare thing to have so many clustered together like this. There are only six such places in the entire kingdom."

"How do you know so much about *wizardly* things?" Cord layered more than a hint of contempt on the word.

"How do you not, living next-door to them?" Jaron replied. He then smiled and explained, "I worked for the cost of a spell to find Valdiroth when it was stolen. Three months doing chores for wizards and you learn a thing or two.

Cord just grumbled at that, keeping his thoughts to himself. When they reached a busy intersection, he proclaimed, "Here we are Dillan, your new home." He pointed across the way to a typical-looking, two-story quad building.

Cindra looked to where he pointed and blinked in confusion at the sign. "The Red Eagle Inn and Stables?"

"No!" Cord said as Jaron laughed. "Around the

corner, just there."

They turned left off the Procession Way and onto a main thoroughfare called the Casselvane Road. Just crosswise from the Mystic College was a large archway and a locked wooden gate. Emblazoned upon each door was the Freekirk coat-of-arms: a black chevron and Balkonian mace on a field of crimson. This version incorporated the mighty white hart of the Daerbrik style, its rack of antlers flaunted menacingly as it reared and flashed its hooves. Above the arched passage was a decorative sign that read:

Daerbrik School of Knightly Combat
Sir Cord Freekirk, Master

Sir Cord unlocked the outer and inner gates with a large iron key and a thrill of anticipation ran through Cindra's body as she entered what would indeed be her home for the next two years. They dismounted and led their steeds through the gate. Before them was a long courtyard partially covered with snow, which was hiding in the shadows until spring melted it or it was tread into the earth. The grass was yellow and stiff, having thinned in the areas where most of the training occurred. To the left was half-a-dozen wooden training dummies lined up along the base of the northern wall, passively awaiting the punishment of the coming months. The upper floor had a covered walkway and a long balcony, upon which mock battlements were built to train in basic castle siege tactics. Below was a wide door leading to the main hall.

The southern wall of the courtyard was a long, plastered expanse upon which a mural was painted, depicting armed men locked in combat, along with diagrams of fighting stances. Each figure was ten feet high and rendered in lifelike fashion, rather than the flat style more often seen in older murals. It made Cindra feel as though she was in the company of giants. Just above the mural was a row of small windows, probably belonging to rooms at the Red Eagle Inn. There was also a stable door in the far corner, likely the scene of Jaron's youthful indiscretion with someone else's betrothed, which all ended badly two years ago.

As they led the horses to the wide doors of the main hall, Cindra noticed a long, sheltered display on the wall. It held dozens of little coats-of-arms meticulously painted on wooden plaques, each not much larger than her hand. She realized it represented the graduates from noble houses that attended at one time, and it saddened her that she might never be able to post the arms of House Corrina among the collection. She saw the Dunlorden arms of a stag's head on a green field as she and Jaron entered the hall, as well as that of House Greenfellow; the two houses had little love for each other and their plaques were as far apart as possible.

Instead of entering through the large doors, they tied their mounts to the fencing dummies and Cord led them to a small door on the eastern wing. It led to a comfortable sitting room called the Master's Hall, where instructors could relax by a fireplace and discuss things privately, away from the ears of their students.

"Normally, you wouldn't see this room unless you were a returning instructor, young *Dillan*," Cord stressed her new name. "But since you're a squire serving a knight, who is also an instructor, you will be required to serve him his meals here." He watched her eyes, looking for signs that she felt such a task was beneath her dignity.

"Yes, Master Freekirk," she said almost meekly.

He just raised his eyebrow and snorted. Jaron smiled.

The walls of the Master's Hall were hung with tapestries of knights on horseback and marching armies, some depicting battles Cindra recognized only because of the standards carried by the opposing armies. Her military history was limited to the battles fought by her house and those of her mother's family, many of which were against each other before her parents' marriage alliance. There was a hart's head mounted above the mantle; the fine animal's rack was broad and imposing, polished and dusted regularly.

Somehow Cindra had expected to see a fine coat of dust on things since the school had been closed for the winter months. There must be a permanent staff, she decided.

Sure enough, the three were met by a man and woman dressed in work attire, which was clean and presentable. The man was old, perhaps more so than Cindra's father; his hair was thin and gray and his face had many lines from years of toil, his body was bent and he walked with a slight limp due to a stiff hip. The man's wife was a bit younger, though she had the rough edges of one who spent much of her life in service. She was plump with smiling eyes, and her dark hair was streaked with silver and tucked beneath a kerchief tied about her head.

The man came forward and clasped hands with Sir Cord, who bellowed a greeting. "Elmore, Celia, good to see you again!" Cord said warmly. "I trust all is well?"

"Well and in order, master. Welcome back." Elmore said as his wife nodded and smiled, her eyes moving to Jaron and Cindra.

"I think you remember Sir Jaron Dunlorden?" Cord turned to present his friend. "He was a student here some five years past; he will be an instructor for the term, and his squire will be in training." He indicated Cindra who stood nearby. "This is Dillan DePort, Esquire. Dillan, meet Elmore and Celia, our school stewards." Cindra and the couple exchanged little head nods.

"You must think me senile not to recall young Jaron Dunlorden," Elmore grinned as he winked at Jaron. "It's not every student what has such a row over a lady!" He chuckled and his wife giggled behind her hands. Elmore turned to Cindra to explain. "This one is a master of more than fighting, mark me. He charmed the bride-to-be of his rival, right under his nose. Found them a-kissing in the stables, he did; twas a duel that lasted near an hour as I recollect, in and out of the doors, over tables and chairs. Took me most of the day to clean up the mess!" He cackled with mirth as Jaron scratched his head nervously.

"And I nearly kicked them both out of the school for breaking its cardinal rule," Cord chided.

Cindra smiled as a boy might at the rowdy tale, but she recalled the story with some bitterness. Jaron had anxiously related the tryst with the woman Deliah to help explain why he and Sir Earnold hated each other so much. The men had a vendetta that began with their fathers, and Jaron seducing Earnold's bride-to-be was the spark that finally led to real violence. During the duel, Jaron gave Earnold a prominent scar upon his cheek, but Jaron had spared him since he knew he was in the wrong.

However, after their scandalous kiss before the festival crowd, Cindra and Jaron learned that they were both victims of a love spell cast upon a pair of roses, roses that Deliah had acquired for Greenfellow by nefarious means. Only Sir Cord's persistence had uncovered the plot. Cindra had no fond feelings for this Deliah woman.

Cord laughed, looking nervously at Jaron and his squire. "That was long ago," said Cord, "He's beyond such nonsense now. No more old stories, lest young Dillan realize his mistake in following this rascal." He clapped the old man on the shoulder and said, "Make sure Sir Jaron's room is ready; he is to share it with Dillan, so there needs to be a second cot or bed, as can be arranged."

"Twill have to be a cot master," said Elmore. "One of the beds was infested with bugs and I had it burned. The other will be needed for yer second instructor."

Jaron asked, "Second instructor? Anyone I know?" He looked to Cord with a bit of concern. The more people inhabiting the eastern wing, the greater the risk of discovering Dillan's secret.

Sir Cord looked surprised for a moment, then explained, "I'd nearly forgotten! I had a student the last two years who asked to return as an instructor for the term. It seems he has few prospects back home and wanted to wait things out while earning a stipend. Good lad, good fighter; name of Gavadaire LuVestra."

"Aurilonian?" asked Jaron, suspiciously.

Aurilon was a neighbor and rival across the Crimson Bay and had faced Calilon in many wars. It was said that the country was possibly in league with the rebellious barons in eastern Calilon and waited for civil war to begin so it might have its pick at the remains.

"Aye, our friends across the sea. Don't hold it against him lad, a student is a fellow until they meet on the battlefield." Cord chided, reminding Jaron of the school's cardinal rule once again.

Jaron and Cindra followed Elmore up the stairs to the masters' quarters. The old man moved a bit slowly, so it was hard for Cindra to follow him, especially with her baggage over her shoulder. Jaron's room was near the end of the hall next to Cord's, which seemed to satisfy Jaron. If this Gavadaire was lodged next door however, and if he was the nosy type, he might overhear something not meant for a stranger's ears. Not that they would be doing anything improper, or at least she hoped nothing *too* improper, but there might be things spoken in confidence that could lead to her discovery. They would both have to keep an eye on this new instructor.

The room was comfortable enough, with a small fireplace and chimney for warmth and a table with chairs to take meals together; Cindra would be expected to serve him as a squire would, but she was relived to think that they might eat together in private once in a while.

Elmore said, "All is in place, there's a wardrobe for your gear and clothing and fresh linens can be had for the asking. Just send the lad down with any requests. Celia's mostly about the kitchen, but not to be bothered before meals, as she's much to do 'round that time." He headed for the door. "Next week is the big day, till then you can relax and take yer ease if you've the mind. I'll stable yer horses for you." He nodded to each of them and showed himself out.

Cindra looked into Jaron's eyes and smiled gratefully, for her dream was becoming a reality and it was all due to his help. She reached up to put her arms around his neck, kissing him on the lips gently as she said "Thank you, love. You don't know what this means to me."

Brushing his hands under her vest, he placed them on her waist as he replied, "Thank me after your first day of bruises and sore muscles; there will be many more to come after that."

"Then you will have to soothe them," she said cooing softly. She held him close and laid her head against his chest, listening to his heart grow faster.

"Lady," he whispered in her ear, "You will be the end of me someday." He embraced her tightly and kissed her lips, all the while listening for noises beyond the door.

Chapter Seven

Battle Lines

The Freekirk School opened its gates early in the morning on the first of day of Balmoth, the third month of the year, which was devoted to the War God Balkon. A table was set up outside the doors of the Master's Hall and Sir Cord sat behind it, facing the gate so that the students would have to cross the length of the yard to sign in. Their confidence, focus, attitude, and personality would be measured by the master's appraising eye.

The attendees had until noon to arrive and present themselves, so Cord and Jaron settled in for a long wait. Cindra kept herself entertained by swinging a wooden sword at a fencing dummy, whacking it about the head and body, feeling each impact jar her arm and shoulder. *I will have to get used to that*, she thought. The *clack, clack* of the sword rang a cadence that echoed about the courtyard.

The Casselvane Road passed through the Trader's

Gate, the one commonly used by merchants, farmers, and herders on their way to market. The street was bustling even this early in the morning, and Cindra was often distracted by a passing herd of sheep, or a troupe of minstrels, or a Galindri caravan ringing with bells and hanging copper pots for sale.

The first person to enter the courtyard was a tall man, fair skinned, well-built, quite handsome, and striding with purpose and confidence. A fine sword swung on a baldric at his side. Cindra stopped her sparring almost in embarrassment. The man was dressed in red and blue tailored silk; he wore a long-sleeved jacket with voluminous shoulders, a cloak billowed behind, and his bombast-breeches gathered decoratively above the knee in the style of Aurilon. His hose fit snugly and his shoes were embroidered with black thread. The toes were long, pointed, and bound to his ankles to keep them out of the way as he walked. He removed a fancy hat made from a styled hood; its long tail was wrapped, pinned, and tucked to make an adornment beyond its original design. His blond hair was long and bound in the back, not in a knight's braided *tipok* knot, but wrapped with a simple leather tie. By his face, he was perhaps a few years older than Jaron. He was clean-shaven, his nose was sharp and chiseled, his eyes bright and blue as a summer sky.

Cord arose from his chair and Jaron straightened his posture, gazing at the newcomer with curiosity and a hint of suspicion. Cord called out, "Gavadaire LuVestra!"

Cindra realized she had been staring as the man passed. She reminded herself she was supposed to be a boy, and returned to smacking the fencing dummy, perhaps a bit more aggressively.

"Master Freekirk!" called the man in a thick Aurilonian accent. "So good to see you again," he came forward and took Cord's grip in an overhand clasp, making a nodding bow in the traditional Aurilonian greeting. "I am honored to return as an instructor; I hope to give something back to the school." He smiled, showing white, even teeth.

"Allow me to introduce another of my former students, Sir Jaron Dunlorden." Cord presented his friend, and Sir Jaron offered his hand and had it bowed to. "He will be an instructor as well, and his squire Dillan will be a student."

Cindra heard her new name and turned, bowing to the man. She thought she might be blushing, so she quickly returned to whacking the fencing dummy.

"I am pleased to meet the renowned Sir Jaron," Gavadaire said. "I well remember your famous duel at the festival two years ago." The man looked on him with admiration, but Jaron became nervous.

"You saw that duel?" Jaron asked, eying Sir Cord.

Cindra turned around and listened, suddenly attentive. *This might be a problem,* she thought, watching Jaron's face.

Gavadaire replied, "Oh yes! I had come to Portshia to attend the school. I arrived a few weeks early, during the Festival of Selvina, and heard of a challenge of honor over the love of a lady. Such things I had only read about in stories of old, so I went to see." He smiled, hands on hips, "The way you allowed your opponent to nearly kill you before turning the battle; it was risky and inspired, a true spectacle. He was once a student here as well, was he not?"

Jaron nodded, "He was, but it was not meant to be a spectacle. He had someone place a spell upon me."

"Is this so?" Gavadaire was aghast. "Was the fellow apprehended?"

"He was never caught," Cord said.

"How dishonorable!" Gavadaire remarked. "Still, you triumphed. Your love must have been blessed by the goddess, for certain."

Cindra was listening intently now. *So this man had witnessed the duel with Greenfellow. Had he also seen me in the grandstand? Would he know my face?* She wandered over silently, the wooden sword hanging in her hand. Cord had not seen through her disguise, and he had actually met her face-to-face before the festival. Surely *this* fellow would not guess her identity.

She asked Jaron quietly, "Was that the lady who was sent to Rokvynnar? The one who died at sea?" She acted timid for bringing up a sore subject to the knight, but she was really reminding Gavadaire that Lady Cindra was dead.

Not standing nearby. Dead.

"Alas yes," LuVestra nodded his head solemnly, remembering. "My apologies, Sir Jaron. I did not mean to bring up such a painful memory."

Jaron accepted the apology with a nod, trying to look miserable.

Gavadaire quickly changed the subject. "I must see to my things; I have a room at the adjoining inn, I hope that is alright, Master Cord? Or do you wish for me to move into the instructor's quarters?"

Jaron gave Cord a pointed look, shielding his face from Gavadaire by scratching his temple.

Cord said quickly, "No, no the inn is fine if you wish. Will your stipend be enough to afford the room for the entire term?" Jaron glared at Cord, willing him to drop it.

"Oh yes, I also received support from home. I shall be well enough." He bowed and said, "Now if you will excuse me, I must see to my gear and the care of my horse. It was a pleasure meeting you." He nodded to Jaron and Dillan before walking out the gate, his cape flowing behind like the wings of a bird.

Cindra watched him go as she moved next to her knight. "So he is to be an instructor," she mused, looking to Jaron playfully and seeing him look back with a dark expression. "What?" she asked defensively.

Jaron said, "I hope you can remember that you are supposed to be a boy. Not that it would discourage *him*, I think." He crossed his arms and leaned on the table.

"You just say that because he's handsome and well-dressed," she said with a smirk.

"And Aurilonian," he muttered.

"I am half-Aurilonian, you cad," she scolded, "Besides I already have a handsome knight to attend to." She teased him with a girlish voice while letting her boyish mannerisms slip.

"LuVestra is not a knight," said Cord, amused by his friend's jealousy, "He is from a noble lineage, but has no family holdings or prospects, and he serves no lord. He was raised in a monastery by Su'Kraal monks."

"Raised by monks," Jaron said, giving Cindra a knowing look, "That settles it; you're not safe around him, boy or no."

She smacked his arm with her wooden sword.

The next few hours saw a trickle of students enter the yard, some together, some alone. The first lad to enter did so with a bit of hesitation, looking unsure and nervous. Cord had to wave him over to the table and Jaron muttered something about the 'first victim' under his breath. Cord gave the nervous ones 'assertiveness training,' which usually involved a lot of yelling.

By late morning most of the students had arrived and gathered into little groups to chat and boast until the master told them otherwise. Baggage was piled by the main hall's wide doors as the young men took in the scene, admiring the large murals and mimicking the fighting stances. Cindra followed Jaron around like a puppy until he made her go mingle with the other students.

"Don't give anyone a reason to single you out. Be one of the boys, don't cling to me like a child to his mother." He spoke to her as Dillan, not Cindra; there was no hidden tenderness in his voice, no softness. It was a tone she would have to get used to.

Cindra, or Dillan, wandered out into the courtyard among the other students, pretending to study her surroundings, but keeping an ear open to conversations. Many of the lads were boisterous and rowdy, sizing each other up in the manner of soldiers.

She had been around those types all her life, though they behaved better when a lady approached.

Several lads had been delivered to the school in the company of their knights, who had since departed. Those boys had an odd look of excitement mixed with abandonment and Cindra figured they might be easier to get to know. She drifted towards four of the less rowdy ones, smiling crookedly and lifting her chin in a funny head toss, like a reverse nod. It was a strange greeting, but Lady Mytha had insisted that it was how boys and men greeted each other and it seemed to work; the two squires responded in kind with the same horse-like head motion. The other two boys however gave a normal nod, head-down-first.

The four lads varied in height and build, only one being shorter than Cindra. The tallest was a blond boy with a handsome face, or it would be once he grew into his ears and teeth. The short lad was freckled and towheaded, with light eyelashes about his blue eyes. He spoke in the most animated manner, but said very little of worth.

The other two boys carried themselves differently; they were squires, like her, (a comical likening when she thought about it) and they took the postures of nobility. They wore no house symbols, since they were all equal as students, yet they only smiled when the other boys laughed, and kept their feet planted firmly, while their companions shifted about like nervous horses.

"Hullo," said the tall lad, adjusting his jacket as Dillan approached. "You squire to that fellow?" he motioned to Jaron with his head.

"Yes," Cindra said. "That's Sir Jaron Dunlorden. I'm Dillan." She kept the introduction informal, lest they start with questions she had not made up lies for yet.

"Adric," said the tall lad, thumbing his chest. "This is Demel and Gaius," he indicated the squires, "and this is-"

"Padison Pemwreth," said the freckled boy with an

earnest smile, extending his hand. Cindra took his hand and the boy shook it vigorously, making her wince. "How do you do?"

Demel, the well-dressed squire with the northern accent said, "You must forgive Padison, he suffers from excess enthusiasm." He turned to the freckled lad and chided, "No need to shake his arm off! It's not a competition."

"But it is!" Padison disagreed, "It's to let people know what you're made of. Dillan here shakes hands like a girl!" He grinned broadly and gave Cindra a little punch in the shoulder; she had a choice to look shocked or laugh, so she chose to laugh.

Gaius asked, "You said your knight's name is Dunlorden? Jaron Dunlorden?" Gaius had a medium build and was Cindra's height. He had chestnut-brown hair, a high forehead, and a stern brow. He looked familiar somehow.

"That's right, yes," she answered, caught off guard by his discourteous tone. "Is that a problem?"

"He brought shame to House Corrina for starters, and got banished for it." Gaius said, folding his arms. The other boys looked from Gaius to Dillan, and their words had caught the attention of others, who began to gather around.

"He and the lady were under a spell; they couldn't help themselves," Cindra replied, keeping her temper. She wasn't about to fight him for his remark, but she wasn't going to let it pass either. "Master Freekirk himself discovered the plot. You aren't calling *him* a liar, are you?"

Gaius relented and unfolded his arms, frowning at Cindra. Then he looked away and said nothing.

"What happened?" asked Padison, eager for gossip. The situation had just been defused, but he never let that stop him. A few other boys came closer to hear.

Gaius spoke, "There was a tournament two years back and Sir Jaron-" he lowered his voice a bit, "Sir Jaron and the count's daughter made a spectacle of themselves before the festival crowd. She was betrothed to a foreign ally at the time, so it was a *huge* scandal. The lady's bodyguard challenged Dunlorden to a duel and got himself killed."

"A fight to the death?" Padison looked impressed. "In front of a crowd? Wow! Did you see it?"

Gaius shook his head, "No, but a fine account of it reached my father's house. The countess banished Dunlorden for two years, some say to save him from the count's wrath. The only reason he wasn't executed was because Master Freekirk found out they were under a love spell, and the bodyguard was behind it all."

"That's a load of river cow crap!" One of the new arrivals spoke up from behind Cindra, making her jump. "They sullied the name of a dead knight. Very brave. Sir Earnold Greenfellow died for the honor of House Corrina, the same house that named him traitor."

The lad walked into the group, hands on hips. He was as tall as Adric but broader in the shoulders with a stronger frame. He had a dark brow that shadowed deep-set eyes, and a sharp nose hanging over thin lips. His hair was dark and short, save for a single tail in back, grown for the day he would braid it into a knight's *tipok* knot.

I know those features, Cindra thought with growing unease. *But from where?*

"And who might you be?" asked Gaius, not used to being called a liar.

"Rejick Ratham of Breega, where the rest of House Greenfellow lives in exile, thanks to the Corrinas." He almost sneered the name. "Sir Earnold Greenfellow was my cousin." He motioned to the lad behind him, "This is Terrus Drakthorne, another admirer of Sir Jaron's handiwork. He saw the whole thing himself." The boy behind him was a bit shorter, with reddish hair and ruddy skin. He was more amused than belligerent as he watched his friend stir trouble.

Cindra looked up at Rejick Ratham, knowing they

were going to be *great* friends. She could feel it, like a hangnail.

Rejick caught her glance and glared back. "If it wasn't for my cousin, your good knight may have knocked up the count's daughter before she got married off. Too bad she couldn't swim."

Cindra was feeling rather Dillan-like at the moment and had the urge to punch the obnoxious lad in the face, foolish though it may be. The top of her skull started burning with rage, her cheeks colored and she balled her fists, but it was Gaius that leaped forward and struck the sneering boy square in the nose. The crowd erupted in shouts and flailing limbs as Cindra found herself in the middle of a row, boys on both sides trying to hold back the combatants as they strained forward, eager for more.

Cord and Jaron rushed over but it was Cord's thunderous voice that brought the fight to an end. "ENOUGH!" he bellowed, making everyone fall silent. "What's this all about?" he demanded of the two boys. Rejick was wiping blood from his nose and Gaius had a bruised cheek. Jaron was looking at Cindra with a worried, angry expression that softened when he saw she was all right.

"A family matter Master Freekirk," Gaius answered. "Won't happen again." Rejick glared at him and nodded to the master, willing to let it go for now.

"I usually say this after registration is over, but I'll say it now: all here are fellows until we meet on the battlefield!" Sir Cord's voice boomed and echoed in the courtyard. "Fighting among yourselves is not tolerated on school grounds! Anyone who breaks this rule will be tossed out on their ear, regardless of who your family is. Do I make myself clear?" He glared at the assembled boys who all nodded.

"DO I MAKE MYSELF CLEAR?" Cord shouted, making the inn's windows shake.

"Yes, Master Freekirk!" they all answered loudly, eager to make him stop shouting.

"Good," Cord said, pointing at Rejick and Gaius. "Leave your family feud outside my doors. I'll be watching both of you closely. House Greenfellow and House Corrina are both loyal subjects of his majesty, so act like it."

House Corrina? At first, Cindra thought Master Cord had accidentally given her secret away, but it took her a moment to realize that he was addressing Gaius! *Of course! Gaius Corrina, my first cousin!* She had never met the lad, though they were the same age. Uncle Aren had visited the castle when Cindra's little brother Argus was born, but that was six years ago, and Gaius had not come with him.

In fact, her father had been visiting his brother in Syngmore Castle when the events at the festival took place. Her mother had sent word by rider instead of the much faster ember swallow, so she might have more than a week to deal with things her own way.

Now Gaius Corrina was a fellow student, one who had just defended her honor against a vile slander. *If only I could tell him,* she thought. *At least I can thank him.*

"Gaius," she said, putting a hand on his shoulder as he moved towards the wall. "Thank you for that," she knew it sounded weak and vague, but it was all she could say.

He looked at her with red-rimmed eyes. "I didn't do it for your knight. I did it for the count's late daughter. We were cousins." He rubbed his bruised cheek and said angrily, "For all I know, what Ratham said about Sir Jaron is true, so don't thank me. It's a family matter." With that, he turned and stalked off.

Demel, Adric, and Padison came up to Dillan, "What was that about?" asked the short boy. "Are their families enemies?"

"It's a long story," Cindra said, trying not to sound hurt. "Sir Earnold's father was banished for cowardice by House Corrina, and Sir Jaron's father, a common soldier, was awarded a knighthood and honors in his place. The Greenfellows hate the Dunlordens, and they're none too happy with the Corrinas either."

"Wow," said Padison, "So Rejick is a Greenfellow, and now he's at school with a Dunlorden *and* a Corrina. Sounds like trouble."

Two Corrinas, thought Cindra, and she nodded in agreement.

Chapter Eight

Priests and Pastries

After registration was concluded, the students were given their bunk assignments in the dormitory, and a footlocker in which to stow their gear. Jaron and Gavadaire acted as shepherds, herding the students, twenty in total, on a brief tour of the school, outlining their daily routine and what was expected of them. There would be one day of rest each week; on Highday, the students were expected to attend services in the Temple of Balkon just down the street, after which they were free to do as they pleased, within reason.

Cindra was looking forward to the first Highday with great anticipation, for it was the day when she and Jaron would travel to Casselvane Keep and present themselves to her parents. To public eyes, it would only be Sir Jaron begging for return to the count's service, but in private it would be a joyous family reunion, the return of a child long thought dead. Cindra had been waiting for this day for two years, though she knew of the grave danger in revealing herself. If those who planned her death knew she was alive and back home, who knows what they would do? The evil men who called themselves 'priests' were responsible for much pain and suffering among the Loyalist Houses, and Cindra's return must be kept quiet until they were found. Yet she could not let her parents suffer any longer.

The next day was the first day of training, and it was a rude awakening for Cindra. She had assumed they would be taught how to hold different weapons and learn fighting stances like in the courtyard murals, but it seemed that Master Freekirk intended to run the students into the ground first. The day began early and ended late, with running laps about the courtyard before breakfast, lunch, and dinner. In between were a grueling series of exercises that stretched, pulled, strained, and tormented muscles she never knew she had. She thought back fondly to her time among the Galindri, earning her 'horse legs' by clinging to the mount and guiding it with her thighs. That training had been painful, but this...

There were hours of twisting to and fro, bending and stretching, twirling the arms about in structured motions as the master called out the counting and the instructors walked up and down the rows, correcting mistakes born of fatigue and pain. It was hardest on Bradric Hyne, a big heavy-set lad with great strength but little stamina. Adric Hywahl, the tall blond boy, took to encouraging him when he faltered, and Padison joined him. The two boys became known as Addy and Paddy, or jokingly as 'the twins,' because they were so very different.

There *were* two brothers among the students as it turned out; though not twins, they were obviously related. Finnas and Ferrol Avenoth had the tanned olive skin and dark hair common in the south, with green eyes that were almost bright enough to hint at Galindri heritage. They were born only nine months apart and fiercely competitive, especially with each other. They had both raced to the registration table upon arriving, kicking up dust and making quite a scene. Now they took to training with a vengeance, which might have been a good example, were it not for their bad attitudes. The elder boy, Finnas, was somewhat likable when he wanted to be, even smiling and joking with other students, but Ferrol was mean and cold, challenging everyone who met his eyes. He spoke threats fluently and everyone gave him his space, all except his brother. They would often come to blows or wrestle, though doing nothing that could get them expelled.

The most exotic students, the ones who got the wary glances and odd looks, were Minas Koorla and Maadi Gaavi. Cindra was not unused to dark skin or odd mannerisms, but these two were not Galindri, and their ways were strange and mysterious to her.

Minas was a native of Portshia, but his family was Maanok, barbarians from the east over the Gartethan Mountains. He was very tall and imposing for his age, with tanned, copper skin and squared features. Tattoos adorned his cheeks, and his hair was long, braided, and gathered in the back. His people once swarmed and raided through the mountain passes into Calilon, but now only the Aurilonians had to cope with them. He was avoided and not trusted by anyone.

Maadi Gaavi was a different sort entirely. He was a young man from Gozhima, a vast and wild country of jungles, plains, deserts, and all manner of unspeakable dangers. He was slim but well-muscled, with umber-dark skin and tightly curled hair, which he kept trimmed so close as to be almost bald. He bore scar patterns on the sides of his head and upon his chest, and his eyes were as dark as onyx. Cindra had been so accustomed to bright green Galindri eyes that dark eyes on dark skin was almost disturbing.

Gaavi's people were known for taming and riding the moku, feathered bird-like creatures with grasping claws instead of wings, and sharp, horned beaks. Cindra had seen one years ago in the Market Square; its colorful plumage did not detract from the menace of the vicious talons and hooked beak. She would have liked to ask him about the beasts, and about how he came to be here, but his accent was thick and his Calilesh was limited. That, and she was frankly intimidated by him.

When Cindra started her dinner in the common hall that evening, she barely had the strength to lift her spoon, and her hand shook when raising the drinking cup to her lips. Jaron gave her a look of sympathy combined with a little grin that said 'I told you so.' The meals were light and bland on the first day, giving many students less to throw up when their stomachs rebelled. Cindra was not among those who got ill, but it was only because Jaron showed her deep breathing exercises to stifle the urge. As his squire, she was expected to serve him during meals, carving his meat and pouring his ale, but he took pity on her that evening.

"This must be how laundry feels after being beaten on a rock and twisted dry," she whimpered. "How much more of this is there?"

"Best not to think that way," Jaron said. "In war, you don't have the luxury of knowing when it will all end. You just persevere."

"I thought I'd get to whack someone with a sword," she said, poking a stewed carrot with her knife.

"There'll be plenty of that, and unlike the dummies, the other students hit back."

"I suppose so," she muttered.

Jaron treated her like any other student in public, but when they were alone, he was much more tender and caring. He was even happy to massage her sore muscles before bed.

"Ow! I think my whole body is one big bruise," she whined as he rubbed her shoulders through her nightshirt.

"Huh, this is nothing. Wait until tomorrow when you

start to get *really* sore." He moved his hands between her shoulder blades, making her gasp as he found another knotted muscle.

"Tomorrow... I don't know if I can manage tomorrow. I feel sick today, especially after listening to poor Bradric wheeze." Cindra had been worried that the big lad would drop dead. It was a good thing the twins were there for moral support.

Jaron said, "Bradric will be alright, and so will you. Just focus on why you're training. If that doesn't help you through it, then maybe you're here for the wrong reasons."

Cindra tried to turn, but found the movement painful, "This wasn't all some trick to get me to quit, was it? Because it won't work," she huffed.

"Heh, it's a trick to get everyone to quit. If they can't take the first month of drilling, then they likely won't complete the course anyway. It helps to weed out the ones who are not so committed."

She took a deep breath and let it out, "A month is it? Fine then; I can manage. Just keep rubbing." She bowed forward, stretching her back and neck so Jaron could knead her pain away.

Highday could not come soon enough, and the students let out a cheer at the end of their first week of training. They got up early, dressed in their best clothes, and donned the school's tabard: the red and black draping emblazoned with the white hart of the *Daerbrik* School.

Cindra dressed with Jaron in their quarters, grateful for their privacy. Because of his status as instructor, she was able to bathe, use a chamber pot, and deal with her monthly blood without being discovered, although Jaron was made to leave the room for those activities as well. At least the dressing routine had become smoother; they'd gotten past the nervous, giggling phase and were often too exhausted for anything else.

The students gathered in the yard for inspection as

Master Freekirk walked up and down the line, straightening a collar here or adjusting a belt there. The students all had different dress clothes according to their means, but the tabard and red cap was the school's version of a uniform and they all had to look presentable in them. Once the master was satisfied, the students filed out of the yard and were marched to the Procession Way. They followed it eastward to the Warrior's Path, a street that began at the north city wall and ended right at the temple door.

Balkon's temple was built of gray and black stone. It had a domed roof with eight large spikes radiating out from the base of the dome, each as long as a grown man. A curved wall supported the roof, along with pillars spaced evenly around the perimeter. Each section of wall between the pillars was adorned with a relief depicting the god Balkon and his winged Kyraine servants overseeing some aspect of warfare. The effect was glorious and daunting all at once.

Kyraine fascinated Cindra. They were female warriors that gathered the fallen on the battlefield, and supposedly once guarded the very lives of ancient kings. They were beautiful and terrible, with clawed hands and feet, like great birds of prey. When first she heard of them as a girl, she wanted to be one, but everyone had told her it was quite an improper pursuit for a lady.

The vaulted interior was dominated by a huge bronze statue of the god of war, adorned in a suit of armor made of beaten and polished metal plates. Torches lined the perimeter, glowing through the fragrant clouds of incense, and the light behind the statue danced and flickered, evoking both the deity's famous temper and the flames of war. There were small, circular windows around the edge of the dome that permitted beams of light to lance through the smoke-filled air. Priests entered from behind the statue's base, bearing black maces that were miniature versions of the enormous one held in the god's bronze hand. They all had red hair, either by birth, or by some strange concoction that reminded Cindra of dark red raspberries.

She and the other students stood in a cluster, surrounded by a few hundred other worshipers. Most were soldiers of some sort: guardsmen of the wall, watchmen of the streets, knights, squires, sell-swords, militiamen, bodyguards, and simple conscripts. Anyone who had to risk his life in arms found his way into the worship of Balkon. Whether they wanted to die an honorable death, or simply do their duty and live to tell about it, men from all fighting classes gathered under this one roof to pray.

All of them are men, Cindra noted.

The high priest, who wore black and red robes with metal plate armor on his shoulders and arms, stood before the altar and raised his mace in the air, calling out to the glowering, silent effigy.

"Balkon, Lord of Strife and Bringer of War, hear our solemn prayers!" He spoke in a voice that echoed to the high ceiling, and the crowd answered their part of the litany with solemn reverence. Cindra would have to mouth the words until she learned them. The reading of the sacred texts followed, and she wondered how long the service would be; the incense and closeness of so many bodies were making her woozy.

The priest's voice rang out, "In the Age of Krythius, when the Anointed King fell into corruption, the Wandering Prophet did speak to the masses gathered at the fortress of Wen. He proclaimed that a king would rise, one who would undo the terrible darkness that was to come. A king of divine blood would he be, yet born of mortal mother, and so the will of Arathus would be made flesh, his purpose clad in an armor of adamant, so that none might lead him astray.

"And so it came to pass that Ashimae, the blessed Lady of Lelova, was made with child by the will of Arathus. She named the boy-child Kraal, for he was destined to gather all under his gaze and be as a shepherd over a flock, a mighty king to unite the fractured land."

The incense was going to her head and she felt light and strong. As the reading came to an end, the gathered throng offered up a mighty shout that seemed to shake the very walls. It stirred something deep in her chest, like the thrill she'd experienced when firing a canon from the castle walls, or when she gathered her courage and attacked Black Will, saving young Nixy. It was a fierce thing, that feeling, as if she could roar like a lion, or grow to a giant size, rivaling the gleaming metal god before her. His painted eyes seemed to dare her to do so, and despite her rising pulse and growing sense of awe, she did not look away.

The service ended and the students filed out with the rest of the congregation, stepping into the bright morning sunlight as it rose over the eastern mountains. Cindra tugged Jaron's sleeve excitedly. "May we go to the castle now?" she asked, barely able to contain herself. Jaron hesitated, and Cindra's face fell when she saw the look in his eyes; he had something to say that she wouldn't like. "What is it?"

Jaron cleared his throat and placed his hands on her shoulders, "Cord and I spoke about this at length, and we've agreed... we don't think you should accompany me to the castle." She began to protest, but he interrupted, "If anyone were to recognize you, all would be undone. We can't risk it!"

"But it has been two years! Jaron, they are my parents!" She hissed the words, trying to keep her voice down even as her shoulders trembled and her breathing came in huffs. "How can you keep me away?"

"Dillan," he said firmly, bringing her mind to how she ought to act, "I shall tell them all they need to know, and nothing more. Our concern is for your safety, and if your parents learn too much..." He glanced around to make sure they were not being overheard. "Anyone at the castle who knows your face can start rumors... rumors that will lead directly to the school."

She became furious, but managed to contain it to her face. "You two only care about the school's reputation! You don't want it known that I'm hiding and training there!"

"That's not true at all!" Jaron retorted, getting angry himself. "Gods above and below, we're already risking everything by following your insane plan! If this becomes public, it could mean our lives for what we've already done."

This sobered her a bit, "What have you done that could possibly cost your lives?"

Jaron sighed, calming himself. "Ci-*Dillan*," he caught himself and took another breath, speaking low, "This deception could get us killed. You are breaking many, many laws doing this, and we are helping you."

"I know, but my father-"

"Your father must keep peace among the faiths. The Balkonittes don't allow women in their temples, and they would demand a severe punishment for such a sacrilege."

"I wouldn't let them put you to death, Jaron!" She tried to be reassuring, but she was unsure herself.

"I appreciate it," he said with a smile, "But if we risk exposing you before the plotters are found, they could use all of this against us. If we are to survive, then we need leverage; something to prove that it was all necessary and worthwhile. Right now, a whisper in the wrong ear is all they need to bring down our plans."

She now felt ashamed of her accusation. *This isn't about me, but my family and the realm,* she thought, *I'm supposed to be the one to remember that.* Her anger relented, but she didn't want to give Jaron a victory so easily. "So you and Master Cord discussed this without involving me. Did you plan to just dump me at the school while you rode off to the castle?" She crossed her arms and tried to look affronted.

Jaron scratched his head awkwardly, "We were going to tell you when we got back from the service," he explained as Cord strode over to join them, "We planned to break it to you gently with some pastries.”

Cord made herding motions with his arms, “Come along you two, back to the school if you want to argue. Plenty of room to fight like cats and dogs in the privacy of your quarters.”

Seeing the discussion was over, Adric and Padison headed over to chat with her. Cindra put Cindra away and slipped into Dillan’s skin, grinning crookedly at the boys as she shouldered Jaron as roughly as she was able. “I *better* get my pastries,” she told him, and went to join her friends.

Chapter Nine

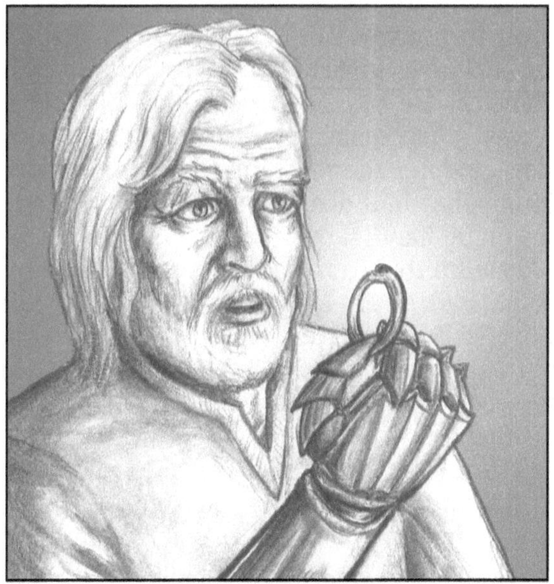

A Trinket of Gold

Ildric Finnael had not done so much traveling since his younger days, but these were dangerous times, and he required information. Two years ago, he had traveled north to the hamlets of Syngmore to learn about the boy Nixyalderthor DuQuayne. More recently, he had great cause to journey west to the city of Waynwell. It had been an eight-day ride along well-kept roads, but his back and buttocks were not as resilient as they used to be. Still, the trip had been worth it. He had returned from his journey bearing the magic golden bracelet he had once given Lady Cindra, but had not the time to meet with her parents about it; the strange visit of the elven emissary had taken precedence. Now he was making up for lost time as he walked up the path to Casselvane Keep. *So many matters of importance, all coming up at once,* he thought. *It bodes ill, or I'm not a wizard.*

Which, of course, he was.

Ildric had dressed in simple gray-green traveling robes for this audience, for he did not want to call attention to himself. He had even left his staff in the tower, choosing instead to carry an old wand for emergencies. He did not try to hide his identity, for there was a particular obviousness about a man in disguise, and he didn't want to arouse suspicion by sneaking about in a deep hood while trying to hide his famous metal hand.

He was admitted to the count's study, the same room where he had given Lady Cindra's parents the good news of her survival over two years ago. Now he must worry them again, but not without need. Besides, he had foreseen that Sir Jaron would arrive and soften the news somehow.

Count Amon was attired in an embroidered vest of dark crimson and hose of burgundy. His graying, receding hair was pulled out of his face by a circlet of gold, and his beard was trimmed and neat. It was his eyes that brought pause to the wizard, however. The count had a drawn and sleepless look, with dark circles of fatigue shadowing his eyes.

Countess Zara wore a dress of deep blue lined with yellow trim. Her golden hair was bound and braided, covered with a gauzy veil that framed her long, stately face. Unlike the count, her emerald eyes were sharp, and her brow furrowed with anxiety. "What news brings you to our home once again, arch mage?" she asked, her voice steady.

"News of caution and danger, not tragedy I am happy to say." He took the offered seat, feeling his spine shift and pop like the gears of a creaky old mill. "One moment, your lordships..." He raised his silver hand and closed his eyes, as if giving a benediction in a temple. The green dragon eye embedded in the palm flickered and glowed, looking this way and that, as if alive. Satisfied, the wizard lowered his hand and opened his eyes. "I have been more careful of late, and I wanted to be sure we were not overheard."

The count leaned forward in his chair saying, "There are no spy-holes or listening horns in *this* room, I assure you. It was made for privacy."

"A wise precaution, lordship," Finnael said. "But there are other ways of eavesdropping, as you must know."

"Only by wizards," the count said.

"Precisely the problem I have come to discuss, my lord."

The countess gripped the arm of her chair, "Please arch mage, the matter of your visit."

She is indeed on edge, Ildric thought. *Best to be direct.* He cleared his throat and began, "Late last year, I was attending a meeting of the Order of Astrellaris. As you may know, the Tower of the Silver Moon is layered with many protections against magical spying and intrusion, yet I felt the presence of another mind seeking me out. It was like a distant call or faint question, like the sweeping gaze of a lighthouse searching dark waters in the fog.

"I believe that had I not possessed the Eye of Omithys, I would not have noticed the intrusion. While the one searching for me was not powerful enough to succeed, I could sense *him.*" Ildric shifted in his seat, uncomfortable from his recent journey. "I turned the inner eye towards the intruder, gaining a few brief flashes of insight before he broke his connection. It was most enlightening."

The countess was growing more restless, and the count was rubbing his eyes as if they pained him. He implored, "Gods save us from wizards and their word-painting. The *matter*, arch mage."

Ildric pursed his lips, biting back a sharp retort. He said, "Someone else knows your daughter is alive, and is seeking her."

They gasped and jumped in their chairs, now quite alarmed.

*Be short with **me**, will you?* Ildric thought with annoyance. Before they could assault him with questions, he chided, "She is safe for now, but what I saw is important. It took me a few moments to make sense of it all, but it came to this: there was a wizard in another part of the realm attempting to locate the owner of a certain magic golden bracelet."

The countess asked, "The one that saved her at sea? Your gift to her?"

"The same," Ildric said, and he took it from the folds of his robe and held it up for them to see. "How he came by this I do not know, but I saw what he saw; he learned that Cindra was alive and hiding among the Galindri."

"The Galindri?" the count exclaimed, "Those nomad horse traders? Gods, arch mage! You did not leave her with them, did you? They are savages and thieves!"

Ildric raised his silver hand to plead for restraint, "My lord, I beg you not to judge them all by a few stories." His tone became stern, "There is not a people in this world who have not had among them both good and evil. As it was, the family she encountered took her in and kept her safe for two years. I would say their ilk is the more common sort that roam the lands, not the exception." He cleared his throat again, hoping for no more silly interruptions. "Since that time, she has departed their company and made her way back to Portshia..." This news caused much hope and cheer to brighten their faces. "... and I have placed a powerful counter-spell upon her, protecting her from another such scrying attempt."

"What of the wizard who was searching for her?" the countess asked. "Did you find him?"

Ildric nodded gravely, "I did. As I said, he was searching for the previous owner, and so found Cindra. But the bracelet was in my possession far longer, and thus he stumbled upon me, and I upon him. Since my efforts to find him were thwarted, I cast my vision out for the bracelet instead, finding it in Waynwell."

"Waynwell?" the count said. "I would have expected a plot to come from the east, from one of the Dissenter Houses. Lord Mamfett of Kelgar Province is a staunch supporter of the crown, and the lord at Waynwell is his son!"

"I do not say the conspiracy has its heart there, my lord. Merely that the bracelet made its way there, possibly following Lady Cindra on her journey back home. Regardless, once the winter storms let up, I set off to Waynwell to find the bracelet and the diviner who read its past. Instead, I found the item in the possession of a different wizard who had purchased it at auction. Apparently, the diviner had been murdered, and his belongings were sold to cover his debts. This was why I could not find him; the dead leave no echoes in the quintessence."

"Murdered!" the countess exclaimed. "That means whomever is truly searching for our daughter is still out there!"

The count offered, "Or perhaps his murder was unrelated and the secret died with him?" His eyes said he desperately wanted this to be so.

Ildric shook his head, "No, I am afraid not, my lord. Whoever hired that wizard either knew she was alive and lost her trail, or they suspected she was alive and had him confirm it. No matter. The villain left no loose ends. He killed the poor fellow on the day I first became aware of him."

"How can you be so sure of this?" asked the count. "It might be that she lost the trinket in Waynwell, and the wizard was trying to find the proper owner when he was slain by one of his lenders..."

Ildric knew the man was grasping at hopes, wanting to be rid of the worry that obviously plagued him of late, draining his strength and taxing his health. Sadly, he could not afford to grant the count any illusions; the stakes were too high. "I can assure you, my lord, that the man's murder was indeed related to the bracelet and the threat against Lady Cindra's life. The culprit left it behind because he knew it could be used to find him, in the same way the murdered wizard found Cindra and myself. Unfortunately for him, it was in his possession too long already."

Zara said, "You have found the murderer?"

"In a manner," Ildric replied, sitting up straighter. "I know he was in possession of the trinket for many months, and that he inquired with many wizards to learn its secrets. There are few in the Mystic College who study the art of reading enchantments, since there are so few enchanted objects to study. No demand for the skill, you see; no jobs to be had. A pity that such matters stand in the way of-"

"But *who is he?*" pressed the countess, losing patience.

"Forgive me, your ladyship. I was rambling," he said. "By his speech, the man pursuing Lady Cindra is of the south, possibly from Portshia itself. He has fair hair with curls, and a like-colored beard. He seldom shows his face, choosing to wear a deep hood or a bestial mask when handling the bracelet. This detail is telling; he understands how divination works."

"You and he have us at a disadvantage then," muttered the count.

Finnael explained, "Divination is the seeking of both the known and the unknown. As one might imagine, the 'known' is by far the easier to find. If the bracelet can be seen with magic, then so can its surroundings, including the one who holds it. The longer an 'unknown someone' is in possession of a known object, the more of a connection they will form; this is why the killer abandoned it in Waynwell after learning it once belonged to me, and that I knew someone was seeking it."

Count Amon nodded, "It would give him away, like a campfire in the night."

"Indeed," Ildric said. "It is my belief that he is here in Portshia, though he has help. Something is masking him from my sight, something he didn't have before." He scratched his white beard, "There are certain enchantments that can veil a person from the Sight, though I can overcome most of them. I cannot see his face or hear his voice, but through the fog of his surroundings I can see this very city." His tone grew low and dark, "He is here, and he is not working alone."

The dread of those words hung in the air like a volley of arrows suspended in time. A sudden knock at the door made them start in surprise. The count took a deep breath to calm himself and called out, "Enter!"

Constable Fingelm strode in, eying the wizard with a bit of distaste. His chagrin at being excluded from these meetings was plain on his face, though he kept his voice even and dignified. "Apologies, milord. There is a knight below requesting an audience; a Sir Jaron Dunlorden... returning from exile, as I recall."

Ildric sniffed at the remark. *Of course you recall, you artless peacock. You read the order before the assembly of knights.* He had little patience for the man, who seemed to think he should be privy to every whispered word.

Before casting the counter-spell upon her, Ildric had seen Lady Cindra in the company of Sir Jaron. How they managed to find each other was baffling, but most fortunate. Ildric told the count, "By all means, see him at once milord."

The count nodded to Fingelm, who bowed and cast a disgusted look at the wizard. "As *my lord* wishes," he said with a touch of irony.

After the door closed and the sound of footsteps faded, the countess said, "Do you think Sir Jaron knows about our daughter's survival?"

Ildric said, "I have seen them together in visions, your ladyship. I believe their paths crossed in the western lands, and they have traveled for some distance in each other's company." He noted the count's discomfort and added, "There is the matter of the scandal that led to his banishment, milord. I understood that a love spell of sorts was used upon them both. I do hope this will be remembered when the lad's fate is decided." He looked through his eyebrows at the count.

Amon Corrina met the wizard's gaze coolly, "I have had two years to consider this, arch mage. My wife did well to banish him so that I might come to terms with those events. My heart is much less troubled and my anger abated. I plan to accept the lad back into my service, for his father's sake if for no other reason."

The wizard nodded and waited for the arrival of Sir Jaron.

Shortly, the knight was ushered into the study by Constable Fingelm, who made as if to stay. "Sir Jaron Dunlorden, your lordships."

The knight sank to his knees. The count motioned to the constable and said, "You may leave us, Fingelm."

Ildric risked a glance at the man. His skin was coloring to match his reddish hair and beard, and the crestfallen look on his face was almost comical. "Eh... yes milord." He bowed again and left with what dignity he could muster.

I shall have to toss the man a bone, lest he falter in his duties, Ildric thought. *A sword will rust faster in its scabbard.*

The count stood before the knight. "Rise, Sir Jaron, son of Fedrick. We welcome you back to the service of House Corrina." Jaron rose but kept his eyes lowered contritely. "Know that all has been forgiven in light of the circumstances," the count looked at Ildric who nodded slightly. "And we hope errantry has honed you further."

"I thank you, your lordship. I believe it has." He unbuckled the sword from his hip and offered it solemnly to the count. "My father gave to me the keeping of Valdiroth, the Firebrand, upon my departure. I return it now to my lord." Jaron waited for the count to receive it.

Amon Corrina only smiled and said, "Who better to wield it, Sir Jaron? You are a skilled and worthy knight, and you have done great service to my family. Besides, your father is no longer able to perform his duties as my personal guard, bless him. I charge you to carry Valdiroth and wield it for the honor of House Corrina, as your father before you has done these many long years." Ildric nodded and Zara smiled in approval.

Jaron bowed with his hand over his heart, his gratitude showing in the slight watering of his eyes. He cleared his throat and spoke to the count, "If I may, I carry news of great importance," he glanced at the wizard, "May we speak alone milord?"

Ildric only laughed, "What could you hope to hide from me, young knight? Tell on, do not keep the parents waiting."

Jaron's mouth dropped as he understood. *They knew.* He nodded and spoke in a low voice, "Lady Cindra is alive and in Portshia, your lordships." The lady's parents sighed in relief, squeezing each other's hands. Jaron had obviously anticipated a great outpouring of emotion and questions, but now he was a bit off balance.

Ildric grinned to himself.

The knight continued, "She was rescued from drowning by a magical bracelet..." he looked at Finnael as he remembered, "...but you must know that by now. She was kept safe by Galindri nomads until late last year, when fate brought us together." He mentally skipped the part about seeing her naked. "I escorted her to Cordoshome, where we stayed through the winter as a guest of Lord Saul and Lady Mytha. We arrived in Portshia only last week. I assure you, she is safe and well, and she misses you both dearly."

"May we see her?" asked the countess softly.

Jaron did not wish to refuse her, nor was it his place, yet he replied, "It was decided by me and Sir Cord Freekirk that she would be safest in hiding; this is why she did not accompany me, as we feared she might be recognized." He reached into his tunic and removed a roll of parchment. "But at great risk of discovery, she sent me with this letter." He handed the scroll to the countess, who took it with shaking hands.

Dearest father and mother,
I must be brief. Though I long to see you both, the

time for our reunion may be far off. There are evil men calling themselves priests who seek to undo the kingdom and any Loyalist house that stands in their way. It is why my ship was attacked; they feared the alliance my marriage would bring. I also believe the priests who worship this 'Countless Lord' are behind the poisoning of my late, former betrothed, and even the king himself. Be careful, for the castle itself may have eyes and ears.

I am doing my part to help in this crisis, but my location must remain secret. Please understand that I cannot contact you directly, but Sir Jaron can deliver any message.

I love you both so much, and long for safer times,
Always your kitten,
CC

Countess Zara began to cry softly, for she had always called her daughter 'kitten' and knew her hand, having read many letters and poems that her child wrote for her eyes alone. The count took the letter gently from his wife and he looked up at the knight with moist, grateful eyes. Jaron stood looking at the floor, being respectful to the break in their composure.

"I recommend destroying the letter, lest it fall into the wrong hands," Jaron offered.

"I agree with the good knight," said Ildric. "Let no sign of these tidings remain."

The countess folded the letter and held it in her hands, composing herself. "It will be done when I return to my chambers; I cannot bring myself to do it now." She dried her tears with a kerchief and took several deep breaths.

"Now Sir Jaron," said the wizard, "I shall tell you what I have told their lordships." He held up the golden bracelet, "This is the trinket that saved Lady Cindra's life, but it somehow found its way into the wrong hands."

Jaron's eyes widened, "You have it? She told me that

she lost it in Pinikal last summer, when she encountered those evil priests! One of them grabbed her, but the Galindri intervened. She thinks that she lost the bracelet during the struggle."

"So all of the pieces fall into place," Ildric said, looking up at Jaron grimly, "Late in winter, one of these 'priests' hired a wizard to scry out the bracelet's previous owner. They know she survived the attack at sea and hid among the Galindri, and they seek her in Portshia as we speak."

Jaron gasped, "No! How-"

"Peace, Dunlorden," Ildric said. "They also know that I am involved, so they dare not move recklessly. I protected her from further magical seeking, but you must be cautious. Do not let down your guard."

Jaron's hand went to the hilt of his sword, "I should return at once. She is safe, but I must warn her regardless."

"Can we not know where she is? Will you not tell us?" asked the countess, deep concern evident in her eyes. The question might have been a command, but she just avoided making it so.

Jaron's eyes darted from Cindra's noble parents to the arch mage, hoping for a way out. Ildric intervened, "I think it wise that her location remain secret, even from us. The smallest hint might lead our enemies to her."

The countess nodded in silent understanding, placing the letter within a pocket of her dress.

Ildric and Jaron left the count's study and strode down the circular hall, heading towards the grand stair. Jaron's steps were rushed, but Ildric stayed the knight with a hand on his shoulder. "A moment Sir Jaron, if you please."

The knight halted, looking anxious.

The arch mage spoke in a low voice, "I think it best if you do not go directly back to our friend."

"But-"

"Our enemies know our friend is here, but they do not

know where, or with whom, or in what guise. You must act as you would if all were normal. See your father. Take your time."

"But-but *our friend* must be warned," Jaron said. "If they are searching the city..."

"They will only go where they have business going. They will make subtle inquiries and pay bribes. They will cast a wide net and hope. But they will watch who comes and goes from the castle with great interest."

Jaron forced himself to relax, "I see..."

"Good!" Ildric said. "Then make no hurry of it. Stop at a tavern after. Enjoy your day of rest from the duties at the Freekirk School." The wizard's eyes went to the approaching form of Constable Fingelm.

Jaron made to depart, saying, "Thank you for the advice, arch mage." Then to the constable, he bowed and saluted, hand over heart.

"Sir Jaron," Fingelm acknowledged, and the knight strode away. Turning to the wizard, the constable folded his arms and said, "More secrets, I presume? Are these going to add to their lordships' worries, or take from them?"

The wizard forced himself to smile at the presumptuous man. Fingelm may be in charge of the count's forces in times of war and defense, and could call upon any knights and conscripts he required within the entire province, but he was still just an adviser and lackey. His duties did not require the subtlety of statecraft or the delicacy of spy-craft. Still, he was a loyal servant and required a measure of respect. Ildric said, "My duty is to keep their lordships appraised of vital and hidden knowledge, not to see to their moods. I hope you do not hold any enmity against them for excluding you-"

"What do you imply, wizard?" The man flushed at the notion.

"I do not imply anything, dear constable. The count has need of secrecy in his negotiations."

Fingelm was taken aback by the morsel of

information, "Negotiations? Regarding the alliance with Rokvynnar? You are involved?"

The wizard indulged the man a bit, "I am somewhat involved. I cannot tell my part in this matter, of course."

"And Sir Jaron is a part of this as well?" The constable frowned.

"Well, he *did* just return from a two year journey..." said the wizard.

"But that was-"

"Please," Ildric said. "There are games within games at play. I can say no more..." He made to go, but stopped as though a new thought occurred to him, "There is something however... You may serve the cause by watching out for anyone, *anyone* who might show too much interest in castle gossip. Don't let on that you know the matter, or what is at stake, just be vigilant. There's a good fellow." He patted Fingelm on the shoulder and strode away.

The constable rubbed his beard in thought, a furrow of worry creasing his brow.

Chapter Ten

Coming To Terms

After his meeting with the count and his conversation with Ildric Finnael, Jaron made his way downstairs to his father's quarters in the castle. Old Fedrick Dunlorden was officially the head of the house guard, as well as the personal bodyguard of the count, but his duties were reduced of late. Even before Jaron was exiled, the old warrior had found it difficult to stand at guard for a prolonged time, and became winded on the grand stair. Jaron's father had the stubbornness and sturdiness of the farmer he was, but everyone had their limits.

He knocked upon his father's door waited for almost a minute before it opened. A craggy countenance peered out at him, its one good eye taking a moment to focus on his face. The top of his bald head reflected the warm firelight beyond, and when the old man's face cracked in a smile, there were more gaps than teeth. Jaron realized how much he had missed that face.

"Jaron lad!" The door swung wide and Sir Fedrick opened his arms to embrace his son. "Welcome back boy! Good to see you, good to see you." He slapped the young man's back hard, as if to be sure he was really there. "I hadn't heard you'd returned!"

"I just got back two weeks ago. I've been helping Cord at the school. I'm going to be an instructor this term." Jaron hoped his father would think well of that, but he got a punch in the shoulder instead.

"Two weeks? You wait *two weeks* to come see your old man? What ill-mannered, grass-crapping billy goat raised you anyway?" He sat heavily in his chair by the fire, looking a bit frailer than Jaron had ever seen him.

"I've been... I'm sorry father. I should have come sooner." He had no excuse, none that he wanted to discuss anyway. "How have you been?" He looked around the room and noticed that things were a bit disheveled. There were dirty dishes on the table, clothing was strewn about, and the housecoat his father was wearing was a bit stale; the smell still clung to Jaron from their embrace.

"Oh, dying I expect." The old man said glumly. "I've been out of sorts for a year now, probably more." He picked up a goblet and swirled the liquid inside before finishing it off, making a face.

Jaron was at a loss for words; he had never heard his father speak like that before, even in jest. "Dying? You're not dying, don't talk like that." He waited for the old man to smile and make a joke, but the elder Dunlorden just looked into the fire.

"I feel it. I get tired too easy now, much too easy. I feel it in my joints, in my chest... it's an ache that won't go away." He took his pipe from the mantle and lit it, relaxing as the smoke wound about his head.

"Have you seen a healer?" Jaron asked, suddenly very worried.

The old man choked on his smoke, "Gods no! I'll keep my blood in me, thank you." He shivered, "I'm not afraid to bleed, but I'll do it in battle, not as food for a bloated worm. Time enough for that after I'm gone."

Jaron pressed, "What about Lelonethan priests? They use herbs, tonics, and that divine alchemy they swear by. I've seen it work wonders. If the expense is too high..."

"No, I've tried some of their tonics. They helped soothe me but the pain is still there. I'm *old,* Jaron lad. There's no use pouring gold into a grave." He puffed his pipe again, sending little rings towards the ceiling.

"Stop talking like that," Jaron said, trying to will the reality away. Deep in his heart, he knew his father was right. He *was* an old man, older than most men got to be, especially in his profession. Most warriors didn't live past thirty, and his father was more than twice that age. He'd seen over a dozen battles and skirmishes, and had the scars to prove it. Still, that didn't mean Jaron had to like the idea. "There must be something that will help..."

"Well there is, come to think of it," Fedrick said thoughtfully. "You could have a chat with the gods and see if they'll let me live forever. Have 'em throw in a good eye while they're at it." He chuckled; it was a choking, wet sound. "That's the way of it, boy. All things die, some sooner than others." His eyes grew sad. "Like the young lady and her brother before her. Tragic, too tragic..." a thought struck him and he asked, "Y-you must have heard, surely?"

Jaron nodded and tried to look heartbroken, unsure if he should tell his father the truth; the fewer people who knew, the better. "Lady Cindra was taken before her time, yes."

Fedrick changed the subject after another puff, "I see you brought back the honor sword safe and sound. I trust you used its power wisely? You didn't use its flames to light your campfires, did you?"

Jaron smiled sheepishly and sat across from his father, laying the sheathed sword across his knees. "No," he said, "But I do have a story to tell..."

Jaron returned to the school later in the afternoon, having spent the better part of the day talking with his father. Sir Fedrick had listened with rapt attention as Jaron related his worst days: losing the honor sword, his quest to recover it, his charitable treatment of the thieves upon catching them, and his life thereafter. Jaron could have sworn his father got a bit misty-eyed hearing of lessons learned and the trials overcome. It was like the old man's greatest hopes were realized instead of the dreary, shameful account Jaron thought it to be.

After that, he did not talk so much as listen. The old man had much to say about the last two years and all the people that Jaron knew, or at least people his father thought he would remember from brief encounters long ago. By the time Jaron made ready to leave, he had learned news about dozens of friends, relatives, local residents, and the less reputable types that his father had kept up on. He never knew the old man paid so much attention to the comings and goings of others; it was like he was turning into a gossipy old woman. *Or maybe it's what someone his age finds important*, Jaron thought.

He returned to the school later that evening, and found Cindra sleeping in their quarters. After making certain she was safe, he went off to find Cord. The school master was in the master's hall, relaxing by the fireplace with a mug of ale and a pipe. Jaron came in and sat down, sighing as he sank into the soft chair.

Cord smiled around the stem of his pipe, "So did the count accept you back with open arms? You still have your head, I see." He knew that the news Jaron delivered might well have earned him a lordship. *So long as he didn't tell them where their daughter was, or what she was doing... and with whom.*

"It went very well, yes." Jaron said, looking around to make sure they were alone. "But there was a bit of ill-news. Arch Mage Finnael was there, and he gave me a warning about *our friend*. He told me the secret is not safe and we must remain vigilant. Our friend is protected from magical eyes, but ordinary ones can still see."

Cord had a wide grin despite the warning. "You sound like a real spy with all that silly, confusing talk. Did the wizard use this doublespeak, or did he say it more plainly?"

Jaron blushed, "I-he... We spoke plainly but carefully. No one knows if there are unfriendly ears in the castle."

"True enough," Cord said. "So... does the brown goose fly at midnight?" He gave Jaron a series of exaggerated winks.

Jaron sighed in frustration. "This is serious. One of those masked priests got a hold of the magic bracelet, and had a wizard seek out its former owner."

Cord sobered quickly. "When was this?"

"Late last winter, when the two of us stayed at the manor. Finnael claims they don't know many details, but they discovered our friend was alive and well, and heading back to Portshia."

"A curse on all wizards and priests," Cord snarled, raising his mug as if making a toast. He finished his ale in a few gulps. "Meddlers and trouble-makers, all of them. At least the priests had the gods to blame once, but no more."

"It was because of Finnael that we know this," Jaron said. "And he has protected-"

"It was another wizard that sniffed out the secret, and a priest who set him to it. One for money and one for the gods. Same as always." He drew too heavily on his pipe, making the smoke taste bitter.

Jaron knew Cord was in a mood now. He had taken a great risk admitting Cindra to the school, and it looked like all their caution might be for nothing thanks to magic. It was the one thing most warriors feared; the one thing they had no reliable way to face. Years of training and all the best equipment were for naught if your opponent could make you blind and deaf with a word, or turn the ground under your feet to mud, or gods knew what else.

Cord puffed his pipe for a while longer before asking, "Did you visit your father?" His voice told that he knew much of the old man's condition.

"I did," Jaron said, "He thinks he is dying, and he talks like it's already over. How long has he been like this?" Jaron frowned, wondering why Cord didn't bring it up sooner.

"He didn't want you to worry; he wanted to be the one to tell you, assuming he survived long enough for you to return. You know him," he shrugged, "he doesn't want people fussing over him, even at his age."

"Well, there's going to be a bit of fussing," Jaron replied. "I told him I'd have some of the castle staff look in on him from time to time and make sure things are in good order. If he needs help cleaning or taking care of himself, then he's going to have to accept it. Better than living like an old bear." He shook his head.

"The son becomes the father, and the father, the son." Cord said with a sniff. "Funny how it all works, isn't it? My own father turned senile little by little, and mother takes care of everything now. If I were living there, I'd be head of the household in his place."

Jaron grinned, "No, your mother would still be wiping your big pale ass for you." Cord laughed and made a remark under his breath, but Jaron's mirth did not last. He said, "He just seems so... comfortable with the idea. Of dying, I mean. He's so calm about it." Jaron stared at the ceiling as he recalled their long talk, the stale air, the resignation in his father's eyes.

"That's just now," Cord said. "The fear comes and goes; as in war, one minute you're ready to charge into the opposing army, the next you wish you were anywhere else in the world but there. He's an old warrior who's lived with death all his life, but this isn't like a normal battle. At his age, death can come in the night while you're sleeping, or drop you in the middle of a shit, and *that's* if you're lucky. There's no easy way to face an enemy like that."

"Poetry, as always." Jaron smirked. "You're a word-smith, let no one deny it."

"I aim to impress," Cord said, and he let out a belch.

The sounds of students coming and going echoed in the courtyard while the men sat by the fire, watching it die into graying embers.

Growing up, Jaron knew his father was older than the fathers of other children. The old man had never looked young to Jaron's eyes, but he had not been prepared for seeing him for the first time in two years. It was as if all of his memories had blurred together during his exile, making Fedrick Dunlorden a man of indeterminate age. Seeing him in his present state had brought that image crashing down, and it shook him to the core. He had never thought of Sir Fedrick, the champion of House Corrina, as *frail*.

"You're brooding again lad. Get some sleep."

Jaron nodded, got up, and left without a word.

Chapter Eleven

Brother Dane

Nixyalderthor sat in the minstrel's gallery overlooking the audience chamber in the east wing of the castle; he was reading a book line by line in preparation for his daily lessons. The count had been very nice in making him a ward, giving him his own bedroom and nice clothes, and feeding him the most wonderful food he had ever tasted, but the count also insisted that Nixy spend several hours a day learning stuff. Not fun stuff like riding horses or chasing ducks, but stuff like numbers, letters and rules.

At least in the Warren there were other lads to play with, lads who respected his accomplishments. Now he was alone, or at least he felt like it. There were other children about, but they avoided him. It was the same with his former friends in the stables; all they knew was that Nixy was once a groom and a slop-shoveler like them, but now he was treated different. It's like he was made again, like the way he'd been made in the Circle of

Gold. Once you were a made brother, everyone knew you'd proved yourself, and everyone wanted to be your friend. But he was a made brother of House Corrina, and the only people who treated him nice and friendly were people you didn't play with. Plus, he didn't know what he'd done to deserve it.

Every day he had to sit in a room with a Eyoronian cleric who would teach him things he might never use. Counting was important, sure, but Nixy knew his numbers well enough to count out his share of a take and pay his dues. Turns out there were far more numbers than Nixy ever imagined; they just kept going on and on. It seemed ridiculous to try and learn them all. Letters were much easier because there were just a few dozen of them, and they made words when you put them together; numbers just made more numbers. Nixy hadn't needed to read much, but now he was learning. Rules were the most annoying thing to learn. There were rules for everything, even eating and walking. 'Sit up straight, stand up straight, use a knife and fork, chew with your mouth closed.' Ridiculous.

He heard footsteps coming down the grand stairs in the next hall. An armed knight appeared and walked back towards the eastern quarters, his eyes downward. He looked familiar and it took Nixy a moment to place his face. *That's it! He was the knight that Cindra kissed two years ago! 'Jarek' or something*. He remembered the knight killed Cindra's grumpy bodyguard in a duel because of that kiss, and Cindra had blamed herself for some reason. He didn't understand at the time, but he was just a kid then; he was twelve now and had a better grasp on the ways of the world: girls were trouble and they could make you do stupid things, and *that's* why she felt responsible.

Girl or no, he still missed her. She was the first person to be really nice to him, even after chasing him and getting her purse back. She saved his life. She brought him home and kept him safe. Nixy watched the knight disappear around the corner and he went back to his book.

He sighed and pushed thoughts of Cindra from his mind. She was long gone and there was nothing to be done. He had made up his mind to try to make her parents happier, so he went through with his studies and learned what they wanted him to learn. It wasn't all fun, but it was important. Besides, if he could cheer them up, maybe he could report the good news to the Circle of Gold and they would be happy with him too. Everyone wins.

It was nearly time for his lesson with Brother Dane, so he dog-eared his place in the book and headed for the main entrance. Before stepping into the entry hall, he saw a figure coming down the grand stairs. Out of habit, he stopped to see who it was. If it was that constable fellow, he didn't want to be seen. The constable didn't like Nixy and always gave him a suspicious look.

It wasn't the constable, but a bearded old man in a gray-green cloak who was leaving in a hurry. Nixy saw a glint of silver from the old man's right hand and realized it was 'Talon' Finnael, the arch wizard. The man had visited Nixy and Cindra two years ago, bringing a little talking purple dragon along. The dragon wasn't with him this time, and the wizard alone was a bit scary.

Nixy wanted to call out and say hello, then reconsidered. *What am I thinking? A wizard, especially **this** wizard, was a very important man and deserved respect. Besides, children are to be seen and not heard. It's one of the Rules.*

What would I say to him anyway? "Remember Black Will? He's dead because the Vemlok who's house I broke into knocked his head off on the roof of the cathedral. Who's the blood-drinking Vemlok living in the city? Oh, nobody important, forget I mentioned it."

He waited for the man to leave before heading for the door. He didn't want the wizard to question him about anything, and he didn't want that spooky green eye in that spooky silver hand looking at him either.

Nixy walked around the castle bailey towards the rectories, were a few Eyoronian, Arathusian, and Lelonethan priests lived. They were simple but comfortable dwellings, each with a large study room and a stained-glass window facing the castle. The bed chambers were in the back, against the curtain wall, and were lit only by small windows near the ceiling.

The castle had its own chapel, devoted to the three most revered gods of the Divine Court: Arathus, king and lawgiver; Eyorona, goddess of wisdom and learning; and Lelonetha, Mother of Mercy. Nixy had been to the chapel once for a blessing after being made a ward. The orange-robed priestess gave thanks to Lelonetha for her mercy, and praised the charity of the count for taking in a 'base and lowly child of the streets.' That part made him sound like a street urchin. *I'm a made brother in the Circle of Gold, not some crumb-grabbing ankle scrambler!* The thought had immediately made him feel guilty as he remembered the real reason he had returned to the castle.

Brother Dane was a Eyoronian monk, not a priest. He explained that his order worked as instructors, often in noble houses. When Nixy asked if the monk worked for the count, Brother Dane replied, "In a manner... but we really do the work of the gods."

Nixy had silently considered what it might be like to work for a god, especially when they no longer talked to you. He figured it was better to have an angry little potato-man like stable master Gorin yell at you when you did something wrong, rather than get no answer at all and find out you were in trouble only after you died. Of course, having a god criticize your work would be pretty unnerving too. He didn't share these insights with the monk.

Brother Dane greeted him as Nixy entered the Eyoronian rectory. It was small and sparse, with a bookshelf, a table and two chairs, the goddess's oak leaf symbol on the wall, and very little color. The books were stacked out of the direct sunlight, waiting to be used for the day's lessons. Nixy took a chair and the monk sat opposite him, his dark green robes looking vibrant in the daylight, especially in this dull room.

Brother Dane was old to Nixy's eyes, but no more than twenty-seven years, his brown hair receding early and his beard grown to a full bushel on his chin. He had dark eyes and eyebrows that almost met in the middle, making him look a bit funny when he was concentrating.

"Welcome back, Nixyalderthor. I hope you are well?" He took one of the books and began flipping to the desired page.

"Yes, brother."

"How is life in the castle?" he asked.

"Good, I suppose. A bit boring sometimes, so I explore when I can."

The monk smiled at the remark, "Found anything interesting?"

"I found a door under the grand stairs, but I haven't gone in there yet. It goes down."

The monk nodded, "It goes to the vaults."

"Vaults? Like tombs?"

Brother Dane nodded again, "Yes, as well as the old dungeon and the counting house."

"All of that's down there?" Nixy was more intrigued than ever.

"It is, though the guards won't let anyone into the counting house but the lord and the treasurer, in case you were wondering." Brother Dane grinned at him and placed a piece of chalk on Nixy's writing board. "The count and countess, they are well?" he asked, still looking through his book.

"I guess so. I haven't seen them all day." Nixy squirmed a bit, "I think they've been busy."

"Oh? Why do you say that?" the monk asked.

"Well, they had a visit from that wizard today, you know Talon Finnael? He was just here. I actually met him once." He liked to drop that fact to impress people.

"Indeed! How interesting," said Brother Dane. "I wonder what that was about? Must be important."

Nixy just shrugged. He had no idea what went on behind closed doors. After all, he was no spy. *No, I'm just a **terrible** spy,* he thought guiltily.

"You are keeping an ear to the ground, aren't you?" Brother Dane asked as he casually thumbed through the text. Nixy looked up in surprise as the monk raised his eyes to meet the boy's.

Brother Dane is Circle of Gold! Nixy realized in a wash of panic.

The monk held the lad's gaze and asked, "You remember why you're here?"

Nixy gulped and nodded silently. He was *never* going to enjoy his lessons now. "I been doing what I was told," he said meekly. "I ain't heard nothing special, honest."

"No one expects you to be privy to any secrets, child." The monk said with a warm smile. "This is just about the happiness of the lord and lady, nothing more. When you see them next, pay attention to their moods. Are they sad, are they relaxed? Do they smile more often, or speak quietly to each other?" The monk folded his hands on the book as if in prayer, smiling comfortingly. "That is the sort of thing they want to know."

"S-so you're not really a monk then?" Nixy had a habit of asking questions of the man, and this seemed like as good a question as any he had asked before.

"Yes, of course I am." Brother Dane smiled his usual smile without a hint of menace, "But like many, I serve more than one master. I serve the goddess Eyorona, I serve Count Casselvane, and I serve, in my own small way, our shared brotherhood."

"Did Dexer send you?" Nixy felt the gaunt man's eyes on him suddenly, peering at him from every dark corner.

"Dexer? I'm afraid I don't know who that is. I'm guessing by your tone that he's not very pleasant."

Nixy shook his head quickly, not fooled by the man's sympathetic eyes. *Are you just another dagger hidden in a friendly hand?* For a brief second, Nixy considered turning the monk in and throwing himself on the count's mercy, begging for protection. In the next second it occurred to him that this monk may not be the only Circle man in the castle, and there might be no safe place at all. That was how the Circle of Gold worked; fear and secrecy both kept you safe and kept you in line. If the monk didn't know Dexer, then he may be trustworthy. *Or maybe that's what he **wants** me to think.* It was a fix he was in, sure enough.

Sensing Nixy's growing unease, Brother Dane offered, "All you need to know is that I am here to teach you to read, write, and learn your numbers, and you are to chat with me about the lord and lady's moods. I do not know what our 'friends' will do with this information, but it is important to someone." Brother Dane gave that friendly smile again.

If he's a killer, he's good at hiding it. There was no hint of threat in Dane's voice, only a gentle reminder. Nixy decided he could probably trust the man not to stab him in the eye, so he relaxed into his chair and opened his book.

"I'll let you know if I see anything," Nixy said with what he hoped was a nice, obedient voice. He looked up at the monk with his most sincere puppy eyes. *You wouldn't stab a puppy, would you?*

Brother Dane nodded and took out a reading lens, holding it over the text. "Now, where did we leave off?" he asked, "Ah, here we are."

Chapter Twelve

Up the Wrong Tree

"Remember, the nobleman I represent wants this to be discreet," said Julen Gordon, wagging his finger. "He won't pay nearly as much if this gets all over town."

"Understood, Master Gordon, I won't breathe a word of it," replied the shopkeeper. He held his hand out for the offered coin.

Julen made a teasing motion, as if reconsidering the bribe, but then smiled and placed the coins into the greedy little man's hand. "A pleasure doing business with you, as always." He tipped his floppy hat and turned to join his wife, who was standing by the busy street.

"Another of your contacts?" Lemorea asked. "I hope you're keeping track of all the coin you're dropping down these rat-holes."

That was Maveezh talking, not Lemorea Gordon. Ghethas preferred his wife's true self most of the time, except when she was criticizing him; this had been happening more often of late.

"I am," he sighed, "and these rat-holes are our best chance at finding her. Unless you have a better idea?"

"Of course I do, husband dear. Cease this foolish search and focus on more pressing matters."

"But she survived! The plan was for her to die, and she did not. I can't ask our horned friends for a refund, now can I?" Ghethas shook his head.

"The wedding was prevented; that's all that is important," she said coolly. "Even if she returns home and the count marries her off again, we have accomplished a delay of two or more years. That will suffice."

"But she saw my face unmasked. What if she recognized me?"

"Assuming she *did* recognize your face *and* remembered your name from that dinner two years past, then we indeed have a problem. If she did *not*, then asking around town about a Gali girl with hazel eyes is sure to implicate you." She motioned to the shop behind them, "How many of these shopkeepers will keep your inquiries secret if the count's men come calling, either with sword or coin?"

Ghethas didn't want to argue, especially since he almost never won. "So what 'more pressing matters' would you have us see to instead?"

"The Mad One," his wife said without pause. "We are counting on this wandering lunatic to deliver our salvation to us, but where is he? The high priest seems content to wait, but-"

"*That*," Ghethas interrupted, "is precisely why we should wait. He has studied the prophecies and knows the will of-" he bent his head and spoke lower, "-of the Countless Lord."

Maveezh was not convinced. "Both of us have read those same prophecies, and we too know the will of Llomaak." Startled, Ghethas glanced about to see if anyone had overheard, but she continued unconcerned, "If the salvation of all humanity rests in the hands of an insane old conjurer, then I would *at least* know more about him."

"You have become dangerously brazen, my dear. If anyone were to suspect-"

"What's to suspect?" she scoffed. "No one believes that Llomaakittes still exist, or if they do, they think of savage little covens, hiding in caves and sacrificing livestock." She smirked, "And so they were, after the Time of Chaos." She shivered with excitement, "When *Mash* extended his hand and twisted the world; when His power was glimpsed by the terrified masses... ooh, it must have been truly awe-inspiring."

"Yes, and the true servants of the Countless Lord were hunted down like vermin, leaving only those 'savage little covens' to persecute," Ghethas reminded her. "The priesthood only survived by keeping their heads and *voices* low."

"Very well, husband. I shall keep my voice *low*," she said, as baritone as she could manage.

He smiled despite himself, "I hate hiding behind masks as well, but they have their uses. You know, if our brothers and I had just a *few* more minutes with that girl in Pinikal-"

"You'd have been killed by a brownie mob, and dragged behind your horses until you were nothing but feet tied to a saddle," she chided. "You don't think ahead, my dear."

"We didn't even know what we had, not until I took that bracelet to be examined. Now that damned wizard in the white tower is looking for me." He put his hand to his chest, feeling the warding amulet beneath his shirt. The high priest had been annoyed at having to lend it to him.

"Don't fret my dear. I'm happier to have you returned safe and sound, dead Corrina girl or no." She adjusted her gloves as she declared, "Today I am going to ask the high priest for more information on the Mad One."

"He won't like it," Ghethas warned. "You know he won't."

"Well, he doesn't have to like it, he just has to hear me out." She turned to him, "We are the only ranking priests in the city! He can't expect to keep us ignorant forever."

"The only priests that we know of," he reminded. "There may be others. Besides, are you in such a hurry for the world to end, my love?"

"No," she sighed. "But if it is to end, I'd rather know where all the pieces are on the board, and how much longer we have." She kissed him and patted his cheek, then left to see the high priest.

The goals of the Llomaakittes seemed like madness when Ghethas first heard of them, but when everything was explained in the greater context of eternity, it made sense. The tales of the creation of humans were numerous and different in every land, but they did not precede written history. The elves were long in the world before humans walked upon Jayde, and were present to record the waking of the first humans, and to hear what gifts the gods bestowed upon the new race. No elf claimed to hold the event in living memory, but their records survived to be copied and translated down through the millennium. The worshipers of Llomaak, or *Mash* as he was called, found them very telling indeed.

Llomaak the Chaotic gave humanity a questioning nature that led them to challenge everything. This was why humans had discovered so much in their short lives, even the use of magic; not through natural talent, but by hard work and innovation.

Arathus the Tyrant gave the new people something far more sinister; he gave them judgment. Every human life would be judged after death to determine its worthiness to rejoin the spirit force of the universe. Those who were deemed wanting would suffer punishment and drudgery, earning their release over uncounted years under the eyes of the gods.

For those like Ghethas who lived according to their own desires, the life after death was sure to be a prolonged crucible of suffering designed to burn away all the impurities and imperfections he had taken so much effort to cultivate. How many people had died and found themselves standing before the blind god Valdak, condemned to a near-eternity of correction for the crime of living life to the fullest? The 'gift' of the Tyrant was the greatest curse ever laid before humanity, and it was the ambition of every Llomaakitte to undo that curse; if the structure of creation had to fall to make it happen, so much the better. All would be free in the end.

But before the world came crashing down, there would be war, chaos, and a Chosen One to carry the Dark Heart. The Mad One knew the identity of the Chosen, and he would reveal it on the brink of war. Timing was everything; if an alliance was made with Rokvynnar, it might postpone the conflict or prevent it entirely. So the Corrina girl had to die. Besides, he had a score to settle with her; she had slipped from his grasp twice and made him look like a fool. She had *literally* slipped from his grasp in Pinikal, though he hadn't known it at the time.

Ghethas had been making the rounds as his alter ego, Julen Gordon, talking to any shopkeeper that dealt with Galindri. He spun a story of a certain anonymous and desperate nobleman who wished to be reunited with his half-Galindri daughter, estranged for some sixteen years. She was his only living family, and he was willing to reward Julen for finding her, and of course Julen would give the one who helped him a substantial cut. She would be known by having eyes unlike other Galindri, more hazel than bright green. This little detail Ghethas recalled from their face-to-face meeting that ended so abruptly, before he and his fellow priests really got to know her better.

Of course there were fraudulent attempts to collect the reward, and there were many false leads. Some fools even resorted to kidnapping, and Ghethas wondered what kind of reward those idiots hoped to receive from the girl's fictional, anxious father. It didn't really matter; if they caught the right fish in such a broad net, then it would be worth all the trouble.

Julen came to the office of a scribe, where the clerk had claimed to have a lead. "So this girl you saw, you think she is how old?" Ghethas asked, keeping his smile friendly.

"Oh, about fifteen or sixteen, as you was looking for Master Gordon," said the clerk, arranging the parchments on his desk to look more presentable.

"And what about her made you think she might be the correct girl?"

"She was dressed as like a Galindri might be, but she was lighter of skin than usual, and her hair was lighter as well." He thought for a moment more, "Her eyes were maybe not as green as you see on the others, though I didn't get a good look; she moved on quick after I saw her." He motioned to the window near his desk, which overlooked the street. "I don't usually look up. Folks like to watch unnoticed, as it were. Some just watch to admire my quill strokes, and others try and read the letters. Oh, but I don't do sensitive work afore the window, mind you." He sighed, "Ah, but the swish of a skirt does draw the eye-"

"Did you happen to notice where she went? Was she with a caravan, or other Galindri?"

The man sat back on his stool, stretching his back as he considered. "I can't rightly say," he shrugged.

"You didn't see?" Julen stared incredulously, "It's a big window. You can see quite a lot, especially if a reward is at stake."

"The memory fades, as happens when there's not so much fuel for the fire, if you follow me." The clerk smiled a little and sniffed.

"Ah," Julen said, "Perhaps *this* will purchase some more firewood." He drew his purse and took out a silver Calimark, placing it on the desk with a *clink*.

"That is a good amount of firewood," agreed the clerk, taking the coin with a sweep of one hand into the other.

"She's staying in the Market Square with several other caravans. Hers is the one with the orange trim and green roof. Likes to go off alone, it seems."

Julen raised his eyebrows in mild surprise, "You watched her for some time then?"

"Enough to be useful," the clerk said with a modest smile. "Not an easy thing, following a girl and not spooking her like a deer. Especially one of them Gali girls; sharp eyes and ears, you know, and skittish too." He poked the quill holder to make it sit more favorably next to the inkwell.

"I shall remember that if she turns out to be our girl," Julen smiled and donned his garish hat, "The lord I represent will be so very happy, as will we both." He bowed to the clerk and left the office of contracts, heading out into the street across from the Red Eagle Inn. A group of students from the fighting school were fooling about near the door while one of the smaller lads read the menu.

Few Galindri bothered with written contracts or documents, so it was a long shot to inquire at the scribe's office. Yet Ghethas figured that if the Lady Cindra wanted to send a message within the city, she would be able to write it herself, but would not have access to ink or parchment. Being a sly girl, she might seek out a scribe's office, write and seal a letter, then send it to the castle by courier. If this Gali girl was indeed Lady Cindra, then his suspicions had been correct and she was looking for writing materials. If not, then she had lingered at the wrong window.

He considered getting advice from his wife, but he feared she would tell him again that he was wasting his time. No, he'd not get her approval; it would either work out as he hoped, or it wouldn't. *I'll either find the Corrina brat, or an unfortunate Gali girl who looks close enough. In any event, it'll be an enjoyable way to spend a cold night.* He headed for the Market Square to meet his date for the evening.

Chapter Thirteen

The Way of the Hart

Cindra was beginning to think her brilliant plan was, in fact, the stupidest thing she had ever thought of. After the first month of running, jumping, climbing, swinging heavy clubs about and nearly falling dead asleep each night, Cindra was considering just calling it quits, returning to the castle to take her chances with assassins. The first week was both torturous and horrific, but afterward it became merely horrific and stayed that way for the rest of the month. Her entire body took on a dull throb of pain, punctuated by a pulling soreness that only hurt when she moved; even Jaron's rubbing and kneading could not make it go away completely.

"Not to worry," he said as he pushed his thumbs along a line of soreness on her lower back. "The worst is behind you."

"The worst *liar* is behind me, you mean." She smiled despite the pain. "We haven't started hitting each other with sticks yet."

"Actually the first stage is grappling and wrestling," Jaron said. He felt his passion stirring as he moved his hands up her spine, kneading the soft, bare skin.

"Really? Is it painful? It sounds painful," she whimpered.

"Only when you stop," he said.

"Mmrrrg," she mumbled, enjoying the massage. His hands moved with gentle pressure along her back, his fingertips brushing the sides of her breasts. She was unbound, having discarded the wrapping before dressing for bed. It made back-rubs easier, but Cindra knew the extra exposure was a distraction for them both. His touch had a way of reviving her and relaxing her, making her unwilling to sleep despite the lovely sense of comfort she felt. Suddenly, she had the desire to roll on her back, pull him down and kiss him, but knew that would be the beginning of something they could not easily stop, even if they wanted to. 'Grappling and wrestling' indeed.

Cindra, or rather Dillan, was at a distinct disadvantage, she could see that for herself. She excelled at the running and endurance exercises, keeping her feet while many of the young men doubled over exhausted. The problem came above the waist, where strength of chest, arms, and back was concerned. She was not as strong as the smallest boy, that being Padison, and was a twig compared to the larger ones like Bradric, or the big Norsican, Stansig.

Cindra was paired off with Padison for grappling lessons, and it had been a rude awakening as she scrambled for purchase, trying to get a hold on him that he could not break with ease. More than once she let him throw her to the ground painfully, rather than have him grab some part of her anatomy that would shock and upset them both. Afterward, Padison would pull her up and try to give helpful advice.

"You gave too much ground that time, DePort," he

said. "You've got to push back so I can't get by your guard like that."

Cindra nodded her head wearily, but thought to herself, *I gave too much ground because you're as strong as a pony, and when I push back, I'm just pushing myself back.* Still, he meant well, so she chose not to resent him much.

"Grappling forms the basis for all your future training," Master Cord was saying. "You will not always have a weapon handy. You may be disarmed, or your enemy might get too close. Learning holds and joint locks, and learning to break free of them, is vital."

Often, the students sat in a circle in the courtyard, creating a ring in which two contenders would spar. It gave them a chance to study their fellow classmates and learn from their successes and mistakes. Cindra noted that of all the students of his size, Rejick Ratham was the most experienced at grappling and close-fighting. She recalled that the *Maurbrik* style, or 'Way of the Bear,' was what his family taught in their fighting school. She had seen the style in action once, when Sir Earnold used it against Jaron; only Jaron's flair for the unorthodox had saved him.

The other premier wrestler was Maadi Gaavi, the dark-skinned Gozhiman. His movements were seemingly random and fluid, making his next move very difficult to predict. He was also very slippery, able to get out of many a hold by twisting and scrambling like an angry cat. Watching him and Ratham spar was entertaining to say the least, and more than a bit scary.

Cord's lectures added new layers of violence. "Strength and speed are obviously important, but you will also learn throws and striking attacks, targeting the eyes, nose, flanks, groin, and below the breast bone. Even with an armored opponent, arms and legs can be broken or crippled with the right application of force and leverage. We will not be gouging eyes, breaking balls, or snapping necks during training of course, but you will learn how."

Cindra had no balls to break, but was glad for the reprieve regardless.

Later in the month they set up a wooden barrier wall that the trainees had to climb or vault over as best as they were able. Gavadaire and Jaron demonstrated the full vault, swinging their bodies up and over. Gavadaire cleared the wall with a little more ease than Sir Jaron, and she took note of the knight's annoyance. She intended to tease him about it later, but when she could only scrabble over the wall with multiple attempts and raw hands, she thought the better of it.

One day, the students were given heavy wooden clubs to swing about. These were to build the arm and shoulder muscles, but to her frustration, Cindra lagged behind the others once again. Master Cord assigned her a few extra activities, such as holding her arms at length and flapping them like a bird when she was doing nothing else. She cringed every time she heard him shout "Flap Dillan, FLAP!"

Luckily, she was not alone in her shame. There were a few others that merited Master Cord's special treatment. Filbert Gaddisen, a tall, lanky boy, was given similar training to strengthen his narrow chest and thin arms. Bradric was made to run additional laps to overcome his excess weight. Padison was often given extra laps for talking too much, which he ran with enthusiasm. Whether his eagerness was real or feigned, Cindra could not tell. Paddy was an odd boy.

"Today," Master Cord's voice boomed, "we will begin learning cuts and guards." He spoke to the assembled students, who had their heavy clubs in hand. "The last month and a half was to beat the impurities out of you, like a blacksmith hammering slag out of a bar of steel. Now, you are going to learn the basics of the *Daerbrik* style."

There was a wave of excitement among the students, tired though they were. Many began to wonder if they would ever see a sword, mace, or shield.

"The Way of the Hart, or *Daerbrik* from the old Norsican tongue. What does it mean? How are we inspired by the stag?" He looked about, not really expecting anyone to speak up. "The hart, or stag, has a fine rack of antlers used for offense and defense, like a sword and shield. They charge and clash with each other like mounted knights, and they lock horns, fighting for leverage. They can rear up and strike with their hooves, landing blows that can crush bone and cut thick hide.

"The hart is a proud and noble beast, a lord of the wood. We train in this style to inspire awe in our allies and fear in our enemies. The Daerbrik warrior holds the line. He charges in with weapon and shield, presenting a fierce offense and a strong defense. He defends as he attacks, and attacks as he defends. He is agile, spirited, and bold. He keeps his enemies at bay, and he stands his ground."

There were nods of understanding among the students, and Cindra pictured herself charging on her spirited steed, raising a battle cry against an unknown enemy. Then she pictured herself with antlers. She shook her head to dispel the image.

Rejick Ratham, who was somewhere behind her, whispered to a friend, "Stag is nothing to a bear though."

"This is a wartime style; a style for armored combat, for soldiers and knights," Cord said. "You are *not* training to duel in the streets like some Aurilonian peacock!" He turned and gave an apologetic nod to Gavadaire, who saluted. The students had a laugh at that. Cord continued, "You will learn to strike with precision using spear and lance, both mounted or on foot; you will learn to get inside the reach of a pike, spear, or long ax; you will master the sword, mace, and shield; you will learn the strength and weakness of every weapon on the battlefield. Whether you go in armored head-to-toe or half naked, you will know best how to defend yourself and bring death to your enemies."

Half naked? Cindra thought. *I hope he's joking.*

The students were divided into four groups of five. Cindra's group included Adric Hywahl, Chatty Paddy (as Padison was quickly becoming known), Inis DeGhat and Morrin LiKeska. It was a fair mix of size and build, as were all the teams. No one team had all the large lads, or all the thin, weaker ones for that matter.

Inis and Morrin were both from noble families, well-educated and lettered. Adric and Padison were of wealthy but common merchant families. Cindra chose to make herself a commoner elevated to a squire, because she wanted to be able to poke her nose into any conversation. Most of the other squires were sons of barons, and not so high that they would shun her company.

Once everyone had gathered in their groups, Master Freekirk addressed them again, "Your team is your new family. For the duration of your training, you will work within these teams. I want you all to learn each other's weaknesses and strengths, aiding one another as needed. Your comrade is your responsibility! If one fails in a trial, your team fails. It is the same in battle; the man who only looks out for himself does not protect his brother's back."

He strode up and down the line of assembled students, towering over most by at least a head-height. "I will be watching you. Every one of you has been under these eyes since arriving," he gestured with two fingers at his piercing blue gaze. "I see more than you realize, and I will know more as the months progress.

"I will divide your training groups among my assistants. You all know Sir Jaron Dunlorden and Gavadaire LuVestra," he motioned to the two men, who stepped forward. "They will each supervise two teams. You may name your teams, if you wish. The tradition is to choose a beast or creature of legend, but I leave that to you all to sort out. For the time being, I will call numbers." He walked left to right, giving each team a number. Cindra's team was 'number one,' a fact that meant nothing but felt good nonetheless.

"Teams one and two, you will report to Gavadaire LuVestra," Master Freekirk said. Cindra felt her heart drop a bit; she had always assumed Jaron would train her. "Teams three and four will be under Sir Jaron Dunlorden."

Jaron seemed disappointed as well, though he gave her a look of apology. *He knew! He must have known, and he didn't say anything!* Cindra's face grew troubled. *Was this Cord's doing, or his? Why have me train under someone who doesn't know about me?*

There was no time to ponder this, because they immediately began drilling with their clubs. Gavadaire called his students over, spacing them arm's-length apart. He held a riding crop in one hand. "Good morning," he said. "Do not let my heritage fool you; this peacock is a dangerous bird." He smiled that charming smile and the students were set at ease. "I will be looking for mistakes, and will correct them with this," he gestured with the crop. "A little touch is for little mistakes. A less gentle touch is for bigger mistakes... does anyone wonder what repeated mistakes will earn?" No one wondered. "Good! We are ready to begin, Master!" he called out.

Cord picked up a club and took a guard position. "We will begin with the four basic guards. Feet apart! Left foot forward, towards your opponent!"

The rest of the day was repetitive motion, drilling the guard positions into their heads. Cindra felt as if her wrists would snap, and her fingers were already blistering. She had some experience with blisters during her time with the Galindri, and knew there would be callouses before long. Jaron had them; she hoped he wouldn't mind if she did too.

Master Cord strode up and down the ranks as the students shifted from stance to stance. "Most fencing styles are similar in many ways. You have cuts, guards, parries, counters, and the like. What varies is the technique used; each weapon has its own technique and each attack and defense has its own timing. You will learn to know these without thinking."

Cindra already felt like she was no longer thinking. All that mattered was the movements and the sound of the master's voice. She was too tired to focus on anything else.

"There are four keys to every technique," Cord continued, "distance, timing, form, and direction. If you get one wrong, it can cost you life or limb. The bruises and scars you receive in training will aid you in realizing these keys. If they don't, you will have to rely on luck, and luck runs out fast in combat."

Cindra reflected on her luck, and decided she had better learn her lessons here.

There was a rest-break before the midday meal, and the students gathered in the hall to get out of the warm spring sun. Elmore was setting up the tables and benches for the lunch that Celia was preparing, and the lads began talking, mostly staying in their new groups.

"What do you think our team name should be?" Padison asked. "I was thinking the 'Mighty Minozhians' would-"

"No!" Cindra barked before she could stop herself. Everyone gave Dillan an odd look. "I mean, they aren't mythical, are they?" She rubbed her sore arms, feeling embarrassed for speaking out.

"I know," Padison said, "but I figured-"

"Flap, Dillan, Flap!" came the usual cry, but it was not from Master Cord. Cindra turned and saw Rejick Ratham, backed by his cronies Terrus Drakthorne and Lukas Korbison, who chuckled in approval. The Ratham boy could not direct his hatred at the man who killed his cousin, but apparently that man's squire would do. "The 'Mighty Minozhians,' what a laugh!" Ratham scoffed at Padison, "You ever *seen* a Minozhian, city boy?"

"Sure, they come into our shop all the time to buy horn polish," Paddy said. Adric and a few other lads chuckled. Cindra was silent.

Ratham loomed over Padison saying, "My uncle Waliss fought them when they tried to raid up the Joshian River. He has a Minozhian head mounted in his study. It sits eight feet high on the wall, same as when the bull-man wore it on his shoulders." He poked the smaller boy in the chest. "A Minozhian raider could lose you in his pants until he took you out to piss." This got some laughter and goading hoots from the crowd.

Padison cocked his head and asked, "You sure your uncle didn't just wander into a field and slay a cow?"

This made most of the students laugh; even Drakthorne snickered a bit. Ratham's nostrils flared and his face turned red. "My uncle is a *Maurbrik* master! You're lucky we can't fight outside of training, rock-nipper."

Cindra frowned at the odd term. *Rock-nipper?*

"Your uncle is lucky he didn't have to pay for that cow," Padison said.

Ratham swelled with rage, but Adric broke in, "Have *you* ever seen a live Minozhian, Ratham?"

"The last person to see a live Minozhian was Corrina's cousin, I imagine." Ratham smirked, looking over at Gaius. The boy's eyes narrowed but he would not be baited again. He would save it for the sparring ring.

Cindra could not help herself however, as Mineth's death and Teya's capture flashed before her eyes. "*I've* seen them. I've seen several."

Everyone turned to look at Dillan DePort, the small boy who claimed to be from Waynwell, which was many leagues from the sea.

"Several," Ratham droned, disbelieving. "You've seen *several*."

His smirk was infuriating, and Cindra wished for a moment that they *could* fight outside of training. An aggressive little fire was burning hot in her belly, rapidly consuming her good sense. "Several," she repeated. "I've seen them at sea, and I saw them on the Red Coast a few years ago." Then, against all better judgment, she added, "I even killed one."

This made everyone laugh, even the older, more experienced students who had not been paying much attention. Cindra's eyes did not leave Ratham's laughing face, nor did she give any indication that she was joking.

Ratham recovered, wiped the tears from his eyes and said, "I've heard of one Minozhian cutting down three armored men like wheat. A scrawny little tree-shaker like you wouldn't last a second!"

Tree-shaker? Oh yes, my 'father' in Waynwell manages orchards. Very clever. "I wasn't toe-to-toe with him," she said. "I shot an arrow between his ribs."

"Really?" Padison asked, finally taking her seriously. "You really killed one with a bow?"

"Yes," Cindra said, realizing what a stupid thing she had done in mentioning it. "I was hunting with a friend and we came across a small camp on a cliff rise. There were three of them around the fire, and their ship was pulled up on shore in the inlet below."

Stansig, Maadi, and Minas, who usually kept to themselves, moved closer to hear. The other lads had gone quiet, their doubts slowly evaporating as Dillan gave details of the encounter.

Cindra figured it was far too late to change the subject anyway. "My friend went to investigate, but was captured. They were going to kill-" she almost said 'they were going to kill *her*' but knew that would only complicate matters. She took a deep breath, "I hid in the undergrowth and shot one between the ribs before he could do the deed. Then I fired some wild shots so they thought there were more of us, and they ran below to get help. I got my friend and we fled."

Ratham snorted a laugh, "The Minozhians ran? That's a good one."

"There were only three," Cindra said, "then two. It was getting dark and they were both fire-blind. They had no idea how many were shooting at them."

Drakthorne asked, "Do you have proof of this mighty

deed, or are we just to take you at your good word?"

Cindra folded her arms, "The proof is upstairs in my locker. I'll get it at dinner."

Celia rang the kitchen bell, signaling that lunch was ready. Dillan DePort's wild boast was momentarily forgotten.

Dinnertime couldn't arrive fast enough for Cindra, since most of the day was spent enduring comments and questions about her run-in with Minozhians. Hopefully, showing off the *Kos* knife would end all the disputes and silence the doubters. She met Jaron as he was heading towards the master's hall for the evening meal.

"Sir Jaron?" she asked, "is it alright if I eat with the other lads tonight?"

Jaron looked uncomfortable, "I suppose so... it's a bit unseemly for a squire though."

"It's only for this meal," she answered. "Please? They want to see the *Kos* knife."

"They what?" he exclaimed. "I thought you were going to keep that a secret."

"I was," she replied, "but we were talking about Minozhians and it sort of... came up."

Jaron leaned in close, saying, "Don't make a habit sharing too much information. Questions are something we've been trying to avoid."

"I know, I know," she said. "I won't share anything more, I promise."

After getting his consent, Cindra ran upstairs and dug the weapon out of her footlocker. She gazed at it for a few moments, her hatred for the thing mixing strangely with her pride. It was not the same blade that killed Mineth, but it could have been. Teya had called it Cindra's *Lok-shíneh*, a trophy taken from her first kill, the mark of a Galindri warrior. She had despised the blade, and had only begun wearing it once T'ózha was born. She had asked Teya why she would want it, and the Galindri huntress told her that it honored 'the lessons that one killed to learn, that one died to teach.' Cindra still wasn't sure she knew what that lesson was.

The students all gathered around as Dillan came downstairs with an object wrapped in cloth. There were gasps and awed silence as the big knife was uncovered and drawn from its sheath.

Finnas and Ferrol jostled each other for a good view. Filbert Gaddisen stretched his long legs and stood on his toes, leaning on Halvoy Quenlorden, who flinched at the unwanted intrusion.

"Wow!" Padison exclaimed. "Can I hold it?"

Bradric slapped the small boy on the head, "Show some respect, Paddy. That's a fine prize there, not a toy."

The blade was curved like a half-moon, sharp along the leaf-shaped inner arc. The iron finger-ring at the hilt and the jagged embellishments above it made it look even more exotic. The horn handle was pointed and capped with metal, making a nasty piercing weapon. The Minozhian symbols on the handle gave it an ominous, tribal appearance. Dillan's forefinger slipped into the iron ring with much room to spare, emphasizing the size of the hand it was made for. No one else asked to hold it out of respect, for the way Dillan looked at it was a grim reminder of how it had been won and what it meant.

"You took it off the body?" asked Mat Belvine, a sell-sword who was only a few years younger than Stansig.

Dillan said, "My friend took it for me; said I needed a trophy."

"Dattiz a fyne trophy, tiz troth," said Stansig in his thick accent. "Eve gayned a far me-selve." Cindra had never heard him speak so many words before.

"Doesn't mean you killed a bull-man for it," said Ratham. Everyone's eyes went from Dillan to Ratham and back again. "Maybe you found it in a burnt-out fishing village, or bought it off a curiomonger."

Cindra did not flinch or waver in her gaze, meeting

Ratham's eyes with a baleful stare. "Or maybe it happened just the way I said it did. Besides, I didn't have time to saw off its head like your uncle did with that cow."

The room burst into laughter, and Demel Victhor slapped his teammate Ratham on the shoulder, urging him away from the confrontation, "Come on, lads. Food is waiting, and I'm starving!" They all collected their bowls and lined up for stew and ale.

Chapter Fourteen

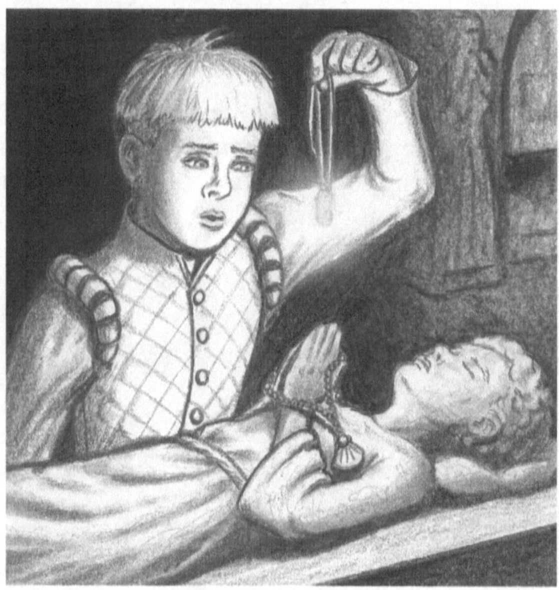

Hope in the Dark

Nixy was bored. He had been living in the castle for nearly five months and things had become dreadfully predictable. Meals were always on time, and that was wonderful, but the rest of the day was painfully dreary and he understood why Lady Cindra had once escaped into the city for a bit of adventure.

Breakfast was the highlight of his morning, after which he took lessons from Brother Dane. The monk taught him letters, numbers, manners, and even history, which was Nixy's favorite subject. The actions of people who lived long, long ago had made the world what it was today, and he was amazed to find that big historical events could have such small, silly beginnings. "So we've been having all those wars with Aurilon because some king had a girl instead of a boy?"

"Essentially, yes." Brother Dane explained, "King Belefor had no surviving male heir, only a daughter named Ziva. Upon Belefor's death, the crown of Aurilon passed to his younger brother, Maladain. Princess Ziva LuKravore married the crown prince of Calilon, Galen Cordobal, our current king's grandfather. By the laws of our country, a royal succession cannot pass through the female bloodline, but in Aurilon, it can. King Galen invoked their own law, claiming that his eldest son would inherit the throne of Aurilon, as well as the province of Maylione, which passed to Ziva through her mother. This did not go over well, and many wars were fought."

Nixy thought on that a moment. "So if Lady Cindra were still alive, she wouldn't inherit her parents' castle and lands?" Nixy asked.

Brother Dane seemed taken aback, but knew of the boy's relationship with the deceased. "The laws for inheritance are a bit different than for royal succession. She would inherit the title of Countess Casselvane, but it would fall to the king to find a suitable match for her. Her husband would become Count Casselvane, and the title would pass to the eldest male heir."

Nixy didn't think that seemed fair. Cindra had been brave and good, and would have made a fine ruler, at least by Nixy's standards.

"Of course, if she had lived," Dane continued, "she would be married to a Duke of Rokvynnar. Either way, disposition of the county would be the king's decision; there is no male heir, the countess is unlikely to be with child again, and the count is unlikely to annul and take a new wife." He cleared his throat, "Speaking of the count and countess, how do they seem to you today?"

After his lessons and Brother Dane's secret spy questions, Nixy would wander the castle bailey or walk the walls until lunchtime. After lunch it was time for sport, which was about as much fun as he got to have all day. Many activities were made available such as falconry, archery, riding, and music. He didn't think much of hunting with birds; it was something birds did on their own anyway, and he was only along to pretend to be in charge. Archery hurt his fingers, which he needed to care for since they were once his livelihood. Riding was fun but a little scary, and he preferred grooming horses to riding them. Music was nice to listen to, but not when he played it. He would have to practice long and hard if he was ever going to make more than a jumbled racket. For the rest of the day he was at leisure, which meant boredom and pointless wandering. He would explore the castle grounds and the stone halls looking for secrets, but there were few to find.

Someone must have noticed his need for something to do, so he was given the chore of feeding Gavagul, the family ember swallow. It had once been Cindra's task, since the fiery bird responded better to young people, but dealing with the creature's heat took some getting used to.

"You aren't gonna flap at me today, are you?" Nixy asked, as he donned the protective glove. "My cheeks are still pink from last time." The previous night, the bird had perched on the leather gauntlet and allowed itself to be removed from the iron cage, but then flapped vigorously, sending waves of heat into the boy's face. "I know you've been cooped up all day, but I want to keep my eyebrows."

"Eyebrows," said the bird, mimicking him perfectly.

"So be nice," he said as he opened the cage. He gave the bird a piece of jerky, watching the wisps of smoke that curled from its tail feathers. It was big for a swallow, but then it probably wasn't related to normal swallows; these birds came from Somewhere Else, somewhere on the other side of the veil. Maybe they had been pets of Tavenji, patron god of thieves and messengers? He knew that this bird had delivered Cindra's last panicked message, and though he wanted to hear her voice again, he didn't want to hear that.

Dinner was hours away and there was little else to do, so Nixy decided to explore some of the upstairs rooms. His own bedchamber was on the top floor, and took up far more space than he needed. It had a fireplace, a dresser, some comfy padded chairs, and even a window with a view of the mountains. He had been so pleased to have his own gigantic room, that he had never bothered to peek into the others. He knew where the count and countess slept; they had separate chambers, which made perfect sense to Nixy. *One of them probably snores*, he figured.

He also knew where the lord's study was, because he had seen many important types meet with the count there. Guards were always at the door when he was inside, so they must have been talking about important things. Nixy wished he could listen in, but he wasn't about to risk his new status for some stupid spy mission. Dexer would just have to be happy with whatever he told Brother Dane.

One of the upstairs rooms was for the lord's attendants, and one was for the lady's. Another was the private chamber of Constable Arias Fingelm, the red-haired adviser who always shadowed the count. Fingelm did not care for Nixy, he could tell that much. He always gave him a suspicious look; not that the man suspected him of spying, rather he looked down at Nixy as if he might be snitching the silverware.

Many of the rooms were unused or filled with furniture draped in linen, a curious waste of space. One such room was just next to the grand stairs. It had a comfortable bed with drapes around it, a cold fireplace, a nice dressing table, a wardrobe cabinet with pretty carved details, and lots of decorations that looked like they might be of the goddess Selvina. Beyond the curtains was a day room with a large seating window, fine rugs, tapestries depicting frolicking ponies, a craft table, a small loom, and some cedar chests by the wall.

When Nixy realized where he was, his skin rose with goosebumps. "This was Cindra's room," he whispered. She had spent most of her days in this place, and he could picture her crossing the room, her dress sweeping along the floor as her hair shone in the warm light of a merry fire. Then the vision was gone, the fireplace was cold, and the warm light of his memory became the pale gloom of sunset. His eyes began welling with tears as he thought of her tragic death at sea; her body resting on the ocean floor without a grave marker to visit.

He wondered as he hurried out of the room if there was a memorial to her somewhere in the castle, someplace with a sense of finality instead of this sad, deserted bedchamber. He used to visit his mother's grave on his birthday. He never knew her, but he always felt a bit closer to her as he sat by her stone marker.

As he descended the grand stair, he watched the guild wizards light the magic lamps, and he smelled the evening meal being prepared in the kitchens. He also noticed two armed guards following a third, who was carrying a locked chest. The men were being led by one of the court officials, possibly the treasurer. Nixy always noticed important looking people with locked boxes, so he watched as the man pushed aside a well-concealed door under the stairs, and he and his escort disappeared within.

Nixy walked casually to the place they had entered and began snooping around for the secret door's latch. It was cunningly hidden under a picture frame; he only needed to press it lightly, and with a soft *'click,'* the door swung inward on silent hinges. A spiral stairway led into the darkness, and he felt a cool draft as the stale smell of dust and earth wafted from below. The door closed slowly behind him as he descended, but there was no need to light his magic glowstone yet, for the flickering orange glow below meant torches. He felt the pull of the shadows, beckoning him to wrap himself in darkness. It was a strange feeling that he didn't quite understand, but he knew it had something to do with his special luck. He didn't think there was any danger below, at least nothing he couldn't talk his way out of.

The stairs led to a landing with some locked doors, and continued down to a dimly-lit guard post, from which two passages branched off. He waved to the guards as he stepped into the room, examining his surroundings with an innocent face. The two men looked up from their card game, more curious than wary.

"Hullo," Nixy said. "What is this place, if I may ask?" It was silly to ask if he could ask after he'd already asked, but Brother Dane said it was good manners.

The guards looked him up and down, noting his nice clothes, his trimmed hair, and the knife at his belt. "These are the vaults," said one guard. He motioned to the portal on Nixy's left. It was a heavy oak door barred with iron and imposing locks, but it was secured by more than just metal tumblers; magic wards were etched into the iron and wood alike. "That's the way to the counting house and coffers." The man then indicated the portal to Nixy's right; it was a vaulted passageway with a pair of decorative doors. The Corrina coat of arms and various holy symbols were carved in relief. "That way leads to the family tombs." He chuckled, "Try to break into one, and you'll end up in the other, eh?" Both men had a good laugh and Nixy smiled. He knew it was a veiled threat, but wasn't going to give them the satisfaction of scaring him.

He found himself drawn to the archway, with the three-pointed crown of Arathus over the blind eye of Valdak, and merciful Lelonetha's open hands on either side. Without a word to the guards, he opened the doors and followed the steep stone path to the tombs.

"Scream if you see any ghosts!" they called after him. He said nothing. *Eyes open, mouth shut.*

A visitor was supposed to bring their own torch, and Nixy hadn't taken one. Instead he brought out his glowstone, the one Ildric Finnael had given him. "*Ilda,*" he said, making it shine like bright moonlight. Holding it before him, he pressed onward.

The path leveled out and the air became still and stale, with the smell of burning torches left far behind. He came to a wide, circular chamber with carved effigies of noble men and women lying on beds of stone, seemingly asleep in their own little alcoves. Above the sleeping figures were several smaller vaults covered with plaques, each bearing the names of Corrinas he had never heard of, some dating back more than a century. He figured they each had their chance at the alcove spots, and were moved into tighter quarters when they became more dusty and bony.

Beyond were small arched passages, no doubt leading to a maze of chambers where even older family members were mingling with the earth. Nixy was no stranger to tombs and crypts, for the Warren was a maze of catacombs altered for the Circle of Gold's purposes. It almost made him feel at home as he wandered around the chamber and read the names, only barely conscious of the fact that he could do so.

In the center of the chamber was a small tomb raised upon a dais of stone; its carved effigy bore the likeness of a small child with curls in his hair, and an elegant robe that draped his little body from neck to ankles. The folds in the sculpted fabric were so realistic that he almost expected them to yield to his touch. A necklace of prayer beads made of white and black pearls was arranged around his folded hands; he recognized the pearl and seashell symbol as the one the countess wore.

A realization struck him and he blinked in the still air, leaning over the little stone face. This was Cindra's little brother, who died at a young age only a few years before. He had learned of the boy's existence at the same moment he had been told of Cindra's death, a fact that had barely registered at the time. Now, as he looked at the peaceful face, he wondered if the little boy and his elder sister were together somewhere in the afterlife, maybe in Haven with Lelonetha, eating the Peaches of Bliss. He hoped they were.

Nixy made a habit of visiting the tombs after dinner. He would nod to the guards and descend into the dark, wandering the deep passages and pondering the mysteries of death. He had never thought much about death, or about being dead, but now he wondered daily what Cindra might be doing on the Other Side. Was she happy? Was she aware? Could she see him, maybe see how well he was doing in his studies? Did she know he was a secret spy, collecting news about her grieving parents for the Circle of Gold? He offered up a daily apology for that, although if the gods no longer heard or answered prayers, he doubted Cindra could hear or answer him either.

It was during one of his pondering sessions that he saw a light in the dark coming from the main chamber of the tomb. The flickering of torchlight danced in the dark passage, making the shadows seem eerily alive. As he padded quietly towards the light, he heard a soft voice echoing in the chamber. It was a low, feminine voice trembling with sadness, sniffing back tears before speaking words in a strange language. He came to the end of the hall and looked in, not entirely surprised to see the countess herself, standing over the effigy of her departed child.

Zara Corrina looked about the chamber, blinking tears from her eyes as she tried to look anywhere but at the sweet face set in stone before her. As her gaze traveled about the room, she glimpsed Nixy in the corridor. She gasped in surprise, her eyes growing wide before recognition dawned.

"Oh! Nixyalderthor," she said, using his full name as she always did. She tried to regain her composure, but it was no use. "I-I did not know you would be down here."

He stepped forward and bowed saying, "I'm sorry, Your Ladyship. I've been coming here every day for a while... I didn't know anyone would, I mean, I-I didn't mean to intrude." He wasn't very good at formal talk, especially with a highborn like the countess. Cindra had been different; she had been his friend.

"Oh, child," Zara took his face in her hands and looked into his face. Her emerald green eyes were glistening and rimmed with red, but she smiled regardless. "There is no need to apologize. If you come here to find peace, I cannot blame you. I come here but one day of the year, so I might honor the life given to me and taken too soon." She turned to look upon the little tomb. "My little Argus; he was to be Count Casselvane one day. Now there is no one to take his place." Her hand brushed his stone curls.

"I was... I was wondering," he couldn't believe he was asking her this now, but somehow it seemed appropriate. "I was looking for Cindra's statue. I know she's not buried here, but I thought maybe... I'd like to say goodbye." His lip quivered as an untapped well of grief arose, taking him by surprise. "I'm sorry," he offered, hoping he had not upset her as much as he had upset himself.

The countess closed her eyes and nodded, placing her hand upon the boy's unkempt blond hair. "Sweet child," she said, "that is a very gracious thought. I too have wanted some remembrance in stone, but neither I nor the count had the will to commission one, for the pain was still too fresh, too near." Her eyes fell to the dusty floor, studying the patterns of tile that radiated from the center of the chamber, like the pale rays of a cold sun.

Her face was sad, but there was something else in her eyes that made Nixy pause. She had the peaceful look of someone who had been through misery and come out the other side. There was a touch of a smile on her lips as she turned back to him, brushing the hair from his eyes with a delicate, ringed finger. "But my husband and I have found that hope can be stronger than sorrow, and everything is not as it seems."

Nixy shot her a curious glance. He always tried to look on the brighter side of things, in fact with a life like his, it was necessary for survival. The countess was maybe being a bit too hopeful, but he didn't dare say so. He knew the lord and lady had heard Cindra's own voice repeated by the ember swallow; heard her last, desperate words before the Minozhian pirates burst in and started killing. They had heard their daughter scream, it was said.

"Do you think she's-" he didn't want to say it. *Alive.* He didn't know if that's what the countess meant, and didn't want to presume out-loud. *Eyes open, mouth shut, stupid!*

The countess's gaze rose to the domed ceiling, following the images painted on the curved surface. "We know something terrible happened, but we know little else. There may yet be a chance that we will see her again. We must not let despair destroy us."

Nixy did not know what to say to that, so he said nothing. It was like the countess had convinced herself that everything would be fine if she only wished hard enough. Nixy knew that such things didn't work, at least not for anyone he had ever met. The hard life on the streets did not get easier by wishing, it got harder. There was a saying about wishes, but he couldn't remember exactly how it went. *'If wishes were fishes, we'd...' Live in the sea? Be buried in fish? Something like that.*

Zara's green eyes fell to the boy's face, and shone like jewels in the torchlight. "Each of us has a fate, a destiny to fulfill. I cannot tell how I know this, but... Cindra's destiny is still before her. We will see her again someday." Without another word, she took the torch from its sconce and waited for Nixy to follow her back to the land of the living.

He approached nervously, not sure whether he should share in her hope, or be truly concerned. He wanted Cindra's parents to be happy of course, both for his mission and especially for their own sake, but this didn't sound good at all.

Chapter Fifteen

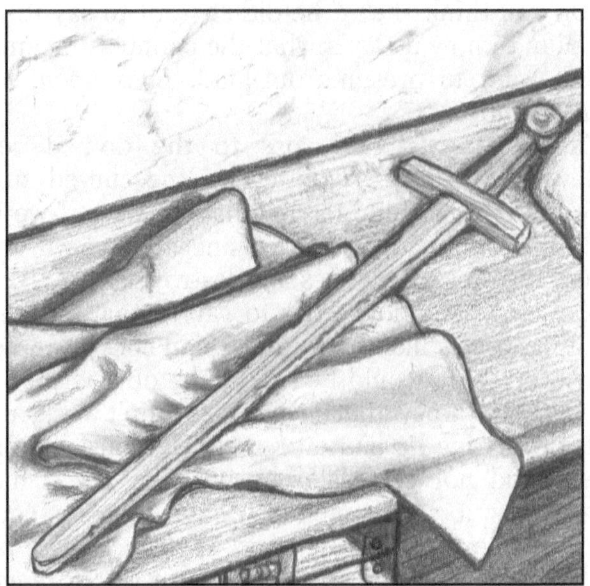

The Maiden Blade

Master Cord stood before his students, who were assembled in the yard. "I have a present for you all," he began. "This is the day we begin training with mock weapons, so each of you will receive a wooden arming sword."

Jaron and Gavadaire came from the storeroom with Elmore the caretaker, their arms full of wooden weapons. A murmur of excitement spread through the assembly, and wicked grins could be seen on the faces of some. The men went from student to student, bidding them to take a sword. There was no patience for students who were picky.

"They are all the same, so don't stand there choosing like a maid-at-market." When it was Cindra's turn to take a sword, she did so with a touch of reverence. Cord continued, "For some of you, this will be your first sword. For others, it is just a toy. Regardless, I want you to treat it like a family heirloom, since the cost of replacement was not included in your training fees. You will keep it with you at all times."

Filbert raised his hand.

"What is it, Gaddisen?"

"Do we have to wear it to mass?" asked the thin lad.

There were nervous chuckles all around as Cord answered, "No, you don't have to wear it outside of these walls. But if I catch you mistreating it, or if you forget to have it with you, there are a variety of embarrassing punishments available. Are we clear?"

"Yes, Master Cord!" they all cried.

Cindra was overjoyed with her new sword. She recalled the play she had seen years ago with Jaron, and the amazing sword dance the heroine had performed in the second act. The princess had wielded a curved saber with a long handle, the kind they used in the eastern island kingdoms. The dance had been graceful and fluid, powerful and stirring. Cindra resisted the temptation to swing the training sword about and twirl, deciding to wait until she was alone in her room. Others were not so restrained.

The swords were only half-way distributed, but already there were lads dueling with them, and the *clack, clack* of wooden blades echoed about the courtyard. The Avenoth brothers had been among the first to receive them, and were now engaged in a heated battle with each other, delivering bruising blows and barbed insults. Stansig was gazing down the length of the wood, as if examining the craftsmanship. Adric, Filbert, and Halvoy all wore silly grins, yet they held their swords without confidence. Padison chopped the air bravely.

The swords were crafted of hardwood, thick and blunt; the hand guards were simple and cruciform, and the handles were wrapped with hempen cord. The pommels were carved as orbs, ovals, disks, and jeweled shapes, all heavy and sturdy enough to take some punishment.

Cindra felt a thrill as she held it at arm's length,

imagining the sun glinting off a polished metal edge. *I need to name you. All the best weapons have names.* She looked at the faces around her; only Jaron met her eyes and smiled. *It will be a secret,* she decided, *I will call you 'Thalyroth,' the Maiden Blade.* She imagined it was one of the Corrina Honor Swords, made especially for her by smiths of old, who had read the omens and foretold her coming.

"Now, into your groups!" Master Cord barked, "We will begin sparring while you're all still pissing vinegar!"

After spending the morning hours putting the four keys of combat into practice, the students began learning take-downs and throws. These were taught by having Jaron and Gavadaire first demonstrate them on each student, so they might learn how to fall properly. Few got away unscathed, though Cindra managed to avoid injuries received by the bigger lads. Bradric got the wind knocked out of him more often than not, and the boys who were mostly legs and arms had the roughest landings. Padison was like a leather ball, practically rolling and bouncing up after each fall, earning praise from the instructors. The Avenoth brothers proved equally resilient, likely due to a lifetime of inflicting such punishments on each other. Grigor DeKenric was hurt the worst after Jaron flung him a little too hard, dislocating his shoulder. Master Freekirk and Celia, Elmore's wife, had experience tending injuries of that sort, and treated him as lessons continued. Cindra made a point of staying in Gavadaire's line.

Later that evening, while dining in their quarters, Jaron asked "So why were you lining up to be thrown by Gavadaire? Don't you trust me?"

Cindra carved the roast beef and served him, saying "For one thing, he doesn't know about me and would not hold back." She carved a slice for herself, adding "And maybe I didn't want you to break me like you did that DeKenric boy."

Jaron sat back and stared at his plate as if he had lost his appetite. "I don't even know why he's here," he said finally.

Cindra was confused, "He seems perfectly decent to me, unlike some I could name; Ratham for example, and those two brothers." She began eating without waiting for him to start.

He tapped his fingers on the table and stared at her. "His family name is *Evenast*, as in 'the son of Baron Drom Evenast.' You are familiar with Baron DeKenric, are you not?" Cindra stopped chewing and looked up at him. Jaron said, "If there is a civil war, Kenric is one of the barons that will rally against the crown and its supporters. They are just on the other side of the Iron Pass, two weeks' march from Portshia if left unchecked." He finished his ale, "And we are training his son to fight."

"Oh," she said around her food. "*That* DeKenric. Still, it couldn't improve his opinion of us if you injure his son."

"Being nice to him will not curb his father's ambitions, or undo the web of deceit that entangles his house. When war breaks out, he will be as good as a spy within the walls. Do you think he will decide to stay and fight against his own father because I was gentle with him?"

She shrugged. Cindra had always thought of the Dissenter Houses as vile traitors with evil mustaches and wicked laughs, planning the demise of the kingdom. She had never put a face on them, and the face of Grigor DeKenric was neither evil nor devious. He seemed nice, but he was to be her enemy apparently. She would have to keep an eye on him for the sake of her house and the kingdom, though she doubted he could do much spying while living at the school.

"Alright everyone, form into teams in the courtyard." Master Freekirk's voice echoed through the main hall as the morning glow spilled over the mountains. "Today we're drilling with opposing teams. Dread Wolves and Thorn Bears, match up! Fire Steeds and Ice Drakes, match up!

Cindra's team had finally settled on "Dread Wolves," and because she had caused such a scene over Padison's "Mighty Minozhians" idea, she didn't want to bring up the fact that dread wolves were not mythical beasts either, and she knew this because she had stuck a spear in one.

She cringed when Master Cord paired them with the Thorn Bears, for that was Rejick Ratham's team. Sure enough, Ratham himself stood opposite Dillan DePort in the first match, and the lad towered over her by at least a head-height. Her teammates fared no better, for the Dread Wolves were comprised of the least experienced fighters in the class. Cindra had practiced archery in her younger days simply to alleviate boredom. Inis DeGhat and Morrin LiKeska were not bred for fighting; Inis was more of a scholar, and Morrin fancied himself a warrior-poet, though he was more familiar with wielding words, not swords. Addy and Paddy had no martial training whatsoever; they were sons of the merchant class who were branching out into new markets as swords-for-hire.

By contrast, Rejick Ratham and Lukas Korbison were brutes who came from warrior families and traditions. Terrus Drakthorne was well-muscled and formidable, but at least he was even-tempered. Demel Victhor was the son of a northern knight and was rumored to have seen combat, and Minas Koorla was a Maanok, a people known for their ferocity. All wanted to challenge the Minozhian-slayer, but apparently Rejick had called dibs. He twirled his sword with a limber wrist as he glared at his opposition. Cindra tried to ignore him, listening to Master Freekirk instead.

"I will call the attacks, students defending will block as they have been instructed." He glared at the Avenoth brothers and said, "Anyone using attacks other than what I call will sit out the exercise." He raised his arm.

"Weapons at the ready!"

The students faced off, one side attacking and the other set to defend. Cindra was on the defending side for the first round, so she steeled herself to receive Ratham's overzealous blows. He did not disappoint. The lad put all the strength of his arm into the called attacks, forcing Cindra to push herself to her limits. As her arm rattled with each impact, she prayed that *Thalyroth* would survive its first day of action. She flinched as she repelled Ratham's attacks, grateful that she knew where each would land. It would take a lot of practice to overcome that instinctive response and keep her eyes open and focused. Fear began to take her as she imagined how deadly it could be if Ratham chose his own attacks. *Could I parry in time? Could I even hope to counter?*

After the first round, the students were made to rotate partners, giving her a moment to recover. She now faced Demel Victhor, who hailed from Rickshome-on-the-Joshian. Victhor was strong but steady, offering no unpleasant surprises and allowing Cindra to relax a little, training her body to the movements.

"Sorry about Ratham," said Demel. "He's not really mad at you, just your Sir Jaron. It's bad luck to follow a shamed knight, DePort."

"He was the Corrina champion before, and is again," she answered. "His shame has passed in the eyes of the count, and should with the rest of you as well."

The cadence of wood impacting wood was the only answer.

Eventually, the rotation came around and she faced Ratham, but this time she would be attacking. She truly wished to whack him on the nose, but she didn't want to get in trouble. Besides, her shoulder was aching badly. The sun had risen over the rooftops and the sweat began to sting her eyes. Ratham was blocking her attacks with force, striking her blade rather than deflecting it. The impact made her wrist ache and she began to notice little dents in the Maiden Blade. It was not a good time to be Dillan DePort.

Before the midday meal, Cindra went to her room and rummaged through her gear, looking for one of the gifts her Galindri family had given her. Her Shadowood bow was unstrung and wrapped in linen, the quiver of arrows lay next to it, and the *Kos* knife rested nearby in its sheath, but she was after none of these. She finally found it: a strip of burgundy fabric embroidered with black thread down the middle of its length, the headband of a *Gatéth-sho'a* warrior. She bound it around her forehead and tied it in back, pulling her forelocks free to hang on the sides of her face. Looking once in a little brass mirror, she straightened it and then left the room.

She went down to the main hall, which was currently set up for lunchtime. Sir Jaron sat with the other two instructors at a head table, but 'Dillan' was free to sit where she pleased at lunch. Not wanting to seem like a mother's duckling, she shared a table with some of her teammates. They eyed the new fashion accessory for a moment, and not attaching any special significance to it, returned to their meals.

"Bad luck about pairing with the Thorn Bears, eh Dillan?" asked Paddy. He had a bruise on his hand from a stray attack.

"Rotten luck," Dillan agreed, rubbing her shoulder. "Not that Master Freekirk noticed Ratham beating on me."

"Oh, I think he did," said Morrin, chiming in with his expressive voice. "Instructor Gavadaire noticed too, but thought it best to let it pass."

"How do you know what Gavadaire was thinking?" asked Padison. "Maybe he didn't see anything wrong with it, or maybe he's no friend of Sir Jaron either, so he let Dillan get beat on."

Morrin turned a derogatory gaze upon Padison and said, "I saw it in his face, dear Chatty. No rules were being bent or broken, yet I saw it troubled him." Turning to Dillan he said, "It may seem harsh, but it will do you well in the end. If Ratham and his mates are hard on you now, you will only be stronger for it later, mark me." He had a look of sagely wisdom on his young face, and his dark, curly hair added to his childlike appearance. He had the 'manner of the manor' as it was called.

"*You* benefit from him next time then," Cindra retorted.

Adric sat back and said, "I was too busy dodging blows to look at the instructors' faces. How did you manage it?" Padison bobbed his head in agreement, wanting to know.

"My opponent was fair with me, pulling no tricks or surprises. All I needed to do was listen for the called shots and block as I was taught. I could spare an eye for other things," Morrin said.

"No good," said Inis to his fellow squire. "Get that out of your head. How are you going to know where a blow is landing if you don't learn the signs? Enemies don't call out their attacks in real combat." Inis was intense in all things, and his steel-blue eyes bored into Morrin as he spoke. His cropped, sandy hair stood upon his head like quills. Cindra could easily imagine him leading troops into battle, but she knew he was just as green as Morrin.

"True enough," said Morrin wearily, "But we have two years to learn such things. I am not just studying to fight, but I am studying the teachers as well. Master Cord and Sir Jaron are both skilled, with great reputations in combat and tournaments, but Gavadaire LuVestra is a legend in his homeland, did you know? He has won every jousting tournament he has ever entered, and he's never lost a duel. The monastery where he was raised is home to many battle-scholars and war-masters, all devoted followers of High King Arathus. It is indeed a high commendation for the Freekirk School that he has chosen to train and instruct here!”

“Aren’t we lucky,” said Adric, between bites of stew, “that we have you here to tell us these things.” Padison snickered as he ate another spoonful.

Cindra remarked, “I think the Freekirk School had been famous long before Gavadaire LuVestra was born, and I’d not go singing his praises too loudly. He’s met neither Sir Jaron nor Master Cord in battle yet, and he’s better off for it.”

“That’s as may be,” said Morrin dubiously, “I certainly hope things never come to that end, for I’d rather have Gavadaire for us than against us. We will leave it at that.” He went back to his stew, which had cooled during his lecture. The others were happy to oblige him and finished their midday meal in peace, talking only about small matters and gossip.

After midday Master Cord had the students assemble in the courtyard for the next lesson. He had them sit and form a ring about the center, which they did gladly. The day was hot and muggy, and sitting in the sparse grass was a welcomed relief.

“We’ve gone over standard cuts and parries, and those movements will become a part of your daily routine,” Cord said. “Now we will include counter-attacks and throws.” He slapped his palm with his wooden sword, “I will need an assistant for these demonstrations, someone with strength and skill...” He turned within the circle, weaving his sword before him like a dowsing rod, as if it could seek out such attributes on its own. “Rejick Ratham!” he boomed. “Come forward.”

Ratham grinned awkwardly at his fellows, not sure whether to be worried or smug; he decided on smug. Cindra and her team made faces at each other, and Padison made a flatulent noise as Ratham stood up. Several students chuckled at that.

“We will begin with the basic counters,” Cord said, “Ratham, I want you to bring each blow with the same enthusiasm you were displaying earlier.”

Morrin LiKeska smiled knowingly at Dillan, whose

eyebrows went up at the remark. *He had seen it after all,* she thought.

"I want you to watch my hands, shoulders and torso," he told the students. "Also, mind my footing. Balance and leverage is vital." He turned to Ratham and saluted with his sword, "*Gher yaas,*" Cord intoned.

That's the Norsican tongue, Cindra thought. *Guard yourself.*

Cord said, "Whenever you're ready, lad."

Ratham blinked uncertainly, not feeling as smug anymore. He took up a guard position and advanced a few half-steps, then swung in an overhead arc towards Cord's shoulder. Before he knew what happened, his blow had been redirected and the point of the master's wooden blade was at his throat.

"Good," Cord said. "Again."

Cindra looked at Jaron who gave her a wink, though his face betrayed none of his mirth. She couldn't help but smile however.

Ratham made a feinting attack at Cord's right shoulder, but turned it into an underhanded slash at his left flank. Cord shifted his defense to block the true attack, stepped inside his opponent's guard, and threw an elbow at Ratham's head. It was not a solid blow, but it knocked him to the ground just the same.

"A good feint," Cord remarked, helping the dazed lad to his feet. "Let's have another."

Ratham didn't look as willing anymore, but everyone was watching and he couldn't back down.

"Guard as you attack, attack as you guard," Cord said, turning the lad's blade as his own thrust into Ratham's armpit, making him wince. "The strongest attack can be redirected, and your opponent's strength will turn against him. Use every part of the sword, from the point to the pommel. Use the cross-guard to trap his blade-" He trapped Ratham's incoming strike with the cross-guard and kicked the inside of his weight-bearing knee, making him fall. "-and be aware of all openings."

Cindra watched with great interest as her tormentor

regained his feet, looking none too happy. *What a fascinating lesson,* she thought with satisfaction. *I think we've all learned something today.*

Chapter Sixteen

Birdbrains

Nixy had stopped going to the catacombs after his encounter with Cindra's mother. Instead, he spent the next few weeks thinking about what she said, and what it might mean. She seemed to believe that her daughter was still alive, but that went against all the signs. It had been over two years since Cindra left home, and wouldn't she have come back in all that time if she could? If she had somehow been saved and made it to her wedding, there would have been word. He just wasn't ready to have that kind of hope.

On the evening of the first day of Valmoth, Nixy went to give Gavagul his dinner. The bird shook out his glowing plumage at Nixy's approach, twittering a lovely song as he sat in his iron cage. A bed of glowing coals served for a nest, shedding sparks as Gavagul flapped his wings in welcome. Nixy felt the warm air buffet his face as he took the thick leather gloves from a nearby shelf, opened the cage, and let the bird perch on his wrist.

The aerie was located in the watch turret above the keep gatehouse, giving a wide field of view from the shelter of the conical roof. Nixy walked the bird around the inside perimeter as he fed him bits of meat, having been told that it was safer than walking the battlements. Ember swallows were intelligent and willful, flying off on errands of their own if their keepers were not well-known to them. Most noble families took care of their own birds so the creatures would develop a loyalty to the house. It had been Cindra's task to feed Gavagul, and she had taken him on her ocean voyage so she might send word of her safe arrival. Instead, he had delivered her final, tragic message.

"It's not fair," he said to the bird. "She was young; older than me, but still young. She has parents who miss her and people who care about her. Nobody would have missed me, but she saved my life. Now I'm living in her house and she's gone. It's not fair," he repeated to the bird.

It blinked and said, "Not fair," in Nixy's own voice.

Gavagul sidestepped across the leather glove, nearing the exposed flesh at Nixy's elbow. It would burn a bit if he placed a claw there; he knew from experience. He nudged the bird back gently towards his well-protected wrist.

"The countess thinks her daughter is alive somewhere," he said to the bird, who blinked a large, red eye at him. "She still hopes for it, and thinks Cindra's still got a destiny." He sniffled as the pity he felt for the countess came pouring out again. "I'd like to think that's true, but I don't see how. Those bull-men are supposed to be meaner than bulls and men put together. That's exactly what they are, I guess." He sighed, "I do wanna see her again, but she's... she's just dead. I know it, and everyone else knows it. I guess it's different for her parents, though. Harder to believe." The bird whistled a song and bent down towards the food pouch on Nixy's belt. "Hey, be patient!" he scolded.

"Hey, be patient!" said Gavagul in Nixy's voice.

After the bird downed another piece of meat, Nixy set him on one of the iron perches mounted outside the main cage. He was supposed to let the bird flap about if it wished, exercising its wings. Once the bird accepted him as a keeper, he could let it fly around the castle a few times before calling it back.

"I want to tell her I miss her. I pray to the gods to let her know, but I don't think they listen." He leaned on the stone and looked out at the city lights, then smiling sadly at the bird, asked, "I don't suppose *you* could give her the message?"

Gavagul blinked and cocked his head. "Who?" he asked, sounding like an owl.

Nixy was taken aback, for the bird had never asked him anything, only mimicked his voice. "Uh, Cindra. You remember Cindra Corrina?"

"Cindra Corrina," the ember swallow repeated, and his large eyes went distant, as if looking far into the night beyond the stars. He swayed a little on his perch and Nixy began to wonder if the bird was ill. After a long moment Gavagul said, "Ready."

Nixy blinked in confusion, not understanding. *Ready? Ready for what?* Then the thought hit him like a brick. "You... you can take her a message?"

Gavagul sat patiently, tilting his ear-hole towards the boy.

Legends said that ember swallows came from somewhere beyond Jayde, maybe even from the lands of the gods. Would he be the first one to ever send a message to a dead person? Or what if the countess was right and Cindra was really alive! What if she was in the clutches of Minozhian pirates, or washed up on a desert island? His mind whirled, his excitement growing as he considered the possibilities.

Gavagul fluttered his wings impatiently, waiting for Nixy to say something useful.

Nixy calmed himself as best he could and said, "Tell Cindra that we all miss her very much, and we're all sorry she's dead, unless she isn't dead. Then tell her that we still miss her and want to see her again, and if she's in trouble or needs help, then send you back. There. That's it, I guess." He panted and waited for the bird to do something.

Gavagul tilted his avian head back and forth as it absorbed the rambling message. He then began looking all about the enclosure, chirping loudly. When the boy just stood there, Gavagul flapped around the window slats and in front of the door, squawking in annoyance.

"Oh!" Nixy said, realizing what was the matter. He opened the door to the aerie, hoping the bird wasn't making a fool of him.

Gavagul beat his wings and flew, circling the castle roof once before racing off like a shooting star, leaving a trail of fire and smoke in his wake. Nixy dashed to the battlements to see if the bird went straight up into the heavens, or off across the sea. He was a little surprised when Gavagul streaked north over the city and dove down, disappearing behind the roof of the distant cathedral.

"No!"

The cry woke the little dweedragon from his uneasy slumber, and he almost fell from the footstool he had curled up on. He blinked his bleary eyes until he saw his master, Ildric Finnael, racing across the room to an open window.

"Master? What is it?" Drahn was fully awake now, though his eyes were still focusing. His concern turned to dread upon seeing the wizard's face as he looked into the night.

"Drahn, I want you to fly to Casselvane Keep at once, before..." His mouth gaped as he peered across the cityscape. "Oh no, we are too late!"

Drahn scrambled over to the window to see what was wrong. He witnessed a little streak of flame arcing from the castle to the middle of the city, where it passed over the cathedral to land somewhere near the campus of the

Mystic College. At first, Drahn thought it might have been a cannon shot, or a fire rocket launched into the city, but there was no sound or explosion. Besides, it had descended rather too suddenly to be anything other than a living thing; an ember swallow, maybe.

"Master?" Drahn asked, a sense of dread growing in his stomach.

Ildric wore a grave expression as he stared at the spot where the flame had landed. His silver hand flexed nervously as the Eye of Omithys glowed in the palm. "Someone has found Lady Cindra," he said. "The protective spell I put in place has been breached by the family's ember swallow. Curse me, but I did not foresee that possibility."

"But how?" Drahn asked, craning his long neck to look at his master. "The power of the eye pwotects her. You said no wizard could seek her out, so how did a silly bird do it?" He was upset that a mere ember swallow broke the power of the Eye of Omithys, which had been created by dweedragons, as it happened. Drahn took it as a wound to his pride.

"Ember swallows are remarkable creatures, able to seek out the recipients of their messages over great distances, finding them somehow," he said. "It must be this one's familiarity with the girl that allowed it to see past my warding spells. I do not think another could manage that feat."

The uncertainty in his master's voice was telling. Drahn asked, "Should I fly to the castle to see who sent the bird?"

"Yes," Ildric said, donning his cloak. "Go at once, but be careful. If it is one of the plotters, they may be dangerous. Don't try anything heroic."

Drahn wanted desperately to help, for he had been so useless these past four months. He had confined himself to his room, taking little food and drink, and wallowing in sadness over the fate of his mother and clutch mates. The elf woman and his master had both tried to comfort him, but he was inconsolable. Master

Ildric had finally lost his temper, saying, 'The evil that destroyed your family is still out there, plotting to destroy the world. You can either stay in your room and weep, or find that evil and fight against it!' Drahn had come out later that evening to join them for dinner.

He now crawled onto the windowsill and launched himself into the night, spreading his leathery wings and flapping frantically towards the castle. Heroics were not on his mind, but if a traitor was lurking atop Casselvane Keep, he would certainly be tempted to bite him. The cool night air rushed past as his eyes fought to adjust to the darkness, his vertical pupils opening wide. He flew over the masts of ships in port, then soared over the Peer District until he saw the crenelated ring of the castle's roof. Little brazier fires flickered in the sea breeze, outlining the figures of the night watch. Drahn's eyes picked out the conical roof of the aerie where the ember swallow was kept, and he noticed a small, shadowy figure there, possibly lurking.

Drahn dipped his wing and circled, trying to get a better look. Some watchmen on the roof were moving towards the aerie, but no one was yet rushing in to capture the perpetrator. Drahn was worried that he might get away, but he noticed that the shadowy figure did not seem to be in a hurry to leave. The culprit was just leaning on the battlements, staring at the ember swallow's smoke trail as it dissipated in the moonlight.

Gaining a bit of altitude, he considered his next move. *If I land on the aerie roof, I can get a look at his face. Then if he tries to run, I can drive him towards the watchmen.*

He came in gently, cupping the air to slow his descent, and landed on the top of the conical roof. He clawed the wooden shingles for purchase as he tried to creep closer, hoping he was being stealthy enough. Unfortunately the shingles were slicker than he had anticipated, and he began an undignified slide towards the edge, hissing as he scrambled for a foothold. He dropped off the aerie roof just as the figure below him looked up, and suddenly Drahn found himself caught in the stranger's arms.

Panicking and twisting in his captor's grasp, he cried, "Twaitor!" and snapped his jaws on the person's nose.

The boy yelped in pain and dropped the dweedragon in a heap at his feet. "Ow! Wha-whudya bide me fow?" Nixy cried, holding his nose and checking for blood.

"Nixy? Nixyalderthor DuQuayne? Oh my!" Drahn recovered himself, getting to his feet and clapping his fore-claws for joy. "You are safe! Wenyssaya will be so pleased!" He blinked and stretched his neck, standing up as tall as he was able to look at the boy. "But did you send the ember swallow? Did you send a message to Lady Cindwa?"

"What's going on here?" asked a watchman who had responded to the noise. His halberd was held at the ready as he eyed the little dragon with the boy. "Is this... your creature?" he asked.

"No," said Drahn cheerfully, "He is not mine, but I am vewy happy to see him anyway!" The guard just stared at the dweedragon, dumbfounded.

"We're fine," Nixy said, "This is Drahn. He's a friend, even if he did bite my nose." Nixy glared and Drahn looked contrite.

The man looked puzzled but he relaxed his guard. "Alright then," he said, returning to his post.

"Sowwy about the nose," Drahn said, "but I thought you were a twaitor looking for Lady Cindwa. Oh, but you shouldn't have done that!"

"What are you talking about?" Nixy asked.

"Lady Cindwa," Drahn said, speaking in a hushed whisper, "You may have put her in gwave danger!"

"Lady Cindra is dead," Nixy said, "...Isn't she?"

"Erm," Drahn cleared his throat, "Eh, well, not exactly." He looked around to make sure they were alone. He took a deep breath and began, "Master Ildwic gave her a magic bwacelet that saved her from dwowning at sea, and she has been in hiding ever since, living with Galindwi nomads for the past two years."

Nixy's eyes went wide and his mouth fell open, but Drahn motioned for the boy to stay calm. "She is now somewhere in the city, but is hiding in secwet. No one must know, for there might be spies in the castle!"

"No one told me she's alive?" Nixy said, trembling. "It's been two years and no one told me?" He wanted to shout aloud, out of joy or anger, he couldn't tell which.

"No one knows!" Drahn said, "Well, no one but the lord and lady, and Master Ildwic. Oh, and myself of course, and Sir Jawon Dunlorden, and maybe the Fweekirks..." His voice trailed off as he realized he was not helping.

Nixy turned his back to the little dragon, his shoulders heaving as he took in great gulps of air, his head turned to the heavens. As his breathing slowed he turned to look at Drahn as if for the first time, a smile beginning to spread across his face with no signs of stopping. "She's alive!" he cried, as quiet as he could manage. He stooped and picked up the little dweedragon, hugging him and hopping about gleefully. Drahn squirmed like a cat, mindful not to claw him or do any more damage, even though his dignity was in shambles.

"Yes, yes, she is alive." Drahn hissed at the boy, trying to rein him in. "Like I said, she is in hiding, but not anymore! The ember swallow you sent could lead her enemies to her!"

"Oh no!" Nixy exclaimed, nearly dropping the dweedragon and running to the battlements. His eyes followed the moonlit smoke trail, now a lazily meandering smear in the breeze.

Drahn was able to twist and land on his feet, though the ungraceful drop made him bite his tongue. He let out a hiss of pain, but considered it a fair trade for biting the boy's nose. Any more mishandling however, and Drahn made up his mind to bite him again.

Cindra was enjoying her dinner in the main hall with the other students, finishing the extra helping of beef that Celia had given her for the sake of healing. A sparring injury had made things difficult this last week, but she was well on the mend.

It happened during sword and buckler training, and Dillan had been paired with Gaius Corrina. The tip of his blade had slipped past her buckler and struck her in the armpit. The pain was sharp and terrible, then her left arm had gone numb. Gaius had apologized adequately, but Jaron made too much of a fuss over her, and Master Cord had to pull him aside for a talk. At the time, she was sure they were going to send her packing.

Cord had given her an earful later in her quarters. "Damn your schemes, and damn my mother for backing you! She must have lost her wits, agreeing to this-this *idiocy*. If I lose my license over your stupid..." He managed to keep his voice from carrying beyond the room, which was quite a feat. He must have been *really* upset, speaking to her that way. Jaron had reminded him that he had the final word, since it was his school.

Jaron and Cord were currently dining with Gavadaire in the Master's Hall, eating their special Highday meal. While the 'special' part was only a pitcher of wine and a roast pheasant, the students imagined a feast of roast venison, a whole pig, fish and eels, and exotic fruits, all served by scantily-clad nymphets. When Cindra had told Jaron what rumors the students had conjured, his eyes took on a wistful, longing expression and Cindra had to punch him in the shoulder.

"Pass that butter, will you?" asked Bradric, who proceeded to smear the thick white mass on his squash and everything else on his plate. He still had a mighty appetite even though he had lost much of his initial padding.

Adric took back the butter dish while some still remained. "Easy on that, mate. It's not cheap, you know."

"Cheap enough if you churn it yourself," Padison said as he dipped his bread roll in the dish, making a butter crater. "We have a dozen cows at home. Milk, cream, cheese, and butter... all you could handle."

"And beef as well?" Bradric asked. "Rath's blood, I'm going home with you, Chatty." He had a way with blasphemy that made Cindra cringe.

She was finishing her drink when she heard a familiar sound from the courtyard, a musical call of a bird unlike any other: the warbling whistle of an ember swallow. She nearly choked on her drink when Gavagul flew in through the open doors and landed in the midst of the dining hall, making the buzz of conversation fall silent. The warm breeze of his entry washed over Cindra's stockings, her eyes went wide, and her heart leaped into her throat. *No! No,no,no,no...* Gavagul fluttered onto the table and hopped over to her, chirping triumphantly and ruffling his feathers, which began to melt the butter.

He looked into Cindra's panicky eyes and began to speak, but Cindra blurted out a command that had been taught to the family's ember swallows for generations. *"Nethimos!"* It meant 'privacy' in Celvestrian, telling the ember swallow to hold his message until bidden to speak. Gavagul made a disappointed twitter, not wasting any time in eyeing the beef left on her plate. It had been a very short flight, but work was work, and he got fed after work.

"Must be for Sir Jaron," she said, nervously excusing herself from the table, and using her wooden spoon as a perch for Gavagul. "I better go and get him at once. Probably very important." She left the room as fast as she was able. The bird gave her a chirp of annoyance as she carried him from the food, but his mood softened and he gave her an affectionate nip on the thumb.

Nixy stood in the castle study, the mounted heads of game animals scowling down on him with no sympathy. The count and countess were there, both dressed for bed. Sir Jaron was there also, his face flushed and angry; he had ridden from the Freekirk School and arrived only ten minutes ago. Jaron had sent Gavagul back to the castle, requesting an emergency meeting with the lord and lady, and Nixy. Drahn, the only one that was in a good mood, had flown back to the wizard tower to give Ildric and some elf woman the 'happy news' about him. Nixy felt small and alone.

"What could you have been thinking?" barked the count, his brow furrowed deeply. He had always been courteous to Nixy, and this direct anger was something the boy was wholly unprepared for.

"It wasn't my idea!" Nixy blurted, his eyes starting to well up with tears. This was apparently not the best answer, for the faces before him paled and exchanged panicked looks.

"Whose idea was it then?" asked Jaron, "Who put you up to this? Gods above and below!" His hand was on the hilt of his sword, eager to draw it and go charging off after the guilty party.

"Speak child," the countess asked. "Who told you to send the bird after Cindra?" Her normally calm face was pinched in distress, her emerald eyes showing real fear.

"It... Well, it was *kind* of my idea," Nixy squeaked. "But it was mostly the bird's."

The count was not moved. "The *bird's* idea? That is not possible Nixyalderthor. Gavagul does not offer to take messages to anyone, he does as he is asked."

"But he did!" Nixy cried. "I was talking to him and said I wanted to tell Cindra I missed her, and I asked him..." the guilt of the bird was sounding less likely the more Nixy spoke, "I asked him if he could tell her, 'cause I thought she was dead, and he says 'Who?' and I say 'Cindra" and he goes all weird for a second then he says 'Ready.' I thought he'd take the message to the afterlife if she was there." He started to cry, his guilt obvious now, even to himself. If Cindra had been put in danger because of his stupidity, he'd never forgive himself.

The countess stood by him, placing a hand on his shoulder. "I am afraid the fault is mine. We spoke in the catacombs when I was visiting our son... I-I hinted that

Cindra need not be mourned, that her destiny was not yet fulfilled."

"Why would you say such a thing?" asked the count, looking exasperated.

The lady responded in her melodious, low voice, with an undercurrent of emotion that spoke volumes. "I was in the crypt to mourn the child we had lost. I could not bear to play at mourning for Cindra any longer. Not there, not in the presence of this dear child, who was grieving for her himself." She stroked his hair protectively as Nixy stared at the floor. "All those who love her deserve hope, at least. I did not think that anything ill would come of it, but I wanted him to have that hope." She lifted her chin defiantly as the count sighed in resignation.

Sir Jaron visibly relaxed as well, his hand going from his sword to run over his sweat-soaked hair. "It was her idea for me to come here." He paced as he explained to the boy. "She brought the firebird to me and we listened to the message in private. She decided it was best for me to rush off to the castle as if I had received an urgent summons; hopefully anyone seeing the fire trail would assume the same. The only question was: did someone put you up to it, or was it your own bird-brained idea?" He smiled at the boy, patting him on the shoulder. "Luckily that's all it was. Let's all hope that no harm comes of it."

Nixy slouched in relief, yet he still felt ashamed.

Jaron knelt down to look into his eyes, lifting the boy's chin. "She misses you too, lad. She misses you too."

It was all he needed to hear.

Chapter Seventeen

Suspicions

Ghethas had avoided the Market Square for a month and a half, until the Galindri caravan belonging to his victim's family had left the city. The clerk who sold him the information had a good eye for detail, he had to admit. The girl had been the right age and height; she had lighter skin and hazel eyes, just as described. Ghethas had experienced a thrill when he took her; certain he would have his revenge on the Corrina bitch who had slipped his grasp twice. Alas, it had been the wrong girl. Well, he couldn't blame his source for that.

Once her body turned up, the city watch made a paltry effort to find a suspect. The Galindri families drew closer together, extra wary and thirsting for justice. If anyone had seen Ghethas in the market on the night of her disappearance, he might find himself on the wrong end of several brownie knives. They often made their own justice, since the local authorities had little to spare. It wasn't lost on him that the god of justice and revenge had the same dark skin.

But Julen Gordon was a merchant, and a merchant needed to mind his business, so Ghethas spent the early evening bidding on shipping contracts in one of the square's auction halls. Maveezh had declined to join him, for she was busy working up the courage to pester the high priest. They needed a business loan, due to losses incurred while doing the secret work of the faith. Ghethas had no desire to be there when she dropped *that* on DuChat's desk.

The man had been in a sour mood lately anyway, since his best source of intelligence in the count's household had dried up. Apparently Constable Fingelm had canceled their weekly lunch at his villa, and had begun acting suspicious of DuChat's increased interest in castle gossip. Not one to be snubbed lightly, DuChat decided to increase the interest on Fingelm's sizable loans.

As the auction hall closed for the night, Julen Gordon made with the pleasantries, smiling and shaking hands with his associates. He donned his cloak, adjusted his floppy hat, and stepped out into the night in the company of a few other men. He had accepted an invitation to a tavern, mostly because it allowed him to walk with a group past the remaining Galindri caravans. He stayed towards the rear, not engaging in conversation as he usually did. Julen Gordon could be truly exhausting, and Ghethas longed to retire him.

The party walked noisily down the Golden Path, heading for what one man claimed was the best tavern in Portshia. The summer evening was cool, yet the paving stones still retained some of the day's heat, and Ghethas longed to soak his feet at home. They turned down the Procession Way, chatting merrily, when one man saw a light in the sky. "What is that?" he asked, pointing. The light glowed like fire, moved like a shooting star. Only instead of burning out, it dove steeply towards the distant rooftops and vanished from sight, leaving a smoke trail that glowed in the light of the full moon.

"Looks like a firebird," said another fellow. "Come from the castle, maybe."

The man who recommended the tavern said, "His Lordship is too impatient to send a courier on horseback, it would seem. Ah, such conveniences."

"I wonder who it's for," Julen mused, as a thought tickled the back of his brain. He declared, "I'm going to find out. Go on without me, lads!" He waved to the men, who made noises at his leaving, but didn't care for long. There was beer in their immediate future.

Ghethas began walking at a rapid pace, his mind whirling. *Ember swallows are only used by Great Houses*, he reasoned. *The smoke trail seems to lead back to the castle, so what could be so important? Who is receiving this message?* His stride lengthened and soon he was jogging. *Which building, which building?* The smoke trail was dispersing in the gentle breeze, but it was enough to still act as a guide. *The Mystic College? No, the smoke leads across the road from there, unless the wind pushed it farther...*

He traced the smoke trail to a neighborhood near the scribe's office, where he had received his faulty tip. *That worm of a clerk had better not have double-crossed me,* he thought.

The scribe's office was closed, as were the adjoining businesses on the south side of the street. The north side housed the Red Eagle Tavern and Stables, and judging by the breeze, the ember swallow must have landed somewhere beyond. He decided to ask at the tavern.

As he approached the building, two things happened. A door in the corner of the stable opened wide, shedding light across the heads of sleepy horses. A young man or boy moved in the dim light, hastily throwing a blanket and saddle on a horse. At the same moment, the ember swallow rose up over the rooftop, circled once, and shot off to the south. Ghethas ran south down the street towards the Temple Walk, glimpsing the fiery dart of the bird as it streaked over the cathedral, then the canal, then...

"The castle!" he exclaimed. His suspicions confirmed, he ran back to the stables, stopping across the street to watch from the shadows. A man emerged from the doorway, said a few brief words to the boy, and mounted his horse. He spurred the chestnut stallion into the night, his cloak flying behind like wings. The boy watched him go, speaking briefly to the stable hand before disappearing back through the door.

Ghethas approached the stable hand in a casual, friendly manner. "You there! Might I ask what that was all about?"

The man leaned on his rake, squinting in the low light. "Who's that? Who wants to know?"

Ghethas smiled, "I own a shipping business and I do some travel abroad. Gordon is the name."

The man nodded, looking him up and down. "Evening, Master Gordon. That was just a man from the school, heading out in a rush."

"The school? Of course, the fighting school," Ghethas said. "So the firebird was for him? Who is he?"

"Don't know nothing about no firebird," said the stable hand. "Didn't see one, as I've been mucking out the stables. As to who he is, that was Sir Jaron Dunlorden. I recall him from his student days, now he's assisting Master Freekirk."

"Dunlorden?" Ghethas said. "Isn't he the knight who was banished a few years ago?"

"Yes, that he was," said the man. "A temporary thing, as I understand it. Now it's all water under the bridge, as they say. He's gone respectable again; even got himself a squire, like a proper knight."

"Indeed," Ghethas said, scratching his beard. "I thank you for your time, good fellow." He tipped his hat and walked towards the tavern. *Dunlorden was Lady Cindra's lover, if the stories are true,* he thought with mounting excitement. *She might have even contacted him.*

The Red Eagle Tavern had a long, narrow common room, with small tables and benches, fireplaces at each end, and several upstairs rooms for rent. Julen Gordon made his way across the common room towards the kitchen counter, smiling amicably to one and all. He was unknown here, but it never hurt to stay in character.

The innkeeper met him at the counter. "Welcome, master! Red's the name. What can I get for you?" Red was a red-faced man with blond hair and a blond mustache, and arms like a bear.

"A room, if you have one," Julen said. "One with a window preferably. Facing north."

"Oh, 'fraid we don't have any on the north side. Only a few there with windows anyway, seeing as how they overlook the fighting school's courtyard. They're up early, drilling and crashing about, and that Master Cord, he's got a voice that'd break the clouds, if you follow me."

"Very well, I'll take whatever is available," Ghethas sighed.

He awoke from a fitful sleep, his legs twisted in the sheets of the modest bed. He had been dreaming of the Corrina girl, painted brown and dressed in those alluringly immodest rags of a Galindri vagabond. He could smell her skin, her hair, her fear. He looked into her wide eyes, and this time he knew her for who she was. He saw through the trickery, saw through her dark skin into her noble blood. The chatter of her Gali speech was replaced with pleas of mercy in clear Calilesh, and the color began to bleed from her face. Then, like a greased pig, she slipped from his grasp and fled, vanishing into a mass of savages.

Groaning and rubbing his eyes, he heard the booming voice of the fighting master shouting at his students. The noise echoed above the rooftops and out across the street. *The innkeeper was right about that voice,* he thought.

He dressed and went downstairs to see if he could get a better look at the courtyard. The streets were bustling with early risers and people heading to work. Steam arose from piles of fresh horse dung as the stable hands took their tenants for their morning walks. Strolling around the corner, Ghethas found the wooden gates of the Freekirk School swung wide open, but its iron gates were closed to visitors. Regardless, a small crowd of onlookers stopped to gawk at the students, hoping to pick up some secret techniques.

Ghethas saw the master standing on the stoop, calling out orders in baritone thunder. Two other men walked among the students, correcting their movements as needed. Ghethas could not be certain if one of them was Sir Jaron, for he had only seen him once, two years ago.

This will not do, he thought. *I need a better vantage point.*

He looked at the south wall, with its large murals of fighting men, and he saw a few small windows overlooking the courtyard. *All of those rooms are occupied,* he recalled. *Pity. I suppose I could create a vacancy, but I'd rather not draw that kind of attention...*

He was getting anxious, the feeling that he was on to something was overwhelming. *Sir Jaron was involved with Lady Cindra,* he thought. *If she has returned to the city, he will likely know where she is hiding. He might have even gone to meet her last night. It's possible she's no longer disguised as a Galindri...*

He went back to the inn and climbed the stairs, eager to get back on the trail that had long gone cold. Walking to the end of the hall, he put his ear to each door facing the courtyard, listening for signs of life. A snore here, a cough there, a shadow moving under the door; every room but one was occupied.

"Finally," he said under his breath. He took out his room key and one of his daggers, coaxing the door open. The lock was fairly cheap, and he was inside in under a minute.

The room had the look of an extended stay. The occupant's luggage was completely unpacked, with selections of clothing arrayed in neat stacks. There was a wash basin and soap, clean linens, and a bottle of wine with one cup. The window was partly open, letting in the blue hue of morning. Ghethas looked out, careful not to be seen.

The students were breaking off into pairs, flourishing their wooden swords. He recognized Sir Jaron clearly now, walking behind a row of young men as they sized up their opponents. The other assistant, a tall and impressive man with elegant but practical clothes, walked past skirmishing students, pointing with a riding crop. Master Cord Freekirk paced back and forth, hands behind his back, scowling.

The students were all dressed similarly, with tight hose, leather shoes, and loose, comfortable tunics bound at the waist. There were few variations: some vests here, some pantaloons there, trousers, tall boots, short sleeves, a red headband. He began to give names to the more interesting students as they trained. There was Ox, Slippery, Coal, Wisp, the Old Man, Broomstick, the Barbarian, Badger...

He watched for quite some time, locking the door as an afterthought. It wouldn't do to have the tenant barge in on him, but he was prepared for that. He had a knife balanced for throwing, and a dagger for close-work. The view was so good that he decided he would share the room with a corpse for a few days if need be. He just had to wait for Sir Jaron to leave and lead him to his prey.

Eventually, the master called for everyone to sit in a large circle. Ghethas felt his legs cramping up, so he shifted from foot to foot, working out the pins and needles. He hoped his waiting would bear fruit. It would be nice to have some good news for his wife, who had told him repeatedly to abandon this hunt. *No faith in me,* he thought.

Master Cord had brought out two metal swords, and

this was causing a bit of a stir among the students.

"From now on, much of our individual sparring will be with metal blades," he was saying. "They are blunted but still dangerous. A blunt-edged blade can still cut if swung with enough force."

Sir Jaron was walking along the outside of the circle, looming over the seated students. He stopped behind Wisp, leaned down, and whispered something. The student shifted his legs and changed position.

Ghethas stared. The student had been sitting in an odd way, at least odd for a boy. He had been leaning to his side on one arm, legs together, bent at the knee. Ghethas had seen his wife sit on the ground like that, but never a boy or man; it would be uncomfortable to say the least. Now the boy was sitting cross-legged, leaning back on both hands, fitting in with the others.

Ghethas frowned as he tried to grasp the thought tickling his mind. He recognized the boy as the one who saddled Sir Jaron's horse last night. *His squire?* he wondered. *Must be.* He examined the lad closer, taking in the light, concealing clothing, the face and auburn hair, that blood-red headband. *The headband... Children of the Abyss! That's a Galindri headband! It's the Corrina bitch, by Llomaak's lungs. She's playing at being a boy!*

His heart began racing, his palms grew sweaty, and a thrill of adrenaline shot through his body, making him tremble. *If I only had a crossbow, I could finish her now. Damn me, why didn't I prepare? There's time, there's time. I can return later with all I need. To the pit with whoever stays here, I need this room. Thanks be to the Countless Lord.*

Later that day, Ghethas returned to his own room with a bundle. He spent the next hour preparing his tools, assembling the light crossbow, coating the bolts and his daggers in poison, and changing into different clothes so he would not be recognized as he fled. If he timed his shot well, he could be out of the building before anyone realized what had happened.

He checked the room across the hall, knocking and listening. No sound, not from the room or the courtyard beyond. It was midday and the students were likely eating lunch. He unlocked the door and checked inside, tensing to strike. *Empty.* He looked down the hall to make sure he was unseen, went inside, and locked the door behind him.

As he checked the room, he noticed a few things had changed: there were clothes missing, the bed was made but rumpled, and the wine bottle was empty. *Lucky bastard,* he thought. *We managed to miss each other again.* He went to the window and looked out into the courtyard, setting the crossbow on the nearby table.

The double doors to the main hall were open, letting the air circulate. The smells of cooked food mingling with sweat and dust wafted up to him, and his stomach grumbled. He could make out the legs of those seated nearest the doors, but no faces. He'd have to be patient.

Lunchtime was over finally, as the benches were pushed away and tables were moved aside. Shortly thereafter, the students began to trickle out into the courtyard. Master Cord stepped out of the hall, followed by his other assistant, the well-dressed fellow with the blond hair and chiseled features. They spoke together for a while as more students trickled out. *Still no 'Squire Cindra,'* he thought. *The audacity of it all. It's a brilliant scheme to be sure, but how does she manage to go undiscovered?* He noticed a big lad, the one he called Ox, stepping into the courtyard and lacing up his trousers. *So after lunch there's a break for the jakes. I'll wager she comes out last. Probably has to use a chamber pot in a privy room, away from prying eyes.*

A few more students assembled in the yard. Master Cord and his assistant finished their conversation, and the assistant hurried off to the school gates, opened them, and left. *Running an errand? Good. One less set of eyes.* He pulled the lever to cock the crossbow, then loaded a poisoned bolt. *Here comes Badger, Spots,*

Coal... There! Wisp, my little Lady Wisp... He hefted the weapon and stepped into a firing stance, waiting for them to line up with their backs to him, facing the master.

The Corrina girl still wore her Galindri headband, a nice, red flag to mark her no matter where she stood. Sir Jaron appeared now, conferring with the school master. The students began to line up in groups of five. Lady Cindra was in the front row with a student behind her, but from this height there was almost no way to miss. He rested the crossbow on the window sill, careful not to expose the weapon more than was necessary.

The breeze blew into the window, refreshing him. He had been sweating more than usual, and he wiped his brow to clear his vision. *I won't be thwarted by a drop of sweat,* he mused to himself. The noises of the tavern were pushed to the back of his awareness as he lined up his sights between the girl's shoulder blades. He took a deep breath, let it out slowly, and rested his fingers on the trigger lever.

A sound broke his concentration, sharp and alarming, the sound of a key turning in a lock. Cursing aloud, he spun and took aim as the latch turned and the door swung open. As soon as he saw the man's chest, he fired the weapon. The power stored in the bent limbs was released with a loud 'thrum' as the thick cord snapped forward, launching the heavy bolt across the room. The man's eyes widened as he responded, shutting the door fast enough for Ghethas to feel the wind of it, shutting it just enough to catch the bolt that would have pierced his heart.

Tossing the crossbow aside in disbelief, Ghethas went for his throwing knife. The door burst wide and a figure rushed in; tall and blond, muscled and furious, with fine clothes and chiseled features. *Holy blood, it's him!* Panicked, he threw the knife underhanded at the man's face, drawing his dagger with his other hand. The man altered his momentum, shifting his body into an uncanny dodge as the knife flew past. Ghethas had only just drawn the dagger when it was kicked from his grasp, spinning across the room.

Realizing he was desperately outmatched, the priest made to flee. He grabbed the crossbow from the bed and swung it at the fighting man, hoping it would distract him as he made for the door. He heard it crash against the wall as he burst into the hallway, going over the escape route he had planned for if things got completely buggered.

Ghethas was almost to the landing when he felt a sharp pain behind his thigh. Gasping, he slammed into the wall, lost his balance, and tumbled down the stairs. The boots of the warrior could be heard at the top of the steps as Ghethas rose in panic, scrambling to get his feet under him, struggling through the pain of his fall, and the numbness growing in his leg. Reaching back, he found the source of that numbness; it was the familiar leather-wrapped handle of a dagger, his own dagger, dipped in venom which was now coursing through his veins.

The numb feeling spread to his calf and buttocks, then to his foot and lower back. When it hit his spine, he fell to the floor, unable to do anything but scream silently. He heard voices, footsteps coming down the stairs. He felt his body lifted by the shoulders, saw a handsome face with piercing blue eyes, shouting angrily. Blackness took over his limbs and surrounded his vision, as if he was being swallowed by it. *I'm drowning, drowning in the Abyss,* he thought, *I am coming, Lord! Mash bah havaath gnen. I am coming...*

Chapter Eighteen

Birthright

The day after the ember swallow incident, Nixy's life had taken a truly odd turn. There were times when he would think about the particulars of it all and burst out in nervous laughter, or sometimes just sit quietly in disbelief. It was the kind of story that orphan children or street urchins all dreamed about, only so much weirder. Fate had placed him in the care of the lord and lady, being fed, clothed, and instructed like a noble-born, but that was only the half of it.

He was also a spy in their household, reporting to the Circle of Gold on Cindra's parents. He only had to tell Brother Dane if they were really happy but pretending not to be. And they were, because Cindra was alive. Would he be betraying her if he told? Would it be like sending up another stupid ember swallow, leading the Circle to the truth? Maybe if he said her parents were happy, but for another reason? These thoughts plagued him daily. Spies weren't supposed to pick and choose what secrets they kept. If the Circle learned that Nixy was holding back, they might think him a traitor, which he was, sort of.

To make matters weirder, Nixy was required to be present at an audience with the lord and lady. He was escorted to the count's study by armed guards, and there were more guards at the door and in the hall. He wanted to ask what was going to happen, but figured that would only betray his fear. *Eyes open, mouth shut. Eyes open, mouth shut.*

He expected to see the count frowning behind his desk, but the desk had been moved to make room for the chairs of state, typically found in the audience hall. The lord and lady were before him, both dressed in blue and gold finery, and crowned with golden coronets. Constable Fingelm was there as well, his normal glower replaced with a curious look. Ildric 'Talon' Finnael was there, and Drahn the Nose-Biter, and also a beautiful hooded woman with enormous, violet eyes. He had seen those eyes before, as if in a dream.

What happened next was something he was totally unprepared for. As soon as the door closed, they all bowed to him. Ildric, Fingelm, and Drahn bowed low, the blond woman curtsied gracefully, and the lord and lady bowed from the neck. Fingelm said, "Royal Highness."

This is a joke. It's some kind of weird joke, Nixy thought.

Fingelm continued, "Nixyalderthor DuQuayne, may I present Lady Wenyssaya of Du-Velthathwe, emissary from the elven lands to the east." She smiled, removed her hood, and Nixy's legs went weak. She was unnaturally beautiful, with large, almond-shaped eyes that shone like amethyst; hair like flowing cascades of gold, swept back to reveal delicate, pointed ears; and perfectly smooth skin that reminded him of honey and cream.

Wenyssaya spoke with a melodious voice, light and clear, "Othiis thayas, reviiam."

It was a language Nixy had never heard, yet somehow he understood, or he thought he did. *'Joyous meeting, my prince.' Why do they keep calling me that?*

"But I'm not a- a prince. I'm just a farmer's son." Nixy muttered. It didn't seem right to argue with such impressive people, but if they were having a joke on him, he wanted it to stop.

The count spoke, "Nixyalderthor, our honored guest. It has come to our attention that certain forces, thought long since departed, have been at work in the world of late. I believe the Lady Wenyssaya can explain everything." He motioned for her, and she nodded to him, taking a step forward.

Wenyssaya said, "I come on behalf of the Lord of the Shadowood, who sends his greetings. He bade me to welcome his lost heir, blood of his blood, the product of his love for a mortal woman who dwelt beside the boughs of his realm." She turned to the lord and lady. "He owes the life of his son to the bravery of your house, and he thanks you for keeping him safe. For this kindness, I am to deliver the undying gratitude of the Shadow Lord, and renew the offer of friendship that has long been dormant."

Nixy was truly confused. The Shadow Lord was supposed to be an elf that ruled the forest by his old home, stealing children who didn't mind their parents. He had never seen an elf before today, but had always believed in them. Still, if there was an elf prince in the castle, Nixy would have discovered it; he had certainly explored everywhere. It was almost as if they were talking about *him*, which was ridiculous.

Yet everyone was looking at him.

Wenyssaya came to stand by his side, placing a strange, painted hand on his shoulder. "I have journeyed a great many leagues to find you, my prince. From now on, I shall be your instructor and protector, until the time you are ready to meet your sire."

Nixy's life flashed before his eyes, back to the days of fear and uncertainty, living with his father in a poor shack on the outskirts of the village. He remembered the way people talked about him when he passed, how they called him 'ill-born,' and the other children were told not to play with him. He recalled his birthdays, when his father would come home drunk and angry; wallowing in bottomless sorrow for his beloved, departed wife, the mother Nixy had killed by being born.

I'm no prince. I'm nobody!

Then why were there monsters after him? Why did he have that cursed 'special luck' that made his life so strange? He thought back to the night he ran away from home, the night of his eighth birthday. He began to see with a new clarity, to examine the details that had been such a blur at the time. How exactly had he escaped that night? His father had come after him with a switch, his watery eyes shining in the flicker of the lone candle. Nixy had ducked into a dark corner to hide, pushing himself deeper into the shadows until... until he found himself outside and running, running for the safety of the woods. He hadn't used a door or a window.

The last thing Nixy remembered of his father was a look of panic on the man's face, the frantic grasping of his hands, his hoarse voice calling his name, growing fainter and hollow as the velvet darkness surrounded him. But if what this elf woman said was true, that man was never his father. His *real* father was an elf lord who ruled the Shadowood with a dark and dread power, stealing wayward children who didn't mind their parents...

Nixy made a huffing noise as his chest contracted. Before he knew what was happening or why, the feeling expanded into panic-stricken laughter that made him double over, made his sides ache. It was the most ridiculous joke that could be played on someone; a prince by birth, living in poverty and misery, stealing food to survive, huddling in alleys and doorways to stay warm, and struggling to impress a dangerous viper of a man so he might dole out an extra share of crumbs...

He collapsed on the floor, his laughter growing more painful as his chest tightened, turning into waves of fear and confusion. He began to cry in the midst of his convulsions, tears pouring from his eyes as his sobs became longer and thinner, stretching out into silent wail from deep within his throat.

He felt arms enclose around him, and a fragrance like wildflowers filled his gasping lungs. A soothing hum reverberated through his soul, calming him with its gentle music. He rocked in the arms of the elf maid, the truth spinning in his head and making him dizzy. The fabric of his life was ripped apart and tossed into the whirlwind, until he didn't know who he was anymore.

In the days following this revelation, Nixy had become withdrawn; he skipped meals or took them in his room, barely eating his favorite foods and leaving wonderful leftovers for the kitchen servants to finish. He even missed his daily lessons with Brother Dane, causing the priest to ask after his welfare, though it was probably motivated as much out of fear as genuine concern. Brother Dane had his own minders to answer to, and did not wish to disappoint them with gaps in his reports.

Nixy's heritage was to be kept a secret, but many could tell that something had changed. Nixy had been moved into new quarters that were reserved for visiting dignitaries, and an adjoining room was provided for the elven emissary as well. They spent a good deal of time together, and when Nixy went anywhere outside the walls, he was afforded the same security as a member of the noble house. Thankfully, he was still allowed to roam the castle grounds without an escort. He always had watchers though.

Wenyssaya did her best to enlighten the young prince about his birthright and did him the favor of remaining informal during their time together, putting him at great ease by calling him by his name and treating him like a normal boy. She answered his questions as best as she could, though often the answers led to more questions.

"What is my real father like?" he asked during one of their sessions.

Wenyssaya gathered her thoughts before answering, "The Shadow Lord is very old, though time does not change our kind as it does for mortals. He is tall and fair, with golden skin and long white hair that flows like water over a cliff face; his eyes are deep and troubled, for many an age has worn upon him, yet they are ablaze with undying fire, as jewels in the sunlight. He wears garments of gossamer silk, dark and fine, woven in the elder days when the forest was young. Upon one hand he wears a ring of silver, set with a gemstone the color of autumn leaves.

"There is a light that shines within the old ones, such as has not been seen among my people for many generations. When he sets his will to action, his power moves through the forest like a gentle breeze, or if his anger is roused, as a mighty wind that stirs the forest from the deepest root to the highest branch. He takes solace in the darkness of the deep woods, and wraps himself in shadow. It is his chosen element, that piece of the world that he calls his own."

Nixy considered all of this and asked, "Is he nice?"

Wenyssaya smiled and replied, "I cannot say I have met him. All that I know of him is from my dreams, and those dreams are strongest when Navithwi is nearby."

Nixy understood seeing people in dreams. He saw Wenyssaya's violet eyes long before he ever met her. "Is it a magic bird?" he asked.

"He is a bird who has spent his life in the Shadowood. He was given a charge to deliver his master's summons, and to be my guide. He has a bond with his master, to be sure, but he is not steeped in the Shadow as some creatures are."

"Like... like wolves?" Nixy asked, almost whispering.

"Perhaps," she said, noting his anxiety. "Have you seen strange wolves?"

Nixy nodded, "A few times, I've seen black wolves. Not just black, but *black* like pitch; so black you can't make out their fur, only their eyes and teeth. The troll that wanted my-" he gulped, "the troll said the black wolves protected me. But I'm scared of them. *Real* scared."

"Sometimes our protectors can be fearsome to behold. Yet, they are our protectors." She offered nothing more on the subject.

"So, why didn't my fa- um, the Shadow Lord send some of his own subjects? Wouldn't that have been quicker? You said you came a long way from the east."

She replied, "None dwell within the Shadowood that he calls kin. The humans fear him, and rightly so, for he guards the sanctity of the woods," she took Nixy by the hand and looked meaningfully into his eyes, making him flinch, "but there was one who did not fear him, one who saw great beauty in the woods; a human girl-child whose innocence and life were as a candle burning in the darkness, and he nurtured it."

"You mean my mother," Nixy said. He had Cutter, the magic knife with the Shadowood handle carved in the shape of a raven's head; he always wore it on his belt now. His real father had given it to Nixy's mother. Maybe he would learn why he let her die?

Nixy said quietly. "She died because of me. Because of him."

Wenyssaya caressed his face and said, "Do not blame yourself or your father for what happened, Nixyalderthor. It is the way of the world, birth and death. Know instead that you were born of love; that your father holds that love still in his heart, and shall do so until the ending of the world. Love for your mother, and love for you."

Nixy bowed his head, accepting her advice, but still found himself unable to follow it.

Chapter Nineteen

Tavern Talk

The training days grew shorter as the year wore on, and the southern heat began to give way to afternoon showers. Regardless of the weather, the training was done in the yard.

"You won't always be asked to fight on a beautiful spring day," Master Cord would bellow over the deluge. "Those of you who will purchase a suit of mail will be in for an even bigger treat! Try slogging through a quagmire with cold mud filling your armor!"

After such a day of training in the mud, the students would strip to the edge of modesty and do their best to clean off, lest they earn the wrath of Elmore the steward. They would carry their bundles to the scullery and launder the garments themselves, hanging them to dry on lines in the dormitory.

Cindra was conspicuously exempt. It was bad enough that the wet fabric revealed her breast wrappings underneath, forcing her to wear a vest on cloudy, muggy days. Expecting her to strip off any amount of clothing was to invite disaster. If she was lucky, most would assume it was extreme modesty, or shame over being the smallest in size, if not in stature. Even the Gaddisen boy was attaining some bulk to his wiry frame, and her fellow Dread Wolves were becoming fiercer-looking to the point of deserving their name. Padison had begun to look like a tow-headed, miniature bull, and Adric... well, Cindra had to admit that his new physique suited him quite nicely.

The natural solution was for her to act the squire again. She would help Sir Jaron out of his wet clothes, take off her soaked pantaloons, letting her long tunic hide her shape, and carry the whole bundle up to their room. Jaron would follow at his leisure while Cindra changed, and the laundry would be taken to the scullery after the other students had finished.

Washing was nothing new to Cindra, though she was unfamiliar with the modern conveniences. Her time with the Galindri had included regular wash days when camped by a river, but it mostly involved beating the clothes on a rock. Jaron had to show her how to use a washing bat, tub, and hog-bristle brush to scrub out the dirt. A twisting rack was used for the heavier protective fabrics.

"Are you sure you don't mind doing this?" Jaron asked her one evening as they prepared for bed. "If you like, I could have Celia do the washing with-"

"Don't be silly," Cindra scolded. "How would it look to the others, having someone else do our work?"

Jaron looked confused, "It would look rather natural, I imagine. The upper classes are expected to make a show of their wealth."

"So now you are teaching me how the upper class should act?" she said. Seeing him recoil a bit, she softened her voice. "I'm sorry. I didn't mean to snap. It's just that I don't want to be treated differently."

He placed his hands on her shoulders, rubbing them through her nightshirt. "I know. You show it every day, trying harder than anyone else just to fit in. I was the same, but for different reasons."

"Your father was a farmer," she said.

Jaron nodded, "Not in my lifetime, but yes. We lived on the farm until my mother passed, then we moved to the city. I'd never seen a building larger than a barn, and suddenly I was living in a top-floor room in Lowcourt."

"It's odd; I feel them judging me with their eyes, especially when it rains and I don't undress like everyone else," she said.

"But you're following your knight's orders," Jaron offered.

"I could do the same thing while removing my wet clothes," she replied. "It's *odd*. They all know it's odd. They think I'm ashamed of myself."

"You have nothing to be ashamed of, my love." Jaron ran his hands down her limbs, feeling the firmness beneath, and he held her, resting his chin upon her head. "I think you are becoming rather dangerous-looking."

"Dangerous looking?" Cindra asked, "Because my muscles are growing? Do I frighten you, Jaron?"

He chuckled and said, "It's just different, that's all. I've seen strong women before, but never so..."

"So what?" she pressed, backing out of his embrace.

He nearly squeaked the word. "Boyish?"

"I am *boyish?*" she asked, looking at him incredulously. "You mean I am boyish when I am not dressed as a boy?"

Jaron retreated, moving to turn down his bed. *Now I've stepped in it*, he thought. "No, not- I meant that... It's not that I don't find you beautiful, Cindra."

She had already undone her wrappings, so she drew her nightshirt tighter to accentuate her shape. "*These* are boyish?" she demanded, and Jaron could not help but look. Her breasts were high, shapely and firm, defying the pull of the fabric. She turned around, "And this?" Jaron sat heavily on the bed, recalling the first time he had seen her bathing in a forest pool. She had filled out even more in the last year; her slim waist and gently-curving hips granting her what boorish fellows referred to as a 'peach bottom.' The linen clung to her thighs, but was high enough to expose much of her strong and sculpted legs.

Jaron, dressed in his nightshirt as well, was greatly stirred and felt the need to climb into bed and pull up the covers. He stammered, "I-I was not meaning your-um, female attributes. I was only speaking of those parts I see regularly, your back, arms, shoulders..."

Cindra turned, letting the nightshirt hang normally. "Boyish," she said, daring him to go further.

"Boyish was a wrong word," he admitted. "I've just never known a woman to look so-"

"Dangerous looking," she said.

Jaron was defensive now, "You are becoming a trained sword- er, woman, or sword-maiden... there's not even a word for it. You are as skilled as any of the new recruits, and your body will grow with your skill." He had not really imagined what she might look like after two years of fighting school, and it gave him pause.

Cindra sensed his uneasiness and asked, "Can you love a woman who threatens you so?"

Jaron sighed, "I *do* love you, Cindra. And you *don't* threaten me."

She folded her arms, noticing his eyes drifting to her chest. "Or perhaps you fear that your tastes will stray towards strong arms and shoulders? Who knows, you might have more in common with Gavadaire LuVe-" her words were cut off as a pillow hit her in the face.

"That's not funny, Cindra." Jaron had his arms crossed too, which meant he was annoyed. "I have only desired the company of women, but this... this will take some getting used to! You dress as a boy, you answer to a boy's name, you train with men for combat," he sighed, "Not many men could adjust to this life, these changes. A woman passing as a man; it breaks the laws of society and nature." He slumped against the headboard in exasperation as words failed him.

"I have had much to adjust to also," she said coolly. "I watched my closest friend die to save me, and I have spent years in hiding." She kicked his pillow back at him and paced the floor. "I am not doing this to make you uncomfortable or to test you. I am doing it to survive, Jaron. I was nearly exposed before the school when Gavagul flew into the hall. The next day that wicked priest is found in LuVestra's room; the same man who caught me at Pinikal, the *same man* who was at my betrothal banquet with his wife! Even now, four months on, there might be eyes watching this school. Must I now worry that you no longer think of me as a woman?" She remembered to keep her voice down when fighting, lest Sir Cord pound on the wall.

"I never said that!" Jaron retorted. This had started with a question about doing laundry, and now she was putting words in his mouth, making her anxieties and trials into weapons against him. That alone left no doubt that she was a woman, but Jaron kept this to himself.

"You were thinking that," she accused.

"Gods, help me. I'm in love with a mind reader," he said. Sarcasm never helped, but it felt better than unconditional surrender. "I suppose I needn't speak at all."

"That would be an improvement," she snapped. She stormed over to her cot and put herself to bed, turning her back to him.

He stared at her for a long time, wondering if she was waiting for him to apologize. He was no stranger to the 'monthly moon madness' as his father called it; he knew her foul disposition would pass, but it didn't make things any easier. He supposed it was especially difficult for her not being in the company of women, who would be more understanding and comforting, not to mention assisting in all the little private measures that no woman was very keen to share. *Perhaps Celia could be trusted with Cindra's secret, to make things easier?*

Now was not the time to ask either of them, so he said, "Good night, Cindra," and blew out the lamp.

"*Good night,*" she growled.

Another Highday arrived and the students marched to Balkon's temple, though Cindra had been very much on guard since the priest of the Countless Lord was found and killed. Jaron and Master Cord had debated in private about keeping her from attending, but she argued that her absence would only draw more attention to her. They relented as usual, and she was allowed to go to mass with her friends.

After mass, several students went to the Red Eagle Tavern for a pint of ale. The common room was dark and cool, with the door and windows facing to the southwest, out of the noonday sun. Cindra occasionally glanced at the foot of the stairs where the priest had fallen months before. A barmaid had burst into the courtyard and told everyone what had happened. Cindra accompanied Jaron, Cord, and a few more curious students to the scene, and she had grabbed Jaron's elbow upon recognizing the dead man. Her urgent look and fierce grip told him all he needed to know.

Cindra sat with her team at a table near the back where the lads could watch the tavern maids with an unobstructed view, sometimes chatting them up while they were trapped behind the serving bar. Bradric Hyne had joined them as well, since his team had not arrived yet.

"Here, she's my favorite," Bradric said of a larger serving wench. "Hips, that's what I like."

"I thought you liked 'em with hooves too," said Paddy, ducking the big lad's swatting hand.

Adric pointed out another woman, younger and slimmer, who was carrying three mugs of ale in each hand. "That's my girl there. Neck and shoulders is what I like. She wears those dresses that show them off, just for me."

"Just for you!" they all jeered, knowing he'd never so much as spoken to her.

"Below the knee," Padison said. "I love those Gali-style short skirts, and those low slip-shoes with laces. The barmaids at the Hawk and Arrow wear them, I hear."

"Below the knee 'cause it's all you can see!" Bradric joked, nearly knocking the lad over with a shoulder slap. Padison laughed, knowing he had earned it.

"Morrin? What about you?" asked Cindra. LiKeska was a curiosity, for he would moon endlessly about the exploits of some hero of legend, and most recently, about Gavadaire LuVestra. She suspected he was either a hopeless hero-worshiper, or a 'shepherd's ewe,' or both.

Morrin sat up straight, gathered his thoughts and said, "I believe the entirety of her person is to be viewed as a work of art, together and complete. Her grace and poise must inspire, her form and beauty, enchant; her wisdom and heart, enliven; and her love, inflame."

Cindra smiled at that, and the others nodded mutely, trying to think of something to say that was half as profound.

"Inis?" she asked.

Inis DeGhat sat up straight, composed himself as Morrin had done, and said, "Tits."

Padison was in the middle of a drink when he laughed, spewing ale on Bradric. Everyone at the table roared with laughter.

Once they had gathered their wits again, Adric asked, "What about you, Dillan?"

Cindra didn't have to fumble for an answer; both men and women had a feature she found attractive and revealing. "Eyes," she said. "You can tell a lot from the eyes; if they're shy or confident, honest or shifty. Words can lie, but eyes rarely do."

What had first captured her attention about Jaron was his eyes. They were deep and honest, full of feeling and sincerity. He could look like a sad puppy or laugh with his eyes if he chose, and no doubt he used it to his advantage. He was charming but vulnerable and it all showed in his eyes.

"May I join you lads?" asked a familiar voice from behind Cindra. Gavadaire LuVestra came down the stairs. He had changed out of his Highday clothes, but still looked elegant. The lads offered him a space on the end of the bench next to Adric and across from Dillan. *Gavadaire has nice eyes*, Cindra thought to herself. *Intense, piercing eyes.*

Instructors did not often gather socially with students; it was bad for discipline. Gavadaire did not seem to care as he called for a load of bread, broke it, and passed it around.

"A delightful pause in the training, yes? Ah, I love Highdays. Go to temple and rest, so unlike the monastery where there was mass every day." He took a swig of his ale, not spilling a drop.

All Cindra knew of his past was from Master Cord, with dubious commentary from Jaron, but she was curious to learn the facts herself, so she took the bait. "How did you learn to fight while living in a monastery, captain?" Dillan asked, using his school title.

"Aha!" he laughed, "I take it you do not know of the Su'Kraal Brotherhood? The Sons of Kraal are warrior monks who revere the Divine King Arathus. As such, they train to be supreme defenders of the law. The army that adds Su'Kraal monks to its ranks is a feared army indeed." Gavadaire smiled proudly.

"Never heard of them," said Padison.

Morrin said, "Well, you are hardly a student of history, are you?" Padison made a face at him.

"Since the days of Kraal the Great, the brotherhood has practiced the art of war. They hold teachings that were passed down by Kraal himself. They study strategy, armed and unarmed combat, even Divine Alchemy to be used in battle against the forces of Chaos." He paused for effect, checking to see if his audience was enraptured yet. "They have not marched to war in over two hundred years, but a lord need only secure their pledge to do so and his enemy gives up the field."

"So no one's seen them fight in two centuries?" asked Inis. "Seems like a hollow reputation, begging your pardon, captain." Young DeGhat was not as impressed by reputation as his fellow squire Morrin, apparently.

Gavadaire only smiled, "Fair enough, but perhaps you would like to learn some of their techniques? Judge for yourself if it is a hollow reputation."

This did get their attention, causing Adric to ask, "When? We already have full days ahead of us."

"Perhaps on Highdays," LuVestra suggested. "We can meet in the yard and practice."

"Give up our one day off?" asked Bradric, holding on tighter to his mug.

Cindra was tempted, but had to ask, "Does Master Cord approve of this?"

"He has consented," Gavadaire said, turning his sky-blue eyes on her. "He believes that if you are willing to put forth the extra work, you will benefit greatly."

They looked at one another, the same question on their minds. Adric asked, "Is it because he thinks the Dread Wolves aren't doing well?"

"No, no!" laughed Gavadaire, "This offer is open to all students, but yours was the closest table." He waited for the relief on their faces to spread before lowering his voice. "In truth," he leaned forward, encouraging them to do the same, "Master Freekirk is concerned about the news from the west, about the death of the king, and what it might mean."

"Civil war," breathed Cindra. The others nodded mutely.

Gavadaire agreed, "It may be in our futures, my friends. It is wise of Master Freekirk to use any advantage he can. Your Sir Jaron, for example," He startled Cindra as he addressed her directly. "He is an excellent horseman and swordsman, and I am sure much can be learned from him. He even has experience in battle, I understand."

"But you yourself have seen combat," said Morrin, as if Gavadaire had forgotten. "You are undefeated, are you not?"

"Indeed I am," Gavadaire said proudly, sitting back and straightening. "But my victories were in single combat, both in duels and tournaments. Sir Jaron and Master Freekirk have seen battle, which is quite a different thing." He looked into his ale wistfully, as if sorry he had missed the chance to fight in a war. "The battlefield is chaotic, full of the clamor of hundreds of men and beasts fighting for their lives; cannons roar like thunder, arrows fall like rain, death surrounds you, and every man is tested to his limits." His eyes lifted, returning to the faces of the young men, who were in rapt attention.

To Cindra it seemed as though Gavadaire sought to prove himself beyond his already legendary accomplishments. According to Jaron, war was a thing best left behind and not longed for. *Perhaps that was the real difference between them*, Cindra thought.

"Perhaps the real difference between Sir Jaron and I," Gavadaire said, "is that I am not bound to a particular lord, and only owe service to the Su'Kraal. I could become a sell-sword, but I was raised for a life of honor, not to fight for the highest bidder. Ah, such is life," he mused, casting a hand in the air in resignation.

"Why have you not become a knight then?" Cindra asked. "You might choose to serve a lord, like Count Casselvane for example. With your reputation, I am sure he would offer a knighthood gladly." She thought to herself, *And we need all the help we can get.*

The other lads looked to LuVestra for answers, though most knew what he might say. It was common for squires to remain squires these days.

"Ah, Dillan." LuVestra smiled, "Cost is the answer. I have no income to speak of, no estates to tax, and none who employ me to stand in readiness." He took another swig of ale, "I attended the school on the good graces of the Su'Kraal, who shall reimburse Master Freekirk for any costs beyond my meager stipend." He gestured to his mug of ale as an example, "Otherwise I could not afford to serve as a knight would be expected."

Cindra thought that odd. "Why then do you stay here at the inn, rather than the available room next to ours?" *Not that I'm complaining. Jaron and I need the privacy, and he killed that assassin priest after all.*

Gavadaire seemed uncomfortable, glancing at the spot where the intruder had lay four months ago. He said, "I... wish to keep others out of harm's way, if possible. I am not as well-loved everywhere as here at the school." He broke into a charming smile, but Cindra had read his eyes.

*Of course! He thinks the assassin was after **him**.* She asked, "Has someone sent a killer after you before?" The other lads waited for an answer.

Gavadaire's smile faded slowly. "Let us not speak of these things on such a fine day. We were discussing knighthood, and the sad state of my finances, as I recall."

The other lads chuckled as Gavadaire explained, "For a knight to go to war, he must first have his own armor, weapons and warhorse, as well as an aide or two in support," he ticked off the items on his fingers as he spoke. "Then there are extra horses, both for riding and baggage. A camp will be needed if he is to sleep warm and dry," he leaned forward, "Then there is the retinue."

"Retinue?" Cindra asked. Jaron had never mentioned any of this at all.

"Yes, a knight is expected to bring more than just himself to a battle," Gavadaire exclaimed, tossing an arm in the air with flourish. "Archers, footmen, light cavalry, whatever he can muster from his own household or lands; typically one man per farm in the case of conscripts. The retinue needs retainers as well, mind you. Supplies, proper cooks, grooms... none of this is paid for by the knight's lord, save for the wages of the fighting men."

Inis added, "Of course, a poorer knight might do with much less; say, a couple retainers and horses, plus the supplies."

"Well, I have my own horse," Cindra said.

"A riding horse, or a war horse?" asked Inis.

"He's a Gali bay pony," she answered proudly.

"That will not do for an armed cavalry charge," Morrin said. "Perhaps as a scouting horse or light cavalry to harass enemy flanks..."

Inis added, "And if you like him, which you seem to, you likely will not wish to ride him into battle. Horses make large targets."

Cindra flinched at that. She had not considered that T'ózha might be killed in battle. It was a sobering thought.

"It's that yearling in stable, yeah?" Bradric asked. "He looks old enough for backing. You got a trainer?"

"Backing?" Cindra asked.

"Riding," Bradric replied. "My dad's a horse trainer, and he owns a yard in town for ground work."

"Oh," she said, "I have only been leading him on walks with Sir Jaron. Is it expensive?"

Bradric shrugged, implying that it was a conversation best held in private.

Gavadaire leaned back with hands on the table, "So, I am without rank because I cannot afford the obligation, nothing more. There is no great benefit to being a knight in this age; heavy cavalry is not so unstoppable as it used to be. Speed of horse is nothing compared to the speed of cannon shot, or a hail of arrows." He sighed heavily, "Ah well, learn as much as possible, that is my advice."

Some of the lads were surprised to hear such talk. Adric asked, "So you think mounted knights are no longer useful?"

"Everything has its time, my friend." Gavadaire replied. "Think of the armies of old, with their chariots and slingers. They dominated the plains of the Bythian Empire, but were useless in the mountains of

Celvestria. The Celvestrians had their tight formations of swordsmen, but they could never hold the thick woodlands of western Hibland, or the lowland marshes against the more agile native armies." He took in the blank stares around him and realized he might be exceeding the known military history of his audience. "The point, as I come to it, is that no army is perfect for all times and occasions. For every attack, there is a counter, though it may take centuries to be widely used. Heavy cavalry has already met defeat against ranks of long spears or cannons. They would devastate an enemy's unguarded flank, but in a direct frontal assault against a modern army... No, times change and so must we if we are to remain useful."

This made perfect sense, though Cindra was a little disappointed that she was training in what might be a dying art. Mounted warriors had been indispensable for centuries, earning a place in the most celebrated of songs and poems. Were they soon to be discarded as newer weapons took the field?

"What do you see as the future of warfare, captain?" Cindra asked.

"Oh, I am no Diviner. But I think perhaps wizardry might have a place one day. Consider how the Mystic College trains wizards to perform useful magic. You think they only learn spells to clean the streets and light lamps? No! They reach into every aspect of life now, making little trinkets that anyone might use. They would be foolish not to look towards warfare, if they are not already. Cannon powder came from their alchemy, and see how it has changed the way we fight? I think there will be armies of wizards on the battlefield one day, mark me."

A voice from the next table said, "Beg pardon captain, but not unless the battle takes place on a spirit well." Filbert Gaddisen had been listening to the conversation with Halvoy Quenlorden and Mat Belvine, two of his teammates. Filbert came from a family in which the men studied at the Mystic College and joined the local casting guilds; one uncle was even in the employ of a high lord in the north. He was therefore a bit of an authority on the subject. "Wizards can't be casting spells all day. It's exhausting work, pulling all that magic through your body and mind. One mistake and you can pass out or worse, and the trickier the spell, the more dangerous it is to cast." He fluttered his fingers in a complex series of motions for effect, making some of the lads flinch. "Wizard towers and schools are built on spirit wells, so casting is much easier," he said as he took a sip of ale, "but once you leave it, it gets much harder and tiring."

Gavadaire motioned in his animated way, dismissing the lad's argument. "In a battle all men grow weary, all is dangerous. And I dare say, a wand is lighter than a sword any day, no?" He smiled at his audience.

Filbert replied, "But concentration is key. All we've got to do as soldiers is shout 'Charge!' and go hit things. A wizard's got to recite Celvestrian phrases aloud, build complex patterns and symbols in his head, then pull the power of creation through his body and hope he doesn't *burn out his brain*." He knocked on the table to emphasize the last four words. "If you think soldiers do poorly when hungry, tired, and sick, then you don't want to be around a wizard in the same condition."

Cindra asked, "But aren't there already war wizards?" She knew there were, but Dillan might not.

Filbert nodded, "It's true, but they are very specialized and *very* expensive. I've only heard of an army employing three at most, and they aren't on the front lines."

"I've seen a war wizard in action," said Mat, the sell-sword, "I was with Lord Voldon's company up north. We were putting down a local rebellion- some baron or another, I forget who. Anyhow, we charge across a grassy field to engage them, and we come to find the ground was thick mud. Hadn't rained in months, mind you. Worse, the grass covering the mud was as sharp as razors. What we thought was a route turned into a trap."

"How did some rebel baron afford a war wizard?" Filbert asked.

"No idea," Mat said. "But he wasn't like any wizard I've seen before or since. Had the look of that Koorla lad in the Thorn Bears. Maanok, or I'm a hog farmer."

"*Were* you ever a hog farmer?" Padison had to ask.

"Vintner," Mat answered.

"A grape squisher!" Paddy said.

"Rock nipper," Mat retorted. Padison made a face at him.

There's that term again, Cindra thought.

Gavadaire wanted to continue his debate and said, "But magic can be stored in crystals, can it not? Spells can be used by the common man using trinkets, glowstones, and the like. Say a magic word and *d'jallé!* You have a spell! I have used these myself, they are fantastic."

Filbert nodded, "All those trinkets cost money, and all lose magic over time. They don't do anything very powerful, mind you; glowstones are small and cheap because they don't need a lot of magic to kindle. Powerful spells take larger and better crystals, even gemstones. I don't think any lord will spend a fortune in jewels for his common soldiers to carry around. Arrows are cheaper and more effective."

Many of the lads smiled at the thought, considering what they would do if handed valuable magic jewels and told to go fight.

"Ha, perhaps not," agreed Gavadaire, "But would it not be amusing if slings returned to battle, throwing spell stones instead of pebbles? As I say, it may be impractical now, but I tell you somewhere it is being studied. It is the way of the world, is it not?"

Everyone nodded, agreeing to consider the possibilities. They also agreed to meet next Highday in the courtyard after mass, so that Gavadaire might teach them the secrets of the legendary Su'Kraal monks.

Chapter Twenty

The Su'Kraal Way

"I don't like it," Jaron said. "I don't know why Cord is letting this continue."

Cindra had a feeling he would respond like this, so she had prepared. "If you recall, *Sir Jaron*, you yourself have a preference for a foreign style," she said. "You have studied the dueling arts of the Storm Isles of Onkanshu, as you keep telling me."

"I do *not* keep telling you that. I mentioned it once or twice," he replied, clearly annoyed. "Besides, those styles are battle-tested. But this Su'Kraal style... what do we know about these monks anyway?"

"They are legendary warriors, from what Gavadaire and Morrin LiKeska say," she replied. "Apparently, their reputation alone can win battles."

"So no one has tested this reputation?" Jaron asked.

"That's actually what Inis said," she had to admit.

Jaron threw his hands in the air, "Well, at least *someone* was thinking straight."

"What do you mean by that?" Cindra asked, challenging him.

"You are *my* squire," he replied, only then realizing how bizarre that sounded. "I do not want someone else filling your head with wild notions. You've been going on all week about the Sons of Kraal, about raising a retinue, buying extra warhorses, using magic artillery... You need to focus on your training and keep your eyes open for threats. We don't know if that priest-assassin was working alone."

"Why, Sir Jaron. You sound so possessive." She raised her eyebrows in that way her mother did when her father was being ridiculous.

"I- you-, ugh!" He stammered and stamped about. "This is not about me, Cindra! This is about your safety. We know this 'Julen Gordon' fellow had a wife, and it's likely she is an accomplice. You said so yourself."

"It has been four months now, and there have been no further attempts," she replied, "Gavadaire thinks *he* was the target. Only you, Cord, and I know the truth." Her voice was confident, but she couldn't help recalling the powerful grip of the masked men as they prepared to do vile things to her. *'My wife is the understanding kind,' that's what he had said. Not 'what she doesn't know won't hurt her.' His wife knew and accepted it. What else could she be but an accomplice?*

"We kept silent about the crossbow and the poisoned blades, yes. But no one has seen his wife since the attack," Jaron said. "She could still be out there, waiting to finish what her husband started."

"She may not even know," Cindra argued. "It happened the day after Gavagul found me, and it didn't seem well-planned at all." Jaron crossed his arms and raised an eyebrow, his doubt obvious. "Think about it," she said. "You have learned where your prey is hiding, and you know she has the same routine every day. What do you do? You bide your time, that's what. You set up in an unoccupied room, you choose your moment. Maybe you use a disguise until the deed is done. Maybe you keep watch, and learn that she goes into the stable every night to tuck in her horse."

"You do what now?" he asked.

"Don't worry, I tuck Vortigern in too," she said. "The point is, if he had learned where I was and told his wife, he wouldn't have done something so rash and stupid."

"And how do you know that?" he asked, unconvinced.

"Because it's a wife's job to stop her husband from doing rash and stupid things," she replied.

Master Cord stood before the assembled students in the hall on the next Highday, after the worship service. "I have some announcements, so pay attention. We are approaching the stage of your training called the focus sessions, where each of you will meet with me in this hall for an hour every few days, to refine your techniques, learn new ones, and be evaluated. Captains Jaron and Gavadaire will oversee daily exercises. I will post the rotations later today, so if you can't read, ask someone who can. I don't want to be kept waiting.

"The school will remain open through winter during the term, although most training will be individual and indoors. We will still have morning and evening drills." This led to some groans and murmured complaints. "This isn't the frozen Peningrand, or even the Casselvane Highlands," Cord barked. "This is Portshia, and it doesn't get cold enough to sit around and get fat."

Several students poked or nudged big Bradric, who swatted at them, saying, "Shove off, rock-nippers! Or by Balkon's balls..." This only made everyone burst into laughter.

Cindra leaned over to Adric and asked softly, "For the love of Selvina, what is a rock-nipper?"

Adric smiled and said, "Portshia used to have silver mines long ago. They would hire dwarfs to work in the smaller shafts, and when they had children, or 'nippers,' they would work in the mines too. A 'rock-nipper' is a dwarf child."

Cindra recalled stories of the dwarf district, an old

part of Portshia where the little people once lived together. Rejected by their families as misshapen or cursed, they started families of their own. *Mystery solved.*

"Quiet, quiet," Master Cord boomed. "Finally, as you may or may not know, our Captain Gavadaire has offered to supplement your training with the techniques of the Su'Kraal monks. I have consented to this because we live in troubled times, and I want to give you all the best experience we can manage in two short years. If you are interested, lessons will begin after midday meal every Highday." Some more grumbling and groaning was heard, but also excited whispers. No one wanted to give up their one day of rest, unless it was for something really worthwhile. "Now go change out of your parade dress and get ready to eat."

Cheers and the shuffle of feet preceded the emptying of the hall.

"What is the best fighting style?" LuVestra asked, striding before his students. Many called out '*Duerbrik*' out of loyalty or since the grand master was standing nearby. Others called out the names of other famous schools, including Rejick Ratham, who shouted 'Greenfellow *Maurbrik*.' Gavadaire waved them into silence, smiling at their enthusiasm. "No, no, the best style is the one that suits your situation, be it aggressive, defensive, quick, or measured. Why then am I here to teach you the Su'Kraal way, if it is not the 'best' style?" he paused, "Because no style is effective if it can be avoided."

This caused a murmuring among the students who were hoping for something grander and more impressive than avoiding combat. There were some disappointed looks, but all were waiting for him to offer more. After all, he did not win so many duels by running away.

"Sir Jaron, if you would please come forward to assist me?" Gavadaire called to the knight, who was leaning against a pillar with his arms folded. Jaron straightened in surprise, unaware that he was to be a part of the lesson. Sir Cord smiled and gave him a slap on the shoulder to get him moving. Gavadaire took up a sword of blunt steel. "If you would be so kind as to strike at me with this?" he asked, offering Jaron the sword.

Jaron took the blade, but said, "I will not strike at an unarmed man, Gavadaire, lesson or no." He had his own honor to think of, not to mention his pride. It would not be fitting if he injured the man in a training exercise.

"Ah, I thought not," said Gavadaire, "therefore I shall have blade also, but I will not be using it in this demonstration." He winked to the students who were becoming interested in the tension between the two men. Everyone knew the knight of Calilon and the adventurer from Aurilon were not fast friends. Gavadaire took up his own blunt blade, swishing it theatrically. "Now, you shall see that which has made the monks of Su'Kraal legendary and feared. I promise not to hurt your Sir Jaron," he added, looking to Dillan, "but I need a man of his skill to demonstrate."

The men faced off in the courtyard. Jaron took the stance of a *Daerbrik* fighter with arming sword, holding it before him in a guard position, while keeping his other arm close so as not to be an easy target, but ready to grapple if needed. His opponent simply stood with feet apart, sword at his side, as if holding it only for the knight's benefit. He nodded to Jaron to begin at his leisure; his face now bereft of its cocky assurance, his eyes taking in his opponent's every movement.

"*Gher yaas,*" Jaron called out, and he stepped up and swung his blade, intent on hitting the man whether he parried the blow or not. He aimed for the man's padded torso, but Gavadaire stepped aside, and the swing passed by harmlessly. Jaron reversed his swing and delivered a crossing blow to Gavadaire's shoulder, stepping in further to insure that it landed. The man bent his back to let the swing pass over his chest, regaining his stance quickly as Jaron aimed a high strike at his neck. The attack was a dangerous one, even if the swords had been made of wood, but Gavadaire only stepped to the side to let it pass before him.

Jaron became flustered as the students cheered; he came on again with a fierce combination of slashes, both high and low, that should have forced the man to block or parry with his blade, but Gavadaire only dodged with more alacrity, bending, twisting, and ducking under every attack. Jaron's strength was spent chopping only at the air.

Jaron made a few more attempts before he decided he was tired of being made to look a fool, so he lifted his sword in salute to his opponent. "Impressive," he said.

LuVestra returned the salute with a polite smile and said, "I thank you for your assistance, Sir Jaron. Well done." He turned to the students with a flourish and said, "That is an example of what I have to offer; the ability to avoid any attack while your opponent tires himself, leaving openings for you to exploit. Not everyone becomes adept at this training, for it requires great reflexes and a keen eye for the intention of another, but to those who are able to grasp the fundamentals, it will prove to be most invaluable."

Cindra could see that Jaron was shaken by the contest. Surely he was now imagining what a real engagement would be like if his opponent chose to attack instead of avoid. She wanted to say something to sooth his wounded pride, but it would have to wait. LuVestra was calling for interested students to stand forward, and Cindra was interested indeed.

Gavadaire spent the next few hours evaluating their response time and ability to anticipate. Luckily he was using a wooden sword, so injuries were few. Many students could be easily faked into ducking or dodging when there was no real attack, while some were at a loss without a sword or buckler. It was a result of constant drilling, and the students were forced to unlearn what had been pounded into them through the year.

Gavadaire would say, "A cup is most useful when it is empty," urging them to open their awareness and not depend on trained responses. Many students grew frustrated, and Cindra thought they might not return for more lessons.

For her part, Cindra did rather well. She was smaller and faster than most of her comrades, and had watched Gavadaire with many other students before it was her turn to face him. She had observed his eyes and shoulders, waiting for any twitch or flicker of movement to foretell a strike. His feet also gave away his intentions as he shifted his weight, indicating whether a blow would fall from the right or the left. While most of the students watched their fellows during the tests, Cindra watched Gavadaire.

When her turn came, she stood before the man with her feet apart as she had seen him do with Jaron. Her eyes watchful for any movement and her experience with other sparring partners sharpening her reactions. She was quite aware of the fact that she was without sword or buckler, and made no attempts to guard herself with her arms. Gavadaire had mostly kept his arms at his sides, using them for balance during his demonstration.

"Ready, Dillan?" he asked, his sky-blue eyes smiling down at her.

She nodded, trying to lose herself in the moment, reacting by instinct alone. The first blow nearly struck her shoulder, but she had read the man's intentions correctly, bending and twisting at the waist to duck under the swing. It had not been overly fast or dangerous, but would have left a bruise if it had landed. The next was aimed at her leg, which was now the foremost target. She shifted her weight and brought her knee to her chest, forcing her to plant her foot down quickly lest she fall. She saw Gavadaire draw the sword back and shift his foot forward. Without thinking, she flexed and snapped her body like a cat, leaping out of the range of his incoming thrust.

"Good!" Gavadaire said, advancing two quick steps, faking right and slashing left. Cindra ducked under the blade and spun aside, but her opponent reversed and leveled a slash at her head. Eyes wide, she arched her back and flexed like a bow, letting the sword whistle through the air above her.

"Excellent!" Gavadaire cried. "You have the grace and balance of a dancer, young Dillan." He patted her on the shoulder and called for the next lad to come forward.

Cindra smiled widely at the praise, the thrill of the trial making her giddy. She was thankful now for her earlier dance instruction, both in her castle days and among the Galindri.

"Well done, Dillan!" said Padison, slapping her on the rump as she sat on the ground next to him. It nearly made her jump back up, and she fought the urge to punch him. *He thinks I'm a boy,* she reminded herself, *and that's what boys do sometimes.* Still, she had even more empathy for those tavern wenches who received such treatment from drunkards every night.

"You did well yourself," she said to Padison. "He didn't touch you either."

Adric, who was nursing a bruised shoulder, said, "When you got a big mouth like Paddy, you learn to duck and dodge a lot. He's like a cockroach, I swear."

Cindra agreed, "Even if you step on him, he keeps running around, mocking you." Padison just shrugged.

Finnas Avenoth, the friendlier of the two notorious brothers, had avoided being hit. His brother Ferrol, who had received a bruised thigh and shin, was sure to make sure he got his fair share later. Maadi Gaavi had no trouble avoiding the blows, since it was a skill he had possessed upon arrival. His people fought with little in the way of armor, relying on quickness and deception to overcome a foe. Cindra's cousin Gaius had avoided receiving a solid hit, suffering only a sore finger. Master Cord and Sir Jaron were also among those tested, and both did very well, as one might expect. Cindra had never seen Cord Freekirk move so quickly and gracefully, and Jaron more than made up for his earlier performance. She was happy he had consented to join the group.

By day's end, Gavadaire had decided which students among those interested were ready to be taught, and which needed to further hone their basic skills. Those who were not interested at all included Stansig and Mat, both of whom were older and treasured their day of rest. Bradric Hyne was strong and fast, but not very agile, and he also liked sleeping the day away. All told, more than half of the students participated, including Rejick Ratham and some of his friends.

Gavadaire put them through a regimen of stretching exercises and drills, meant to train the body in the basic evasions of the Su'Kraal style. As he led them through the movements, he shared nuggets of the philosophy of the Sons of Kraal.

"Like the wind, I cannot be hit. If you attack me, you must approach me. If you approach me, I shall yield and strike, defend and attack. The wind blows fiercely, but cannot be struck." He recited this as they practiced stepping and twisting, weaving their bodies from side to side. "In principle, this is not unlike your former training," he said. "But instead of using weapons to turn a blow and counterattack, you will learn to use minimal effort to avoid blows entirely, looking for openings in your opponent's defenses.

"Ducking can include an attack on the feet or legs, a sidestep can precede an upward slash or a thrust. An opponent's force can be used against him, throwing him off balance to devastating effect."

This and more they learned throughout the day, which ended only when Celia rang the dinner bell.

Chapter Twenty One

Twist

Brother Dane ran his fingers through his beard as he stared out the rectory window, his brow knitted in worry. He had been informed that his daily lessons with Nixy DuQuayne would resume today, but the source of his worry was not that they had been out of contact; it was what the boy would have to say. Of course, Dane had to report the suspension of their lessons to the Circle of Gold; there was nothing to be done for it, and he told them all he knew, which was little.

He feared for the lad and his new guardian, the glorious, golden woman who was rumored to be an elf. The Circle had been too interested in the advent of her arrival and the sequestering of the boy. His contact seemed most disturbed about it, and the man was disturbing enough as it was. Dane would see Nixy and the elf woman on occasion as they walked through the yard, and he wondered if he should warn them, but he dared not approach. Assuming he could overcome the distraction of the woman's beauty, it would be difficult to explain how he knew they were in danger.

Dane straightened and smiled broadly as Nixy entered the rectory office. "Welcome back, young Nixy!" he said. "I missed our studies. I hope you have not forgotten all I have taught you?"

Nixy smiled and shook his head. "Nope," he said, "I've been waiting to find out how House Cordobal got the crown."

The lesson went on for over an hour as the pair got back into their routine, culminating when Brother Dane had to ask the inevitable question, "So, how are the lord and lady today?"

"They seem really happy," Nixy said, although Dane saw the reluctance in his face. "Things have been going well, I guess."

Brother Dane was much encouraged. "They are happy, though they try and hide it?"

Nixy nodded, "Yeah, I mean, yes, even when they try and act sad, it seems like they aren't."

"Have you any idea *why* they are happy?" Dane asked. "Have they hinted at anything?"

"Nope," Nixy said, though he squirmed a bit. "All I know is that they cheered up all of a sudden."

"When did you notice this?" Dane pressed. *I must be sure that this effort is not wasted,* he thought. *My debt will be wiped out for certain if I can give them more.*

Nixy squirmed some more, clearly reluctant to talk. "I-I guess it started when our lessons stopped; when the Talon- er, I mean Arch Mage Ildric Finnael, when him and Wenyssaya- she's the elf woman- they came to see me. Them and Drahn, the little purple dragon."

"So their mood changed after that meeting? What did they discuss?" Dane tried to keep his voice calm and casual, for Nixy was becoming more uneasy. *He must see me as a friend, not a threat.* "Does it have something to do with Sir Jaron being summoned the night before?"

Nixy jerked his head up, "Uh, no! Not-not really. I

mean, that was... That-that was about Sir Jaron's father. He's been sick, and they thought it might be his last night. He got better though, so that's good."

"I see," Brother Dane said. "So what did the wizard and the elven woman discuss with the lord and lady?"

Nixy explained, "It was about me, actually. They says-uh, they say that I'm kind of, um," he blushed and scratched his mop of blond hair, "They say I'm a... prince."

This remark took Brother Dane completely by surprise. "A-a prince? A prince of Calilon?" He wondered if the boy was making a joke, but he seemed too distressed for that.

"Er, not Calilon," Nixy squeaked. "A prince of the um, Shadowood Forest." Dane stared blankly. "Wenyssaya says my real father is the Shadow Lord, who's a really old elf. That makes me half an elf, and a prince, kinda."

Dane just sat and stared at the boy, digesting this information. "This is news indeed," he finally muttered. "I-I think that will satisfy our friends. Thank you, Nixyalderthor. I hope this is the end of our mission, but not our lessons or friendship." Dane truly liked the boy, who was eager to learn once he found something to interest him. He stood and gathered the books, ruffling Nixy's hair. "Highness," he said with a smile.

Later than evening, Dane made his way to the tavern where he met his contact. He had positive news for once, and he prayed that it would please the man. If Dane was lucky, he would be out of debt tonight, and would never see his contact again.

He entered an old but prominent tavern on the waterfront called the Brass Dolphin. It had a reputation for good ale and better luck for those who drank there before setting sail. Dolphins were the favored creatures of Obesh, so the men who gathered here drank with reverence and as much dignity as sailors could muster. Dane ordered an ale and edged past the evening crowd, heading toward the back where his contact waited at a more discreet table. The tavern was built with high rafters like a warehouse, and decorated with hanging nets that tended to catch whatever was tossed into them. Over the course of the evening, the nets would release debris, so Brother Dane knew to cover his drink when walking under them.

The table at the back was deep in the shadows, out of reach of the glow from the fireplace and the hanging oil lamps. A man waited there amid the gloom, lounging in the wooden chair with one foot resting on the table. His clothing was dark and discordant, a yellow-green linen shirt the color of seaweed; a vest of burgundy that bore deeper, redder stains; leather breeches of navy blue; and green leather boots laced with yellow cord. A cloak of dark gray fabric was draped over the back of his chair.

What made him so unnerving was his face, which was an uneven collection of features that seemed to have been selected and arranged by a blind man. His eyebrows were set oddly, with one arched higher than the other, the lower one having a wild tweak of hair that curled upward. His eyes were different colors, one blue and one green. His nose was long and kinked in the middle, probably the result of a well-placed punch. When the man smiled, it was a crooked, half-smile, revealing yellowed teeth. He had a long chin and square jaw, though at times it seemed to pop and shift. Dark hair hung like a mop over his head, and he kept it at bay with frequent brushing of his fingers. He called himself 'Twist,' and it suited him well.

"Good evening Brother Dane," Twist said with a light, lilting voice. "I hope you have some news for me this night, for I do hate wasting my time." The man tapped his fingers randomly on the table, his mismatched eyes boring into the monk as he took the opposite chair.

"Yes indeed," Dane said with a nervous smile. "In fact, I think we have found what you're looking for." He took a long drink of ale to bolster his courage.

Twist stopped his tapping and raised his chin with

interest. "Oh? The boy has noticed a change?" He inclined his head in a curious manner, cracking his neck audibly.

"Yes," Dane said, wincing at the sound. "Nixy has told me that the lord and lady-" Twist motioned for him to lower his voice, "...the lord and lady have been very happy of late, even when they try to act as if they are not."

"When did this start?" Twist asked, his voice a monotone.

"Four months ago, the day our lessons stopped." Dane replied.

"After the ember swallow was sent into the city?"

Dane nodded, "Nixy claims that the elder Dunlorden was dying, though apparently he has recovered. I am not certain that he was telling me everything..."

Twist waved the air as though shooing a fly, "Never mind that. What about the wizard and this supposed elf woman? What is their part in this?"

Dane sat back and allowed himself to smile. "It's rather difficult to believe, actually," he said. "It seems that she is indeed an elf, and she informed Nixy that-" he chuckled despite himself. "-that he is actually an elven prince, the son of the fabled 'Shadow Lord' himself! Absurd, isn't it?"

But Twist was not laughing.

"I mean, it has to be some kind of joke or diversion, does it not?" Dane asked. "Perhaps that is why the lord and lady are happier, or perhaps the elf woman has charmed them somehow? It says in the stories that elves would play tricks upon-"

"No! No, no, no," Twist shook his head. He was becoming agitated, squirming in his chair as if no position was comfortable for more than a few seconds. He pointed a finger at Brother Dane as he thought aloud, "The firebird; that was a signal. Sir Jaron was delivering something... a message? No, the bird was sent back, but he left just the same..."

Brother Dane did not want to offer his thoughts while

the man was so restless, so he only watched with morbid curiosity.

"The wizard and the elf arrived the next morning. Your lessons stop and the elf woman becomes his guardian, always with him. Why? Doesn't make sense... something isn't right." He fixed Dane with a fierce look and said, "The bird must have been a feint, a smokescreen. No! Wait..." he cleared the air with his hands, waving his previous words away. "An alliance. Yes, it has to be an alliance!"

"Between whom?" Dane asked, too engrossed to mind his own business.

Twist peered at him and began drumming his fingers again. "Are you sure Dunlorden was alone when he rode to the castle?"

Dane shrugged, "I did not see him myself. I only learned he had arrived, and in great haste."

"So he may not have been alone," Twist muttered. "The heir of the Shadowood and the heir of House Corrina..."

This made no sense at all, for Dane knew as well as anyone that Lady Cindra was long dead. "What Corrina heir do you mean?" he asked.

"Listen," Twist reached out and grabbed at the air between them, as if he were pulling Dane closer. "Don't ask the boy any more questions. Let him relax... let him relaaax." He drew out the word, making the hairs on Dane's neck stand up. "Don't come here again. We'll contact you when the plan changes."

"And my debt?" Brother Dane asked. "It is now paid?"

"Once this is over," Twist smiled his crooked smile, "you're a free man."

The meeting was at an end, but as he left the Brass Dolphin, Dane was not relieved. He did not understand what the Circle of Gold was so very interested in, or what they had at stake, but he had a strong feeling that things had taken a turn for the worse.

Chapter Twenty Two

Cold Steel

It was growing colder by the day as Tavenmoth turned to Eyoromoth, the eleventh month. The trees along the Temple Walk were beginning to color the street with a carpet of golden leaves, but the training at the fighting school continued as usual. Highday courses continued as well, and many of the students were learning fast. Cindra was happy to be among them, and the constant praise from Gavadaire didn't hurt either. What she lacked in strength, she made up for in speed and balance.

In the middle of Eyoromoth, the individual training began. After the morning drills, students were encouraged to sit and watch in the hall as Master Cord gave special attention to one student at a time. This would last for an hour, with half-hour breaks in between. Those who did not choose to attend could do as they wished, although it was wise to spend time perfecting their techniques. The master noticed who took the time off and how they used it, and could make focus sessions appropriately miserable for layabouts.

Cindra's team was in the first day's rotation, and she was scheduled to have the last session. Jaron had spoken to her about it the night before, saying, "Cord and I have discussed this, and we both agree that your focus sessions will be dangerous. He cannot be easy with you in front of the other students."

"I have never asked him to be easy with me," she had replied. "I wish to learn as the others learn. Besides, it cannot be much worse than Ratham beating on me when we spar."

"About Ratham," Jaron had said, "Part of the training involves steel sparring with other students in a focus session. Whoever is called forward can challenge anyone."

"Splendid," she said, and she turned over and pretended to sleep.

Now she was standing in the middle of the hall across from Master Cord, with most of the school seated along the walls. She wore a heavy, quilted tunic for protection, her usual hose and pantaloons; soft leather boots with laces; thick fencing gloves; and a padded, metal face guard that protected her forehead, ears, and cheeks. *Thalyroth*, her Maiden Blade, was upstairs in her quarters, its wooden length nicked and dented by countless parries and strikes. She now held a blunted, steel arming sword in her right hand, and held a metal buckler in her left. She absently wondered if she would ever wield her wooden sword again.

Master Cord saluted. "*Gher yaas*," he said, and he raised his own sword and buckler.

"Go, Dillan!" Padison cried.

"Don't distract him," scolded Adric, smacking his arm.

Cindra and Cord circled each other, swords at the ready. Cord's eyes were grim and determined, and it occurred to Cindra that this was the first time she faced someone who knew her true identity. Cord was her father's vassal, and if the lord's daughter got hurt in these sessions, it would be Cord's doing. *He is a proud and honorable man; my father's 'faithful hound.' This must be a very difficult thing for him to do.*

He moved so suddenly that Cindra barely had time to raise her buckler, deflecting his thrust. He knocked her sword away, his arm now poised overhead like a scorpion tail, the tip of his blade inches from her chin.

"Focus, DePort," he grumbled, "Or go back to your orchards." He backed a few paces away and readied himself. Derisive chuckles could be heard among the onlookers.

Cindra knew not to look at the faces of her fellow students. Not only would it disrupt her concentration, but certain looks on certain faces would make her angry and resentful, leading to more carelessness. She raised her sword and shield, advancing.

Her blow struck Cord's shield, and she managed to block his strike, her arms ringing with the impact. He was definitely serious about not coddling her, as his next attack proved. He swung up under her guard, striking her in the ribs. Even with the padded armor, the pain was intense and she gasped. Still he came on, bringing his buckler down on her sword hand, making her drop the weapon.

Fearing her bones were broken, she watched him raise his blade for a finishing strike. Without thought, she ducked low and rolled, striking his knee with the edge of her buckler for good measure. Cord grunted in pain as Cindra scampered to her feet, looking for a way to reach her sword.

"Damn it, DePort! That hurt." Cord said, and he lowered his weapon. "A good escape. You are still disarmed, but a shield can be a weapon too. You might have used my moment of pain to get the advantage on me instead of backing off."

Cindra straightened painfully, holding her side. "Backing off seemed like a better idea at the time," she said, and the students chuckled in agreement.

"I gave no quarter after that blow to your ribs," Cord explained, "because you must be able to fight through pain and injury. Now, let's go over the proper way to break a kneecap..."

The southern winter marched on, the leaves browned and blew from the trees, and the mornings grew chill indeed. Rather than suffer on the cold cot with nothing but a smoky brazier for warmth, Cindra decided that sharing a bed with Jaron would be preferable. He did not approve at first, but took very little convincing.

"Think of the fuel we will save," she said as she slipped under the blankets. "We're just being practical."

"Eh, practical, yes," Jaron agreed. His heart was beating so strongly, as was her own.

"What are you getting me for my birthday?" she asked.

"Uh, I hadn't thought of it, really," he said. He was so very warm.

"Not a thought?" she asked, putting his arm around her and snuggling close, resting her head on his chest. She felt his pulse like a drumbeat, entwined her leg about his, and grew giddy as their scents mingled.

"I swear, you will be the death of me, Cindra." Jaron sighed. "Although, I have a gift in mind now."

"A sword?" she teased.

Jaron made a heavy sigh, "No, I've seen how you treated your Maiden Blade. Besides, there is your honor to think about."

"So worried about my honor," she said, stroking his chest. "I think I've besmirched my honor beyond hope as it is."

"All the more reason to resist," he said. "I would not risk your maidenhead."

She thought on this for a time and said, "Did you know that my mother raised me to revere Selvina?"

"I had noticed the decorations in the castle," he said.

"Then you know that Selvina has rules for what is acceptable and not acceptable before marriage. You and

I are lovers, after all." She kissed his shoulder.

"Selvina is not here to vouch for us," he said, his voice growing breathy. "If she was, I might never have been banished."

"Her ways are mysterious," she said, enjoying the feel of the linen nightshirt sliding between them. "If you want to learn what is acceptable, you could always go to her temple. The priestesses are happy to instruct, but I prefer you ask them for words, not... acts."

"I would never- I mean, I don't," he stammered, making her giggle. Then he had a thought and asked, "Did your *mother* tell you about these 'acceptable' things?"

"No," she answered. "They were not deemed suitable for me, but I know they exist. Reverend Sister Lyneth told me."

"Of course she did," Jaron sighed. "H-how many weeks until your birthday?" he asked, almost whimpering.

The month of Kraamoth was the introduction to the longsword, which had a lengthier blade than the arming sword and a two-handed grip. It reminded Cindra of the sword used by Princess Moon in her dance, but that blade had been curved, and did not have such a large cross guard. Nevertheless, as she watched Master Cord demonstrate in the main hall, she decided she liked this weapon best.

"The longsword was originally designed for cutting," Cord said to the gathered students. "Footmen would use it against opponents with weak armor, cleaving through the ranks with sweeping, powerful cuts." He sliced the air to demonstrate. "However, things have changed in the last few centuries; heavy cavalry and elite footmen now wear plate armor, and regulars will often have chain shirts. So the longsword masters developed more thrusting and piercing techniques, using the point to attack weak spots at the face, neck, and joints." He performed a few thrusts, even grasping the blade midway up its length. "Even the dimensions of the sword have changed."

"Most of our traditional arming swords are double-bladed, as you know. In Aurilon, the popular style is a more rigid blade with no cutting edge, but a very strong, piercing point. Both can be used like so," again, he grasped the blade with his free hand, using the sword more like a spear or staff. "This is known as a half-sword grip. It is commonly used when an enemy gets too close. It provides leverage for a more powerful thrust, and allows you to land a blow from either hand, using the pommel or cross guard as a club." He demonstrated a few swings from either hand. "Of course, the most important thing to learn here is how not to cut your hand..."

Cindra had seen that technique before; Sir Earnold Greenfellow had used it against Jaron in their duel. At the time it seemed like cheating, but she had since learned much more about real combat. Duels were not pretty or graceful; they were intense, vicious, and often very short. In a fight to the death, nothing was off-limits.

"No shield," Padison muttered. "Got to use both hands."

Master Cord heard him and said, "Not true, Pemwreth. A buckler is small enough not to hinder you, and the sword can be used with one hand, if needed."

"If you're longer than the sword," cracked Halvoy. Laughter bubbled up from the crowd.

"You're not that long yourself, Quenlorden." Padison replied.

"My sword's longer than yours," Halvoy said.

"Only because you tug on it all night," Paddy shot back. Whoops of mirth rang in the hall, and Halvoy made an obscene gesture.

"That's enough," Cord said. "Cold as it is, none of us can brag. Now, shut up, all of you."

Cindra smiled but remained silent. She really had nothing to add to this conversation anyway.

The longsword became Cindra's new love. She had never felt strong enough to match blades with a one-handed grip, but the longsword gave her new confidence. In her focus sessions, she learned how to merge her earlier training with the new style, facing off against Master Cord as he demonstrated attacks and counters, parries and ripostes. She learned the circling, predatory dance that preceded an attack; the quick, shuffling steps of the aggress and egress; and how to exploit the reach of the longer blade. She learned new trapping and joint-locking moves, as well as new ways to use her whole body to attack. Of course, she learned most of these things by having Master Cord demonstrate them on her, and he was not gentle.

The chill of late Kraamoth made Cindra's aches and pains seem worse than they were. Still, the simple act of undressing made her wince, drawing Jaron's concern.

"Are you going to be alright?" he asked, moving to help her.

She nodded, accepting his assistance. "I will be. It's too bad I can't give him as good as I get." Her arms, hips, and back were covered with bruises, and her joints ached. "He deserved a bloody lip for laying me out on the floor today."

"That's the spirit," Jaron said, smiling. "I can't tell you how many times I wanted to knock him on his back."

"Did you ever get to?" she asked, as they sat on the bed.

"Once or twice," he admitted. "Later in the focus sessions, there will be measures."

"Measures?" She had not heard of this before.

"It's like a test every few months," Jaron explained. "You show what you've learned by sparring with the master. It's all made as safe as possible, and there are special rules."

"Like no strikes to the knees?" She smiled, remembering how Cord had limped for a few days after her first session.

"Like that," he nodded. "Also, no lethal or crippling moves, or they will be reciprocated, if possible."

This gave her pause. "Have people tried to kill him during these measures?"

Jaron said, "Not him, no. But it's an old rule that has been in place for many generations. Apparently one of his ancestors was maimed by a vengeful student, and had to kill the man. His life, personal honor, and the honor of the entire school were at stake."

"Honor," she intoned. "I'm still not sure I know what that means. You used to speak of it often, as I recall."

"Used to," he agreed. The thought seemed to demoralize him.

"I think I understand it better now," she said, putting her hand on his. "As a girl, it was easy to scoff at the honor of men. They are always fighting each other for this offense or that, and it all seems so childish. It felt as if my honor was everyone's business, and I resented people 'protecting' it, especially you."

Jaron turned to her, "And now?"

"Now... I can defend it myself, and I think I hold it more dearly." She leaned against him and said, "As a woman, I would feel helpless, depending on a brave knight to fight my battles. It became easier not to care so much about how others saw me. But now that I live as a man does, now that I can stand on my own..."

"It becomes your responsibility," he said. "No one will defend it for you."

"Yes," she agreed. "Now I want to show my worth. I don't want to feel helpless, or let anyone think that I am."

Jaron put his arms around her and said, "You are worth the world to me, and you are the least helpless woman I have ever known."

She returned his embrace, snuggling against his chest. "I do love you, Jaron Dunlorden."

"And I love you, Cindra Corrina," he said. "But..."

"But what?" she asked.

"Now that you're all 'honorable' and such..." he gave

her a squeeze.

"Hmm?"

"Well," he said, "Tomorrow *is* your birthday, after all."

She smiled and ran her fingers through his hair. "And I thought you'd forgotten," she breathed, her words tickling his lips just before they kissed.

The Long Night, the eve of the New Year, was once marked by solemn prayers and vigils into the late watches. The Gartethan calendar began on the winter solstice, marking what had become known as the Age of Omens, when the gods abandoned the world. Every year ended with the hope that they would return to guide and speak with their children once again. However, after 1117 years of waiting, most people now spent the Long Night with wine and good company.

The first day of 1118 was like any other at the fighting school, except morning drills were canceled to give the students an extra hour to deal with their hangovers before breakfast. Cindra joined her fellow Dread Wolves as they enjoyed their bacon, eggs, sausages, and biscuits.

"Morning Dillan," mumbled Adric. By the dark circles under his eyes, he had not slept well last night.

"Morning, all," Cindra said, trying not to look too chipper.

"You are not eating with Sir Jaron?" Morrin asked. "I thought he only gave allowances for the midday meal."

"Oh, he said I only need worry about the evening meal now," she replied. "He wants me to enjoy some camaraderie, rather than carving meat and pouring drinks."

"He sounds like a good knight to serve under," Morrin said. "Maybe he'd like another squire?"

Cindra didn't know whether to be amused, jealous, or both. "I doubt he could handle another squire. He's not a wealthy knight, to be honest."

"You been sick, Dillan?" Padison asked, catching her off guard.

"No," she said, with a curious expression. "Why do you ask?"

"I been hearing noises down the hall the last few nights," he said. "Sounds like you're... I dunno, in pain or something."

Cindra nearly choked on her ale, but managed to cover it with a laugh, "Oh! No, no, that's not... No, I haven't been sick."

They all looked at her, awaiting an answer. Morrin seemed more amused than curious.

"It's-" she finished clearing her throat as her mind raced, "It's just that Jaron has been helping me with my recovery."

"Recovery from what?" Inis asked, concerned.

"You know, injuries," she replied, rotating a shoulder and making a face. "Between Master Cord's focus sessions, and the Su'Kraal training, I've been beaten up and twisted out of shape. Sir Jaron does this... massage technique. I don't know, I think it's foreign or something. Anyway, it hurts, but it helps." She felt a blush coming on, so she coughed to cover it up.

"I do stretches myself," Padison said. "Sometimes I get ol' Bradric to help. He does this massage thing on my back; he says it's like they do on horses. Feels like I'm being kneaded like a lump of dough."

"Maybe Sir Jaron could show us this massage technique?" Morrin asked, his face innocent.

"Er, I don't think he's likely to share it," she said, blushing again. "He claims it's an 'ancient secret' or something." She took a gulp of ale to wash down her embarrassment. "So, has anybody thought about steel sparring next week?"

Master Cord stood in the center of the main hall with a six-foot oak staff in hand. The students were seated on the cold floor around him, creating a large ring in which the duels would take place. They were all dressed in heavy arming doublets, and had their protective gauntlets and headgear by their sides. There was nervous anticipation in the air as everyone sized up the competition, wondering who would be chosen.

"Alright then," Cord began, "We will go over the rules. These fights are meant to measure your skill against your fellow students, not to carry out feuds or vendettas. If one of you gets injured, it is only an unfortunate consequence of the training, not something that must be avenged. If any of you tries to inflict a serious injury on another student, I will eject you from the school with as much force as I deem necessary. Is that understood?"

"Yes, master!" was the mass reply.

"Good," he nodded. "The rules are simple. Blows can be made with any part of your weapon or body, but a scoring blow must be made with the edge or point. Avoid striking the face; most of you are ugly enough as it is. The first competitor to land five scoring blows wins the match. However, instant victories are accomplished by disarming, immobilizing, or flooring your opponent, all while remaining in a dominant position.

"Now, I will call a name, and that student will come to the center of the hall and choose an opponent. He will also choose a weapon for both to use. This is steel sparring, so obviously all the weapons are blunted steel; we have daggers, arming swords, longswords, bucklers, and kite shields.

"I will be watching whom you pick and what you pick, for it will reveal where you believe your strengths and weaknesses lie. You will be judged not only by whether you win or lose, but on your choices as well." He gave that a moment to sink in, then added, "Oh, by the way, this is my clobbering stick." He spun the staff from hand to hand, making it hum through the air. "I will use it to keep the duel within bounds, and to tap you when I want a tussle to end. When I tap you, the fight will stop and you will return to guard positions. Failure to do so will result in a clobbering. Understood?"

"Yes, master!" came the reply.

"Excellent! Now, our first challenger will be Adric

Hywahl." He gestured to the lad, who had gone a bit pale. His fellow Dread Wolves gave words of encouragement as he got to his feet. "Hywahl, choose your fight," Cord said, and stepped back to give the lad some room.

Adric turned in a circle, as if considering each student. In truth, the Dread Wolves had discussed this for the last few days, as had the other teams. Adric wanted a good, fair fight, so he said, "Halvoy Quenlorden."

Halvoy was about Adric's age, though a bit shorter, and thicker about the shoulders. He grinned to his fellow Fire Steeds and got to his feet, and they gave encouraging shouts.

"Choose your weapon," Cord said.

"Sword and shield," Adric said, and they donned their gauntlets and headgear. Jaron and Gavadaire also fitted both lads with throat guards, and extra protection for the legs and knees. Once they were ready, they met in the center of the hall.

Adric and Halvoy saluted with their swords and shouted, "*Gher yaas!*" They circled each other, testing one another's nerve, then moved together with a clashing of their swords and wooden shields. The fight lasted for six passes, with each fighter scoring two hits, and ended when Halvoy tripped up Adric to send him tumbling to the floor. The Fire Steeds cheered their teammate as the victor helped his opponent to his feet. Cheers and applause went up for a good match.

"*D'ravos!*" Halvoy cried. Cindra translated the Celvestrian in her head: *Victory!* It was a cry that had doggedly followed her Norsican ancestors from the old world to the new.

"Good match," Adric said, his breath heavy and steaming in the cold hall.

"Same to you," Halvoy replied. He had a confident grin as he sat back down among his team.

The matches went on for the rest of the day, often

ending sooner than it took to choose weapons and gear up. Cindra learned much from watching the short bouts, for example, aggression often trumped caution; speed usually won over power; and footwork was more important than any other aspect of a fight.

The longest duel so far had been between Maadi Gaavi and Mat Belvine, lasting ten passes. The nimble Gozhiman danced all about the seasoned sell-sword, scoring four good blows, but Mat had learned to anticipate his opponent's erratic moves and tripped him up in a rush, ending the match with a blade at Gaavi's throat. Until then, Cindra was not sure the dark-skinned foreigner could be beaten.

Ferrol Avenoth predictably challenged his brother, Finnas, and Master Cord had to break it up with his clobbering stick. Their match had been close and frenzied, and had quickly degenerated into head punches and rolling about; it was all very entertaining.

But when Master Cord called Rejick Ratham to the floor, Cindra felt a quiver in her bowels. *He is going to pick me,* she thought, and the idea gave her goosebumps. Ratham turned slowly, taking his time, though his teammates were smirking and whispering among themselves, looking in her direction.

Finally, Ratham's eyes came to rest on his choice. "Corrina," he said.

Cindra felt a shiver go through her that had nothing to do with the winter cold, but it was quickly washed away as she noticed her cousin rising to his feet. A thought struck her as she saw the loathing on Ratham's face, *He is challenging Gaius, and by extension, House Corrina and all who serve it.*

"Longsword," Ratham said, choosing his weapon. The pair armed themselves and faced off in the center of the hall.

"Begin!" Cord shouted.

The lads saluted and took up guard stances. Ratham made the first pass, beating Gaius's sword aside and lunging at his chest. Gaius parried and counter-attacked, forcing Rejick to disengage. Another assault began, and the sliding clatter of steel against steel filled the hall.

Don't let him get close, Cindra thought, hoping Gaius had studied Ratham's moves as she had. *He's a Maurbrik fighter, so don't let him get close.*

Gaius advanced, struck high, and reversed his attack to strike his adversary's hands from below in an attempt to disarm him. Ratham parted his arms to avoid the blow, leaving his chest wide-open, and Gaius lunged forward. In one deft move, Ratham looped his sword through his opponent's arms, twisted and locked his joints, spun about, and flipped him to the cold floor.

A gasp went through the crowd as Ratham stood over his vanquished foe. "*D'ravos*," he said calmly, returning to his seat. Master Cord, scowling, moved to tend to the fallen Corrina. Cindra also started forward, but Gaius waved her away.

"I'm alright," he was saying, though his eyes looked a bit unfocused. He grunted in pain as Cord lifted him by the arms, but he was able to return to his place among his fellow Ice Drakes.

"Well, *that* was scary," Padison said under his breath. "I only seen that move once before."

"Obviously he's been practicing it," she said. "Gaius got too close."

Adric frowned across the hall at the smirking Thorn Bears. "He didn't have to be that brutal. He could have disarmed him easy without throwing him."

"That was a message," Cindra said. "He hates House Corrina, and he's none too fond of those who serve it."

"Lucky he didn't pick you then," Padison said, patting her shoulder.

She had to agree.

Chapter Twenty Three

A Grim Assessment

The lessons with Brother Dane had become more enjoyable now that the priest was no longer asking about Nixy's spying assignment. He didn't say anything about having to go back to the Warren either, not that Nixy would have, even if he had been ordered to. There was no way he could live in those catacombs again, shivering in the dark, eating runny gruel and stolen bread. He was a prince now, with fine clothes, servants attending him, and a beautiful elf woman for a teacher. It was like he had died and gone to Haven.

One day, early in the New Year, Brother Dane had not been feeling well. He asked if Nixy could have his lessons after dinner, and Nixy agreed, arriving at the rectory as the sun was creeping down towards the horizon. There was a single lamp lit in the study, casting a warm blanket of light over the frozen ground. As Nixy approached, he could see Brother Dane's illuminated form through the narrow window, waiting at the table with his books. Another robed and hooded figure moved beyond. *Another monk?* he wondered. *I hope he's not a replacement. I like Brother Dane.*

Nixy was let inside with a cheerful greeting, though Brother Dane's heart wasn't in it. *Still sick? Monk food must be bad.* The other monk kept his back turned, his green robes darkening in Brother Dane's shadow. As Nixy was offered a seat, he noticed that the lamp light made Dane's robes the only source of cheer in the cold, dreary chamber.

"Are you feeling better, brother?" Nixy asked.

"Yes," Dane said nervously, "yes, I am better. Thank you, my little prince." The monk glanced at the man in the back of the room, and that was when Nixy saw that Dane had been crying. "I... I need to step out for a moment, Nixyalderthor... forgive me." Dane rose shakily and left the rectory in a hurry.

Nixy felt bad for him, wondering why the monk didn't just reschedule for tomorrow. *Poor Brother Dane,* he thought.

The other monk went to the door and locked it, then stood before the window, his hooded frame blocking the view. Nixy realized too late that he had been ignoring his instincts; they had been screaming at him, but he felt too safe to listen. *Something is very wrong, very wrong and very dangerous.* He scooted his chair back with a wooden screech as the hooded man raised his head.

It took all his nerve to keep from crying out as he beheld the monk's face exposed in the lamplight. It was pale and skull-like, with piercing gray eyes that bound Nixy in place, chilling his blood. The hairless brow, bony cheeks, thin lips and hawkish nose were well known to him. They belonged to Dexer, the man who had been more like a father to him than anyone, and who terrified him all the same.

"Nixy my boy... good to see you. We were so worried..." Dexer had used those very words the last time Nixy found himself in a surprise meeting with the man. They held the same naked threat as before, but this time something was different.

Different is bad, very bad. Nixy's insides were quivering, as if he were full of bugs. He felt sick. No wonder Brother Dane left in such a hurry. *'Forgive me,' he had said. Gods, what was going to happen?*

"I've been asked to have a little chat with you, see... the Boss knows that I can always tell when one of my boys is lying." He smiled coldly as Nixy shriveled in his chair. The man's grating, raspy voice played on the boy's nerves like a handsaw played a harp. "You were asked to report on the Gold Cat's moods, if he and his lady were happy..."

Nixy nodded rapidly.

"And you said they were..." Dexer glared.

Nixy nodded again.

"Do you know why?"

Nixy squirmed and shook his head.

Dexer dropped a dagger from his sleeve into his hand and began digging the point into the table, twisting it about. "You sure boy? Because I've been let in on a little secret," he said, allowing Nixy's terror to build. "I was told why you're really here. It's the girl, your little friend who saved your life. She's not as dead as we've been led to believe, yes?"

Nixy twitched involuntarily. *They knew! They knew Cindra was alive, and they sent me here to see if it was true!*

Dexer didn't wait for him to confirm or deny the story however. "That's wonderful news!" He smiled his frosty smile, trying to look compassionate and failing miserably. "I've seen how sad you were before; I know how much she meant to you." He laid the dagger flat on the table as he spoke. "You don't know where she is, by chance?"

Nixy shook his head saying, "No one told me." *That's true at least. No one told me exactly where she was.*

"That knight, Dunlorden; he brought her out of hiding, didn't he? Is she in the castle now?" He nodded over his shoulder towards the white stone wall outside. "You two sharing a room?"

"N-no, Dexer! I dunno where she is, honest! I wouldn't lie to you!" he blurted. "No one told me nothing!"

"But you know she's alive, don't you? Who told you that?"

Nixy grasped for a name that could possibly intimidate Dexer. It was a short list. "Ildric Finnael," he said.

Dexer's eyes narrowed and he seemed to relent. "Fair enough. But there's one more thing I gotta know, the big thing on everyone's mind: this golden goddess of an elf wench shows up, out of the blue, and you get moved to nicer quarters," he reached out and felt the fabric of Nixy's sleeve, making him flinch, "you get nicer clothes. You're with her all the time... why? What does this divine creature out of my grandma's faerie stories want... with... you?" He poked the boy's chest with the last three words.

Nixy decided this was his chance to be free of the Circle forever, to deliver his Straight Arrow, his resignation, right to Dexer's face. He just hoped it would be accepted and not get him killed. "I'm a prince," he said with less confidence than he tried for, "A half-elf, and a prince."

He thought when Dexer heard that, he would do something, anything; laugh, or smirk, or get mad. Anything would have been better than what he did.

"Is that so?" was all he said. His face hadn't changed, he hadn't moved an inch.

"A half-elf, and a prince," Nixy repeated, in case it hadn't registered. "My dad in Syngmore isn't my real dad." His voice gained a little more confidence, and he counted on his 'special luck' to see him through. "My real dad is the lord of the Shadowood. He sent Wenyssaya to thank the Gold Cats for protecting me." He hoped Dexer read into that last part. *I'm protected.* Though at the moment, he didn't feel very protected.

"Shadowskipper," Dexer said, using Nixy's chosen name. "The kid with the special luck... the kid who could do the impossible." The man straightened and moved slowly around the table, leaving the dagger within reach. "I always wondered about you; always knew you was a better pickpocket than anyone had a right to be. You got in and out of Clavemont Manor 'cause you got magic, ain't that right boy? Your special luck isn't luck at all." Dexer sat on the edge of the table and rested his foot on Nixy's chair, making it harder for the boy to move in a hurry. "So the elves decided to get all diplomatic and cozy again after a thousand years, just for little ol' you? Just because some stump-squatting, pointy-eared, faerie lord couldn't keep it in his pants any longer?"

Nixy nodded, "W-Wenyssaya wants to take me to meet my father." *So if you kill me, he'll be real mad.* He had learned to read Dexer's face as a survival skill, but he'd never seen the man like this. It's like he was thinking of doing something he didn't want to, or wanted to do something he shouldn't.

"Nixy DuQuayne," he said, pulling a crooked smile. "I always figured if I had a son, one I gave a damn about, he'd be like you. Clever, talented, and a little bit... odd. But the Boss, he's got this grand scheme, see? And in the grand scheme of things, the king's men can't have a winning hand."

"W-why?" Nixy whispered, finally understanding what Dexer meant to do.

"Who knows?" Dexer shrugged. "Maybe the Boss is looking to move up in the world? Maybe he's got his eye on the crown itself? All I know is..." Nixy saw his eyes narrow and his lips tighten, "...I got my orders."

Move! shouted Nixy's instincts, and Nixy listened.

Dexer came at him with the knife, his slash missing by a hair's breadth. Nixy launched himself off the chair and rolled to his feet as Dexer's robe billowed, looming like a barrier before the only exit. There was just one place to flee to, so he darted into the small sleeping chamber at the back of the rectory. The room had only a cot, a small table, and a smaller window. Nixy leapt on the cot, trying to open the shutter and escape into the cold night, but the window was too small, too high. The little chamber grew even darker as Dexer stood in the doorway.

"Don't make this harder than it has to be," he said, almost with a hint of sympathy. "You made yourself more trouble than you're worth, and now we gotta clean up the mess." The metal of the knife glinted in the dim light as Dexer entered the room.

Nixy jumped off the cot, fumbling for Cutter, his magic knife. He had worn it every day since his last encounter with Black Will and the troll on the cathedral roof, but he had never drawn it in defense before now. The fear made his hands fumble and his arms feel like limp bits of rope; his eyes darted about the room frantically, looking for anything that might aid him. All he saw was the surrounding darkness.

I can use that, he thought desperately, trying to remember what Wenyssaya had said. *My father's home is in the shadows*, he recalled. *It's his element, and mine too*. He felt himself back away from Dexer, though he didn't actually move. He pushed against the darkness, and the darkness took him, like a spoon sinking in thick porridge.

Dexer came up short, moving to let more light in the room. He cut the air before him with the knife, slashing at the spot where Nixy stood, but the knife found nothing to bite. "This one of your magic tricks, boy?" he whispered. "Impressive, it really is." He backed up and closed the door, trapping Nixy in the room with him. "I can hear you breathe, kid. I can smell your fear. You can't hide forever." He took out another blade and weaved them about, searching.

Nixy wasn't hiding, exactly. He was watching Dexer move around, watching the knives slash in the surrounding dark, watching the intense look on the gaunt man's face. He could see fairly well, as if the dark bedchamber were moonlit, as if the shadows gave off their own pale radiance. He saw that Dexer's eyes were wide and blind, useless in the dark. For the first time in Nixy's life, he was consciously moving within the Shadow, and it was frightening and exhilarating all at once.

But if Dexer didn't like the game, he just changed the rules. The gaunt man reached into the neck of his robe, and drew out a small crystal hanging on a leather cord. He held it before him and said, "*Ilda*," invoking the spell within the glowstone. Dim light flooded the room and Nixy felt the pressure of it against his skin, as if the comforting darkness was now pushed against him like a heavy blanket, making the air thick and stuffy.

Dexer peered into the little room with intense eyes, pulling back his hood to free up his ears; only Dexer had no ears, just holes where they should have been, like a bird or a lizard. The flesh about the sides and back of his head was melted and scarred, as if he slept on a pillow made of fire.

Nixy willed himself to sink deeper into the waning darkness, pulling what was left of it as close as he dared. He began to feel smothered, as if a wet cloth had been placed over his nose and mouth; the shadows about him became darker and more primal, fighting with the intrusive light emanating from the glowstone. Suddenly, he felt as if his back were to a yawning chasm, a vast, empty blackness from which he would never return. He felt drawn to the edge though he wasn't moving, and he grabbed for the wall to steady himself. But the wall wasn't the solid anchor he was hoping for, and his hand felt like it was pushing through mud.

He also felt a presence in the dark; a powerful will that focused that emptiness into substance and purpose. The shadows deepened and Dexer's light appeared to dim like a dying faerie bug. Nixy dared not turn around, for he felt as if the Abyss was just over his shoulder. He felt something moving there, felt it tickle his back with a cold finger of dread.

Dexer stopped his advance, drawing back cautiously. The gloom was deepening, despite his glowstone. He held his knives at the ready, the cold steel poised to sink into soft flesh at the first opportunity. Instinct told him he needed more light, and he always heeded his instincts. Backing towards the exit, the gaunt man found the latch and swung the door wide open. Lamplight cut a path through the darkness, and standing there against the wall was Nixy DuQuayne, pale and sweating with fear. Dexer threw a knife, pinning the boy to the wall through his fine tunic. Nixy barely flinched, as if he had bigger things to be afraid of.

The man twirled his remaining knife and gave the boy a little smile. "I got to hand it to you lad; you would have made a legendary thief. It's a damned shame…" He began to move in for the kill.

Nixy was terrified, but not just by Dexer; something was in the room with him, something that came from that horrible blackness. He looked straight at his executioner, trying to avoid the man's shadow as it grew to cover him.

"Any last words?" Dexer asked, his blade at the boy's throat.

"Ru-ru-run," Nixy stammered.

Dexer hadn't expected that. He also didn't expect the deep, rumbling growl that emanated from the shadows to either side. Cold yellow eyes appeared, and gleaming fangs below, and the darkness coalesced into the shape of two black wolves, both as large as ponies. Dexer pulled his second knife from the wall, freeing Nixy to move, and he backed slowly to the door. He was just at the threshold when they lunged, clamping jaws on each arm and pulling him this way and that, trying to rip him in half. Nixy darted between his legs and scrambled into the rectory study, shouting for help as Dexer's cries grew in pitch and volume. The bedchamber door was knocked shut in the struggle, and within moments, the noise died.

Guards poured into the rectory, swords and spears at the ready. While two of them pulled Nixy to his feet, several others approached the door.

"No! Don't!" Nixy cried, but the men did not listen. They swung the chamber door open and peered inside, ready for anything.

But they found nothing; only a few bloodstains on the floor.

Chapter Twenty Four

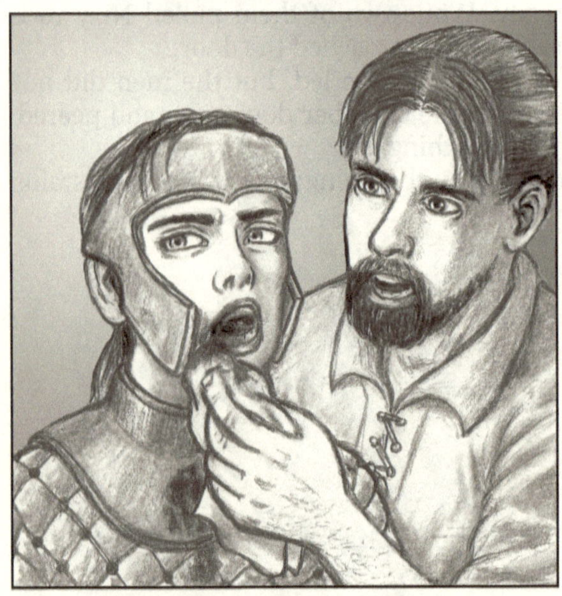

Step, Beat, Glide, Whirl

"Something needs to be done," Cindra muttered. She was sawing Jaron's portion of beef with too much vigor, and she had nearly overfilled his cup. She wished to be conspiring with her teammates, but she had her duties at the dinner table. "Someone needs to do *something*."

"Indeed," Jaron said, half expecting to be splattered in blood when she cut him another slice. "Someone needs to calm themselves, first." He glanced at Master Cord, who shrugged.

"I *am* calm," she said, slapping the beef on his plate. She turned to Cord and asked in an accusing tone, "Master, why didn't you eject him for that?"

Master Cord gazed sidelong at her and said, "I will answer that in two parts. One, he did nothing wrong, not by the rules and not by his training. Excessive? Yes, but not wrong." Then he looked her hard in the eye and leaned forward, "And two, this is the *Freekirk* School, not the Corrina School. I don't take suggestions or orders regarding who stays or goes. If you feel so strongly about it, then *you* challenge him."

Cindra was taken aback, but had the sense to be properly abashed, not angry. Cord had not been addressing Dillan just then, but Lady Cindra. He had gone right past her armor and struck her person, and the blow rendered her silent.

"Don't give my squire any ideas," Jaron said, knowing full well she had the idea already.

Later that evening, as she and Jaron visited their horses in the stable, she asked, "How would you fight Ratham, if you could? And don't try to talk me out of anything, because I will have to face him at some point in the next year, I am sure of it."

"As am I," Jaron admitted. "And I wasn't going to try to dissuade you."

"There is a first time for everything," she said. "So, how would you fight him?"

Jaron did not need to consider long. "He is a taunter; he likes to draw his opponent in and fight close, tempting them by lowering his guard, or making an opening. When he attacks, he never overextends, keeping himself stable and centered. He also likes to grab and trap his opponent's blade."

"He falls back on his *Maurbrik* training," she agreed.

"I would fight in circles," he said. "Slash and move, no thrusting unless it's to his flanks. Also, never let him back you into a corner. If you run out of room to maneuver, he will have you."

Cindra nodded. "The Su'Kraal training is all about maintaining your exits. Ratham will know this, but I don't think he likes it as a style."

Jaron agreed. "He thinks it is too passive, yes. I also noticed that he is not very flexible in his lower back; possibly some old training injury."

"Really?" she asked. "I hadn't noticed."

"I oversee his team on daily drills," Jaron said. "His back bothers him, and he can't bend back as far as the others."

"How will that help?" she asked.

"That," he said, "is something I will let you work out for yourself, my young squire."

The next day of duels began, and Cindra was more focused than usual. She tried to observe every change of stance, every step, every shift of weight that the sparring students made. Her attention was especially focused on those who had acquired some fighting experience before attending the school. While they were all trained *Daerbrik* fighters now, it was inevitable that their earlier habits would present themselves.

Mat Belvine would crack the bones in his neck with a tilt of the head, rotate his shoulders, and shake out his free hand; he did this to intimidate his opponent, or fool them into making a brash attack which he was always ready for. He had been a bodyguard and sell-sword, and likely faced many nervous brigands in his time.

Stansig Gebthor was altogether different, not bothering with luring anyone in. He would shout, growl, and make the floor vibrate with his stomping advances. It was like facing down a thunderstorm, or an angry bear. This did not mean he was careless however, just very, very scary.

Maadi Gaavi was scary in another way. His movements were less erratic and confusing than they had been months before, but he was still capable of bursts of chaos when the need arose. He would also make an eerie hiss-chatter noise, while spinning the tip of his sword in little circles towards his opponent's face. She wondered what kind of battles he had seen in his native land, and if they had been against other men, or some of the strange creatures that were said to inhabit the continent.

Demel Victhor, Lukas Korbison, and Terrus Drakthorne had very similar styles and habits. They had not seen combat, but all came from local noble families, and had been raised in the martial tradition from an early age. It was likely that their early instruction was in some variant of the *Daerbrik* style, and they were more proficient with its principles and forms than any other student. It was what Jaron called "One seed, one breed."

He had explained, "On a farm, you want to avoid using one kind of seed crop, or one breed of animal. Too much inbreeding can lead to a weak line. This is true of fighting styles as well."

She saw that weakness when those students were faced with an unpredictable opponent. It was just like Gavadaire had said, 'The best style is the one that suits your situation; be it aggressive, defensive, quick, or measured.'

Her thoughts were interrupted when she heard her name, or rather Dillan's name.

"Dillan DePort," said the voice, but it was not Master Cord's. It was Halvoy Quenlorden, and he was choosing her as an opponent.

She rose to her feet amid shouts of encouragement from her teammates, and walked to the arming table where Jaron and Gavadaire were waiting.

"Weapon?" Cord asked.

Halvoy replied, "Dagger." This caused murmurs around the room, for no one had chosen that weapon yet. It was not exactly a battlefield weapon after all.

The amount of protection needed was minimal, requiring little more than a face-guard, so Halvoy removed his heavy doublet. Cindra did the same, but remembered that she had not worn her vest over her shirt today. Her breasts were still wrapped as usual, but the wrapping could be seen through the fabric if it got moist with sweat. She hoped the match wouldn't take that long.

Jaron gave her an encouraging look, but said nothing more. She could see the worry in his eyes however. She wished he wouldn't fret so much, especially in front of her. It was a little demoralizing.

"Why the dagger?" she asked, as they secured their

face-guards.

Halvoy shrugged, "I always carry a dagger, so I might as well learn to be good with it." Then he grinned and said, "You might thank me for this if you ever have to use that big, scary Minozhian blade in a fight."

"What makes you think I haven't?" she asked. She hadn't, but he didn't know that.

He flipped the dagger about as they walked to the center of the room. "Then I guess you'll know to get a lot closer with a shorter, thinner blade?"

They saluted each other and began the match.

Halvoy darted in and out, testing her defenses. Cindra weaved her dagger nervously, not caring for the lack of reach or protection it offered. *One seed, one breed*, she thought bitterly. *I've gotten spoiled with a sword and shield. Let that be a lesson to me.* She advanced and made two crossing slashes at his body, but his blade found her forearm on the second slash. *Damn.*

"One hit, Halvoy," called Master Cord.

"Closer and quicker," Halvoy said as they circled. He slashed at her face and attacked her free hand when she raised her guard.

"Two hits," Cord said.

Both forearms would have bruises tomorrow, but if his blade had been sharp, she would now have little to fight with. *Time to see if he falls for his own tricks*, she thought. Stepping forward, she slashed at his head with a probing strike. He leaned back, and at the same time brought his dagger up to slice at her arm again. This time she was ready for him, and she turned her thrust into an underhanded slash that caught him on the hand. Then lunging to his right, she brought the blade across his neck at the collar. He had reached up to grab her arm, but the blow had already landed.

"Two hits for Dillan!" Cord called, and her teammates cheered.

"Well done, DePort," Halvoy said, rubbing his neck.

"Thanks," she said as they resumed guard positions. A wash of pride overtook her, and that fierce little spirit within her chest kindled. This wasn't life or death like it was before, when she saved Nixy from Black Will, or Teya Two-Knives from the Minozhian pirate. No, this was fun. She had something to prove to everyone here, especially herself, and she was going to enjoy doing it. Win or lose, she was no longer afraid.

The combatants circled again, but this time Cindra was feeling light on her feet. She hopped forward and back, and side to side with graceful dance steps, or bounced on the balls of her feet. Halvoy smiled a little at her display, testing her new tactic with a combination of slashes, first striking at her blade to beat it aside. She ducked her blade out of the way, keeping it moving, and returning his attacks with counters of her own. Halvoy retreated a few steps to reassess his situation.

Cindra took advantage of his hesitation, made a gliding step forward to provoke him, and backed away quickly when he retaliated. He knocked her dagger aside with his free hand and slashed at her belly, but she flexed to avoid the blow, grabbed his wrist, and brought the point of her dagger towards his armpit. Not to be killed off so easily, Halvoy grabbed her wrist and held the blow in check, then spun her about, intent on putting her in a headlock. She managed to duck out of his hold and deliver a back kick, and then she rolled and spun into a guard position.

Halvoy fell to the floor with a grunt, his dagger clattering from his grasp. Cindra turned to see him curled in a ball, holding his groin in pain. Sympathetic groans went up around the room, and Cord came over to help him up. Cindra was still in fighting mode however, and it took a moment for her to calm down and realize she had won.

"I'd call that a finishing blow," Cord said. "Three hits, Dillan has the match."

She went to Halvoy's side, elated but feeling terribly guilty. "I'm sorry, Halvoy. I didn't mean to hit so low."

He shook off the master's aid and straightened to face her, saying, "No, was a good escape, good match,

DePort. Maybe we'll dance again sometime." He limped to his teammates, who slapped his back and laughed.

As Cindra returned to her seat amid the cheers of her friends, she felt that fierce little spirit within her leap and flash, fed by the fuel of victory. Still, she was sorry she had injured Halvoy, who seemed like a good and decent lad. If it had been Ratham, however...

Fights resumed after the midday meal, once the tables and benches were cleared away. It had been a light meal, for which Cindra was grateful, for she had requested to be chosen as the next challenger. Her morale and confidence was at an all-time high, and she didn't want to let it go to waste.

"Are you sure you're ready?" Master Cord had asked. "Ratham hasn't fought today, and he'll be fresh." It was no secret to Cord who she intended to challenge.

"I'm sure," she answered. "There is no point in putting it off. Besides, I'm feeling my oats today."

"Ha! Very well, DePort." Cord winked. "Take care now. I don't want to answer to your father if you get broken."

She winked back and said, "I trust in my superior training, Master Cord."

"Ass kisser," he said, "Dillan DePort! You're up!"

Cindra strode to the center of the hall, tugged at her gauntlets and flexed her hands. Without looking up, she called, "Rejick Ratham!"

Murmurs abounded at the unlikely pick, and Cindra's teammates whispered excitedly among themselves. Ratham got to his feet and stood over his challenger, staring at the top of Cindra's head as she dusted off her doublet. She wouldn't meet his gaze; in fact, she was practically ignoring him. It was all part of her plan.

"Weapon of choice?" Cord asked, slightly amused.

Cindra waved the question away. "Whatever Ratham likes will be fine," she said. This increased the volume of the murmurs to a dull roar. No one let their opponent choose the weapon!

"I think your recent victory has gone to your head," Ratham said, sneering and looming over her like a storm cloud. "Beating a fishmonger doesn't make you good."

"Actually, I understand he's from a family of coopers." She deigned to meet his eyes, channeling her mother's best patronizing expression. "They make barrels?"

Ratham growled, "I *know* what a coop-"

"Weapon of choice, Ratham! We're waiting," Master Cord boomed.

"Longsword!" Ratham called back, almost snarling at the master.

Interesting, Cindra thought. *He would have the biggest advantage with a dagger, but he's uncertain now.* She gave him a little smile, tilting her head towards the arming table.

Jaron was there, giving her a look that she knew quite well. It said *'I hope you know what you're doing.'* Thankfully, he didn't say anything out loud, but proceeded to help her with her face guard and neck protection.

Ratham kept his comments to himself until they were armed and in the center of the hall again. Then he said for all to hear, "Your knight's going to want a new squire when I'm done with you."

She just gave that patronizing little smile and replied, "What do you say, Ratham? Shall we pit bear against cat and see who wins?" This got the attention of more than a few people, including Gaius Corrina. Bear against *cat*, not bear against hart. The message was clear: this was about House Corrina's honor.

"You're not a cat yet," Ratham scoffed. "Just a kitten who learned to pounce."

"Ready?" Master Cord asked.

"Ready!" Ratham replied.

"Let's see if this bear can dance," she said, saluting with her sword.

"Begin!" shouted Cord.

Ratham came on immediately, advancing with his

sword in a series of lunging attacks, thrusting high and low. Cindra retreated a few steps, parrying as she went, before skipping to the side. Ratham kept pressing the attack, swinging his sword in controlled chops, beating at her blade.

Cindra switched to a scorpion-like Fire guard, holding the sword over her head, point towards the enemy. Ratham pulled back into a Water guard, sword held waist-high, point at his opponent's face. He shuffled back a few steps, lowering into an Earth guard, his sword pointed at the ground. *Trying to lure me in*, Cindra thought. *He's not angry enough yet.*

They shifted through guard stances, anticipating, adjusting their distance and position, locking eyes and watching for an opening. Ratham goaded her by tapping the end of her sword. Cindra kept her feet moving in a little dance, starting right then reversing, backing away then returning. She attacked with a shout, stamping her foot and thrusting at her opponent's armored neck. Ratham parried and countered, gliding his blade along hers, stabbing at her arms. The combatants traded several more blows in this manner; feet moving, arms pumping, blades barely separating as metal rang with abrasive music.

The moment she saw Ratham's hand leave the handle, she made her exit, performing a whirling step that would have made her dance instructors proud. Her sword followed through, landing a blow on the hand that Ratham had intended to grab her wrist with. The young man hissed in pain, cursing.

"Hit, DePort!" Cord said. Cindra's friends cheered, as did a few others who didn't care for the obnoxious Ratham.

Cindra's chest swelled with confidence, but she quickly calmed herself. *It was a good hit, but only one hit.*

Ratham flexed his hand, grimacing. Master Cord asked, "Ratham, can you continue?" The lad nodded, glowering at his foe. He gingerly gripped the pommel with only a finger and thumb.

They resumed starting positions and began again, this time with Cindra on the offensive. She came on with a series of cuts toward Ratham's side, sending impact shocks down the blade to jolt his injured left hand; the hand that was meant to give leverage to his blows. She was certain he could swing quite hard with one hand, but every little bit helped.

Rejick was not in a pleasant mood, and it manifested as an overly-aggressive series of thrusts and cuts, which Cindra chose to avoid rather than parry. Her Su'Kraal training made her aware of the space around her and of her entire body, allowing her to duck, dodge, and sidestep his assaults without using her sword. Unfortunately, this meant that Cindra's guard was not as strong as it should have been.

Feigning a thrust at her face, Ratham redirected his attack to strike the top of her foot. Cindra cried in pain, moving her injured limb out of harm's way, and slashed in an attempt to drive him back. He parried the blow, used the cross-guard to hook her blade aside, and then smashed his pommel into her chin. Blood flew as Cindra was made to bite her tongue.

"Hold!" Cord cried, bringing his staff between them. "Two hits to Ratham. Jaron, see to your squire."

Jaron was already halfway there with a linen rag, and he cursed under his breath as he saw the damage. Cindra had a wide gash on her chin, and blood was streaming from her mouth, coloring her teeth and lips in crimson gore. Luckily her tongue was intact, but it had a nasty gash. Her eyes were tearing up with the pain, and she was favoring her right foot.

"I think this match is over," Jaron said.

"Nhu!" Cindra shook her head. "Umarrite!"

Jaron looked her in the face, clearly worried. "Are you sure?" he asked so only she could hear, "You're a mess."

"Show ish he," she said with a fire in her eyes. She wiped them dry and took her position as the students applauded.

Cord said, "LuVestra, go and fetch Celia, tell her to bring her needle and thread." As the man left, Cord gave Jaron a long-suffering look before calling, "Continue!"

"*Gher yaas*," Ratham sneered. He advanced with confidence, watching her hobble on her bruised foot. Swords clashed as he pressed the attack, but Cindra had lost the mobility that had been her saving grace. He closed too quickly, knocking her blade aside and striking her in the head with his injured hand. He cried out in pain and anguish as his opponent went down.

Cindra fell to one knee. The face guard absorbed a little of the impact, but it still made her ears ring and her vision blur. She dropped her sword, raising her arm in time to block the knee he aimed at her addled skull.

But Ratham had pulled his punch; his hand was broken, and he could not bring himself to smash it into anything with much force. He was distracted by the pain, taking precious seconds to adjust his grip for a finishing strike.

She picked up her sword in her left hand, and with her right, she grabbed Ratham's ankle. She sent the point of her blade under Rejick's fuzzy chin, pushing up and back while lifting his foot out from under him. He tipped back, unable to flex enough to avoid the blade, and fell with a crash to the floor. Cindra was on him in a second, her knee on his chest and her longsword in a half-hand grip, pointed at his throat.

"D'waavuss," she said around her swollen tongue, her blood dripping on Ratham's chest.

"*D'ravos!*" cried her teammates, who rushed forward to slap her back and help her from the hall.

"*D'ravos*, by the gods," muttered Jaron, rubbing the blood back into his face. *There'll be no living with her now.* He shook his head and went off to see to his wounded squire.

Chapter Twenty Five

Whispers

Maveezh had waited long enough. She had mourned her husband for a year, wishing for vengeance but powerless to act. He had obviously found the Corrina girl at the fencing school, but had missed his chance to kill her before she was spirited away to the castle. *Now my beloved husband is dead, and I am in hiding, unable to even visit his grave.*

All of the high priest's information pointed to a marriage alliance between the Corrina heir and a half-elf noble boy, a boy who was sent to the Corrinas by DuChat himself, ironically. Both were secured in Casselvane Keep, unreachable even by the high priest's Circle of Gold assassin, who had disappeared without a trace shortly after the New Year vigil.

Now she sat across from DuChat in his private office, as she had done so many times before. Only this time, she was not begging for scraps of information, but demanding action. *My husband would be horrified at my audacity,* she thought. *But he is dead, suffering whatever judgment the Tyrant has in store for all of us.*

"What you ask is blasphemy, Maveezh," he said with a dangerous calm. "You want to *test* the prophet of Mash?"

"I want to be certain that he *is* the prophet of Mash," she said. "If the Countless Lord would speak to us, then we would know for sure."

"The gods do not speak any longer," he stated. "Everyone knows this."

"So we must trust our fate to old prophecies and omens? Why not be certain? Llomaak's faithful *rejoiced* when the gods fell silent and we could make our own destinies. Are we truly free, or are we not?" She sat back, calming herself. "What is the worst that can happen when you are trying to end the world?"

DuChat considered and said, "How would he be tested, exactly? What methods would you use to confirm that he bears the blood of our god? I am most interested to hear."

At least he is entertaining the idea, she thought. "We might at least ask to *see* the Dark Heart. There is the Incantation of the Blood; I used it before on that stone your man acquired in Aurilon." Her brow creased and she added, "Speaking of that, what has changed since then? You did not trust in the Mad One so implicitly before. That's why you were interested in that large amethyst in the first place."

DuChat took on a brooding look, folding his fingers as he ran the tips through his beard. Maveezh realized that she had never seen him as uneasy as he looked just then. "I was impetuous. I had... doubts. It was a crisis of faith, Maveezh." He looked up at her with a lidded stare, the scar upon his eye pulling tighter. "Do you know how I came to hear of the Mad One's arrival?"

She shook her head, uncertain why he was sharing this. He was never this forthcoming.

"I heard it as a faerie story, told by a business

associate. He claimed that far in the north, a merchant from Port Kiron learned of a mad old diviner, possibly a wizard or holy man. The merchant sought him out, hoping to use his powers for profit. He paid for the stranger's passage across the Eshlin Bay, but the old man seemed to be cursed. Bizarre things happened around him, and the crew almost put him over the side out of fear. Finally, they made port at Eshlin-Keska. The old man said he was heading south, claiming he had 'business of the heart' in Portshia.

"The merchant left the mad fellow behind, racing his caravan ahead to tell the tale. The story traveled south from Eshlin-Keska, then to Rickshome-on-the-Joshian, and eventually down the trade routes to here. I heard it four years ago, and only because I made small talk with a visiting supplier. I wasn't even planning on being at the warehouse that day."

Maveezh waited for more, but he had finished. She said, "I don't understand why this-"

"It was *mere chance*," DuChat snapped. "I am the *High Priest* of Llomaak, not just in Calilon, but in all of Gartetha! Yet I received no omens, no dreams, no indication that the prophet had arrived. We might have prepared, might have sent someone..." he trailed off, regaining his usual calm, cultured demeanor. "I was *annoyed* with the Countless Lord, do you understand? I felt slighted. I do not take it well, not even from a god, it seems."

Maveezh understood perfectly well, for she felt her role had been marginalized also, but she did not say this. Instead she offered, "Yet word did come to you, though seemingly by chance. Is that not equally as amazing as having a prophetic dream or sign? Is chance not the province of chaos?"

He smiled, "I thought the same upon reflection, once my wounded pride had healed. While your dearly-departed husband was away on his errand to the west, I considered how things had turned out. The stone Dexer recovered was not the Dark Heart, but that meant we could use it to pay the Minozhians instead of betray them; now they might aid us again for the right price.

"There is something in the prophecies after all, and it is foolish to try to work against them." He leaned forward on his elbows and said, "Some of our scholars have an interesting theory, did you know? They believe that the Mad One who was foretold is the same individual that made the *original* prophecy; that he was speaking of *his own* return."

Maveezh had not heard this, and she said with mouth agape, "That would make him well over a thousand years old!"

"Indeed," DuChat said. "If it is true, he may be a power to be reckoned with. Are you certain you want to test such a one?"

She thought for a moment, weighing the risks.

My beloved husband is dead.

Finally, she replied, "I am certain. Ghethas died in the service of the Countless Lord, and now he is suffering the judgment of the Tyrant. If this Mad One indeed caries the seed of the world's destruction, then I will have it hastened to us. If not..." She cursed herself as tears clouded her vision. "We were going to see it together, he and I. We were going to live life to the fullest, and laugh when it all came tumbling down."

DuChat reached out and took her hand. "We have all lost someone we loved, Maveezh. We all have those for whom we are willing to pull down Creation; if not for the sake of all, then at least for one. Is it asking so much to just have faith in-"

"It is," she snapped, wiping her eyes. "It is."

He sat back in his chair, knowing that there was only one way to deal with *her* crisis of faith. "Very well," he said, folding his hands before him as he often did when closing a deal, "If you must, send five of the brethren to test the Mad One. See if he has it with him, and if he is false, then kill him." He leaned forward with a warning look, "But don't send anyone you care about."

Maveezh sat in the cool, darkened gloom of her bedchamber, adjusting the polished mirror upon the vanity table. Candles had been lit, dripping wax on their little clay dishes and flickering with the draft from the open window. Though the weather was nice for late spring, the evening was more breezy than she would have liked. Regardless, an open window was required for the ritual.

Divine Alchemy, like wizard's magic, needs what it needs; only a fool ignores this.

She poured a special concoction into a small copper bowl that she had blessed with her own blood under the new moon. The amber liquid gave off a rank odor that stung her nose; she figured she would never get used to it, and perhaps that was the point. She opened a leather pouch and withdrew a few pinches of ash gathered from a funeral pyre. The dead man had been a fellow priest and a friend, happy to forgo traditional burial so that his brethren might acquire the valuable material upon his demise. When the ash hit the liquid it gave a squealing hiss, releasing a sickly, yellow wisp of smoke. It reeked of sulfur and death, pungent and vile.

Calling across the veil between worlds was risky, especially when inviting a demnox to partially cross over. Whispers couldn't possess a body like some other demnoxa, but they were very unpleasant if allowed to roam unbound in one's mind. The mirror served to focus the summoning and keep the Whisper contained, but accidents could happen. "*Kwaath ni haazh, een dizhwa vess, Lom kewa Haaviss!*" Maveezh completed the spell and waited, staring calmly into the mirror.

The candles flickered violently, her reflection shimmered like a heat mirage, and the woman in the mirror changed. The image twisted its mouth grotesquely, baring teeth in a grimace, moving lips as if unfamiliar with them. The image spoke, and Maveezh watched with morbid fascination. Its voice was the faint, rasping whisper that gave the things their name.

"Aaaah, flesh... rather, a reflection of flesh, but twill suffice..." Its sibilant hissing made her ears itch and her skin crawl. Maveezh clenched her teeth as the familiar face before her rolled its eyes and worked its tongue inside its mouth. *"What service do you ask of us?"*

She had thought on this for months now. There was a cabal in the north that might intercept the old lunatic on his way to Portshia, but she needed to contact them first. Whispers were good for that, and much more discreet than ember swallows. The firebird messengers were as subtle as rocket flares, as Ghethas would no doubt agree. *Poor Ghethas.*

"I need to send a message to a priest of the Countless Lord, one of my brethren, Omiras Bevek. He lives in Rickshome-on-the-Joshian in the Calione Mountains," she watched her own face contort like a madwoman's.

"Ricky-joshy-cali-mounty..." it hissed in contempt, *"this means nothing to us. All here is blackness and wind, no mountains, no cities. We need his face, his eyes, conjure him for us."* The woman in the mirror shuddered and shook with inhuman speed, her eyes bulging from their sockets hideously. It was a trick of course, to make Maveezh want to close or avert her eyes. Any such distraction, even taking too long to blink, would allow it to hide in her mind instead, haunting her dreams before she could dictate the terms of its service. She had no intention of letting a Whisper run rampant behind her eyelids.

She brought a face to her mind, the face of the one she wanted to contact.

"No, this one will not do," the Whisper said with amusement, *"This one is dead, rotting in earth. His soul is not here with us, or I would have heard his screams..."*

Maveezh glared hard at the Whisper as its face became that of Ghethas for the merest instant. Her heart pounded and her breathing grew heavy, but she dare not turn away. *Damn you, idiot woman!* she cursed herself, *Concentrate, or this thing will wear his face in your dreams and drive you mad!*

She kept her gaze on the repulsive reflection, calming herself as she pictured the man she had met years ago. Omiras Bevek was a lean, hawkish-looking man with a short beard and hair that was cropped to a graying stubble. His eyes were hard and black, like little pieces of coal over a sharp nose. They had met during a social event at one of Lord Clavemont's famous parties; Maveezh and Ghethas were playing the annoying Gordons, and Omiras Bevek had been the bodyguard of a wealthy northern merchant. Bevek had the look of a steely killer, so the part suited him well.

The Whisper made a satisfied sound that resembled escaping steam and bubbling water. Her reflection grinned, pulling its lips back to show receding gums and exaggerated teeth. Stretch-lines formed around the tortured mouth as it cocked its head. *"Yesssss, that will do. That will do nicely."* The gurgle in its throat made Maveezh want to cough, but she composed herself, keeping her expression tranquil. The impulse to mimic the reflection made her facial muscles twitch, even as she was sickened by it. She watched the mole on her reflection's face start to shift and grow. *It's no wonder people go mad dealing with these creatures*, she thought.

As if it heard her thoughts, it croaked, "Mad... mad-mad-mad-mad-"

"I need you to give him an urgent message," Maveezh said forcefully. "When he accepts the message, he will give the benediction 'Mash bah havaath' and you will leave him. Do you accept?" She stared herself in the eyes, which rolled back to appear white, then darted about spasmodically. Maveezh wanted to blink, but she only narrowed her eyes instead, keeping the demnox in sight.

"We accept," it hissed softly, *"What is this **urgent** message?"* Her reflection stared past her into the room, grinning at the flickering shadows as if there were more if its kind within them. The thought gave her

goosebumps, but she dared not turn and look.

"Tell him that the Mad One is taking the Casselvane Road to Portshia. He must be intercepted and relieved of his burden. Choose four trusted brethren to assist, use caution but move with all haste. The High Priest is waiting." The last bit was to offer extra motivation. What did it matter that DuChat was only indulging what he thought to be her foolishness? His doubts would evaporate when he held the Dark Heart in his hands.

"The Mad One's burden... what could it mean? Hrmmm, a riddle, a riddle," the Whisper scratched thoughtfully at its chin, drawing blood; Maveezh felt a sympathetic tingle on her skin as the breeze from the window made the candles flicker even more. *"We know a great many mad ones here, and all have mighty burdens. What's the burden that can be relieved so? Something big, something small?"* The Mirror Maveezh took a thinking pose, tapping its bloody chin with a clawed finger.

"I didn't call you to discuss the message, only to deliver it. Do it tonight, do it until he gives the benediction and you are dismissed." Her mouth tightened into a line as she glared at the maddening demnox wearing her reflection. She had a pain behind her eyes and a deep desire to close them, but it was the last thing she was going to do. This Whisper seemed more churlish than others she had summoned in the past. Maybe it sensed that the End was near?

Mirror Maveezh darted a long, black tongue, licking the blood from its chin. Then it grimaced and made a choking bark, a vulgar kind of laugh that made the woman flinch. It bowed its head in mock deference, all the while looking slyly up at her past its eyebrows. *"Sssssh temper, temper. We will do it, we agreed."* It winked at her, then closed its eyes as a gust of wind blew from the room and out the open window, extinguishing the candles.

Maveezh looked at her reflection in the mirror,

making sure the loathing and tension on the face were truly her own. Satisfied that the Whisper had gone, she placed the mirror face-down and closed her eyes, rubbing her temples. She hoped Omiras Bevek would not hold a grudge for her sending such a messenger, but it could not be helped. She made herself ready for bed, shuddering at the thought of what dreams Omiras might have as the Whisper carried out its task. She had a feeling her own might not be pleasant either.

Chapter Twenty Six

Bridges and Trolls

Omiras Bevek awoke in a cold sweat, his heart thumping in his chest, threatening to break out with its thunderous beating. Fear and loathing gripped him as he fumbled for the proper phrase. He could still see the chattering teeth and spinning eyes in the darkness, making it nearly impossible to concentrate. "*Mash bah havaath!*" he blurted into the shadows. The window shutters clattered with an unnatural breeze, blowing out from the room into the dark night beyond. He heard a sound like a hissing snake breathing a sigh, or perhaps a gurgling death rattle, and the eerie noise faded into the peaceful chirping of crickets and the rustle of leaves on the trees.

"A Whisper," he said to the darkness. The woman beside him stirred and let out a mumbling question, followed by light snoring. The demnox messenger, twisting a pleasant remembrance of the evening's pleasures into a hideous nightmare, had used his woman's face. The visage of the sender had been used as well, shifting under falling hair, spitting bile into his eyes. He was no stranger to depravity, but some things were best reserved for the Abyss and its mad children, not the world of mortals.

Bevek heard the message ringing in his thoughts, spoken by a forked tongue and burned into his mind with goat-pupil eyes, all sitting neatly in the face of the woman beside him.

"The Mad One is taking the Casselvane Road to Portshia; he must be intercepted and relieved of his burden. Choose four trusted brethren to assist, use caution but move with all haste; the High Priest is waiting." It had repeated this until the dreams became more unsavory and finally unbearable. He spoke the words of confirmation over and over, but to no avail; the wretched thing held him until he awoke and uttered the words aloud.

Getting out of bed and hearing the chimes of the hour before dawn, he washed his face in cold water and got dressed in the dark. They would need coin, supplies, weapons, and probably a few items of Divine Alchemy to supplement their arsenal. He would be pounding on the doors of his fellows within the hour, rousing them from their peaceful sleep and warm beds, bidding them make ready for a long chase. The Mad One was to be caught and the Dark Heart was to be taken. He wondered whose idea that was?

Marvek was not happy to see him, having been in a particularly warm bed having a very peaceful sleep. Bevek had little patience for his complaints and told him, "Be happy you did not receive the summons. She sent a damned Whisper."

"Rath's golden balls," Marvek swore. "Must be important." His attitude softened and he was silent for the rest of the morning, except to scold others who complained. No one wanted a visit from a Whisper.

The preparations were completed by late morning, a small miracle for a Highday. It was with heavy hearts that the company passed the gates of Rickshome-on-the-Joshian, leaving the soft lives they had worked so hard to secure for themselves. If the world was to end soon, they wanted to spend their last days here, but duty was duty, and the world wasn't going to end by itself. They bid farewell to the clear waters of Lake Lumiras and the shining city that was called the Jewel of the North.

Bevek took the lead, his hooded cloak draped over the back of his horse, making the two look like one peculiar, fused creature. Marvek, the most senior acolyte, rode second. He was a big man, red of hair with ruddy cheeks, his unruly mane braided behind his head in the northern manner.

The third was Colm, a quiet acolyte from the town of Cantra in the northern province of Shylith-Dromah, where the Llomaakitte priesthood once held its most sacred rituals among the stone circles.

Fourth was Helvert, a fellow sell-sword that had accompanied Bevek on many missions, both as an honest mercenary and a devotee of the Countless Lord. He was a thin man with a bland face who could vanish in a crowd, blending in with his remarkable ordinariness, making him an invaluable spy.

The fifth man was new to the order, having earned his place with a grand show of enthusiasm, poisoning the well in the village where he was raised. The local lord, fearing a plague, had the bodies burned in their homes and set fire to the fields and livestock as well. It was a fine amount of bedlam created with little effort, marking him as particularly efficient and ruthless. His name was Felithor and he showed great promise, even if he was a bit too eager.

"So this old man we're tracking, is he the real thing?" Felithor asked.

Marvek called back, "That's what we're off to find out. Scared?"

"Hardly," Felithor answered with bravado. "Prophet or no, he's just a man. Men bleed and men die."

Helvert called over his shoulder, "What were you taught of the Dark Heart, newling?"

"It is the blood of the Countless Lord, the essence of chaos, imbued with malice for the works of both men and gods," Felithor recited. "It brought the Bythian Empire to ruin, wiping it from the face of Jayde. It caused the Time of Chaos, rending the natural order asunder. And this time," he looked at the sunlight through the dappled treetops, "This time it will end all things and set us free."

"Not bad," Helvert said. "But you neglected to make mention of the Chosen who bear the Heart. That nameless Bythian Emperor was a Sorcerer King. Legends say he used the power of the Dark Heart to conquer whole kingdoms, level mountains, and even make his queen immortal and eternally beautiful."

"I've heard the legend, but–"

"When this land was known as Calilaar, the Tyrant himself chose a mortal king to rule. Orthicus the Great was a mighty king; then we presented him with the Dark Heart, and it changed him to the core. He devastated entire armies, razed castles to the ground, and rent the veil between this world and the next."

Felithor rolled his eyes, "I know the histories, Helv–"

Marvek interrupted this time, "What our good friend is saying in his round-about way is that the bearer of the Dark Heart is not to be underestimated."

"True enough," Felithor said, "but he's just a courier, basically. He's supposed to give it to the priesthood and tell us who the Final Chosen is. He's not the chosen himself."

"But he may be the Prophet of Llomaak," said Helvert. "What do you know of him?"

Felithor thought for a moment. "His coming was foretold by the last prophet. What else is there to know?"

"What if they're one and the same?" Helvert asked.

The junior acolyte scoffed at that, then noticed no one else found it particularly funny. "He can't be the same," he said. "That's impossible."

"Not impossible, just unknown," Helvert said. "One should always fear the unknown."

The majestic Calione Peaks seemed no smaller by midday, but the city above Lake Lumiras was dwindling, so that only its tallest spires could be seen above the trees. Runoff from the surrounding mountains created the lake, which then fed the mighty Joshian River, flowing west and south, all the way to the sea.

The summer floods were abating, but the river would still be fast and high due to winter's heavy snowfall. Bridges crossed it at many points, connecting villages along the edge of the Shadowood as it stretched its boughs eastward. Water oxen plied the currents after spring thaw, drawing laden barges up and downstream.

Bevek wished they could travel by passenger barge, but the Mad One was reportedly taking the Casselvane Road, which was at least fifty miles south of the river's course. They would have to cross the river, trek south along the High Forest Road until it met the Casselvane, and then determine if the old man had passed by or not. If so, they were on their way to Portshia. If not, it meant following the road northeastward around the foothills of the Calione Peaks. That being the case, Bevek was certain their moods would be sour by the time they intercepted the old man, and their 'testing' would reflect that.

"Now that's a sight," Felithor exclaimed, and the others turned to look. Brightly painted Galindri caravans sat in the shade of the aspen trees, as their owners moved about in colorful attire. White clouds drifted on a gentle breeze, tearing themselves upon the distant peaks. High spires of the city gleamed like shards of ice topped with fluttering banners, and the haze of its hearth fires gave a dream-like quality to the scene, as if they viewed a faerie story come to life.

We leave all of this behind to chase down a wretched

old man on a long and lonely road, Bevek mused. *He'd better be the one.*

The first few days were relaxing, even with their haste. The men rode until sundown, staying at whatever passed for an inn along the way. Upon reaching the town of Selvanor Crossing, the company headed south on the High Forest road, a lesser-used path through the eastern arm of the Shadowood. The road was twisting and narrow, plagued by landslides and overgrowth, and it offered few amenities, but it would take a few days off the journey.

"Such a charming road," Marvek remarked as they cleared some large stones from the path. "It's a wonder we haven't met anyone yet."

"It was used more often a few years ago," Helvert said, dusting off and mounting his horse. "But people started going out of their way to avoid it."

"Why?" asked Felithor. "Not because of what that innkeeper said, surely?"

Helvert nodded, "True or not, people were afraid. Besides, for all we know, it could be true."

After three days on the forest road, they came to the Woodcliff Bridge, a sturdy structure that spanned a small ravine through which the Joshian flowed. The currents broke into whitecaps over the jagged rocks below, and the roar of the water was both inspiring and terrible. Barges could not pass safely, so they would have to unload upstream and cart the goods to moorings below the gorge.

Bevek, who had been leading the way, urged his horse to cross the bridge first, for there was hardly room for two riders abreast. The horse was reluctant, but with a bit of urging, it headed across. Hooves clomped on the wooden planks, which were at least in good repair.

Bevek had never had a problem with heights, but upon glancing over the side of the bridge, he was overcome with a bout of vertigo the likes of which he had never experienced. His horse either suffered as well, or feeling his master's weight shifting, was inclined to veer closer to the railing. The other men called out to him in alarm, fearing he might tumble headlong into the rapids below. However, the sensation passed as quickly as it came, and he hastily righted himself in the saddle. Fear surged within his chest, and he heard his pulse pounding in his ears.

A deep, grating voice croaked from below the bridge, "None shall pass..." It echoed about the canyon walls and over the roar of the water, "...unless payment be made." The men drew weapons, and the horses shied from the evil noise, neighing in alarm.

"Who is there?" Bevek shouted. "Who demands a toll on the lord's bridge?" He had an inkling of what it might be, but waited just the same.

From below the far side of the structure came a clawed hand, gray and mottled green, with skin like that of a toad. Another hand followed it, and the owner of the voice pulled itself up the side of the structure, clamping onto the railings with horrid strength, making the timber groan under its dry, bony fingers.

Its head was misshapen; crowned with twisting horns and a spiny brow. A long hooked nose bent over a mouthful of needle-sharp fangs above a pointed chin. Its ears were pointed and swept back, ridged like serrated blades. Its body was spindly and thin, like a starved corpse; the skin stretched tightly over skeletal joints and ribs. Thin, thorny protrusions sprouted from its spine, flaring like the quills of a porcupine when the thing bent its back. The other men cursed and recoiled in fear, but Omiras Bevek steadied his horse and raised a hand in greeting.

"Guadim T'drall," said Bevek, as he identified the monstrosity. "*Mash bah havaath.*" *Mash be exalted* was the greeting given between the servants of Llomaak. 'Mash' was the god's ancient name in the old Bythian language. *T'drall* meant 'fell creature' in the same tongue.

The Guadim glared as it thumped onto the bridge. It

stood hunched over but still eye-to-eye with the man on horseback. "*Mash bah havaath,*" it replied with irritation, looking at the other four men and the meat they were riding. "Leave your food, and I shall allow you to pass." It bared its needle teeth, casually blocking the way. The smell of rotting vegetation and bad eggs wafted across the chasm.

Bevek looked uncertainly at the Guadim, spreading his hands to his sides in a peaceful gesture. "We are all servants of the Countless Lord. Surely you will not extract a toll from *us?*"

The Guadim was unmoved. "Will I not?" it said.

"We are on important business for the High Priest in Portshia," he said, praying DuChat's reputation meant something to this ancient abomination.

It spat a yellowish glob that sizzled on the wood, staining it permanently. "Portshia," it croaked, "Speak to me not of Portshia. Were it not for another of the Countless Lord's children, I would be there still."

It seemed more than a little annoyed that Bevek was making conversation instead of cowering in fear. "The high priest sent you away?" he asked, confused.

"*The high priest!* Hah! Such arrogance," it sneered. "Your little human hierarchies do not interest me. No, it was a vemlok; one of the rare, tamed ones. The pompous bloodsucker bade me to leave and never return to his city. *His* city!" It glowered, making Bevek's horse stamp and toss its head. "I was doing the will of Mash, carrying out orders as old as man. Still, he thwarted me, the traitorous swine." It leered at the men anew, leaning forward and making the horses retreat. "Now... your food."

Bevek dared to be bold, "So this is how you serve Mash now? Lurking under bridges and waylaying travelers? I had only heard of such things in faerie stories and laughed at them." The other men exchanged nervous looks, wondering if this course of action was wise.

The Guadim grumbled deep in its throat and replied,

"It was a temporary setback, and I do what I must to survive. Time is my ally, and patience is my weapon." He chuckled and said, "Your high priest could learn a thing or two about patience, if he has sent you to seek the Mad One. Do you think him powerless and frail? Could he acquire the Divine Blood and deliver it if he were merely a doddering old fool?"

Bevek stared in shock. "I have said nothing of the Mad One. How do you claim to know of our errand?" He felt for his sword handle with his elbow, making sure it was in easy reach; not that it would aid him much.

"Give old Paugh some credit," it said mockingly, "I have many friends in the Abyss, many old, old friends. They *whisper* to me."

The Whisper, thought Bevek. *Gibbering blabbermouth*. He said, "So we seek the Mad One, what of it? Do you have information to aid us, or do you only wish for a handout?" The Guadim tensed, a murderous look in its eyes. The horses shied and snorted, and Bevek's mount got too close to the railing, bruising the rider's leg. *That remark may have gone too far*, he thought.

The foul creature seemed to dwindle slightly as it forced itself to relax. It rumbled from deep in its throat, "Hrmm, so Llomaak's gift was not wasted on humans; every one of you touches the flame to see how it burns. Very well, leave half of your food and I shall tell you what I know."

The five men sat around their campfire, the bridge and the guadim a whole day behind them. There was enough food if they ate sparingly, but each knew they would go to sleep with stomachs rumbling. At least they were alive, and they had new information on their quarry.

"Do you believe it?" Marvek asked, rubbing his beard. "That the Mad One is neither wizard nor sorcerer, but more dangerous than both?"

Felithor spoke up, "He walks with a staff and bizarre

things happen in his wake. The power of the gods is no longer felt in the world, so it must be wizardry."

"The Dark Heart is the power of a god," said Helvert, his face impassive as he stared into the fire. "He does not have to be anything more than the Prophet of Llomaak."

"Whatever he is, we have our mission." Bevek said, throwing bits of kindling into the fire to watch them curl and blacken. "A servant of Llomaak would not refuse to prove himself, and he would surely appreciate what aid we could offer. However, if he *does* refuse..."

"We knock him about," Felithor smiled.

"Well," Bevek said, "if we gain his trust first, he will lower his guard."

"Is *that* what madmen do?" asked Colm, speaking for the first time that day. The men considered this in silence.

"Regardless, we have our mission," Bevek said. "Thanks to our guadim friend, we know the Mad One spent the winter in Velloness, which means he could be in Portshia by now."

Marvek said, "I doubt it. The foothills of the Calione Forest Road are a tough march for a soldier, let alone a shunned old man."

"Shunned?" Felithor asked.

"Likely," Marvek said. "The trouble that follows the Mad One would make him an unwelcome guest in any village. He might get on in a city for a time, since few would immediately see him as the cause. I'm guessing he lives worse than any beggar; sleeping where he can, eating what he can."

Bevek shook his head, "There must be a reason why the high priest ordered us to take it from him. According to prophecy, the Mad One will deliver the Dark Heart to the faithful and choose the scion to receive it."

Felithor offered, "Maybe the high priest has someone else in mind? Maybe he's chosen himself?"

Marvek scoffed, "Rubbish. Even if he *were* of the

secret bloodline, he'd not be suitable. The Dark Heart corrupts those who follow the ways of the Tyrant, turning order into chaos. Neither the high priest, nor any of Llomaak's faithful could be subverted, seeing as we've devoted ourselves to opposing the Tyrant and his ways."

"Well, he must have some plans that diverge from the scriptures," said Colm.

Helvert said quietly, "There is one thing we have not considered," the others turned to look at him as he spoke into the firelight, "Perhaps *we* are the test."

"What do you mean?" Felithor asked.

"Perhaps the high priest is confirming what he believes, that the Mad One is legitimate. By sending us to take the Dark Heart, he is hoping not for our success, but for our failure."

"Sending us to die," Marvek said glumly. "I had a suspicion."

Felithor asked, "What do we do then?" He searched the faces of his companions for a fear like his own and found none.

"We try and take the Dark Heart from the Mad One," said Bevek. "We try our best and pray that we fail, for the sake of the greater goal."

Felithor resolved himself along with the others, nodding and breathing deeply. Death was the eventual goal, death for the world and everyone in it.

Only then would everyone be free.

The week wore on as they traveled the High Forest Road, gaining fresh supplies at the first village they came to, replenishing what the guadim had demanded for his scant information and passage over the bridge. At the end of their eleventh day of travel, after passing many farms and homesteads, they arrived at the junction where the High Forest met the Casselvane road.

The Casselvane was one of the old Celvestrian highways built during the century of imperial rule, when vast work projects connected cities across the expansive continent. The High Forest Road was little more than a wide dirt trail; prone to flooding in the rainy season, creating a ribbon of mud that stranded travelers along its length. The Casselvane Road was built over twelve centuries ago, and built to last.

The community built at the junction was called Casselward, a mining town in the foothills of the Cassel mountain range. The short buildings were poorly constructed and in a constant state of disrepair, owing to the haste of the town's founding. A modest, walled keep was situated to protect the mine and the smelting facilities, which were built on a sheltered rise. The region around the town was bereft of trees for several miles, having been clear-cut to fuel the furnaces.

Felithor looked at the wary faces of the townsfolk. "What's their problem, do you think?" he asked.

Marvek answered, "They likely haven't seen travelers arriving by the forest road since that guadim took up residence."

"Or those that have were shaken down and shaken up," quipped Helvert.

As the others saw to stabling the horses and finding an inn, Bevek and Marvek approached the city watch, asking about a strange old man.

"Been here sure enough," said the watchman. "Passed through over a month ago, and left none too soon." He called over to his fellow, who was chatting up a maid. "Hey there, Kam! Remember the old codger who stumbled through a'moth past?"

Kam stepped up and nodded, "Can't forget him that easy. Was late Jay' or early Lelomoth. Strange time, that was."

"What happened?" Bevek inquired.

"All the forges went cold, for starters. Brought work to a standstill. No one could explain it." Kam scratched under his helmet. "Then there was the dust."

"Aye, blowing dust came in from the east, choking the lungs and settling like new snow," said the first watchman. "Was after the dust blew in that we seen the old man wandering up the road, dirty and worn, like he'd been walking the trails all his life. We didn't think nothing strange of him, just thought 'Poor old gummer got caught in the freak storm.' Was a while later we guessed he was the reason."

"You think these things were caused by the old one?" Marvek asked.

"Don't know if he was the cause or not, but bad things all came together that day. Old fellow wasn't in his right mind, I tell you. Whether he means ill or no, I think trouble follows him, or he follows it."

The other men had collected similar stories from the townsfolk, some too absurd to believe. There was always going to be exaggeration when strange events came to a sleepy town, but it was undeniable that the arrival of the old man heralded far more sinister happenings than could be explained.

The watchman asked, "What are you going to do when you catch up to him?"

Bevek smiled and said, "Take the poor man home, where he can cause no more mischief." The watchman looked dubious, but nodded his head politely.

The journey to Portshia began early the next morning, and the men rode at the fastest pace their mounts could maintain. There were a few small villages by the highway that confirmed the old man's passing, all relating strange occurrences that preceded and followed him. Milk went sour, animals dropped dead, a flock of birds flew into the wall of the local temple; all of these things and more were contributed to his presence.

Some villages had been forewarned, and drove him away with stones and other unsavory projectiles. A pall hung over those communities now, as though all the life had been sapped away, leaving the residents with drawn faces and little hope or care for the future. The priests became more unsettled and wary as they followed his trail, and the warnings of the guadim haunted them. The men had little cause to trust the creature at the time, but it seemed that it had been completely forthright with them. Sometimes the truth was just too good to hide, especially when it was difficult to believe.

Chapter Twenty Seven

Summer Heat

The summer became hotter, as summer is wont to do, but not within recent memory had the sun beat down so fiercely on the lands close to the sea. 'Unnatural' some called it, as if another force was working its will.

The sea breeze offered no relief within the city, for the weather only enhanced the odors of the wharf which were thick with runoff from the sewers. The harbor stockyards were worse in the heat, for while most people loved the smell of meat cooking on the spit, it created a horrendous odor as it cooked while still mooing and eliminating.

Taverns did a brisk business as bedraggled striders crowded within, downing pints of weak ale as they escaped the sun. The finer establishments hired wizards to chill and move the air, making the normally stuffy drinking houses feel fresh and cool, as if an autumn breeze were blowing through. Tavern maids adopted the midriff baring style of the Galindri women, both to stay cooler and increase sales.

"I wish I could hire a wizard to cool this room," Jaron said. Cindra was sprawled on the bed, and Jaron sat in a chair by the window. "I can't remember a day so hot."

The sounds of horses and striders echoed from the street below as Cindra fanned the hem of the large nightshirt she was wearing, moving the breeze beneath it as she lay against the pillow. "Gavadaire claims the summers are like this in Aurilon's western peninsula," she said, "something to do with the currents, trade winds, and latitude. He's really quite well-read about all manner of things; I expect the monastery has a wonderful library."

Jaron was growing tired of 'Gavadaire this' and 'Gavadaire that,' so his tone was rather more annoyed than he intended. "Yes, it sounds dreamy," he said, standing and leaning out the window frame.

"No need to be sharp with me," Cindra said as she sat up, her bare legs kicking over the side of the bed. "There's nothing wrong with book learning."

"I'm not-" he took a breath to calm himself. "I don't mean to be terse Cindra; it's just that..." he ran his hand through his hair, which was unbound and hung loose about his shoulders. "Most of your time is spent with him, you know that? Your team is under his watch, you are one of his favorite students in Highday training, he talks about you often at meals..."

"Does he?" Cindra asked, unable to help herself from teasing.

"Yes!" Jaron answered angrily, "Yes he does." He exaggerated LuVestra's accent, "Bedween you and I, dat Deellan will be quite de warrier!"

Cindra hopped off the bed and swayed over to the window, flipping the hem of the nightshirt playfully; it was obviously no time for teasing. "Don't be cross, Jaron love," she said, touching his arm, "This is silliness and you know it."

"Is it?" he asked, turning to look at her, "He's got his eye on you, which is bad enough, seeing as how you're supposed to be in hiding. You don't have to encourage him by acting like his pet student."

"Pet?" Cindra said, taken aback. "I act like his pet?" She dropped her hand from his arm.

"It's 'Gavadaire said this,' and 'Gavadaire did that,' I hear his name from your lips all the time!" He stalked around the room, "It gets tiresome. He makes you his assistant during training, he calls on you more than anyone else-"

"Or perhaps you hear him call 'Dillan' because you're listening for it," Cindra said, folding her arms. "And he uses me as an assistant, I believe, because I am one of his better students. And I talk about him because he is our training captain." She softened her voice to calm him, "Besides, if you were my training captain, you would likely get tired of me."

Jaron searched her eyes as his face grew warm.

Here it comes, thought Cindra.

"You don't have feelings for him, do you?" His ears reddened as he said the words.

"Just admiration, not love," she said calmly. "He is a remarkable man, but he is also arrogant, flashy, and thinks too much of his own sense of humor."

"You might have described me the same way once," he said.

Cindra stepped close and placed her hands on his chest, looking up at him, "Think. If I had feelings for him, I'd have to give away my secret," she poked his chest, "and if you're so right about his tastes, and he has feelings for me, then he will be expecting a boy, and shall be quite disappointed."

Jaron was still not put at ease. "That hardly covers everything," he said. "If he learns your secret, and prefers women, and if you found you had feelings for him-"

"Jaron love," she said, placing a finger on his lips, "if all had happened as it was supposed to, I would be married for over three years now, possibly with children. Neither of us is living the life we should, so it's foolish to dwell on what might be. We have each other now, which is more than either of us could have hoped for." She kissed him tenderly, standing on her toes to reach him.

He returned the pressure of her lips, holding her close as he leaned in. His arms encompassed her with gentle pressure, his hands seeking out the curves under her nightshirt. She ran her fingers through his loose hair, pulling him closer and deeper. Her hips moved against his and she moaned with anticipation, feeling the hem of her nightshirt lifted to her waist.

It had been too long since they dared such intimacy, and both had suffered from the restraint. Reason was lost as they moved from the window towards the rumpled bed, fumbling at each other's garments with reckless abandon. The summer heat fanned the passion that burned within, and a sudden breeze blew into the room, begging to be enjoyed with bare skin.

After an awkwardly austere dinner following their tryst, Cindra and Jaron visited the stables. Cindra liked to bring nightly treats called 'horse biscuits,' which were little baked cakes of oatmeal and honey. They served as equine travel rations during wartime, but the kind she bought were sweeter than usual, which suited the horses just fine. With almost two hours of daylight left, the pair decided to go riding beyond the walls. They had their horses saddled and harnessed, and made ready to find their way through the busy streets to the Trader's Gate.

T'ózha, Cindra's dark bay pony, had been strong enough to accept a rider since early spring. He was spirited, but his training at the Hyne Horse Academy was paying off, and he was getting used to noisy crowded streets. Jaron's chestnut stallion tried to set a good example of proper horse behavior, standing still and moving only when his rider indicated.

"I can't wait to let him run!" Cindra said, patting her mount's muscled neck. "He's been getting so strong."

"Headstrong," Jaron said. "Just like his rider." He smiled and drew a finger under Cindra's chin, feeling the little scar where Ratham had struck her.

"He's just feeling his oats," Cindra remarked as she scratched the scar. It had healed quickly once Celia applied a tiny bit of salve over her stitches. It was a bit of Lelonethan divine alchemy, but Jaron jokingly called it 'beauty cream.' He had also referred to her stitches as 'whiskers,' since the thread poked out a bit.

They had not gone far before they were met by a funeral procession coming down the road from a nearby temple, forcing the riders to wait until the company turned eastward towards the cemetery. Mourners followed the body of a young woman, who was born on the shoulders of eight pallbearers. Her once-lovely features were now gray, beginning to sag in death; her bright, red hair was arranged about her head like a wreathe of flame; and she was dressed in a long, simple, white gown that might have been a wedding dress. A garland of vibrant wildflowers adorned the litter. The mourners wept piteously, and wore black ribbons and sashes.

Cindra watched sadly as they passed by, wondering if the heat had caused the woman's untimely demise. She said a little prayer to Valdak to be merciful on the woman's soul, then she and Sir Jaron rode towards the Trader's Gate.

The sun cast long shadows as it sank towards the farmlands between Portshia and the Joshian River. Cindra and Jaron rode through the gate and into the Outwalls, the hooves of their mounts clomping on the drawbridge that crossed the empty moat. Lamplighters began kindling oil lamps along the main road, and street sweepers carted away horse dung and other refuse, all by traditional means. Cindra had gotten used to seeing guild wizards performing these tasks with spells, but it was a different world outside the city walls.

The knight and his squire drew little attention as they passed, though most kept their eyes downcast and moved aside for the horses. The general attitude of the populace seemed to change outside the city gates, reverting to a more manorial relationship between noble and commoner. That division was obscured within the bounds of the city proper, where wealth, not birth, served as the greater measure of status.

Farther down the road, Jaron and Cindra eased their horses into a cantor, hoping to reach open fields before the sun sank too low. The last people they passed before turning off road were two ragged men, both looking as if a long, trying journey was at an end. The younger man, perhaps ten years Jaron's senior, had an anxious look about him, watching Jaron and Cindra with dark, haunted eyes. By contrast, his companion was quite chipper and lively despite his great age; his bright eyes were so fixed on the city before him, that he missed the approaching riders. The younger man had to pull him aside lest he be trampled.

Cindra spared a look back at the odd pair before she and Jaron departed the road, making for the farmlands that stretched all the way to the river. Spurring their horses onward, the pair raced over the gentle hills and open fields of the Portshia Meadowlands. Cindra's heart leaped with joy for T'ózha's first full gallop with a rider; his eagerness to show off soon gave Jaron's horse a challenge.

She whooped with delight, wishing her Galindri family were here; wishing to see Hanni clap excitedly and Teya give a rare smile of approval. But the caravan could be anywhere by now; they might even be in Portshia at this moment, though she could not risk a reunion.

She let her pony run himself out, his gallop slowing before they intruded on one of the outlying farmhouses. Vortigras came up behind, panting but determined to make a good showing as Jaron patted his muscled neck.

"He's going to be a fine charger," Jaron said. "We'll be starting mounted combat soon, so it'll be good to put him through his paces early."

"*T'ózha, j'ámo tima, tima,*" Cindra complimented her pony as she stroked his black mane. It had been many months since she had spoken the language of the *Gatéth-sho'a* and she felt out of practice. "He's fast like his mother, my good boy."

Jaron marveled at her, the girl who had wandered so very far and seen so much. "What was it like, living with the Galindri?" he asked, looking to the striped burgundy headband on her brow that, as he understood, marked her as a warrior among them.

She looked to the eastern peaks as the setting sun painted them with light and shadow. She took in the scent of wildflowers and tilled earth, breathing deeply before she replied. "Freedom," she said. "The whole of the land was open to us, and we could go wherever we liked, asking no one's leave." She patted her pony's neck, "Once the herds joined us in the north, it was like a huge family reunion. It's as if every person I knew was only half of a whole; rider and horse." T'ózha bent to graze as Cindra sat back in the saddle, "I was there when this little one was born. Majii-ama, my adopted father, gave him to me."

Jaron had never heard her refer to the old Galindri man thus; he knew old Majii had treated her like a daughter, but Jaron did not know she considered him as a father. It was almost unseemly for one of her station to think in that way, but then Cindra was the most unseemly woman he had ever known.

"Do you think you can go back to a life of duty, after so much freedom?" he asked.

"What do you mean?" she replied, it seemed a silly question since she had given up that freedom to return home already.

"Well, if you become a knight, assuming no one decides to hang you for acting as a man," he looked sidelong at her, as if she needed a reminder, "you will answer to a lord; if not your father, than another who will require service of you. Knights are expected to garrison their lord's castle for a time, to ride to war when needed... in short, they are required to make themselves available." He waited to see if she took his meaning. He was not altogether sure she meant to take this deception so far, but if so, she had to realize what was expected of her.

Cindra considered and said, "I've thought about that for a while, ever since listening to Gavadaire talk about the costs involved and such," Jaron winced at the mention of the man's name, but she frowned to silence any remark, "Shush. You never spoke of such things before, only how hard the training was. Anyway, I figured that once I became a knight, my lord, whomever that might be, would not want me around. He'd be happy to see me go off on errantry and not have to bother with me." She looked rather pleased with the idea.

Jaron groaned inwardly, "So you do propose to go through with it, even to the point of attaining a knighthood? To what end?"

Cindra looked defensive, "To gain my freedom, of course. To keep from being bound up in a castle and made to have babies, to be able to face my enemies instead of run from them. I'm sure I mentioned this at some point." *Why was he bringing up arguments that he had already lost?*

Jaron said in a grave voice, "War is coming Cindra. The Dissenter Houses will soon challenge the new king and all who support him. Casselvane will likely be one of the first battlegrounds. Duty may hold you to defend your home rather than lose yourself to wild wanderings."

Cindra was petulant for a bit, but the weight of Jaron's words sank in. War was indeed coming, for the evil men who sought her life were part of a scheme to make it all happen, keeping the Loyalists weak and without allies. Perhaps there would be a call for all fighting men, even if one was a woman, and she would be duty-bound to answer. Perhaps the freedom of the open road and the endless horizon was a dream that would elude her. She recalled something her dear Mineth had said long ago, *'Soldiers march for miles and miles, but go where they are told and have death as a constant companion. No one really travels just to see the world.'*

"If I have to stay and fight," she concluded, "then I shall make the enemy wish they had left well enough alone."

A slow smile spread across her face as Jaron shook his head and laughed.

Chapter Twenty Eight

The Mad One

Syngmore was the largest city in northern Casselvane province; a 'five-temple town' as the natives proudly boasted. The lord's castle stood upon a looming hilltop, watching vigilantly over the surrounding lands. Banners of blue and gold hung limply from their masts, awaiting the negligent breeze. The walls were strong and impressive, though they were currently unmanned.

Bevek and his men approached on horseback after a two-day ride from Casselward. The dread had been growing in their minds as they rode from village to village, seeing evidence of the Mad One's passage, and it was a little reassuring that the walls of Syngmore were still standing.

They arrived at the eastern gate, where two sentries in blue and gold Corrina livery stood guard. The gates were shut, which seemed odd for the time of day. There were people working in the fields, and carts trundling down the road, but the traffic expected of a busy city in the middle of summer was not apparent here.

"Where are you from and what's your business?" asked the first guard perfunctorily.

Bevek spoke in his most polite 'city' voice, "We have come from Rickshome-on-Joshian in search of an old man traveling alone. He is travel-worn and disheveled, and has lost his wits. Mayhap you have seen him?"

The guard said curtly, "Don't you 'mayhap' me, mister Rickshome-on-Joshian. I'm asking the questions. No room for yer fancy city-talk here." He looked over the other riders suspiciously. "Bounty men, are you?" he demanded, firmly planting his pole-ax. His companion tried to look stern, but just didn't have it in him.

Bevek hated this kind of fellow; little men who used their meager authority to feel powerful, expecting greater forces to back them up when they pushed too far. The Tyrant bred that sort with his precious laws and hierarchies. Maintaining his calm demeanor, he asked, "What makes you think so?"

"That's another question out o' you," the guard pointed out. "Any men who come looking for another are moved by either coin or vengeance. You five come with swords on the saddle and knives on yer belts. So I ask you again, are you bounty men?"

Bevek smiled despite his mood and said, "We are indeed. You are most perceptive, good man. The Lord Duke of Selvane himself has charged us with capturing the mad old fellow and taking him back to his keepers. Anything you could do to aid us would be worth a handful of silver, at least."

The guard shifted a bit saying, "Do you have a charter then?"

"What?" Bevek stared.

"A charter," the guard repeated, "showing that the Lord Duke himself has charged you with catching the old coot and returning him to his keepers."

Bevek's patience had just about run out with the little man as he weighed the option of killing him against carrying out their mission. It was almost worth the risk.

"No, I don't have a charter. Bounty men do not need a charter in Selvane," he said, hoping the guard didn't know better.

"This ain't Selvane, this is *Cassel*vane." The guard annunciated, as if he was talking to an idiot. "And we require a charter here."

"We tracked him out of Selvane and into this province," said Marvek, "We didn't have time to get the proper forms."

"Bad planning if you ask me," The guard said mockingly. "Can't rightly release anyone into your custody without an official charter."

"So you have the old man in custody," declared Bevek, happy to have gotten a smidgen of information out of the vile man. "We can take this up with the jailer, surely."

"Busy man, the jailer. Doesn't like to trouble with those who don't have their forms in order..." the guard shook his head.

"How does anyone enter this damned town?" blurted Colm, speaking for the first time that day. The outburst did not help as the guards shifted into a ready stance.

"Oh, toss him some coin and let's be off," said Helvert.

"Bribes now, is it?" exclaimed the guard. "That's an illegal act, or I'm a milking cow."

"Look," Bevek said, "We have traveled far, and this old man is very important to our lord. If Baron Syngmore needs to send a firebird messenger to Lord Selvane, then so be it. I trust you will explain everything to your baron? Lord Aren Corrina, is it not?"

The argument had gone far beyond the guard's little sphere of influence, so he grudgingly backed away and let the men pass. The gates opened with a loud creaking, making the men wince.

The five men rode into the town, examining the defenses. Upon closer study, it had been a wise decision not to cause trouble at the main gate, for they would never have gotten the Mad One out of town otherwise. As the men rode through the narrow streets, they took note of many sentries walking patrol upon the walls. The avenues were also patrolled heavily, and the faces of the common folk were marked with fear and worry. If the Mad One was indeed in town, his disturbing presence had already established itself among the residents.

The jail house was a stone block building with iron bars on the windows, and a strong, iron-shod door. It was located in a corner of the second district, surrounded by some of the more odiferous trades, such as tanners, butchers, and soap makers. Stocks and rusty gibbets decorated the grounds in front of the jail. The law favored more leniency in these enlightened times however, so the old tools served as a frightening reminder of the alternative.

Bevek, who had been in a few jails himself, knew that something was not right. "There are no guards in this area," he said. "Guards are everywhere else, thick as flies, but not here. See? None on the walls either."

"What do you make of it?" Marvek asked.

"I figure we're on the right track," said Helvert.

The men dismounted and entered the jail house, leaving Felithor to draw from a nearby well to water the horses.

The building had a small official area where the jailer would stay; there was a table, a few chairs, and a small fireplace with a cook pot. A mixture of sweat, dust, mold, and an occasional whiff of human waste were the odors that greeted them. *Typical of a jail house*, Bevek thought.

"Hello?" Helvert called into the dim room. There was no immediate answer, so the men took the liberty of exploring. The only outside light came from the high, barred windows near the ceiling. Farther into the room, they saw six doors with small slats, one at floor level, one at eye level; there was also a stairway leading down.

Marvek began peering into the door slats. "Here, I think I found our man," he said. The others came over to see for themselves, anticipation quickening their hearts. The cell was in a darker corner of the room, but each was lit within by a small barred opening in the ceiling. The noonday sun sent a shaft of light into the gloom, revealing a pale, shriveled figure in a shabby robe.

A shuffling was heard from the stairs, and the men turned with knives drawn. From the basement came a haggard looking prison guard dressed in a dirty uniform, his cap sat askew over his far-gazing eyes, which were sunken and dark. "Hullo," he called in a toneless voice.

"Are you the jailer here?" Bevek asked. The man, who looked like a prisoner wearing the jailer's uniform, nodded his head. "We have come to collect your prisoner," Bevek said, and the jailer nodded again as if he did not care.

"When did this old man arrive in town?" he motioned to the door in the corner.

"Arrive? But he's always been there. He's... no, wait..." The jailer looked at the ceiling absently, as if the answer was written there. "A month? A month or more?" he said, then mouthed something silently.

Marvek asked, "Did anything strange accompany his arrival, any odd happenings?"

The jailer stared at him and began to shake with a giggle, which became louder and more peculiar, sending a shiver down the men's spines. He stopped when his gaze fell on the cell door in the corner.

"We'll take that as a 'yes,'" Marvek said.

Bevek pressed on, trying to get the poor jailer to focus his wandering sanity, "Was he carrying anything with him, a large jewel perhaps? This is most important to our employer, for we are to retrieve it along with the old man."

The jailer looked at his hands, searching for something on his dirty palms. "No jewel," he said, "no peace, no future, not for anyone." He looked up at Bevek with fresh tears in his eyes.

The men turned as one to look upon the cell in the

corner. Finally Helvert came forward and took the keys from the man's belt. The jailer made no complaint, but only nodded absently. Helvert unlocked the cell, opening it wide.

The putrid smell of waste and unwashed flesh wafted into the room as the door groaned open. Within the small cell sat a decrepit old man, seemingly asleep. His robes were filthy, tattered, and torn; his long hair and beard were a mat of knotted strands, the color of ash; grass and bits of debris were caught within his beard, like insects in a web. He stirred as the air of his cell was exchanged with the stale but fresher breeze from without. Yellow teeth caught the light as he smiled, and his wiry, unruly eyebrows rose with expectation. Bright eyes glittered deep within their sockets, above his hollow, bony cheeks. His nose was long and crooked, as if it had been broken more than once. He muttered something unintelligible, stretching forth a gnarled hand.

"Come along old one," Bevek said as he reached to help him, figuring he'd wash his hand thoroughly later. "We're here to get you out and help you on your way." The man took his hand in a surprisingly hearty grip, grinning as he was pulled from the cell.

Felithor came in from tending the horses, and wrinkled his nose at the old man. "That's him?" he asked, unimpressed. "*That's* the Mad One?"

The old man seemed to remember something important. "My effects!" he croaked in a hoarse voice. He gestured to the guard, who avoided his gaze, "my cloak and my staff!"

The jailer pointed to the stairway and mumbled, "Down there."

Bevek motioned to Felithor to go collect the old man's things, praying silently that the Dark Heart would be among them. The young acolyte frowned, disappeared down the stairs, and soon returned bearing a filthy white traveling cloak and a staff of white ash, slightly bent and cracked. *Like its owner*, thought Bevek.

The old man reached for his things, but Bevek said, "Let's get you washed up first, friend." His eyes stung from the pungent miasma that hung about the man's ancient body. "There is a well outside." He instructed the others to lead the old one out and turned to Felithor, saying, "Hold on to the staff for a while. If he is a wizard, he will need it to cast spells. No sense in arming the old fellow." Felithor nodded. Bevek took a last look at the jailer, who was rocking to and fro gently, watching the old man depart. Shaking his head at the poor man's fate, he followed the others outside.

The old man sat on a stone bench near the well as the other priests drew water in a bucket. Marvek held his breath and dumped the cold water over the old man, washing away the first layer of filth.

"Aahh!" the old fellow cried, sputtering and wiping his eyes clear. "Cold, it's cold. Not my favorite, like this. Better warm," he said in a wavering voice, "Fire's not so good though." Another bucket of water hit him. "Oohh!" he cried, "I miss the warm sands, warm lands. I want to go home." He shivered in the afternoon air, even though the sun was warm today.

"We'll get you a clean robe before we leave," Bevek said, and he crossed the street towards a shop that sold textiles. A simple length of wide cloth would do, hung about the old man's thin shoulders and tied about the waist. Anything would be an improvement.

As he crossed the road, he suddenly realized that the street was deserted. When they had entered the jail, there had been people going about their business, but now all doors and shutters were closed. No one had been near the jail, but at least there had been people about.

Ignoring the closed door, Bevek entered the textile shop, where he found the owner and his wife sitting at their worktables. There was a loom standing against one wall, and a spinning wheel against the other. Shelves of linen rolls adorned the back wall, and there was work on the loom, but the couple was doing nothing as far as Bevek could tell. They only stared at him with wide eyes, as if death itself had entered.

Outside at the well, Helvert and Colm were busy trying to scrub down the old man with a grooming brush while Marvek drew more water. They might have to kill the old man eventually, but he needed to be suitable company in the meantime. The outskirts of the town stretched for miles, turning to sprawling farmland that came up against the Shadowood Forest, so they would have to ride with the old codger for some distance before having the privacy to 'test' him. Colm had nicked some soap from a closed shop stall, and it helped their task immensely.

Felithor was sitting on the bench near the well with the tattered white cloak folded beside him. He held the staff in his lap, studying it with head down, rolling it slowly across his legs as he traced the tiny carvings that wound around its entire length. It was not unusual for a wizard to carve mystic runes into his staff; some claimed it aided their concentration or increased the potency of their spells. Felithor was no wizard, but the carvings fascinated him just the same.

Bevek soon returned with a swath of white linen folded over his arm, shaking his head in disbelief. "The pair of them in the fabric shop, the owner and his wife," he began, "seems the old fellow has them terrified, same as everyone else. Gave me this linen for free when I said we're taking him with us." They all looked at the befuddled old man shivering on the edge of the well, his formerly filthy skin scrubbed pink and clean, or at least clean enough. Bevek said, "A series of strange and terrible events have occurred since our friend stumbled into town nearly a month ago."

"Like what?" Marvek asked.

"Little things," Bevek said. "Accidents, small fires, sudden deaths. Nothing unusual in the course of a year, but they all happened when and wherever he wandered in town. Soon he was locked up for his own safety. The people here are frightened, that's for sure."

"Why didn't they drive him out of town?" Helvert asked.

"Or kill him?" added Colm.

"It seems no one wanted the job either way," Bevek answered. "Lucky for us."

"It will make our task easier at least," said Marvek, "As long as the guards don't stop us."

Helvert and Colm went to wash themselves after the dirty job. Bevek draped the linen over the man's frail, bony shoulders, and had him stand so he might arrange the fabric into a makeshift robe.

The old man smiled and looked into Bevek's coal dark eyes with sudden recognition. "You're the one," his reedy voice cracked and wheezed, "You're the one who *lived.*"

The two acolytes at the well heard the odd remark, and exchanged looks.

Marvek began, "What do you-"

The staff clattered to the ground as Felithor got uneasily to his feet. He looked at the other men with a look of despair on his face, then he gave a cry and ran at the jail house. The other men clutched their weapons as their eyes sought whatever had alarmed him so, but they were alone on the street. Before they could do anything to stop him, the distraught young acolyte ran head-first into the stone wall; his head and neck made a sickening crack, and he collapsed to the ground. Fresh blood stained the wall and pooled around Felithor's head, soaking into the thirsty earth.

"Gods!" shouted Bevek, leaving the old man teetering on his spindly legs. He rushed to the fallen lad's body, stopping short of touching it lest the curse jump to him. The other men approached more slowly, swords drawn. Their eyes darted between their fallen comrade and the withered elder, who smiled as he blinked at the sun.

"What in the name of Mash was that?" cried Helvert. "What came over him?"

Colm muttered, "The Mad One knows." They looked over at the old man as he moved to collect his cloak, throwing it about his shoulders and appearing much happier for it. He leaned on the side of the bench to brace himself as he stooped for his staff.

"No!" Bevek shouted, pointing with his sword. "Keep the staff from him!" Colm rushed to intercept it, pulling it out from under the gnarled fingers.

"Fiddlesticks," said the old man, casting a squinting eye at Colm. "Smoke and ash." He shook his head and looked expectantly at Bevek. "Well, are we off then?" he asked, ignoring the body on the porch. "Have a spare horse?"

Poor Felithor would be buried by the townsfolk, without the blessings of the Countless Lord. His soul was probably standing before Valdak the Judge this very moment; his transgressions against the laws of the Tyrant recited by the blind god before being sentenced to an eternity of punishment and redemption. It was a tragedy, dying so close to the End.

No one troubled the men on their way out of the city. People watched silently from their windows, not daring to cheer or call out lest it bring more misfortune upon them. Bevek noticed the grateful and sympathetic looks he and his men received as they rode by, and this added to his growing sense of dread.

The strange old fellow sat upon Felithor's horse while Helvert walked beside, holding its reigns in one hand, his own horse's in the other. The old man held on to the muscular neck of the animal and chuckled to himself constantly; the novelty of riding upon a beast seemed undiminished after more than an hour. Colm carried the wizard's staff in hand as he rode, resting the cracked base upon his toes in the stirrup, as might a knight carrying a lance or a battle standard. No one spoke as they left the outskirts of Syngmore behind them, heading out into the surrounding farmlands.

Bevek was ill-at-ease as he considered their mission. One man had already died, and they were still many leagues from Portshia. If the prophecies were true and the Mad One was bearing the Dark Heart, they might all die soon. *And that would be a good thing*, he told himself. It meant that all was according to the will of Llomaak and the End was at hand. Felithor would be freed along with every other soul. *That was a good thing.*

Before the End would come an age of celebration, the likes of which had not been seen since the Time of Chaos; the constraints of society would break down and laws would be forgotten, and the strong would rule. It would be a paradise, followed by the freedom of oblivion; no judgment, no punishment, no unending toil to right wrongs in the eyes of the Tyrant. *That was a good thing.*

Bevek had always wanted to see those days of celebration, to live without rules by the strength of his own hands. What troubled him was that their mission could cut his life short, depriving him of that much-anticipated time. But one thing gave him pause; the old man had said, *'You're the one who lived.'* What did that mean, if anything?

The men left the road before nightfall, stopping near the edge of the Shadowood Forest. They made camp within the dark trees, out of sight of the farmhouses and curious eyes. They built a fire, bright and hot, for they would need good light for their dark work. Each man had experience in taking lives, but this was no ordinary life; if he was indeed the Mad One, he would be required to produce the Dark Heart or die. A cold, nervous tingle was nestled in the stomach of each man. It mingled with hunger, but it was never wise to eat before opening up a person's body.

The old man was oblivious to the danger awaiting him as he gnawed on a piece of bread. He hugged the linen robe and white cloak about him, happy for the fire, for the nights were still cool in this part of the province. He would occasionally stare at his staff, which was still in Colm's keeping.

Colm held it in his lap as he sharpened his knife, ignoring the old man's gaze. He did not want to alarm their prisoner with his thoughts, which would surely have shown in his eyes if he returned the stares.

Bevek did not wish to begin the interrogation with threats, so he used his most kindly voice, hoping to set the old man at ease. He began, "We are servants of the Countless Lord, the faithful of Llomaak. It is said that you are his prophet. Are you the one called the Mad One, who carries the jewel known as the Dark Heart?"

The old man smiled, nodding to the fire as if the question had emanated from the flames.

"Do you carry it with you now?" Bevek asked. "For it is said that you must deliver it into our hands to herald the end of days."

The Mad One snorted a laugh as he looked up, his face starkly lit by the fire. "Must I? Must I now? There's a face under a face I seek, and it's not yours." He cackled as hot sap popped in the fire, "Portshia is where I'm bound, and I must move along." He eyed his staff again, fingers flexing.

"A face under a face?" Marvek said, pondering the words. "A face under a mask, perhaps?"

Bevek stared across the fire at the old man, his eyes dangerous and intense. He put an edge to his voice, "If we are to take you to Portshia, we must know if you have it! Show us the Dark Heart, so we know you are the true prophet of Mash." The men all waited for the response, readying themselves for a violent search.

But the old man only sighed and said, "It's locked away in my chest, safe and sound." A smile cracked his weathered face.

"Where is this chest?" Bevek asked impatiently. "You did not mention a chest back in Syngmore, only your cloak and staff." The old man kept smiling. "Is it buried near Portshia? Is it far?" He was rapidly losing his temper, and felt like torturing the information out of the old fool, prophet or no.

Helvert grumbled, "There's no hidden chest. He's

probably got it stuck up his bunghole."

The Mad One looked thoroughly confused for a moment, then he turned to Helvert and snapped, "The master of these woods is no friend of yours, that's what!" Then he muttered, "Had his fill of your god and his mischief..."

"That's it," said Colm. "I've heard enough; let's get started." He stood and tossed a fresh log on the fire, thrusting the cracked end of the old man's staff into the glowing embers. But the fire leapt up the staff like an angry serpent, engulfing Colm's body in an instant. It lit up the small clearing with an intense, white glare as his screams grew in pitch, and his fellows leapt away from the intense heat, shouting and cursing. Colm's hair and skin were consumed first, curling and vanishing in wisps of smoke; his eyes burst and became smoldering holes; and his agonized shrieks degraded into gurgled spurts of air. He staggered back two steps before crumpling to his knees, the charred bones now visible through the black, fire-ravaged flesh. He slumped over as if in prayer, and the flame died down to a low flicker. Putrid smoke rose to befoul the treetops.

The staff lay by the fire pit, unmarred by the flames, and the Mad One went to retrieve it. "Smoke and ash," he said, shaking his head as he picked up the gnarled, white wood. "Fiddlesticks."

Helvert withdrew a small vial from his tunic and smashed it to the ground at the Mad One's feet. It exploded in a burst of violet light and smoke, which caused the old man to teeter and nearly loose his balance. Helvert moved in with his knife at the ready, but a flock of ravens descended from the trees, pecking, scratching, and flapping wildly at his face. He cried, "What-?"

"The master of these woods is no friend of yours, that's what!" repeated the Mad One as he gained his bearings once again. "Had his fill of your god and his mischief..."

The acolyte slashed frantically at the ravens, but his

blades kept his fellows from helping him. He turned and fled into the forest shadows, and his cries quickly became distant and muffled. No one dared follow him any further, for it was as if the forest had swallowed him.

Marvek spun and drove his short blade into the Mad One's belly, and then viciously cut upward and shoved the old man off the blade. His victim staggered where he stood, his eyes going glassy and wide as they saw the damage.

"My chest!" he cried, "You opened... my chest..." The wound was large, gaping unnaturally as his gnarled fingers pawed at it. From within bled a deep, amaranthine light; a light that did not warm the night or banish the shadows, but which seemed to feed on them. It pulsed slowly, and the fire seemed to diminish in deference to it.

Bevek and Marvek stood dumbfounded as the man opened the wound further, looking into his own ribcage at the sinister paragon that nestled there. It was a jewel the size of a man's heart; a jewel of terrible, dark beauty that beat with slow pulses of light, and a low, throbbing hum that seeped into the listener's bones. A sickly web of incandescent tendrils spread from it into the surrounding flesh, pumping malevolent power through the body of the Mad One.

"The Dark Heart," whispered Bevek in awe, "It's true." He dared not move.

Marvek stood back in fear, for the Mad One was pushing the wound closed, and his flesh knitted itself shut in moments.

Bevek's eyes darted about the campsite and he saw that the horses had fled, breaking their tethers. Helvert was gone, and Colm's body was a charred heap. Now the old man was looking at his attacker with a dark scowl that evolved into the face of a wrathful god. Bevek watched in terror as his last remaining fellow dropped his sword. The Mad One raised his staff, and the campfire leapt in response.

"You, servant of Llomaak," the Mad One called in a voice that was now strong and bold, "You wish to know the nature of the Abyss, the home of your Countless Lord? I will show you the heart of your precious Chaos!"

There was a deep rumbling that could be felt in their bones, almost too low to hear, like the yawning of a gigantic crypt far beneath the earth. Marvek's body stiffened and he opened his mouth to scream, but what issued forth was a hissing chatter, like the voice of the Whisper that visited Bevek many nights before; then it was joined by the throaty roar of a wild beast, unlike any that walked the earth; then the wailing of tortured, agonized creations that had never known a moment's peace in an eternity of existence.

Marvek convulsed violently but managed to stay upright, like a puppet dancing on a string; his mouth spewed the vile speech of the bottomless pit, where dwelt their lord and his legions. Bevek covered his ears and squeezed his eyes shut, but that only allowed an intruding sample of what Marvek was experiencing to seep in, and he could not bear it for more than an instant.

The priest had seen visions of corrupt bodies; unborn, malformed, slick and scarred from endless writhing against one another to reach a solitude that did not exist. Smells had assaulted his nostrils as he gasped for breath; so horrid and foul were they, that he snorted them out again, and his lungs ached for air. He had felt the movement of tentacles across his brain; long, soft, boneless fingers sliding under the surface of his skull, feeling out the wrinkles in his gray matter and caressing the smooth bone that shielded it.

All of this in an instant. Bevek looked to his friend and could not bear to think of what the acolyte was going through.

Blood began to appear in Marvek's sweat, making his ruddy complexion even more crimson. His bowels evacuated, as if to make room for the horrors trying to fill him up from within. Countless voices spoke their names through his mouth in a cacophony of wails, screams, and roars, all repeating, all joining together to form one single, terrible name.

Marvek's head fell from his body and into the fire, as Omiras Bevek put his comrade out of his misery. He stood panting before the feeble old man in the makeshift robe. "Enough," he said, and he dropped his sword. He wanted to run but could not move, he dared not move, lest the curse that had killed his brethren befall him also. "Prophet of Mash, I am at your mercy," he said, and fell to his knees.

The Mad One was turning his staff with one hand, running the finger of his other hand over the carvings as they twisted around the length, as if reading them by touch. He smiled that befuddled, peculiar smile as he nodded. Only the crackling of the fire and its recent fuel made any noise until the old man spoke.

"You're the one," the Mad One said, as his voice cracked and wheezed, "You're the one who lived!"

Bevek didn't think he wanted to anymore.

Chapter Twenty Nine

The Coming Storm

The sunlight was waning as Cindra and Jaron made their way back to the road and into the clustered buildings of the Outwalls. The evening sky was a rosy haze, and as the moon rose over the mountaintops, its orange face drew the worried attention of all who saw it. The stars were veiled, and an ill wind blew down from the east, sending flecks of dust into squinting eyes.

"Dust storm?" Cindra asked.

"I guess so," Jaron said. "This heat must have baked the soil on the mountains, or maybe..."

"Maybe we should hurry along?" Cindra said.

The wind soon vanished and the air grew still, but the dark sky was still bereft of stars. There were no clouds to be seen, yet the moon wore an aura of sickly yellow light. By the time Cindra and Jaron reached the heart of the Outwalls, a strange fog had settled upon the city. The oil lamps made a path of ghostly halos that faded into the distance, marking the way.

Cindra coughed, and pulled the collar of her tunic up over her nose as best she could. "This is bizarre," she said. Jaron nodded in agreement.

The city walls and towers had vanished altogether in the haze, and the eerie stillness of the air made the hair on Cindra's neck prick up. The horses were snorting with displeasure, and Cindra tasted dirt on her lips.

She tried to keep the worry from her voice as she said, "We have to get indoors, Jaron. The horses too."

"Can you see any signs?" he asked. Neither of them was very familiar with the Outwalls, though it could be assumed that there were inns and stables near the main road. "Anything at all?" his voice sounded overloud in the dead calm.

"Nothing," Cindra said. "I've never seen a dust storm that settles like fog."

"Neither have I," Jaron replied with a cough. The clomping shoes of their mounts echoed around the empty streets as ghost shapes moved in the distance. Faint light could be seen ahead and Jaron pointed towards it. Taverns often had glazed windows to entice travelers with their warm glow; now they acted like a beacon in a storm. The glow resolved itself into a series of windows, with a hanging sign above the entrance that read 'The Dancing Cow.' Below was a painted image of a cow doing a jig. Cindra remembered seeing it on the way out of town and estimated they were nearly a quarter mile from the north gate.

Jaron and Cindra dismounted and Jaron went to the door of the tavern, now closed against the eerie storm. He knocked a few times; faces appeared in the checkered windowpanes but no one answered. He tried again, this time shouting, "Open in the name of Count Casselvane! I am a knight of his lordship!"

There came a fumbling of the latch and the door cracked open. A wary and wrinkled face peered out with a rag over his mouth. "What do you want?" he croaked, as a wisp of dust was drawn into the room. "It's an evil night to be out o' doors."

"Yes," Jaron replied, "we were caught in the storm and need a place to wait it out." He gave a look over his shoulder to Cindra. "I need stabling for two horses and a room for me and my squire, unless this dust clears sooner." He used his most authoritative voice to imply that his polite request was not a request at all, in case the innkeeper moved too slowly or should be given a chance to think about it.

The old man nodded, took a lantern from a nearby hook, and with a deep breath through the rag, plunged into the shrouded night. He quickly led Jaron, Cindra and the horses to the stable in the adjoining building, opened the barn door and ushered them inside. The air was cleaner here, though a little dust could be seen sifting down from the roof slats. "Right peculiar weather this is," he mumbled through the rag. "Came down out of nowhere, but I suppose you know that, sir knight."

"Indeed," Jaron said. "There was hardly any warning. It's a lucky thing we weren't riding farther from the city."

The innkeeper nodded, "Like a blizzard up north, from what I hear. Snow falls so thick in the air you can't tell up from down. Folks get lost in it, they say, wind up dead and frozen not but a few feet from home." He saw to the horses, sacrificing the use of his rag to do so. The man's face was careworn and leathery, the corners of his mouth drooped into jowls, his hair formed a gray drapery around the back of his head and his eyebrows were a mangy tangle. "Fisk's the name, proprietor of the Dancing Cow, at yer service." He gave a perfunctory nod and helped Cindra unsaddle the horses. "Bit of a crowd tonight, as you might expect; mostly people who got caught out o' doors as you were. All of us are waiting out the fog, or dust, or whatever it might be. Normally I'd be happy for whatever brings people into my house, but not tonight. Everyone's fearful. Trouble's in the air; thick it is, like this dust."

He rambled on as he went about his work, giving

Jaron and Cindra the chance to brush the clinging grime from their horses and themselves. When the horses were fed and watered, they left the barn and hurried to the inn. Cindra wanted to ask why the inn was called the Dancing Cow, for surely there was a funny story behind it, but the opportunity never arose.

The inn's common room was nearly full, as regulars and a smattering of travelers huddled over drinks, all talking about the same thing. The dust storm was an ill omen if any had seen one, and each patron had a theory about what it might portend.

"It's the dust of a great army on the march," said one man, a local by his speech. "Probably coming over the mountain pass by the look of things." This gave rise to a great deal of nervous talk, leading some to question the knight and his squire about the readiness of the city's defenses.

Jaron replied to numerous questions, "The city is always ready to repel invaders, but if there were an army on the march, we would have more warning than the gathering of dust, mark me." His confidence set some at ease, but Cindra wondered if he was right.

"Sir Jaron," she said, "I'm reminded of our talk about Grigor." Her fellow student, the son of a Dissenter baron, had been on her mind lately. "Do you think he would be called away if there was any trouble?"

Jaron smiled. She had worded the question carefully. He said, "I'd imagine that would be the first sign of trouble; 'rats leaving the sinking ship' as they say."

"Rats!" A shrieking voice came from behind. They turned and saw a tattered old man sitting at a table near the wall, and a younger man beside him with his head in his hands, as if in deep thought. The elder had a long, bedraggled beard, wiry hair, and bright eyes that reflected the fire in the hearth. His linen robe might have once been white, but was now soiled with the dust of a long road, and it hung in a rumpled mass about his bony shoulders. A crooked, pale walking stick leaned against the wall, its base cracked and blackened as though it had been in a fire.

The younger man looked up at the elder's outburst, a flash of fear in his coal-black eyes. His hair and beard had once been closely trimmed, but now had a wild look to them, as if he had been long away from a mirror. His sharp nose was reddened and runny. He wore filthy traveling clothes, once decent, but now frayed and soiled with neglect.

Cindra recognized the men from the road into town, recalling how she thought them to be father and son. They did not look related up close, but they seemed connected somehow, as if there were invisible ties binding them together. The younger man did not appear to be happy with the arrangement and the elder seemed rather oblivious.

"Rats," the old man repeated, nodding as if he finally understood something that had been eluding him. The younger man watched him closely for a moment, almost suspiciously, as if waiting for a sign. When one was not forthcoming, he gave Jaron an angry look, as if the old man's outburst was somehow his fault.

Jaron ignored them, as if cackling old men shouted 'Rats!' around him all the time. Cindra could not help but look however, for there was something very disturbing about the old man. He was looking about the room as if seeing it for the first time, but when his eyes landed on Cindra, he paused. She gave him a little smile and looked away, but it was too late.

"There's blood on your hands girl," he said in a reedy voice, chilling Cindra to the bone. The other man looked up in alarm, following the old man's gaze. "Blood of friend and foe, old blood from long ago." Cindra gasped in surprise, and the old man's keeper shot her a fearful look. Jaron turned when he realized his squire had been called 'girl.'

Omiras Bevek stood and leaned towards them, "You should go," he hissed, his palms flat on the table. "Go before anything happens." He was unarmed and looked rather under-fed, but his eyes were hard, and burned with great intensity.

"Where would you have us go?" asked Jaron calmly, resting his hand on the hilt of *Valdiroth*. "There is a choking fog of dust out there, as I'm sure you noticed."

"Anywhere!" said Bevek, as the old man fumbled about for his walking stick. "Please, you don't understand..."

Jaron was about to tell the man that a knight was not to be ordered around by the likes of him, when all the lights in the room went out. There was a collective gasp followed by a shriek from one of the serving maids, who was in the middle of delivering a tray of drinks, nearly tripping in the sudden darkness. The flames died rapidly in the oil lamps, candles, hearth, and even the cook fires in the kitchen. The ghostly glow of the street lamps were now the only source of illumination, seeping in through the dust and checkered windowpanes.

Jaron was on his feet, sword drawn at the first sign of treachery and ready for a fight. *Valdiroth* ignited with a *whoosh* as blue flame ran up the length of the blade. Patrons cried out in alarm, many falling back in their chairs, eager to get away from the magic sword.

Cindra stood and turned, staring at the old man as he squinted in the cold, azure fire of the blade. He seemed confused and annoyed at the whole situation.

"Oh, phooey on that," he croaked. Cindra saw him flick his finger and *Valdiroth's* flame went out, as if snuffed by a mighty wind, though the air in the room was undisturbed.

There was a moment of silence in the dark hall as people tried to understand what had just happened. Jaron stood motionless with the cold sword at the ready before him, and Cindra could see a look of shock and fear spreading on his face in the dim light. Confronting a wizard of unknown power was not something they were prepared for.

She felt him jump when she took his arm, but her voice stilled him. "Jaron, we should go," she whispered, the urgency in her tone reflecting her growing dread. "This is all *very* wrong." Her eyes did not leave the space where the old man was sitting. She swore she could make out a dim, violet glow coming from behind his robes, but the sword's flame had spoiled her night vision, so she dismissed it.

"I think you're right," Jaron said as they backed away towards the door. It was not a silent retreat; they bumped into many chairs, tables and patrons as they left, all the while keeping their eyes on the dark shapes at the far table.

Fisk the innkeeper could be heard cursing as he tried to strike up a fire, determined to get things back to normal. Many of his guests either made their way towards the door, or further back into the inn, away from the strange old man. Braving the choking dust was beginning to seem preferable to sharing a room with a mad wizard.

Jaron and Cindra made it out the door and stepped into the brown fog, taking their bearings in the lamp light before heading to the stables. The barn door creaked open as they ducked inside, blinking the irritating grains from their eyes. It seemed as good a place as any to stay, assuming the inn didn't suddenly burst into flames.

"Someone should tell the Casting Guild about him," Cindra said in a huff. "There are laws against using disruptive magic like that, frightening people and making a scene." She folded her arms, mostly to hide her shaking hands.

Jaron was more occupied with the Corrina Honor Sword as he attempted to ignite the blade. He waved it around, slicing at the air and cursing under his breath, but the blade remained cold and dark. "This might be a problem," he said.

Cindra knew nothing about magic swords or spells, but said, "Surely someone from the Mystic College, or the Order of Astrellaris can fix it." Another thought occurred to her however, "Do you think this dust has something to do with that old man?" she asked. "It fell after he came to town."

Jaron sheathed the sword and considered, "I've never heard of a wizard who could affect the weather like that. It would be a fine trick on the battlefield if they could."

Cindra jumped, "Gavadaire thinks that wizards somewhere *have* to be working on spells to aid in war, that it would be foolish of them not to." Jaron raised his eyebrows at the mention of that name, but Cindra pressed on. "What if this is the prelude to an attack? What if this wizard is blinding us to an advancing army?"

Jaron thought a moment and said, "An invading army would have to get past our watchers, spies, and outposts. If they came by the Casselvane Road, then your uncle in Syngmore would have sent word. The watchtowers would have raised the alarm if anyone approached from the mountain passes or the sea." He drew the sword again and huffed in disappointment, for it remained dark. "If there is an attack coming, it's not from an army."

"The man with him seemed scared," Cindra said. "He warned us to leave before anything happened."

"Maybe he's responsible, maybe he's not," Jaron replied. "Let the other wizards handle him. We need to see to getting home." He gave *Valdiroth* one last ineffectual wave before sheathing it and saddling his horse.

They waited for a few hours in the stuffy barn, peeking outside to see if the weather had changed. The moon was high above, appearing as a dirty ghost light in the sky, before Jaron thought it safe to brave the streets. They noticed the lights were lit again in the tavern common room, though neither wished to look inside to see if the old man was still there. Using the lampposts as guides, they led the horses to the city gate. A fine layer of dust had settled on every surface, painting the buildings in drab sepia shades. Shapeless figures moved in the shadows like haunting spirits, calling for the missing. Cindra and Jaron spoke very little as they walked, hoping to keep the intruding dust from their mouths. A stray dog crossing their path paused to whine at them, as if demanding an explanation for the peculiar weather. Cindra gave the dog a shrug and it moved on.

The dark walls of the city loomed ahead through the dense haze; the torchlight blazing on either side of the gate like a pair of eyes flickering in the gloom, its gaping maw and iron-shod teeth waiting to swallow unwary travelers. The wooden gates were closed however, offering the guards limited shelter while on duty, and making it harder for suspicious types to sneak about. Jaron knocked on the wicket door and stood back to be viewed in the torchlight. The eye-slot slid open and the guard within called, "Who goes there?"

"Sir Jaron Dunlorden and squire, returning to the Freekirk School," Jaron declared. The wicket door opened and the guard stepped out into the dusty haze.

"Fine evening isn't it, sir knight?" the guard remarked, looking them over as he leaned on his spear. He looked at the layer of dust covering the horses and their masters. "Been out in this very long?"

"We have been staying in a barn," Jaron said, not wanting to go into detail.

"Ah well, got to make do with what ya can, I expect," the guard said, and he stepped through the wicket door, unlocked the large gate, and allowed them to pass.

Before leaving the gate, Cindra said, "There was an old wizard at the Dancing Cow Tavern that was making a bit of trouble. You might want to see to him before he causes more mischief."

The guard nodded and tipped his metal cap, unsure of whom he could send out in this unnatural haze to scold a trouble-making wizard.

The freak storm was the talk of the town for the next day as life slowly returned to normal. Daylight and the sea breeze drove off the oppressive gloom and remaining dust, and gathering rain clouds on the horizon promised to wash away what remained of the powdery soil that coated the city.

The students in the fighting school had been worried about Sir Jaron and Dillan the night before, knowing they had ridden beyond the walls. They listened eagerly to the strange tale of the mad wizard, his fire extinguishing trick, and their journey back to safety. Cindra left out what the old man had said to her before the trouble started, *'There's blood on your hands, blood of friend and foe, old blood from long ago.'* It was probably just mad ramblings but it still made her deeply uneasy.

The wind picked up, sending billowing grit down the streets; clouds rose over the mountains, and the city was soon covered in a patchwork of light and shade. After the students swept the school clean, Master Cord began focus sessions in the hall. The weather was cooler than usual, so most of the students decided to train in the yard; before long, the practice dummies were expelling puffs of dust when struck, and everyone had sweat stains rimmed with brown mud to decorate their clothing.

Few noticed when the light rain began to fall, but smiles appeared on their upturned faces as the cleansing sunshowers increased in strength. Curtains of rain danced between the bright gaps in the clouds, and dirty rivulets ran down the walls as the dust from the previous night washed off the rooftops and ran into the gutters.

Everything works itself out, Cindra thought, as she fought in the rain. She was sparring with her unknowing cousin Gaius, who was trying to get past her defenses. She felt silly for being scared the night before, letting superstition get the best of her. No army had come in the night, and no disaster had befallen the city. *All is well.*

She blocked a thrust from Gaius and moved to counterattack when something hard struck her on top of her head. At first, she though another student had gotten too close and tapped her with a stray weapon, but then she felt another impact on her arm and saw a little white object drop to the ground. The patter of rain on the rooftops was becoming louder, more urgent; the other students paused to look about as the cleansing rain turned to pebbles of ice that stung where they landed, punishing those who dared to look up in wonder. The sun was shining past the scattered clouds, and the weather was nice but hardly cold, yet it was hailing nonetheless.

The students ran under the covered walkway to escape the pelting, and stood before the doors of the main hall, exchanging nervous glances as this new freak storm moved across the city.

"I never seen nothing like this," Padison remarked.

"Hail in Obamoth, right in the middle of summer," Gaius said to no one in particular.

"What do you think it means?" asked Grigor DeKenric, who's focus training had been interrupted by the freak storm.

Master Cord answered, "I think it means we train indoors until it stops. Those of you in wet clothes, change them before you muck up my clean floors." He gave the sky an accusing glance before heading inside.

The odd weather let up only after the streets were covered with a coating of small hailstones. Sparring had resumed outside when the hail stopped, for Master Cord reminded them that fighting might occur in any weather, and this was good experience. The students reluctantly returned to the courtyard to spar on the crunching ice, driving thoughts of ill omens from their minds as best as they were able. The physical activity helped, but once dinner was served and they had a chance to unwind, the strange events of the last two days took the forefront.

Cord, Jaron and Gavadaire were seated at the head table, listening to the chatter of the students and sharing thoughts between themselves.

"I don't pretend to understand the ways of the gods," Cord began, "but these freak storms have got to be omens of some kind. Something is coming, mark me."

"Wise words from the tavern sage," said Jaron. "Every man with an ale in hand is saying that very same thing right now." He could not bring himself to be too derisive, however. He had only managed to ignite *Valdiroth* a few hours ago, greatly relieved that he didn't have to go knocking on some wizard's door to have a look at it. The incident at the Dancing Cow had shaken him more than he realized.

Gavadaire missed the sarcasm in Jaron's voice as he came to Cord's defense, "I think these may indeed be ill omens, Sir Jaron. I have not lived here for long, but surely this is strange? It is said the Times of Chaos began this way, with odd weather and storms out of season." He took a sip of ale before continuing, "The Su'Kraal monks kept excellent records of the dark times, as one might expect, since they are the heirs to Kraal's legacy."

Jaron was becoming annoyed, "What does that mean exactly, 'heirs to Kraal's legacy?' Do the Su'Kraal really see themselves as literal sons of Kraal? Isn't that a kind of blasphemy?" He leaned to look around Cord's bulk, his patience at an end with the man's pride in his precious monastery.

Gavadaire touched his fingers together to make a steeple over his plate, giving Jaron a look reserved for unlettered cretins as he explained, "The Su'Kraal are obligated to be vigilant against the forces that made Kraal's existence necessary. Kraal opposed the Lord of Chaos and his servants, and warned of the return of dark times. It would be folly to ignore the signs, when they are so plain, do you agree?"

Jaron was having none of it and replied, "So, as a champion of Kraal, what do you propose we do about it? Do we raise an army and garrison the walls because hail fell in summer? I don't suppose Arathus or Kraal left instructions for weird weather?"

"Now who is talking blasphemy?" replied Gavadaire coldly.

Cord broke in before the argument could escalate. "Quiet, both of you. The last thing I need is for my captains to bicker like old women in front of the students." He scowled at Jaron the longest, for he was growing tired of settling his young friend's arguments. "If there is something to be done, it is for our betters to decide. We are soldiers and do as we're told. Let the priests figure out what it means, let the king decide what to do. You two are neither kings nor priests, so it's none of your damned business." He stabbed at his tray with a vengeful fork, stuffing the food into his mouth before he could say anything else.

Jaron backed down but kept his exasperated tone, "Very well, Master Cord, it is not for us to decide. But what shall we do about riding practice next week? If this strange weather continues, we may have trouble renting horses, to say nothing about using the Commons."

Cord sat back and took a drink, happier to be discussing less touchy subjects. "Kylie signed a contract to provide at least two good horses for our training. I don't care if it's raining fish, he'll have them for us. As for using the Commons, we will be there, rain or shine... or fish." He let out his belt as he finished his meal saying, "Only something truly dangerous will postpone our training. The students need *some* experience on horseback, whether they can afford one or not."

Jaron nodded glumly. These students were training more rigorously than he had in his day, having so much packed into so little time. It was needed of course, for despite the odd weather, there was a storm of another kind approaching and they all needed to be ready when it struck.

Chapter Thirty

Dangerous Games

Kylie Hyne the horse seller was true to his word, delivering four good horses for the Freekirk School's mounted combat training. He and several stable hands brought the animals early in the morning to the Portshia Commons, where Jaron had fought for his life against the treacherous Sir Earnold Greenfellow years before. The students were all sitting in the eastern grandstand, out of the morning sun, which shone over the mountains and past the spires of the royal Winter Palace.

Sir Jaron and Gavadaire sat at opposite ends of the stands; Jaron waiting in silence for Master Cord to call for him, while Gavadaire held court with some of his admiring students. Morrin LiKeska, Inis DeGhat, Demel Victhor and Halvoy Quenlorden were all sitting about him, listening to stories of jousts held during the festivals of Arathus that he attended on behalf of the monastery. Cindra sat next to Sir Jaron, but her friends called her over for a chat and she joined them happily.

"Hey Dillan, is that your animal?" asked Bradric, pointing to the fine bay pony tethered near the stands, "Gali breed, ain't it?"

Cindra nodded, "Yes, a pure Gali," she said proudly. She knew Bradric had a good eye for horses, since the big lad's family business was horse breeding; in fact his father was supplying the animals for the practice. "He's just over a year old and fast as the wind." She didn't mean to gush over her beloved T'ózha, but she couldn't help herself.

"Balkon's balls, he's a beauty," Bradric said, making Cindra close her eyes and wince.

Someday the gods are going to get him for that, she thought.

"Be right back," said Bradric, getting up to greet his father as the older Hyne met with Cord to collect his payment.

Adric and Padison watched him go with a grin, for they enjoyed hearing Bradric curse almost as much as they liked watching Dillan's reaction to it. Filbert and Mat sat above them on the grandstand, so they couldn't enjoy Dillan's expression.

"I wish he'd stop that," Cindra said, "The gods are still there, after all."

"True enough," said Adric, stretching his long legs out on the grass, "But maybe it's his way of getting their attention."

Padison piped up, "My favorite is 'Vina's tits,'" he giggled. "That gets me every time."

Cindra punched his arm. "Have some respect for the *goddesses* at least!" she scolded. "Does your mother know you talk like that?"

Padison looked properly abashed, for mention of his mother could still frighten him, "I was just saying it's funny when *he* says it," Padison squeaked meekly, "It's not like I go around using it all the time, or at all." His sudden change of attitude made the others laugh.

Master Cord called for their attention and the

students formed two rows before him on the field. "I know times are different now-a-days," he began, addressing them with his booming voice, "Training a squire was once a knight's duty, and the boy would learn everything from helping his master into his armor, to the art of war itself. Now there are fewer knights, fewer still who take on squires." He glanced at Jaron, "But the need for trained horsemen and footmen is as great as ever, so schools like mine have taken the place of more traditional arrangements. As a result, some of you have never been around horses or experienced what it means to care for them. This you will learn, along with your fighting skills, so that you may all become more complete warriors."

The day began with demonstrations of the basics of horse handling and harness, each student was made to saddle and unsaddle the steeds, adjust the gear and see to the animal's comfort. Few of the students had experience with horses; Bradric was the most senior, having spent his life among them, though he felt less at home in the saddle than on the ground. Stansig, Inis and Demel had their own mounts, though Stansig was more familiar with caring for it himself; the other two young men had always had grooms to do it for them, since neither had been raised as traditional squires. Maadi Gaavi had always ridden moku, the feathered beasts that resembled large birds with grasping claws instead of wings. It was said that moku hunted and ate horses, making them unpopular in this part of the world.

By afternoon, most of the students were able to ride around the circumference of the jousting field, the horses obediently cantering at an even pace, having been picked for their temperament and lack of independence. T'ózha seemed to think it was a timed competition however, and gave Cindra a difficult ride. This led to some outbursts of mockery from Rejick Ratham and friends, who still believed that Dillan got special treatment somehow. The fact that Dillan owned a fine horse served to confirm their suspicions.

"Keep going, horse!" Ratham shouted, as T'ózha sprinted for the edge of the commons, "Drop him off in the cemetery!" Cindra was able to turn him before T'ózha got very far onto the paving stones, scattering pigeons and a few bystanders in the process.

Towards the last hours of daylight, the students were made to carry a long pole as they rode, simulating a lance, spear or standard. Some found it hard to control the horse with one hand occupied, while others had trouble with the pole slipping down or getting in the way. Ratham and Korbison performed quite well to Cindra's chagrin, for they had both learned riding as young boys and the rented horses were no problem for them. Ratham even set his pole in a lance charge, riding his last lap purely for show.

Adric was unimpressed, "Easy to do when there's no one coming at you," he called out. His own time in the saddle had been unsteady but passable. Like many, it was his first time.

Once night fell the horses were led back to the Hyne stable and the students returned to the school for dinner. It was a lively meal as the lads related their time with the beasts, talking about cavalry tactics and what was the best weapon to use from horseback. Many a lad found it hard to sit on the flat benches comfortably, blaming it on saddle sores. Cindra had to laugh, for she recalled what real saddle sores were like and how long it took her to earn what the Galindri called her 'horse legs.' She offered what advice she could, unsure of how males were supposed to deal with their extra anatomy; it amazed Cindra that men could ride at all.

The next day began early with more lessons in handling, making some of the students groan; they had assumed they would be charging down target dummies by now, lopping melons in half from the saddle.

"It will be a week or more before we do any real combat training," Cindra informed her eager friends,

"Sir Jaron says we need to be at home in the saddle before we get knocked out of it." This made some of the lads anxious, for they had not considered that they might be unhorsed in training.

"Does it hurt when you fall?" asked Padison.

"Certainly it hurts," Cindra said, though her own experience was limited. "You can break your neck if you're not careful." She remembered getting the wind knocked out of her once during her riding lessons among the Galindri. It hadn't been pretty.

Adric joked as he slapped Padison's shoulder, "Paddy won't get hurt; he bounces."

Padison replied, "I can fall off my own feet well enough, but I dunno about horseback."

"Can't do much worse than the Avenoth boys," said Filbert quietly, lest they somehow hear him from across the field, "They don't have a way with animals." The brothers were cursing at their horse, trying to bully it into behaving as Ferrol tried to climb into the saddle.

Bradric roused his considerable bulk, bristling at their antics. "If they don't get stepped on or kicked, I'll do it myself," he huffed. The brothers were pushing their luck with the large, powerful beast, and the horse wasn't too happy either.

T'ózha had been saddled at the stables, but Cindra had to unsaddle him to show she could do it herself. Heaving the heavy leather saddle onto his back had gotten easier as her strength improved, and climbing into the seat was becoming almost second nature. It helped not to have to worry about a dress and sidesaddle; she couldn't even imagine going back to that now.

Her second day of riding was easier as T'ózha got used to the small field and the tighter turns. He was accustomed to open grasslands and greater speeds, but now he would have to slow down just as he got going. Cindra wanted to take him outside the walls, but the training on the town commons would be enough exercise for now. Besides, she didn't trust the weather.

Midafternoon brought the promise of storm clouds from the sea, making everyone uneasy. Lightning flashed in the far horizon and the breeze picked up, carrying with it the smell of evergreens and blossoms from the Winter Palace. Talk of more freak storms prompted Master Cord to call everyone together, lest they forget why they were here.

"We are going to continue, rain or no!" he bellowed, "You're not a company of minstrels on parade, you're supposed to be damned soldiers! You'll ride and get wet and like it. If it starts raining daggers, then we'll call it quits." Cord said a silent prayer to Hwessa, goddess of winds and weather, and Pokaht, god of rain, to please hold off if they had daggers planned for today.

Dark clouds loomed over the harbor, driving waves before it to slap upon the hulls of ships, tossing the smaller boats at their moorings. The wind picked up at the base of the mountain, buffeting the trees as it whistled past the high spires of the Winter Palace. Thunder echoed over the sea, rolling in like war drums as the students were put through their paces.

Gavadaire asked Master Cord, "It occurs to me that the horses might be spooked by the lightning and thunder, is it not dangerous to continue?" The rain had not fallen yet, and the clouds were just beginning to block out the sun, so Cord was becoming exasperated with all the worry.

"Kylie assures me that these horses are conditioned for battle," Cord said dismissively, "Most were trained for war but the buyers couldn't pay. They'll be fine." Gavadaire nodded, but if he had misgivings, he kept them to himself.

In the hours that followed, the storm crept farther north over the city, painting the sky in a gray gloom accented with the distant flash of lightning. The wind was cool and steady, driving away all thoughts of summer as it picked up the dust of the horses' passage, carrying it over the flagstones and down the street. Most of the townsfolk were heading indoors now, pulling in laundry from clotheslines and rounding up playful children. The storm might have been taken in stride had not the last few days seen peculiar weather, and now people were less likely to take their chances. Even the spectators who watched the training from the grandstand thought the better of it, and went in for a pint by a warm fire. Soon it was as dark as gloaming, though there were still a few hours of daylight left. The guild wizards began making their rounds, lighting lanterns that were impervious to wind and rain.

As for the students, the ill weather gave cause for bravado as each lad braced himself for the coming storm, calling out encouragement to his fellows and trying to out-shout the thunder. Even Cindra was not immune as she let out a whooping Galindri war cry, much to the amusement of the others. She rode T'ózha around the field, guiding him with her knees and one hand on the reigns as she had been instructed, freeing her other hand for an eventual weapon. The rain began to fall in little faint droplets, like a mist of fine spray thrown up by the surf. The dirt began to turn light brown and the smell of wet mossy earth permeated everything. The beating of hooves on the damp grass was like music, his snorting breath kept time with the rhythm as she bounced in the saddle, dancing to his tune.

In the flash of a lightning strike, Cindra saw a lone figure walking down the street from the northeast towards the commons, white fabric fluttering in the breeze. The figure was too far to make out, especially in the darkness after the flare, but whomever it was, they picked an odd night for a walk.

She turned her horse into another lap, her hair growing damp now in the rain. She held her hand in salute to her friends, who sat under cover of the grandstand. They cheered as she rode by, calling out, "Heyo, Dillan! One more lap, Dillan!" The longer she stayed out in the rain, the longer they could take shelter, but Cindra found she didn't mind at all. Three other students were riding laps as well; Halvoy, Padison, and Terrus Drakthorne were being similarly cheered on.

Cindra turned at the end of the field again and saw up ahead that Terrus had brought his horse to a stop. He was watching the figure walking towards the commons, waving back to his friends to get their attention. Padison rode up behind him, followed by Cindra, then Halvoy, all stopping to see what the matter was. Cord was barking something that got lost in the thunder, but his tone was clear enough.

"Come on," Halvoy said, "We aren't done yet, Master Cord's getting cross."

Terrus turned to him and said, "Would you look at this?" He pointed at the figure that was becoming clearer in the waning light, as distant flashes cast it in a brilliant white flare. It was a woman with thin limbs, flowing red hair, and a light, billowing gown that clung to her body in the falling rain. She swayed gently as she came on, her arms held out at her sides as if to catch the breeze, or keep her balance. Her steps were slow and deliberate as she trod the slick paving stones with bare feet. Cindra could not make out her face very well, but even at this distance her eyes looked dark and keen, fixated on the riders as they stared back at her.

"Is she alright?" Padison asked, as he tried to keep his horse still. "She looks a bit... off."

"Dillan!" came Jaron's voice, and Cindra turned to see him marching up the field, his hand resting on the hilt of his sword as it did when he was angry, "Get back to the field, along with the rest of you! Training's not over yet!" He could not see what they were looking at, for the horses were in the way.

Cindra turned back to the woman, who was no more than a hundred paces away. The horses were stamping nervously, flashing the whites of their eyes, and laying back their ears. T'ózha suddenly made a lurching break, spilling Cindra from the saddle as he bolted towards Jaron, who had to leap aside to avoid being trampled.

Gaining his feet, he ran towards Cindra, who was stunned but slowly sitting up.

"Ci-Dillan!" he corrected himself in mid-panic, running to his squire's aid. The other horses were the danger to her now, for even though they were battle trained, they stamped fearfully, threatening to bolt with or without their riders, who were all too green to control them properly.

Cindra regained her breath as Jaron pulled her to safety. She heard Cord and Gavadaire calling as they ran to get control of the horses before T'ózha's panic became infectious.

"Ooh," she moaned. "What got into him?"

Jaron checked her for blood and bruises, and gave her joints a little squeeze to make sure everything was in place. He said, "At least you don't have any bones jutting out. What in the name of-" He stopped speaking and just stared, looking over her shoulder.

Cindra turned to see what he was staring at, and her blood ran cold.

It was the strange woman, who was now close enough to see clearly. Her mouth was open, her colorless lips parted as a low moan escaped her throat. Dark, sunken eyes held points of red flame, like sparks cast off from a fire. Her hair was borne up on the wind and danced about her pale face. Her pale, sunken features, once lovely, now held sharp angles as the lightning flashed. She leaned into the wind and spread her arms; the gauzy fabric flowed like wings, and the breeze lifted her body like a kite. She closed the distance in seconds, flying like a bird of prey upon a mouse, as the pitch of her hollow voice becoming a high, bestial shriek.

The scene became chaos as the horses squealed and snorted in terror, throwing their riders as they made their escape. Halvoy flipped over the back of his mount, landing on his hands and knees. Terrus managed to hold on for another few seconds, crashing down a short distance behind him. Padison landed near Terrus, and took a hoof to the ribs as his steed leaped away.

The woman came down like a great barn owl, landing on Halvoy Quenlorden, her feet pinning him as her fingers found his throat. Her hair fell like a red curtain over the boy's face, and his screams mingled with the feral roar of the thing that now fed upon his blood, draining it through the iron clutches of her fingers. Her mouth sucked in his dying breath with a horrid croak.

As she saw the creature set upon her classmate, Cindra blanched in horror; it was a monster of legend come to life, something that had made her hide under the covers at night. Halvoy's death throes sent a chill of terror down her spine as she recalled the name: *vemlok*.

Padison was crying in pain, huddled in a ball as he clutched his side. Terrus was on hands and knees, gaping at the woman as she raised her head to seek new prey. The fire in her eyes was brighter now, shining beneath the damp red locks. Her mouth hung open, yawning like a bottomless well, and her hands were like claws, pink and warm-looking as she removed them from her victim's neck. She pounced like a cat, bounding on hands and feet to reach her new prey, and she fell on Padison as he thrashed helplessly beneath her.

"No!" Cindra cried, reaching out in vain as Jaron held her back.

Cord ran up to Padison and his large, booted foot came crashing into the woman's face. There was a sickening thud, followed by a peal of thunder; the woman only raised her head and hissed at him, her bloodless face bore not a mark. Cord uttered a curse and drew his sword as the woman rose over the injured boy. The big knight slashed the woman's throat, opening a gash in the gray flesh, but the wound did not bleed, and soon closed itself. Hissing in anger, she lunged at Cord. Her blow lifted and hurled him backward, and he slid to a stop in the mud.

Jaron released Cindra and drew his sword, but the moment he did, she rushed to help her friend. The smell of moldy earth covered Padison, and he groaned as

Cindra dragged him by the arm, but he was heavier than he looked and her feet were slipping in the mud. She turned to Terrus, who seemed ready to flee.

"Terrus, help me!" she cried, pulling his attention away from the creature. Terrus blinked, swallowed the lump in his throat, and ran to Dillan's side. Together they pulled their wounded classmate towards the other students, who had left the grandstand but had not entered the fray.

Gavadaire came to Cord's aid, launching himself at the ghastly figure. He drove the point of his sword into her breast, but the vemlok reached out and clutched his face with both hands. Her thirsty hiss became a cry of pain, and she released him; her eyes now wide with shock and confusion. She planted a foot on his chest and kicked him back, pushing herself off the offending steel. Gavadaire landed in the mud, but he held his sword before him still; his vision had darkened, he felt dizzy, and her touch had numbed his face.

The vemlok had glided off his blade with her feet hovering inches from the ground, saving her the indignity of a fall in the mud. She floated before them now, the dark pits of her eyes boring into Gavadaire with hatred and malice; the wound in her chest closed beneath the soaked funeral gown. Her hands clutched as the thirsting spirit within pushed her to feed, to kill and feed again. But there was hesitation in her eyes now, and she did not notice Jaron moving up behind her until it was too late.

She spun around as the knight swung *Valdiroth* in a deadly arc. Its blade was alight with blue fire; the rain hissed and steamed upon it, leaving a vapor trail in its wake. The sword cleaved her neck, severing head from body, scorching cold flesh as the vemlok's hideous shriek was cut short.

Constable Fingelm, Sir Jaron and Arch Magus Finnael met with the count later that evening after the dead and wounded had been seen to and everyone was safely back at the school. Jaron was warming himself by the fire, his clothing properly soaked by the rain. Ildric had been summoned immediately, but he hired a carriage to take him through the heavy weather. He was accompanied by Drahn the dweedragon, who now sat by the wizard's chair, ready to help if he could.

"My lord," said the constable, nervously running his hand through his wavy red hair, "I think it best to keep this quiet, lest there be a panic." Fingelm seemed quite shaken, as if *he* had been the one who faced a vemlok this night. Jaron just looked at the man impassively, for it was not his place to speak.

The count turned one of his rings around and around on its finger. His graying hair was tied back from his face but he still managed to look haggard in the firelight. "You are sure this woman was a... a vemlok?" he asked Jaron, hoping the man would change his story.

The knight nodded saying, "I witnessed her funeral procession last week milord, and she came from the direction of the graveyard. She threw Cord like a doll after he cut her throat, and the poor Quenlorden boy was drained of blood..." His voice trailed off as he thought of how close Cindra had come to being a victim of the creature. The count did not know she had been present during the attack, or that she was training as his squire, and Jaron thought it best to keep it that way for now.

"It was lucky you severed her head," said Drahn from beside Ildric's chair. "It is one of the few ways to kill a vemlok."

"It's one of the few ways to kill just about anything," replied Jaron, unused to the little talking dragon. "I wasn't acting on any special knowledge."

"Just the same," said Ildric, motioning with his silver talon, "severing the head is only the first step under normal conditions. However, you carry an enchanted blade, which likely finished the job with one stroke. Still, I would take care to dispose of the body properly."

"Fire," Drahn offered, "or direct sunlight will do,

unless the sky is still overcast tomorrow," he thought for a moment and added, "Also, I would keep the head and body separate until then."

The constable said, "I would suggest manning the grave towers again, in case there are more of them."

The dilapidated watchtowers around the graveyard had not been used for two centuries, not since the great palace haunting of 910, when the royal family received nightly visits from those who died building the new Winter Palace.

Ildric said, "I shall convene a meeting of the Order of Astrellaris at once. There have been many peculiar tidings, the latest coming from your lordship's own brother in Syngmore... may I, milord?" The count nodded. Ildric continued, "There seems to be a singular individual at the heart of these affairs, if the stories from the north are true."

Jaron turned his attention from the fire, "A single man, you say? You think one person is behind all of these events?" There was a quality to the knight's voice that made the wizard study his face closely.

"Yes," Ildric said, "there are tales of a mad old wizard, one who might be the cause, or harbinger, of ill times. The stories have followed this man from his road out of the north, and we believe he was headed here, to Portshia." He watched Jaron's face. "Have you seen such a man?" he asked.

"I have," Jaron said, "My squire and I went riding before that dust storm hit; that was also the same day we saw the woman's funeral. There was an old man at the tavern where we took shelter. He and his companion made a scene and... well, all the fire went out at the same time, the lamps, the hearth, even *Valdiroth.*" Jaron felt safe bringing that up now, since the sword had performed so well this night. "We left at once, for the man's companion gave us a warning that seemed wise to heed."

"Only one companion?" Ildric asked. "The message said he left Syngmore proper in the company of four men. Most interesting."

"So this mad wizard is here, now, in Portshia?" Fingelm blurted, and his red beard quivered as he spoke. "We must find him at once and arrest him!"

"If he is indeed the cause of these events," interrupted Ildric, "then he has a power that is beyond any wizard of the Order, to say nothing of the Casting Guild." Drahn looked up at his master nervously as Ildric continued, "Not since the Time of Chaos have such things been known, when the barriers between the world of Jayde and the Worlds Beyond were made thin or broken. If such times have come again," he paused at the weight of his own words, "then confronting this mad wizard may do more harm than good."

"Then what are we to do?" asked the count, trying to keep the frustration from his voice, "There are enemies on all sides, and now..." he gestured helplessly, "...now you speak as if the dark times have returned, as if the Dissenter Houses and civil war are the least of our worries."

"We must watch and wait," said Ildric. "Acting without knowledge is often more dangerous than doing nothing at all. We must learn what our enemies are trying to achieve; only then can we decide how best to fight them."

The meeting concluded and the count gave orders for Fingelm to set every spy and informant to search for the mad old wizard, wherever he might be. Ildric pulled Jaron aside before departing, leading him to a dark alcove nearby. Drahn kept watch, stretching his neck to peer down the curving halls.

Ildric pulled the knight close and spoke in a whisper, "Am I to assume that this squire of yours, the one who was present when you encountered the mad wizard *and* the vemlok, is in fact our dear Lady Cindra?" He looked gravely into Jaron's eyes.

"She is," Jaron said, "but she is in disguise..."

"This is a dangerous game you are playing, Dunlorden," Ildric said. "Could you not find a safer place than a *fighting school?* I suppose she is training with the men?" His silver hand flexed, producing a mechanical squeak, which made Jaron flinch.

"It was *her* idea," Jaron replied, "She can be quite persistent." *And persuasive*, he thought, although he did not want to share her methods.

"Of that I am sure," said Ildric. "She is her father's child, and a young woman besides. No doubt she has learned how to manipulate the minds of weaker men..."

Jaron raised his eyebrows at the remark but could not disagree.

The wizard leaned on his staff and said, "For now, I recommend keeping that sword by your side at all times. It may be a coincidence that your squire was in the monster's path, but it may not. Nevertheless, her safety is your primary concern. Try to keep her out of danger, will you?" Ildric said, with more than a hint of exasperation.

"I will defend her with my life," Jaron said, "I have sworn to do as much already."

"Defense is easier if you avoid trouble altogether," he offered in a normal voice, making ready to leave, "However if trouble finds you..."

"We can only do our best, Arch Magus." Jaron said.

The old wizard nodded and together they left the darkness for the light, Drahn in tow.

Jaron returned late to the school. Most of the students were sitting up in the barracks, unable to sleep. Others met in the main hall, speaking in low voices about the death of their classmate. Halvoy's body had been taken to the temple of Balkon, where the priests would see to the funeral preparations. A messenger would be sent to Cordoshome in the morning, where the Quenlorden family would be informed of the death of their son, and decide what rites they wished observed.

Jaron found Cord in the master's hall, where the big knight was nursing a bruised ego. He had a goblet of brandy in one hand, and a long-stemmed pipe in the other, but he was enjoying neither at the moment.

"Well done lad, well done," he said as Jaron sat down in one of the upholstered chairs. "There would have been more deaths tonight if you hadn't been there with that silly sword of yours." He motioned to the sheathed weapon the younger knight had unbuckled and laid beside the chair. "Gods know I wasn't of much use."

"No, no you weren't," Jaron agreed, then watched for a response. Cord only stared at the floor. "Oh, come now," said Jaron, "You were of great use! If not for your intervention, the Pemwreth boy would be dead too. You gave the rest of us time to act." He took his own turn looking at the floor and said, "I was too busy keeping 'Dillan' from rushing in to save her friend. Once I let go..." He shook his head as he marveled at the girl's bravery and foolishness.

"Vemloks," Cord muttered. "I never thought I'd come face to face with one. There hasn't been a recorded vemlok attack for centuries." He took a puff of his pipe, releasing the fragrant smoke to curl around the hart's antlers above the mantle. "Now I have a dead student and a lot of explaining to do back home."

"You're leaving?" Jaron asked, not too surprised.

"If the family wants him buried in Cordoshome, then yes, I am." He took a long drink of the brandy. "Halvoy was my responsibility. I talked to his father about him attending the school, and I gave my word I'd send his boy home a warrior." He sighed heavily, "Now I'll be sending him home in a box."

Jaron sat back in the chair and said, "If it makes you feel better, this may only be the beginning of our troubles." Cord looked at him to see if he was making a bad joke. He was not. "Arch Magus Finnael says his Order has been following grim stories from the north, all having to do with that mad old wizard I told you about. They're looking for him now, but don't know what to do when they find him. Seems he may be more powerful than they can handle, if all these matters are his doing."

"Yes, yes that makes me feel *much* better," said Cord, taking another swallow.

"So our troubles may be dwarfed by what's to come, that's all I'm saying." Jaron stretched out his legs, balancing heel on toe as he pondered what the future would bring. "If your finger hurts, try cutting off your arm."

Cord muttered, "I hope you don't think this is cheering me up."

"Not at all," said Jaron, "I just think the students need to be prepared for anything, and that needs to start with you. Enjoy your gloominess tonight, because tomorrow you need to rally the troops." Jaron stood and took up his sword. "Now, where is my wayward squire?"

Cord sniffed a laugh at his one time student, wondering where he had acquired his recent leadership skills. "Dillan is likely in my quarters. Padison is being treated there." He finished his brandy and said, "Go and see to your charge and stop acting like my mother."

Jaron chuckled, leaving his mentor to settle his thoughts. He headed up the stairs to the master's quarters to find Cindra.

Priests had been summoned to attend Padison, and they had done all they could. Now the boy was sleeping quietly, and Cindra got up to talk to Jaron as he entered the room.

"He's going to be alright," she whispered, "He lost a little blood and a rib is broken, but the priests were able to ease his pain. It's lucky Master Cord got to him when he did."

"You might tell him later," Jaron said, "He's downstairs moping about how useless he was."

"I hope you set him straight?" she said, knowing their brand of humor.

"I did. Well, not at first, but I did," Jaron said with a guilty smile. "Come on, you need to change clothes and get some sleep." He guided her to their room next door. "Celia will tend to him," he said, and closed the door as quietly as possible.

The next half hour was spent in silence as Cindra changed her clothes and Jaron prepared a warm basin of water so she might bathe. He did not speak of his meeting with her father and the wizard, nor did she ask, for it was nothing she needed to think about tonight.

After she had cleaned herself and dressed for bed, Jaron came up behind her, placed his hands on her shoulders, and kissed the back of her head. It was a simple act of affection, but she began to cry, shaking gently in his arms as she wiped at her tears with her sleeve.

"I almost lost another friend tonight," she sniffled. "Halvoy is dead and Padison almost died. I didn't know Halvoy that well, but he was nice enough; he didn't deserve that." Her body trembled at the image in her mind, and the sounds, the sounds...

"No one deserves to go like that," Jaron said, "Hopefully that will be the end of it." He hadn't the heart to tell her that it was likely just the beginning. After all, she needed her sleep.

Cindra turned to face him, wrapping her arms about him desperately. "I don't want to lose you, Jaron! I couldn't bear it! I don't want to lose any more people I love!" She buried her face in his chest and sobbed greatly, perhaps already mourning the inevitable. "What would I do without you?"

He held her tightly, burying his face in her auburn hair. "I can only hope you would find a way to go on," he said, "But I am with you tonight."

They embraced each other by the glowing hearth, immersed in the warmth of their love as the past and future fell away, leaving only the pure intensity of the now.

The Author

Mark Rude, also known as Markalf the Going-Gray, is a wizard from Phoenix, Arizona, deep in the land of Mordor. He studied the Arts at Northern Arizona University, in the age when painting was done with paint, not pixels, and a photo shop was a place where you worked with something called 'film.'

It was in this age that he forged the story of Cindra Corrina, intending to make the story into a graphic novel, though it was not overly graphic, and not entirely novel. The comic book he called *Passage* kindled the spirit of the story. Three issues were forged in the land of Mordor, in the fires of Phoenix, before the effort was abandoned; yet the spirit of the story endured.

Cindra's tale was of epic proportions, untellable in quarterly comics that came out only once a year. Yet there was hope. Using fewer graphics, and with more emphasis on words, Cindra's story grew like the light of dawn over a darkened land. Markalf was able to spin his yarn as never before, making a nice sweater, some hand warmers, and a scarf.

Markalf the Going-Gray lives alone in a high tower, where he plots the doom of characters great and small.

www.markrude.net
www.facebook.com/markrude.net